DEFENDER

GX TODD

HEADLINE

First published in Great Britain in 2017 by
HEADLINE PUBLISHING GROUP

First published in paperback in Great Britain in 2017 by
HEADLINE PUBLISHING GROUP

Lyrics from 'Stone Wall, Stone Fence' by Gregory and the Hawk, reproduced
with the authorisation of FatCat Records

Extract from 'The Love Song of J. Alfred Prufrock' taken from
Collected Poems 1909–1962 © Estate of T.S. Eliot and reprinted
by permission of Faber and Faber Ltd

Library card image © Beverly McQueen/Shutterstock

1

Cataloguing in Publication Data is available from the British Library

ISBN 978 1 4722 3310 3

Typeset in Bembo by Avon DataSet Ltd, Bidford-on-Avon, Warwickshire

Printed and bound in Great Britain by Clays Ltd, St Ives plc

Headline's policy is to use papers that are natural, renewable and recyclable
products and made from wood grown in well-managed forests and other
controlled sources. The logging and manufacturing processes are expected to
conform to the environmental regulations of the country of origin.

HEADLINE PUBLISHING GROUP
An Hachette UK Company
Carmelite House
50 Victoria Embankment
London EC4Y 0DZ

www.headline.co.uk
www.hachette.co.uk

For my parents,
Veronica and Gerry.

(Pops, I miss you every single day, without fail.)

'Man hungers to get back the lost voices.'

Julian Jaynes (*Harvard Crimson*, 12 May 1977),
author of *The Origin of Consciousness in the
Breakdown of the Bicameral Mind*

LETTER #24
July 4th, Monday

Dear Stranger,

  You and I will never meet. This letter is our only connection — from my thoughts scribbled on a page, to your eyes and your mind. That is a meeting of sorts, one we must be grateful for.

  I suspect this letter will find you in despair, or lonely, or lost. That is how we live now. We have all become strangers to each other and, worse still: enemies. The human spirit that once tethered us together has now divided us as surely as any ocean ever could. But let us forget all that for now. For now, I want to tell you a story.

  Once upon a time, there was a girl called Ruby, and she was a normal girl in every way. She lived in a normal house with her normal family, and spent her normal weekends working in a care home looking after normal old folk. But there was one person in Ruby's life who wasn't normal, and his name was Mike.

  Mike lived at the care home. He and Ruby played chess, and took walks together, and good-naturedly argued over who could spin a better yarn — Grisham or King. Mike reminded Ruby of her little brother (which went some way to explaining why she loved Mike so much). But the abnormal thing about Mike wasn't that he thought Grisham was the superior storyteller, it was that he spoke to a voice in his head called Jonah, and had done for over sixty years.

Mike told Ruby that soon countless other voices would come, destructive voices, and many people would die, but that she shouldn't be afraid because it was the first step to a better, brighter world. And so, on his death bed, Mike gifted Jonah to her, and Jonah became Ruby's new friend. And along with Ruby's brother they explored this newly broken land, and wept and laughed and bled together, and eventually found an Inn by the sea to call their home where they lived happily ever after.

Now, the moral to all this, Dear Stranger, is simple: that wisdom can sometimes be mistaken for craziness, and that strangers can often be friends in disguise.

Please try to remember on the hard days and cold nights to come that all the deaths weren't for nothing. It's going to take a while, because all change takes time, but it will get better, I promise.

Your friend,
Ruby

Ma, I'm addressing this diary entry to you because you're not coming back. You're dead and I need to see those words in writing.

Words aren't difficult for me. Al and I have been writing notes to each other since we were little. We drove you crazy with all the scribbling and giggling, but words were a lifesaver for both of us. I think they always will be. But words have power, and I must treat them with care — especially words I've kept secret for so long.

A staggering amount of people are dead. This isn't a secret. They were killed by their own hands and others (still not a secret). The fact it took almost three weeks before the killing died down also isn't a secret, although it was a shock to many.

So here's the first real secret: None of this came as a shock to me. I was warned. You remember Mike, Ma? One of the old guys I looked after at the home? Liked cherry tobacco and distracting me from chess with raunchy tales from his travelling days. The staff told me Mike had dementia, but Mike didn't have dementia. He was the sanest man I ever met. He told me what would happen if the voices came. I believed every word he said.

As I write this, I keep looking up and catching glimpses of Mrs Jefferson. She's lying on her front lawn, her skirt around her hips, her hair in curlers. The shovel Mr Jefferson hit her with is lying next to her. I can't see Mr Jefferson, but I heard a gunshot not long after I watched him kill his wife, so I'm pretty sure he's dead, too. The same as everyone else on our street. I wish you would come back, Ma. I miss you so much.

I have to go now. Al is back. I love you.

PART ONE

The Man Who
Was Pilgrim

CHAPTER 1

At the beginning, Pilgrim missed a great many things, things that were by their very nature impossible not to miss once they were gone. Imagining a hunk of cooked cow, for example, could torture a person. It was easy to visualise a medium-rare steak, feel it melting as soon as it hit the tongue, molars sinking through the meaty plumpness and an explosion of juice gushing out. It was enough to make his stomach cramp up like a fist and sit there just under his ribs in a solid, unignorable ball of *want*.

Then the next week he would miss something else. Mashed potatoes, perhaps, or fried okra. There was a period of a month or more, near the beginning, when he would have travelled non-stop for a thousand miles if only at the end of the journey waited a thick, cold, strawberry milkshake. The inanity of a craving couldn't prevent it from rubbing on him like clothes on an open sore.

Quite often there was an absence of such culinary cravings, but those times were worse, for the ghosts of loved ones and more deep-seated longings would creep around him instead. Those he'd kept tightly bottled up for fear that if opened they would froth and volcano forth never to be contained again.

And so he'd waited for a time when such longings were past him, when they became as beaten down and untrodden as the roads he travelled. He knew the passing years would eventually have his memories overgrown with the clutching vines of day-to-day concerns, and that the haunting ghosts of time past would be buried in the old dead world where he'd once belonged. The wait for their interment had been long and exhausting, but each day added another layer of dirt to their graves until finally a huge mound had piled up and rendered them invisible, even to his sharp eyes.

Now he lived only for the day, and longed for nothing.

Time and movement had aided his forgetting, but when the bustle of travel failed to occupy his thoughts, there were plenty of other things to keep him distracted.

A bottle of beer. Capped. Untouched. The label peeling at one corner, the writing faded. The glass was brown, and brown glass was good: over time it allowed less light to infiltrate and molecularly alter the contents. Pilgrim checked the expiry date. It was out by seven years.

He glanced around the dusty bar. It was a watchful, alert glance, one expecting to see nobody and nothing but made up of a diligence born of necessity. One day, when the undertaking of such a searching glance was forgotten, a hidden shadow would be waiting, bent on taking away what wasn't theirs, willing to maim or kill for it. Of course, today wasn't that day – there was no one in the room, only the multifarious projections of his own reflection shot into long, disjointed shards in the cracked bar mirror running along the back wall.

He took his beer and a stool outside. He gazed up at the sky, noting the absence of clouds and the crisp, clear blueness that stretched from one horizon to the other as if it had been steam-rollered out, flawless and smooth. The summer sky had already marked the day to be a beautiful one, but to him the sky didn't denote beauty, the brown glass bottle of beer in his hand did. It was a lost token of a world gone to ruin.

He was in the middle of nowhere, western Texas. The signpost at the town's limits had claimed a population of 539, but Pilgrim doubted more than the 39 remained, and none of them had organised a welcome party. Which was how Pilgrim liked it. It was safest to stay out of each other's way. Parts of the town had suffered fire damage, the gutted, blackened skeletons of homes standing like rotting teeth between the untouched buildings. The burnt husks had still been smoking and giving off a dull heat when he'd passed by, and even now an acrid smell reached his nostrils whenever the wind picked up.

Carrying the stool to the middle of the empty street, he placed it on the centre line of the road. He sat down and rolled the bottle between his hands. It felt hard as granite and smooth as soapstone. It was warm, which didn't bode well for the contents, but he could live with that – it was his favourite brand. Licking at his dry lips, he twisted the cap off. White suds foamed into view. They reminded him of bath bubbles, but the waft of malt and hops was the furthest thing from soap-scented. He groaned quietly and lifted the neck of the bottle to his nose and breathed in deep. Warm, yeasty beer: it had never smelled so good.

He licked his lips again, placed the bottle to them and paused as a shadow flicked past the corner of his eye. Only a small flicker, off to his left, maybe just a cloud passing over the sun, or a splinter of sunlight dancing over a broken windowpane, but still, it was a distraction. All he wanted was to drink his beer in peace.

Pilgrim sighed through his nose, took the bottle away from his lips and stared at the window of the convenience store until the shifting shadow inside retreated and went away. He stared a while longer to make sure it didn't reappear and, keeping one beady eye on the storefront, tilted his head back again, letting the liquid lap against his pursed lips, beer moistening the dry skin. Teasing himself. Then he let it roll inside – a welcome wave of amber nectar flooding his mouth. His throat locked mid-peristalsis, automatically wanting to swallow, and he almost choked on the beer before he could spit it out.

Clearing his throat, he filled his mouth with another long

pull and swilled it around his teeth and gums like mouthwash. He spat that out on to the ground, too, until soon there was a small river of beer snaking its way back towards the bar, heading for the gutter.

He took a long time swilling that beer and spitting it out, wanting to ingrain the malty taste of it into his fading and tattered memories. It was going to have to last him a while.

He would have liked to swallow the frothy beer down, feel it bubble deep within his warming guts, but the danger of drinking something so far past its prime wasn't worth the risk.

I knew you wouldn't chance drinking it, Voice said from that dark place at the back of Pilgrim's head.

Pilgrim closed his eyes. Not because his peace had been broken, but because any sense of peace he ever hoped to achieve would be only an illusion, for Voice was always with him and always would be. He was demon and angel and conscience all wrapped up in one, and there was no escaping him.

Hefting his pack higher on one shoulder, Pilgrim turned right and headed for the alley where he had hidden his bike. He tried to ignore the black cat padding along behind him.

It's still following us.

He tried his best to ignore Voice, too. Voice hadn't been speaking to him all morning, having taken umbrage at something Pilgrim had said. Or hadn't said. Pilgrim didn't know which and didn't much care. The silent treatment suited him just fine. In fact, he wished Voice would employ the tactic more often.

It'll be wanting food next. Mark my words.

They had picked up the tail not long after entering town. Pilgrim concluded the cat had once been domesticated or at the very least had recently been in the company of other people. It was far too friendly for its own good. Most animals had learned that humans weren't to be trusted any more, and knew to keep well out of reach or else chance getting served up as shish kebab. This cat didn't understand the dangers, and had followed him in and out of stores, padding close on his heels, darting away only when Pilgrim stepped into the back courtyard of the bar. He had seen a kicked-over dog bowl by the rear door and a shoddily built kennel in the yard's far corner and figured the scent of its owner still hung around. The cat recognised its old enemy, if not its newer one.

By the time Pilgrim had sat down on the stool in the middle of the road and finished his beer, he had forgotten all about the cat. So when it jumped up on the hood of a car he had snatched his gun out, his finger already squeezing around the trigger before identifying the small black animal as his earlier stalker.

He had directed a cuss word or two at the cat, but it didn't stop it sauntering towards him, unheeding of the gun's barrel tracking its head. For a moment, Pilgrim had considered pulling the trigger anyway, even went so far as to cock the hammer.

The cat gave a low, plaintive meow. It stared up at him with wide yellow lamps for eyes. They appeared lit from the inside, luminous and unblinking.

It meowed again.

Exhaling quietly until his lungs felt strangely deflated, Pilgrim had carefully lowered the hammer back into place and holstered the gun.

'You wouldn't look so endearing with a hole in your head.'

The sound of his voice was all the welcome the cat needed. It slunk forward to wind itself around his legs, purring as if a little motor hummed inside its small body.

You're gonna be stuck with the mangy shitball now, Voice said.

'Can always choose to shoot it later,' Pilgrim replied, leaning down to scratch the cat behind one ear.

The cat had paused to lap at the beer staining the blacktop, its tongue flashing out pink and quick. It gave a delicate sneeze and shook its head and left the rest to dry in the sun. Pilgrim didn't blame the animal one bit; the beer had already left a bitter coating on his tongue.

Sometimes things were best left forgotten.

A smile touched one corner of his mouth when he saw the motorcycle tucked in behind an old, rusted dumpster. The bike was scratched and dented and cracked in places, but she ran sweet and had lasted more than eight months so far. That was three months longer than any other bike he had appropriated. He wheeled her out, one hand swiping a line of dust off the faded gas tank. He slung a leg over the fraying seat, the engine rumbling to life with one crisp twist of the key and a single depression of the starter button.

Shucking his pack on to both shoulders, he righted the weight of the bag until it was comfortable. It felt heavier than it had in weeks. He had dug up more supplies than he'd expected to here, but there was nothing else of any use. The decayed bodies hiding in back rooms and garages and basements, most marked with self-inflicted wounds, offered little companionship.

Besides, you've got me for company, Voice said.

'I thought you weren't talking to me.'

I wasn't. But I got tired of waiting for you to apologise.

'Apologise for what?'

Exactly! You don't even know what you did. I'd have been waiting for ever.

Pilgrim stopped listening. Maybe he *should* consider lying low here for a while, conserve his gas, before the need to restock forced him to move on.

You'll get itchy feet, Voice said. *You know it, and I know it. And who knows where the next meal or cache of gas will come from if you stay here too long?*

As much as Pilgrim didn't want to admit it, Voice had a point. Besides, Pilgrim preferred to keep moving. He'd rather have the open sky as his roof and the horizons as his borders than the walls of a town stacked up all around. Easier to see what lay ahead that way.

The locals won't take kindly to us staying, either. The cat is the only one who'd welcome us.

Pilgrim's eyes automatically found the cat. It stalked back and forth next to the bike, searching for a safe way up.

Bring it along, Voice said. *Could serve as a good appetiser at some point. Or a bartering tool.*

Pilgrim grunted.

Might as well name it while you're at it.

'Maybe I will,' Pilgrim said.

He leaned over and gripped the cat by the scruff of the neck, lifting it high and settling it on the tank in front of him. Its hind quarters slid back until they rested in the V of his thighs, up against the crotch of his jeans.

'If there's even a hint of claws going anywhere near my balls, you're getting a one-way ticket off this bike.'

Pilgrim gave the throttle some gas, watching for the cat's reactions to the throaty growl of the engine. The animal gave a quick, sharp yowl but settled down almost straight away.

Grunting quietly, Pilgrim lifted the glacier sunglasses from where they hung around his neck. Like always, the world became a whole lot more tolerable at a lower brightness level. Next, he lifted the dusty neckerchief tied loosely at the nape of his neck and tugged it up over his nose. He took a moment simply to sit with his eyes closed, absorbing the heat of the day like a lizard, allowing himself to be warmed from the outside in. He breathed deep through the cotton at his mouth, the bike vibrating soothingly through his bones. After a slow count of fifteen – because fifteen had always been a good number – he heeled the side-stand up, knocked the bike into gear and aimed its nose towards the sun.

There wasn't much to see any more. Pilgrim kept his eyes on the road and on the horizon, on the abandoned cars and on the places where ambushers could be lurking, and on the blacktop ahead for sharp items designed to puncture tyres. He had a set number of things to be alert to (for example, signs for supermarkets or gas stations, pharmacies and hospitals, libraries even), but other than those few places, and the wariness of being jacked for his belongings and maybe even his life (and now the cat, he supposed), he generally felt no interest or curiosity in much of anything.

Until he spotted the girl.

She was a distance off yet but immediately she was a splash of colour that drew his eye. And even so, the sighting invoked only a mere flash of curiosity, a reading which barely registered.

The teenager was sitting on a folding chair at a roadside stand, a handmade sign painted with the words '*Fresh Lemonade for Sale. Drink Up or Pucker Up*' propped up next to her. It had been beautifully painted with green vines winding through the script and plump yellow lemons adorning each corner.

Curiosity killed the cat, Voice said in the back of his head. *And satisfaction won't ever bring it back.*

CHAPTER 2

The sun shone bright and strong outside the netted windows. Inside, the farmhouse was dark and shaded and silent. Lacey sat in her grammy's armchair, legs tucked up, a heavy knitted blanket wrapped around her shoulders. The chair was an old wingback, fraying and threadbare, each of its wooden legs scarred pale from the countless times Grammy had knocked them with her walking stick. The winged sides where she had rested her head held no material at all, the pale yellow padding showing through.

Lacey hummed a little under her breath as she turned a pair of wire-rimmed spectacles over in her hands. She used a corner of the blanket to polish the lenses and lifted them to her eyes. She squinted around the dusty room and peered hard at the blurry pictures on the walls.

'God, Grammy. You were blind as a bat.'

She lowered the glasses and the pictures came into focus. Family photographs of Lacey and her big sister, mostly. One where they were sitting on the floor of Karey's bedroom, Grammy's antique vinyl records scattered around them, a six-year-old Lacey beaming up at the camera while carefully holding a black record cupped between her palms by its edges, exactly how Karey had shown her. Karey wasn't looking at the camera. She gazed at Lacey with a worried expression, as if counting the seconds until her baby sister dropped her prized recording of *Sgt Pepper's Lonely Hearts Club Band*. Her worries had been unwarranted; Lacey hadn't dropped it. In fact, she hadn't dropped it for another five whole days. It had hit the floor edge first, snapping clean in two.

All the tears and apologies in the world hadn't saved Lacey from her big sister's wrath (and Karey knew *exactly* what punishment would cause the most heartache). For two solid weeks, Karey hadn't spoken to her. Not a single word. It was the thing Lacey hated most. Silence. Those two weeks had felt like an eternity.

In the cold, silent sitting room, Lacey sighed and slipped her grammy's glasses back on, transforming the family pictures into a myopic blur. Sometimes, looking at those familiar faces made the house feel emptier, the silence weighing a thousand times heavier.

A creak from the hallway made her stomach tighten. She knew it came from under the stairs. It always came from under the stairs. She squeezed her eyes shut and whispered, 'There's nothing there, Lace. Just ignore it. The house makes stupid noises all the time.'

The creaking came again, but she wouldn't give it the satisfaction of looking. She *wouldn't*. The farmhouse was old: it creaked, it moaned, it ticked sometimes as though a spider army was marching to war under the floorboards. It was just her ears playing tricks.

The creak came a third time and, before she could change her mind, Lacey threw aside the blanket as she jumped up, snatched the glasses off her face and dashed to the cupboard. She yanked it open, but the small space inside was empty. Painfully so. It mocked her with its emptiness because she was the one who'd cleared it out in the first place.

She slammed the door shut and leaned her forehead against the wood.

'I have to leave this place before I go crazy.'

She breathed deeply for a time and went back to humming – 'She's Leaving Home', her fifth-favourite Beatles tune – making it to the second verse before she could straighten away from the cupboard and return to the sitting room. She picked up the blanket she'd tossed aside and neatly folded it into halves, then quarters, then laid it on the seat of the armchair. Her boots were already on, but she double-checked they were securely fastened. On her way to the front door, she stopped by the hallway table to pick up the cold metal flask she'd left there. She didn't look at the small cupboard under the stairs.

Leaving the house, she made sure the front door was closed behind her, rattling the handle for good measure, then started the long trudge out to the road.

The idea for a lemonade stand had been a stroke of genius.

What would a weary traveller want more than anything? Lacey had asked herself, gazing out of the kitchen window, past the plants her grammy had cultivated (the cucumbers weren't ripening like they were supposed to – Lacey killed everything she touched, no matter how hard she tried; Grammy had delighted in calling her Leper Hands) to the perfectly rectangular heap of overturned earth behind them. The lantana she'd transplanted to the spot had survived nicely, despite her leper hands (she'd studied her grammy's gardening magazines in detail before even attempting the replanting), and after ten weeks she was both happy and relieved to see the grave blooming with red, orange and yellow flowers. Beside the grave, two potted plants housed stunted little lemon trees.

When life gives you lemons, squirt lemon juice in the booger's eye! Grammy often cackled after bestowing such pearls of wisdom. She also showed Lacey how to make lemonade. She knew lots of handy tips like that.

From the two lemon trees, Lacey had plucked the last ten lemons. In the basement, she found a fold-up table, a chair, an old siding from a crate and a bunch of old paint cans. She'd brought everything upstairs and sat for an hour in the backyard, painting. Then she traipsed out to the road with all her things and plopped down to begin her wait.

After five days, she almost threw everything back down the basement stairs.

After seven, she left everything at the roadside, not caring if it was still there in the morning.

After ten days of waiting, she was worried and resigned in equal measure, but trudged out every morning and afternoon anyway because, as Grams said, giving up was worse than not starting at all.

What else did Lacey have to do, anyway? It wasn't like she was missing an invite to her best friend's birthday party. Courtney Gillon had no doubt celebrated all the birthdays she ever would. The last one Lacey had attended, eight years ago, was probably the best party Courtney could ever have hoped for. There'd been a woman dressed up as Elsa from *Frozen* and a full-size Iron Man complete with gloved hands that lit up. Lacey could barely remember what her best friend looked like, but she could recall to mind the blue beading on Elsa's dress and Iron Man's red gauntlets as perfectly as if they'd been standing in front of her only yesterday. Memories were funny like that.

She didn't really feel sad about Courtney Gillon any more. Back then, birthday parties, and Elsa and Anna, and Iron Man had been important things in Lacey's life, but they all seemed stupid to her now. In the last seven years she had learned what was important: food, fresh water, health, family. And so she continued to man her lemonade stand, and she continued to wait.

Fifteen days and counting. Yesterday, Lacey had used the last of their sun lotion. Already her hair had bleached two shades lighter from sitting in the sun for so long.

So far she had seen only one other person; an old coot on a pushbike. He had been in a bad way – his skin red and shiny with raging sunburn, the deep wrinkles of his faced lined with grime. He hadn't even glanced at her when he rode stiffly by, not even when she called out to him and jogged at his side for three dozen yards, trying to ask where he was going, where he'd come from, what's happening, man. She'd even offered a drink of lemonade on the house, but he hadn't heard her, wasn't even aware she was there, the next push of his foot on the pedal the only thing he lived for. She had stopped jogging and stood, panting, hands on her hips, watching him pedal away.

In the past, her approaching strangers would have resulted in a swift, severe rebuke from her grandmother, probably followed by a run-through of the kinds of scenarios that could result from such foolishness, none of which was a bedtime story. Sure, there had been that one time Grammy ran off a scrawny man who'd hunkered in the front yard, muttering to himself, and refused to move unless they fed him. Lacey had wanted to give him something – in those days there'd still been plenty – but Grams had vetoed her. It'd be like feeding a stray cat, she'd said. Once they took you for a soft touch, you'll never get rid.

The muttering man went hungry.

Another time, a group came by, two men and two women. They threw things and smashed the front window. Grammy had fired the rifle to encourage them to leave, but when they'd started yelling, 'Shit!' and 'Fuck!' and even the c-word at them, Grams fired a second and a third time. Lacey was sure she'd shot one of the fellas in the shoulder, but Grams insisted she'd only winged him. They'd left soon after, the smaller, unwounded man dropping his pants and squatting, leaving a gift for them in the dirt.

They weren't the norm, the cursing people or the muttering man. When other folk had approached, a waving rifle had been enough to have them retreating pretty quick and without any trouble. On the whole, Lacey didn't think two altercations merited so much suspicion. Still, whenever traffic appeared, her grammy's habit of snatching up their rifle and hurrying to take position at the door, where she could spy out the side window, was a long-standing practice in their house. And when Grammy wasn't there, Lacey was expected to do it in her stead. There wasn't a whole lot of charity left in the world, Grams told her, and she'd do well not to forget it.

Sun hot and high in the sky, her shadow casting a second slanted Lacey on the ground next to her, she gazed unseeingly at the tabletop and nibbled on her nails, worries crowding her thoughts. She hummed tunelessly to herself, her third-favourite Beatles song, 'Blackbird'. She was finding it hard to keep her mind off the last two tomatoes in her pocket. Her echoing chasm of a stomach was insisting she eat them, but her brain told her to abstain for just a little longer.

The silence broke. Lacey dropped her hand and sat up, a prairie dog on point. All her concerns about food and sun lotion fled when she heard that sweet engine note in the distance.

The motorcycle wobbled in the heat haze, difficult to make out at first, but it sharpened and solidified the closer it came. She watched it anxiously, all set to fake a faint if the rider didn't slow down, but the drop in engine tone told her it was losing speed, moving down the gears, readying to pull over. She sat back and tried to appear nonchalant.

Lacey knew her grandmother would *not* have been happy about this plan, but Lacey didn't see as she had any choice. Not if she wanted to keep hold of her sanity. Not if she ever wanted to see her sister again. There was only so much hunger and silence a girl could take.

CHAPTER 3

Pilgrim had already made a cursory scan of the area and could find no place for any thieves to be lying in wait. Indeed, the girl had set up the stand on a deserted stretch of highway with nothing but an old farmhouse a half-mile or so up the ways.

Mmm, lemons, Voice commented. *You like lemons.*

Pilgrim rolled to a stop next to the stand, within arm's reach of the plastic cups lined on the fold-away tabletop, and cut the engine. Each time Pilgrim's eyes wandered from the hand-painted sign, they returned a few seconds later. Something about the yellow of the lemons stirred a memory, something deeply buried beneath all that protective dirt. He didn't dig for it, though. There was little point in disturbing the graves.

A long beat of silence went by while the girl looked him and his bike over. He returned the favour, using the cover of his sun-glasses to study her; she was clean, which was the first surprise, and she appeared healthy. Her eyes were bright and clear and held little of the wary suspicion he'd grown accustomed to. He would put her in her mid-teens, but it was hard to tell with her sitting down – height was a good indicator of such things.

Sixteen, that's my bet, Voice said.

Pilgrim didn't enter into bets, especially not with disembodied voices.

'Nice cat,' the girl finally said, finished with her inspection.

'Nice lemonade stand.'

A ghost of a smile was there and then gone. 'You want a glass? Squeezed the lemons myself.'

'That would depend.'

'Depend on what?'

'On whether you'll take a drink with me.'

She was quiet again while she stared back at him. It was a searching stare, as if she were trying to gather some hidden meaning from his request.

'You want me to have a drink with you? That's it?' Her tone clearly conveyed her distrust.

He gave a nod. 'That's all. Scout's honour.'

This time when she smiled it hung around for a while longer. 'You don't look like no Boy Scout I ever saw.'

He doubted she had ever seen a Boy Scout in actuality, but didn't argue the fact. He became aware of how windswept his hair must look but made no attempt to neaten it. 'Appearances can be deceiving,' he said.

He wasn't especially thirsty; there was still a canteen full of fresh water and another two bottles stowed away in the bike's left-side pannier. It was the quenching of his curiosity that was of more interest to him today.

'You seen anyone pass by here?' he asked. 'Any groups of people?' He'd sighted a large travelling troop, five or more vehicles in convoy, only a few days ago. A distance away, they had made a strange sight, their dust cloud eating up the road around them. Nomadic groups of that size were unusual. The speed and direction of this one had appeared purposeful to Pilgrim, though, and he'd wondered briefly where it was heading.

The girl was already reaching for the big silver Thermos and pouring out two cupfuls, one piece of lemon dropping into each. 'No, sir. I've been looking out for folk, too. All I've seen are a fella on a bicycle and now you. Why? You looking for someone?'

'No,' he said. 'No one in particular.'

She set the flask aside and lifted both cups, offering one to him, having to lean far over the table to reach. The reflections from the lemon slice dappled a dancing yellow over her fingers, her skin seeming to absorb the colour until her fingertips glowed with it. The golden light dissipated slowly, fading until the glow winked out altogether, her fingers returning to normal as he took the lemonade from her. He hid his surprise when his hand closed around the cup.

Another surprise? *You'll have to be careful not to overexcite yourself and have a coronary*, Voice said.

Pilgrim paid him no mind. He was wondering how the girl had chilled the lemonade, especially since useable gas was scarce and only a generator could power a refrigerator for any length of time. Electricity hadn't run through these lines for years, the grids shutting down in a matter of weeks in some lucky places, only days in others, their systems sabotaged from the inside by angry, scared, self-destructive workers with whispering devils in their ears. For so long, humans had been resigned to the probability of nuclear bombs dropping, or wars breaking out, or the fickle tantrums of Mother Nature putting them back in their place, but nothing had prepared them for an internal attack. No defences had been built against the dangers hiding within. So, in fear they had scattered, running away from each other but unable to hide from themselves. Paranoia and survival became the new laws of the land.

And I became your trusted compadre, Voice said, somewhat smugly.

Pilgrim hmphed, unconvinced. Less 'trusted' and more 'burdened with', he'd say.

That's unfair, Voice complained. *I could be a whole lot worse, you know.*

The girl held her plastic cup aloft in a cheery salute, oblivious to Pilgrim's internal meanderings. 'Chin chin,' she said.

He lifted his own cup while pulling down his neckerchief.

She chugged hers down, the yellow glow from the lemon

dappling over her slim throat as it moved with her quick swallows. Pilgrim watched closely until half of it was gone before taking a mouthful of his own. It was tangy, verging on being sour, but a perfect measure of sweetness balanced it out so that, when he swallowed, his mouth was already watering for more. He drank the entire cup in three long pulls and gasped slightly when he was done, his tongue licking at a drop he had missed which was winding its way down the side of the cup.

The girl was watching him with a self-satisfied smile. 'It's good, huh?'

He narrowed his eyes at her, even though she couldn't see it from behind his sunglasses. 'It was OK,' he allowed.

She laughed at that, the sound high and tinkling and natural. It pulled him up short, its effect surprising him. It had been a long time since he had heard laughter.

Strike three! Voice crowed.

'Now,' the girl continued, 'on to the payment part.'

The payment part. Of course.

Pilgrim remained silent.

She reached towards the sign and tapped her finger against where it said '*Sale*'.

'Nothing's for free, my man,' she said.

'Right. So what do I owe you?'

'A ride.'

His stomach tightened and a sinking sensation lowered his brow into a frown. 'No,' he said.

His dark look and blunt refusal didn't faze her.

'You should have asked my price before you drank my wares. You didn't, you drank, and now you have to pay up.'

'A glass of lemonade isn't equal trade for gas.'

'Maybe it isn't. But such times call for inflated pricings.'

He didn't answer.

The girl frowned. 'Look, you can either be a decent fella and pay your side of the deal, like an honourable trader, or I can sit here till another traveller passes on by and hope to get a ride from them. Who's to say if the next traveller is honourable, though? Or isn't set on kidnapping a girl such as myself? Even set on having their *way* with me.'

The way she said 'way' left no doubt in his mind what kind of 'way' she meant. A sixteen-year-old who didn't use the words 'rape' or 'fuck' and believed that some kind of honour system still existed. Such old-fashioned beliefs and ways of speaking. He squinted up the road to the farmhouse. How long had she been holed up here?

And how does she know that we *don't want* our *way with her?* Voice asked.

The cat, which had been in some kind of vibration-induced stupor through most of the exchange, roused itself and gave a languorous stretch. It hopped from the bike on to the tabletop and began sniffing at the empty cup Pilgrim had placed there.

The girl absently reached out to the cat, her fingers stroking between and around its ears. The animal delighted in the attention, tilting its head and rubbing its face into her hand.

'C'mon, Boy Scout,' she said quietly, looking him dead in the eye. 'I just need a ride to Vicksburg. It's in the direction you're heading anyhow. Then I'll be out of your hair, I swear.'

He glanced away from her again and stared into the distance, his thoughts turning over.

Even if that convoy didn't come this way, Voice said, *doesn't mean there aren't others roaming about. She'll get herself hurt hanging around out here, asking strangers for rides. But if you want to drive off and leave her here, that's fine by me. The cat disembarked, too. Could be me and thee again: two hombres on the open road. Catch us some quality time togeth—*

'To Vicksburg, and no further,' Pilgrim said, cutting Voice off, keeping his eyes on the road's faded yellow centre line winding its way to the horizon. He made a point of not asking why she wanted to get to Vicksburg. It was none of his business.

'No further,' she agreed.

He didn't have to look at the girl to know she was smiling. He could hear it in her voice plain as day.

'And bring the lemonade with you,' Pilgrim added.

The girl had slipped neatly and easily on to the pillion seat behind him, despite the rucksack on his back. She wouldn't reach the top of his chest if they stood side by side. He wondered how she had managed to survive so long by herself.

She directed him to the farmhouse and asked him to make a quick stop so she could pick up her stuff. He pointed the bike off road and headed directly for the house. He admitted he wanted to scare the girl a little, deliberately going too fast for the uneven terrain, maybe scare her out of coming with him, but on every bump and accelerated slide he heard an exhilarated giggle from behind him.

He eyed the farmhouse as he approached, checking for twitching curtains or shadows passing behind windows, but there were no signs of life. The large picture window at the front had been boarded up and slats were missing from the roof. The siding was bleached a pale, sickly grey, its paint peeling away like flaking skin. It had seen some hard living, this house. A decaying, sepulchral vibe emanated from it. He kept his guard up regardless.

Jamming the brakes on, he skidded to a halt in front of the porch steps and waited for the girl to climb off. He met her smiling eyes and felt something akin to a rock being dropped into the deep well of his gut.

'You're going to be trouble,' he said. 'I can tell.'

She grinned wider. 'Don't be so negative. I'll be right back, OK? Don't go nowhere.' And with that she disappeared inside, leaving the front door wide open.

She's going to be more than trouble. She'll probably get us killed. Voice sounded resigned at the thought.

'That's even more negative than what I said,' Pilgrim said.

It's my job to be extra negative. You're too dull-witted to consider such things.

'She'll only be with us a couple days. She'll be long gone before we even know her name. Besides, it was you who talked me into it.'

What can I say? My good senses deserted me for a moment.

Pilgrim spent five minutes stroking the cat before impatience got the better of him. He nudged the cat aside with his boot and took the porch steps in two strides. He halted just inside the door, his eyes darting around, probing every nook and crevice and cranny.

The place was tomb silent but very bright. Sunlight streamed in through all the front-facing windows, the musty net curtains doing little to dampen its power. A fine covering of dust lay over everything: the banister, which led up the staircase in front of him to the first floor, the floral-patterned carpeting, the side table, where an old-fashioned rotary-dial telephone sat, with a walking stick propped up against it. He took another step, his boots sounding heavy and hollow on the thinly carpeted wood flooring. Through an arched doorway to the left was a comfortable-looking parlour with plump sofas and an old flagstone fireplace, and to the right, through a second archway, an unused dining room. The large fake-flower arrangement, which formed the centrepiece of the eight-seater dining table, was faded and grey. Of the girl, there was no sign.

He wanted the kitchen, so he headed right and cut through the dining room. He removed his shades, the light no longer stabbing daggers into his eyeballs, and left them dangling from their cord. His hand came to rest on the grip of the 9mm semi-automatic holstered at his hip.

He pushed the flat of his palm against the swinging door and pushed through into a bright and airy kitchen. This room was spotless; not a pinch of dust in sight. The centre island was covered with an assortment of bowls, jars, spoons and a scored and well-used chopping board. There were a few lemons left over from the girl's earlier preparations. But still no girl.

He caught a flash of movement out past the window and spied her in the backyard. She was kneeling down next to some sort of rock formation.

She'd better not be praying. Gods and religion are tricksy things these days.

'Hush,' Pilgrim said, distracted, moving closer to the window to watch.

A loud clatter had him half ducking and spinning, his hand snatching out his handgun. The cat was licking at the sugar that had spilled on the table, an upended jar rolling next to its back paw. It seemed oblivious to the fact it had a gun pointed at its head for the second time in one day.

I think it wants *to get shot.*

'It's going to get it, too.' He holstered the gun and turned back to the window. The girl was on her way towards him, a dripping aluminium container clutched in her arms. She passed between a child's swing set and a long mound of earth with a blanket of flowers sprouting from its top.

He met her at the back door.

'What's in the box?' he asked.

She flashed him a suspicious look. 'What's it to you?'

'Well, if you want to take it with you, it's going to have to fit on the bike. And because it's my bike, I get final say what it carries.'

She frowned at him, and he had to fight an amused stirring at the stubborn tilt to her jaw. She let out a sigh and said, 'Meat.'

'Meat?'

'That's what I said. *Meat.* You deaf?'

'No, not deaf. Just surprised. Where did you get meat from out here?'

She smirked. 'Same place all meat comes from – an animal.'

She traipsed past him and dropped the container on to the centre island. The cat gave a surprised yowl and streaked off the tabletop and out of the kitchen.

The girl went to the larder and disappeared, coming back out with a roll of greaseproof paper and a reel of string. She talked while she went about transferring the meat from box to paper.

'Grammy kept chickens. A couple goats, too. Though goats aren't too good to eat – they're kind of tough and stringy. Their milk lasted some before they dried up and turned into glorified lawnmowers. They sure did keep the yard nice and trimmed, though, I'll give them that.'

He was impressed with how quick and efficiently she wrapped the meat packages up. She'd obviously had practice.

'Once I done decided to leave this place' – she ran the string lengthways over one side of the package, flipping it over to repeat on the other side, doing a neat little twist then flipping a final time to make a tidy crossed-stringed parcel – 'there was little reason to leave the chucks out here by themselves. The things would only starve – they're sure not the brightest eggs in the box. They'd stopped laying, too. So I killed and cleaned 'em up so I could take 'em with me. Left them down in the well to keep cool until I got me a ride.'

'A well,' he said, an *ahhhh* of realisation yawning in his head. 'Explains how you chilled the lemonade in the first place.'

One mystery solved, Voice said.

'Yup. Grammy showed me the trick. Our genny was always conking out during storms when the electricity cut off.'

Pilgrim noticed she used the past tense when speaking about her grammy. Next to the sink, on the counter, he spied a single glass and an empty bowl. He also remembered the dust-covered walking stick propped up against the telephone table in the entrance hall. It appeared Grammy was no longer in residence.

There was sure to be a long, sad story behind that observation, but he didn't ask. Everyone's story was long and sad.

The girl wiped her hands on her faded jeans, all the meat now safely wrapped in greaseproof paper. She had made four compact packages.

'You think you can just about fit these on to your bike, Mr Boy Scout?'

He gave her a patient look, deliberately leaving the silence too long. 'I think we can manage.'

She seemed to hesitate a moment and then came over to him. When she slipped her hand into her front pocket he slid his hand to his gun, but all she pulled out was a small red ball. She offered it to him.

He eyed it warily.

'If you don't want it, I'll eat it. I had two but I already ate mine outside.'

A tomato. Of all things, she was offering him a tomato.

'I don't like tomatoes,' he said.

Her head went back, an expression of confoundedness dropping over her face. '*What?* I bet it's been years since you even *saw* a fresh vegetable, never mind tasted one, and you're passing it up 'cause *you don't like tomatoes?*'

'Correct. And it's a fruit, not a vegetable.'

'A fruit. Whatever. You really don't want it?'

He shook his head. 'No. But thank you.'

'Going once, twice . . .' She slowly lifted the fruit to her mouth, patently expecting him to stop her. He didn't, and she popped the entire tomato in, bypassing the time to savour it, eating it whole.

He openly watched her while she went about the business of chewing.

She spoke to him through her mouthful. 'You're not gonna tell me your name, are you?'

He became cautious. He didn't want to exchange names. 'It's

two days to Vicksburg, then we'll be parting company. No need for names or personal histories. It's easier if we keep things simple.'

Her head cocked to one side while she considered him. 'You're going to be a tough nut to crack.'

He decided to treat her like he did the cat. Ignore her. He turned on his heel and headed for the swinging door, directing his words over his shoulder. 'Gather up your stuff. You've got five minutes, then I'm pulling up stakes and heading out.'

'Yessir,' she said.

He had the feeling she saluted him, too, but he didn't pause to look back and check.

CHAPTER 4

She didn't know what to make of him. He was brusque and his eyes were too watchful and she was pretty sure he didn't know how to smile, but to chance waiting any longer for someone else to pass by would be stupid. And Lacey wasn't stupid.

Even if, by some crazy miracle, another traveller did appear – which, frankly, was unlikely, considering this man and the bald old fella on the bike were the only two people she'd seen in the past three months – how did she know their intentions would be any worse or any better? The answer was she didn't. As it stood, her gut wasn't sending up any alarms, and neither was any other body part, and that was all she could hope for.

This would mark the second time she had left the farmhouse since her new life started (a life consisting of the farmhouse's four walls, her grammy, their animals, the yards, and her daily, never-ending chores). Six years had passed since the first and only time, and that had been a run to collect supplies from the nearest town. The journey had been short and fast, and Grammy had given her the strictest of instructions to keep her eyes on her feet and *don't look up*. Lacey knew better than to disobey; she was getting pretty good at gin rummy and didn't want her punishment to be Grams refusing to play with her, especially now she was finally getting close to actually winning.

As they had driven into town, Lacey had glimpsed the bodies, but only from the corner of her eye (she hadn't been brave enough to sneak a look from under her bangs). She had kept her eyes glued to the footwell of their old station wagon, her heart pounding so hard she almost missed Grams telling her it was finally safe to raise her head. By then, they had pulled up outside the store.

Stepping out into the hot day, Lacey had been struck by how quiet it was: no running traffic, no rattling wheels of shopping carts, no din of people talking or outbreak of laughter, no kids younger than her crying, miserable at being dragged around the aisles and not allowed to touch anything. No *bloop-bloop-bloop* of items being scanned at the checkout. Nothing but the uneven *clomp* of her grammy's boots and walking stick as she came around the front of the car.

The wind had changed at that moment, blowing Lacey's hair back, and with it came a smell of eggs, rancid and sharp, as if the store had been built on top of a landfill, all the waste underfoot now rotting into a soupy, festering mess. The next second, the wind had changed again and the stench disappeared.

They had spent the next hour loading their car with food and bottled water and tools and supplies and more food. Lacey hadn't moved more than ten feet away from her grandmother the whole time, the wall of silence a teasing presence at her back, tapping on her shoulder, wanting her to turn and look and maybe find a line of corpses pressed up against the glass windows of the store, gaping in at her. There had been people lying in the aisles, mainly the household-hardware aisles where the claw hammers and hand saws were. At one checkout an employee was slumped over the conveyor belt, her long blonde hair trapped in the mechanism. Lacey hadn't looked too closely at any of them, and her grammy had hustled her along quick-smart whenever they came across one.

The entire trip had lasted two hours, and by the end of it Lacey had been glad to be back home, breathing in the dry desert air, the sweet scent of her grammy's plants welcoming her.

She could laugh about her childish imagination now, the silly fears she'd had while she was inside that store, but she couldn't forget how intensely she had urged the station wagon to speed up, her grammy to drive faster, wanting as much distance as possible between her and that ghost town.

She had already packed most of what she would take, and what that came down to was surprisingly little. Everything in the farmhouse had memories attached to it, and to carry things around simply for sentimentality's sake seemed pointless. Lacey had been taught to use everything to hand; if there was no use for it, there was no point in keeping it. Her travelling gear had been sitting ready beside her bed for the past two months.

She carted her stuff outside, stepping around the cat, which was daintily licking itself in a warm strip of sunlight at the top of the steps.

'I hope this is everything,' the tall man said, his pack open at his feet and the lid of one of his bike's side-box thingies levered up.

'That's it.' She dumped everything beside the rest of his belongings and dusted her hands off. 'So where have you come from? Where you heading? Have you seen many other people?'

He raised an eyebrow at her, then bent down and started stuffing her gear into his bag. 'Sure, lots. Most of them dead husks, though.'

She stared at him for a moment, lost for words. She licked her lips. 'Dead as in killed themselves?'

'Dead as in dead. Doesn't much matter how it happened.'

'Grams said everyone went crazy.' She watched him carefully, wanting to see his reaction. He didn't even bother looking up at her.

'They lost their minds, all right,' he said.

'So you *have* been to the bigger cities, then?'

He nodded, pulling the elastic cord tight on his pack and fastening the top.

'There must be folks there, right? Communities and such?'

'Cities are dangerous. Only people you'll find there are scavengers, ambushers and those who haven't got a civilised thought left in their heads. You don't go in unless you have to.'

'So where are they?'

'I've come across settlements elsewhere, but they don't take kindly to strangers stopping by.'

'Why not?'

He straightened and propped his hands on his hips. He regarded her for an uncomfortably long time with those watchful eyes. 'Trust issues.'

'What do you mean?'

He looked past her to the house, squinted up at the windows, his eyes lazily scanning its façade before coming back to rest on her. 'You've been here a while.'

It wasn't a question. She frowned, feeling defensive, and answered him anyway. 'Yeah. We went out some when we still had gas,' she lied. Grammy went out; Lacey wasn't allowed. 'To gather supplies and stuff. But never far. Never near to the cities.'

'Wise choice. Look, here's the deal. If you're lucky enough to find somewhere you can stockpile and grow food and not be attacked for it, then it's in a place that isn't easily located. Kind of like here. In fact, it's safest to stay away from other people altogether. I've seen men kill each other over a wrong word. I'm not kidding.'

She believed him. Even suspected he didn't know *how* to kid.

'Still want to leave?' he asked.

Her chest felt tight. She realised she hadn't taken a full breath since she'd started the conversation. She inhaled slowly, being careful not to suck it up in a way that revealed how much his words had affected her.

She thought back to the very last phone call she and her grammy had received – something she did most days, and especially in the last few months, since her grandmother had passed.

The telephone was a spin-dial, loud, and it had shrilled through the house like an alarm bell.

Grammy's voice came from the hallway: 'Talbot residence.' A pause, then: 'Sweet One, calm down, I can't hear you.'

Lacey's ears perked up. Grams only called her and Karey Sweet One. Putting down her bowl of Cocoa Krispies, she left the sitting room and wandered into the hall. Grammy had been wearing a housedress, one of her favourites, the one with the pink roses printed all over it. Work boots and socks made up the rest. Back then her hair had been short, grey but for two dark wings at each temple, soft as feathers.

'No. She's right here,' Grams was saying. 'Yes . . . Yes, of course we're OK . . . What's going on? I can hear the baby crying.'

Lacey hadn't made a sound as she came up behind Grammy, but her grandmother turned as if she'd sensed her. When Lacey saw her face, she stopped dead, fear slicing through her middle.

'Grams, what—?' But her grandmother's hand snapped up, palm outwards, and Lacey immediately shut up.

'What do you mean, David is—' Grammy's eyes widened and then narrowed into slits, lips disappearing as she pressed them into a thin line. 'Yes, you told me the strange things Susan was saying last week, but I . . . No, I don't have the TV on, but I can—'

Lacey bit into the inside of her cheek, anxiously watching her grandmother. She didn't know anything about a conversation Grams had last week about Karey's next-door neighbour.

'Listen to me, my darling,' Grammy was saying. 'Listen now. He doesn't sound like himself. You need to—' She paused to listen, shook her head quickly. 'No! Don't do that! Take

Addison up to the top floor and barricade yourself in. I don't care what he said! Do as you're told. Do it. Do it right now!'

'Let me speak to her,' Lacey said, reaching for the receiver. 'I need to speak to her.' Something was happening, something that even Lacey's nine-year-old brain understood as being Bad with a capital B. She *needed* to speak to her sister, but her grandmother caught hold of her hand and squeezed it so tight it made her wince in pain. Lacey's face felt hot. Frustration pooled thickly in her chest and rose into her throat, almost choking her. Tears were close, but she swallowed them back.

'Karey?' Grammy said. 'Karey, what's going on? Speak to me.'

Then she heard her sister's voice, shouting, *scared*, so loud Grammy's head flinched away from the phone. *'Don't come here, Grams! Don't bring Lacey here! Something's not right. It's not just David – there's stuff happening out in the street. He's saying the scariest things. Promise me, Grammy! SAY YOU PROMISE!'*

'I promise, my darling! But I don't know what—'

'Oh my God! Oh my God, David! What's happening! What're you—' Her sister's voice cut off.

Lacey didn't care any more – didn't care that Grams would have serious words with her later about her ill manners – she snatched the receiver out of her hand and pressed it to her ear. It was hot against her skin.

'Karey! Karey, it's Lacey! Hello? *Karey?*'

Dead silence.

She slammed the phone down, picked it up. Dialled her sister's number from memory. Listened. Slammed it down again and dialled it a second time because her fingers were shaking so badly on her first attempt she might have misdialled.

Grammy must have gathered by the look on her face that it wasn't working. She had gone straight to the TV in the sitting room and flicked it on.

Chaos. News channels filled with screams, crying, guilt-laden monologues of regret and despair and self-loathing, the rushing views of live camera feeds thrown from height and zooming incredibly fast as they plummeted to Earth; clips of frantic people running in front of speeding cars. Grammy had switched it off before Lacey could see anything else, and from then on it had remained turned off whenever Grammy was around. Even when Lacey sneaked a few minutes' viewing time, none of what she saw made sense, most of the images just a jumble of confusion, their rambling commentaries filled with strange messages. She would hear the TV during the nights when Grams thought she was sleeping; Lacey would sit on the top of the stairs in her PJs, the shifting white-grey flashes from the TV shining out of the sitting room, the volume turned too low to hear. Soon even Grammy had stopped her secret TV-watching, as the networks shut off, one by one.

Did she want to leave? he'd asked. Looking at the tall man staring back at her, waiting for an answer, Lacey tried to slow her breathing, make it look normal. *Did* she?

'Yes, I still want to leave,' she heard herself say.

'Fine. Is there anything else you need? I want to leave sometime today.'

'Oh. Sure. Could you give me five minutes?'

He nodded, and she hurried away, shakily jogging up the steps and into the shade. Winding her way back through the house, sliding one hand along the walls to steady herself, she made a beeline for the kitchen, not pausing there but going straight out of the back door and into the yard. She dropped to her knees in front of the mound of dirt and flowering lantanas where her grammy was buried and panted for breath.

'Maybe this is bad idea, Grams. A *terrible* idea. Jesus.' She glanced over her shoulder to make sure he hadn't followed her. 'No, I can *do* this.' She squeezed her eyes shut. 'Don't be a wuss, Lacey. Come on. Suck it up.'

When she opened them she found herself staring at the grave.

Her breathing had levelled out. She felt calmer, steadier. 'I'm packed, and I'm going. I can't stay. I'll die here.' It suddenly felt silly talking out loud. She glanced awkwardly across the yard, first at the dilapidated fencing that was in desperate need of weatherproofing, and then at the pitted rust creeping up the poles of her swing set. She chewed on the inside of her cheek and forced her eyes back to the dry, greying soil in front of her.

'I'm sorry, Grammy. I wish I didn't have to leave you like this. I wish I could just lie down on the ground and go to sleep and when I wake up everything will be OK.' The lantanas blurred in front of her and she glanced away again. 'You know what the hardest part is?' she whispered, staring fixedly at the seat of her swing, where she would sit as a kid and squeal, her grammy pushing her higher and higher, always higher than Lacey thought she'd ever dare push. 'It's not even leaving this place. It scares me, sure, but I'm OK with being a little scared. What bothers me most is leaving you here.' For all her attempts to hold them back, tears spilled over and a sob caught in her chest. 'I know you're just a body under all that dirt, and I know you can't even hear me, but I really don't want to leave you here alone. It's really hard to leave you all by yourself.'

For the last two minutes of her allotted time, Lacey went over to her swing and sat there, nudging at the ground with her toe, rocking herself back and forth and imagining it was her grammy doing the pushing.

CHAPTER 5

The girl travelled light, for which Pilgrim was grateful. He had managed to transfer most of what he usually carried in his rucksack to the bike's side panniers, had then shoved the meat packages and a limited assortment of cans and tins into the girl's smaller rucksack, along with a wad of clothes for her, and stuffed the whole lot into his now almost-empty pack. When he next looked up, she was striding back towards him with a rifle slung over her shoulder and a box of spare ammunition. She handled the weapon competently, comfortably even.

The natural naivety she wore folded back a little to reveal something tougher underneath. It surprised him; she'd been sitting out on the road with nothing but a flask of lemonade, after all, but someone, at some point, had taught her how to use that gun. The old battleaxe with the walking stick she had mentioned? He glanced over at the boarded-up window again, then back to the girl. It was a miracle they had both survived this long.

'You any good with that?' he asked, nodding at the rifle.

'Good enough.'

He grunted and held the rucksack up to her. 'You'll have to carry this while we ride.'

She scrutinised the pack, sizing it up. Unslinging the rifle, she leaned it against the side of the bike and turned her back to him. He helped her slide her arms through the straps and lowered the weight on to her shoulders. It wasn't too heavy, but he could hear her muttering under her breath about pack mules.

'What's wrong with your eyes?' he asked when she turned back to face him. They were red and bloodshot. He hoped she wasn't sick. That could be a problem.

The girl wiped her nose on her sleeve and sniffed. 'Nothing's wrong with them. I'm fine.'

'Hm. Need any bathroom breaks before we go?'

He was rewarded with an arched eyebrow. 'I'm not three. I still have control over my bladder. I don't need to go.'

'That's good. Don't want to be five minutes down the road and you asking me to pull over.'

He dragged his neckerchief up over his mouth and was mildly amused to see the girl pull out a long, thin cotton scarf and wind it around the lower part of her face. It was a dark red colour and had tassels. She also produced a pair of sunglasses and popped them on. They had big lenses. She resembled a baby fly.

He had to stifle an urge to smile when she bent down to pick the cat up and ended up stumbling forward a few steps, unaccustomed to the weight of the pack. Even from behind her sunglasses, the irritable glower she sent him was discernible.

He swung a leg over the bike and settled down, accepting the mangy fur-ball and setting it on the gas tank. Then he spent the next couple of minutes holding the bike steady as the girl struggled to climb on behind him.

'Hold this,' she said curtly, thrusting the rifle at him.

She ended up half pulling his shirt off by the time she had managed to clamber on.

She patted his shoulder. 'All set.' Her hand reached forward for the rifle, and he passed it back to her.

He started the engine and felt the girl wiggle around behind him as she settled herself. It felt strange to have a warm, breathing person nudging up against him and even stranger to have the insides of her jean-clad legs pressed against the outsides of his.

Don't be getting used to it, Voice warned.

'I won't,' he said, too low for the girl to hear.

41

CHAPTER 6

There was no conversation – the wind was too loud in their ears for that – but when they passed the signs for town, Lacey twisted to stare over her shoulder at the exit ramp. She couldn't help shouting, 'Look! That's it! The marker! This is as far as I've been!'

She laughed breathlessly, a thrill of excitement making her feel weightless, fidgety, as if she were embarking on some kind of organised trip that promised wonderful sights and the adventure of a lifetime or your money back. As she continued to stare over her shoulder, the bike's passing having kicked up a haze of dust that obscured the town's sign, her laughter grew hazy along with it.

She must have been gripping the man too hard, because he shrugged under her hands, an irritable roll of his shoulders. Easing her hold, she settled back down, facing forward. For just a moment, she bowed her head and lightly rested her brow against his right shoulder. Maybe if she kept looking at the back of his shirt, she wouldn't think about the distance stretching out between her and the only life she'd ever known, the miles racking up, the link between her and her grammy growing thinner and thinner, elongating like a piece of elastic. Soon it would snap, and all ties would be severed.

Isn't this what you wanted? she asked herself sternly. After years of worrying and wishing, there's finally a chance of getting to Karey. To Addison. And now you're getting cold feet?

No, she thought. *No*, this is what I want. It *is*.

She lifted her head, the rush of air hitting her full in the face and whipping around her sunglasses. Her eyes teared up. The wind flipped under her scarf and the tassels smacked her in the face. She struggled to tuck it inside her shirt.

They rode for three hours, and she drank in the sights. They passed a burnt-out café and Lacey called out, 'Look!' and pointed. A trickle of smoke rose up from its charred roof. 'People!' she yelled, straining to see any movement inside the café as they swept by.

The sign of smoke gave her hope. Things didn't just set themselves alight.

They went past a disturbing display of animal bones that some sicko had arranged in a bleached, jutting pyramid, and that slither of hope shrivelled up a tiny bit. She wasn't sure if she wanted to meet the person who'd made that.

Then came the billboard signs, each one defaced with jittery lettering dribbled in blood-like ribbons of red paint. The first one, for self-storage containers, had 'Your all liars!' scrawled across it. A little further along, 'Death is a sweet release' was painted over an advert for fast food. Next, a smartly dressed man advertising a firm of lawyers now advertised the phrase 'FREE YOURSELF'. And on the final billboard, smeared across a close-up of a pretty woman with a brilliant set of white teeth, was a message in dried red scribbles: 'LISTEN – The Darkness Speaks', and next to it a sloppily painted spiral, going round and round and round.

The man said nothing, and Lacey felt herself grow more and more despairing with every mile that passed.

CHAPTER 7

Pilgrim didn't stop for anything the girl pointed out, and she didn't comment when he sped past in silence.

They passed no other oncoming traffic, although they did come across an old guy on a bicycle travelling in the same direction, pedalling arthritically yet determinedly. Pilgrim had geared down to match the old coot's speed, glancing over to ask if he was doing OK. The guy never once acknowledged them, his bloodshot and rheumy eyes fixed on some unseen goal in the distance.

'That's the fella I saw two days ago!' the girl shouted near to Pilgrim's ear. 'He didn't speak to me then, either. God, look at his head.'

The poor man's bald head was glowing red, blisters already forming, filled with fluid. It must have hurt like hellfire, but the old guy gave no indication of discomfort, his bony knees slowly rising and falling, rising and falling, with each rotation of the bicycle's wheels.

Pilgrim pulled away from the cyclist and opened up the throttle, wanting to leave the man far behind.

The girl was quiet after that, not even directing his attention towards the handful of buzzards that were circling a crater a hundred yards out in the sparse brush. The black bodies took turns swooping low and vanishing into the pit before flapping skywards again. He didn't want to know what was laid out down there, but it didn't stop Voice from conjecturing on the matter.

Probably a recent suicide grave. Or maybe a bunch of murdered folk who got found out they heard a little voice like moi. Sun sucked all the moisture from the bodies, et voilà! A stockpile of ready-made jerky for the wildlife.

Pilgrim shut him out.

They silently chased after their lengthening shadow as the sun looped its way to the west, lighting their backs with a dwindling fire and leaving their faces in dimness. The sky took on a deep pink tinge with streaks of deep orange, as if a war waged beyond the horizon.

In the back of Pilgrim's head Voice sang in a low, eerily sweet voice. *Your stories are so old you just tend to keep them. Long winding road, you've got a secret but you won't share it.*

There had been signs for a Route 83 motel for the last ten miles. Normally, Pilgrim might have chosen to continue riding for a while as the sun set and the gloom gathered to full darkness, but he felt a need to get off the road today. A feeling in his gut. Or a case of the cold and squirmies, as Voice sometimes called them. Either way, he took the marked exit and leaned into the curve of the exit ramp, the asphalt humming smoothly beneath the bike's wheels, the rushing air pushing back his hair and combing through its strands with invisible fingers.

Big, open land, you hold the weight of the air in your hand.

Once they left the open highway, the roads became steadily worse. There were abandoned cars, hoods propped open and engines sporting gaping holes where parts had been removed. Trucks without wheels, doors flung wide and the interiors covered in dust and home to a collection of detritus. Pilgrim had to reduce his speed considerably in order to weave and navigate around the relics. The few cars which had been abandoned on grass verges had now been claimed by the verdantly smothering vines of kudzu spilling down from nearby trees. The plant had anchored itself to undercarriages and axles, crept up the cars' fenders and latched on to doorframes, crawling through broken windows to twine throughout the cars' innards, fusing around steering wheels, levers, pedals, until each vehicle resembled a leafy, slumbering beast.

He didn't brake for the traffic lights – they had been extinguished and dead for a long time – and turned on to the main street. It didn't consist of much more than ten or twelve stores, a two-pump gas station and a small town-hall-type building. Halfway down the main strip hung the motel's welcome sign. A twenty-foot gap in between the store fronts led to its parking lot; the main office was just off to the left as they pulled through. The parking lot opened up into a square courtyard lined with twelve rooms, each with a designated space in front for a car to park. A lone sedan, beige, nondescript, had been slotted into a bay on their left. Bashed up and unloved, it might have been parked there for years or days, it was impossible to tell.

When he pulled to a stop and killed the engine, the girl's first muffled words were, 'We're staying *here*?'

He twisted to look back at her, tugging down his neckerchief. 'Yeah. Why?'

She slid her sunglasses on to the top of her head like a headband, pushing the loose strands of her hair back and pinning them into place. It left her forehead smooth and bare, apart from the dirt and grime that had streaked across her unprotected brow. He was reminded again of how young she was.

She pulled her scarf down to free her mouth. 'It's just we can stay anyplace we want, and you've picked a cheap motel?'

'Right,' he said, without explaining further. 'You getting off anytime soon? I want to stretch my legs.'

'Oh. Sure.'

Her dismount was as inelegant as her mount, but at least she was off the bike in a matter of seconds and didn't keep him waiting.

The cat leapt to the ground and skulked off, no doubt

annoyed at having been kept prisoner on the gas tank for so long.

Pilgrim stiffly climbed off the bike and stood massaging the small of his back, arching his spine until he heard it crack back into place. He crouched down to stretch out his thigh muscles before rising to his full height, his head slowly swivelling as he took in the place. He lazily rolled his shoulders, his eyes skipping over each window and door, resting for a few extra moments on the solitary car parked in front of the room marked number 8. He was done with his stretches by the time his gaze passed over the girl (who had already shucked off the pack and was grimacing and rubbing her shoulders) and came to a halt on the motel office.

'Let's see if there are any vacancies,' he said.

He removed his shades as he strode towards reception, his eyes roaming restlessly, making little saccadic movements as he peered in through the large glass windows.

The tinkling bell over the door had barely had a chance to chime before he was drawing his gun and thumbing back the hammer, the muzzle pointed over the counter.

The girl's hushed voice came from directly behind him.

'What's—'

He held up a hand to silence her, nodding to the peg board fastened to the back wall where all the room keys hung. The key for number 8 was swinging in its place, the slight pendulum motion conspicuous in the otherwise still room.

Pilgrim leaned to one side, trying to get a look through the open doorway behind the counter. He glimpsed an arm and a hand coming up to level at him. It was holding something that looked like a slingshot.

Something flashed past him, sharply nipping the edge of his ear, and *thunked* into the wall behind him.

Cursing, Pilgrim ducked, and yanked the girl down with him. She hissed in pain and pulled her arm away, already bringing her rifle up and shouldering it, aiming towards the counter.

'Hold fire!' Pilgrim called out. 'We're not a threat! Take it easy.' He trained his own gun on the doorway. Being so low, he could only see a foot or so at the top. The ceiling in the room beyond was yellowing and cracking, parts of the paint having broken free, leaving greyish, mottled plaster underneath.

'*What do you want?*'

The voice sounded brittle, full of panic, and female.

'We just stopped for a room. That's all.'

There was a long pause. Then: 'For real? You want a room?'

Pilgrim nudged the girl in her side and nodded towards the back room, indicating she should answer.

She rolled her eyes but turned away and raised her voice. 'That's right. My travelling companion here thought it'd be a swell idea to stop off at a cheap motel – you know, instead of simply finding a nice, big, old, empty house to camp out in.'

There was a rustle of movement. The woman's voice was now a little closer and a lot less panicked. 'I'm gonna come out, OK? Don't . . . *do* nothing, OK?'

'We won't,' Pilgrim said, although he didn't lower his gun.

A thatch of tangled hair came into view first, and then the woman stepped around the edge of the counter. Young – no older than twenty-five – she looked like she could do with a damn good wash. The front of her shirt was splotched with stains, as if she had eaten a fair few meals since its last laundering. She held what he had first thought to be a slingshot but could now see was a small homemade crossbow pointed down at the floor and off to one side.

Lowering his gun, Pilgrim carefully stood, making no quick movements, and slid it back into its holster. The girl stood up beside him but kept her rifle centred on the woman's chest.

'Hey,' Pilgrim murmured to the girl, gesturing for her to lower the gun.

She kept the tangle-haired stranger sighted for a few extra seconds, probably to get her point across, and finally relaxed her stance.

'Hey, man, I'm real sorry about that.' The filthy woman winced as she gestured towards Pilgrim's head. 'Wasn't sure if you were with a gang or something. Can't be too careful.'

Pilgrim reached up and was surprised when his fingers found the tackiness at the tip of his ear, the split in the cartilage seeping fresh blood.

'It's fine. It's just a nick.' He pulled his hand away to look at the red stain on his fingertips.

The woman gave a funny huffing laugh. 'A Nik gave you a nick.'

Pilgrim frowned.

The woman stopped laughing. 'Uh, Nikki. My name's Nikki.' And she transferred the crossbow to her left hand and offered her right.

Slanting the girl a look as he reached for the hand Nikki proffered, Pilgrim said, 'You can call me Boy Scout.'

The girl beside him snorted. 'Right. And you can call me Lacey, 'cause that's my name.'

Lacey, Voice said. *Suits her.*

Pilgrim was about to agree but was struck so hard in the back of the head he never got the chance.

CHAPTER 8

Lacey flinched at the hollow *thwack* that came from the Boy Scout's head. He staggered, folding inward, bending over at the waist, legs buckling at the knees. As he went down his head bowed forward, as if he were greeting the floor on his way to meet it. It was a slow toppling – he was a tall guy and had a long way to fall – yet Lacey had no time to try to catch him. The whole reception office, windows and all, seemed to shake when he hit the ground.

She had half reached a hand down to him when she was grabbed roughly from behind, two arms winding around her and pinning her arms to her sides. She cried out and doggedly held on to her rifle. Strained to raise it. Couldn't. She struggled to break free, but it was as if she were bound by strips of iron. Kicking back as hard as she could, the heel of her boot connected solidly with her captor's shin and she felt a bright flare of pleasure when there was a male grunt of pain.

'*Let go!*' she yelled.

Nikki rushed forward and snatched the rifle out of her hand.

'*You bitch!*' Lacey kicked out at her, but she danced out of range. Lacey reversed her kick and drove her heel back into her captor's shin again, eliciting a second pained grunt.

Lacey swung her leg up for a third kick.

'Get her feet, for fuck's sake!'

The rifle clattered on to the counter and Nikki leapt forward and caught Lacey's boot, then ducked down and grabbed her other, flailing foot. She was lifted bodily off the ground.

'*What're you doing? Hey!*' Lacey frantically tried to catch a glimpse of the Boy Scout, but he was crumpled up on the floor and hadn't moved.

They shuffled with her around the counter.

'*No!*' Lacey wrenched upwards, trying to twist her way out of their hold, but their hands clamped down on her, grips cruel. '*What do you want?*'

'A screamer,' Nikki said happily. 'My favourite.'

'*Let me go! Help!*' Lacey directed her shouts at the Boy Scout, but there would be no help coming from him.

Oh my God, he's *dead*. How can he be dead? This can't be happening! I shouldn't have left the farmhouse! I was an idiot to leave! I should have stayed and taken my chances!

'Hurry it up,' the man said, his breath hot on her head. 'He might wake up.'

Wake up? He's *not* dead? A burst of something – hope, happiness, relief? – had Lacey redoubling her efforts to squirm free.

'Stop struggling or I'll snap your neck.'

Lacey stopped. She tried to calm her breathing, her racing heart, but they were out of her control. She concentrated on taking one breath at a time, panic close to overwhelming her, to drowning out that small, rational voice telling her to keep calm, take it easy, she'll be OK. She breathed through her nose, which was a mistake, because her captors' odour made her gag. How could they smell so *bad*? And it wasn't just stale sweat and unwashed bodies and filth; there was something more. Lacey glanced down at the woman's hands, locked around her ankles. Dirt was embedded under her nails.

Not dirt, she told herself, her body stiffening. *Blood*.

They entered a corridor, and the smell only got worse. She fought her rising urge to vomit. Between them, they carried her to a door at the far end. Nikki went backwards, shouldering it open, and a dimly lit set of stairs led downward, a faint pool of light spilling across the floor at the bottom. Nikki started down and, with each step, Lacey's terror grew, as if she could hear a den of rattlesnakes stirring under the treads, their warning rustles growing louder the further they descended.

'Take whatever you want,' Lacey gasped in a rush. 'Just take it and let me go.'

Nikki snickered breathlessly. Carrying her was obviously tiring the woman out. Lacey was glad. She hoped the shitbird had an asthma attack and collapsed. 'Oh, we'll take what we want, sweetie-pie. Don't need your permission for it, neither.'

The temperature dropped noticeably when they reached the bottom. They took her into a room where a lamp lit the space in a sallow glow, jaundiced light filtering over a messy, unmade bed.

Lacey talked fast. 'Listen, you don't need to do this, OK? Please, let's just talk this out. No one has to do anything. You're a *woman*,' she blurted at Nikki. 'Why are you *hurting* me?'

'Aw, I don't want to hurt you.' Nikki was looking over her shoulder as she navigated the foot of the bed, but she took the time to send Lacey a sly glance. 'There's not so much choice as there used to be, my lovely. Me and my brother got needs, too, you know. And it gets a little boring messing around with each other.' Nikki grinned over Lacey's head at the man. 'Am I right, bro? Variety is the spice of life, right?'

They dumped her on to the bed, and Lacey scrambled to the other side. Hands caught her and dragged her back. They flipped her, held her down while they wound wire around her wrists. She fought but took a punch to the gut that left her wheezing and curled up. They finished lashing her hands to the bed's headboard.

She half-heartedly kicked at the blankets, but quickly stopped when the wire pinched painfully into her wrists. She lay still and panted, eyeing them both.

Nikki beamed down at her, but the man, who she was seeing

properly for the first time, was expressionless. He was big and stocky and stared back at her. Meeting his eyes was difficult, but Lacey didn't look away, even as her heart threatened to pound its way out of her chest.

'Relax,' he told her. 'Enjoy your stay here. Take in the view.'

There were no windows. They were in the basement.

'Fuck you,' she said.

Nikki tutted. 'Naughty, naughty. We'll have to sort out that dirty mouth of yours when we get back.' Her smile was fixed in place – this was a whole lotta fun for her.

Lacey didn't bother to answer; she'd tried talking and it had gotten her nowhere. Instead, she watched silently as they left, stubbornly refusing to let her tears fall until their footsteps had faded away to nothing.

CHAPTER 9

Pilgrim didn't open his eyes straight away. He left his head hanging down, his chin on his chest, and tried to come to terms with the grating pain in the back of his skull. It was like having shards of glass scored across his nerve endings – a constant jagged violin-stringed concerto. He also kept his eyes closed because he wanted to gain as much information as he could before revealing he was conscious again.

He was sitting upright in a chair. It was solid beneath his rump and thighs and back, and had absorbed his body heat while he had been sitting on it. Tensing and carefully flexing his muscles, he leaned imperceptibly to one side. Centred himself. Leaned to the other side. The chair didn't lean with him, or give at all. At his best guess, he was sitting on an unpadded, well-constructed wooden chair. His forearms were tied to the chair's arms, and his ankles to the legs. The ties they had used felt like wire. Bound tight, as well. Any sort of struggle or forceful movement and they would saw right into his flesh and cut deep, possibly even to the bone.

That's a good thing. Voice's words echoed down a long, distant tunnel.

And Pilgrim had to agree. If they had tied him so securely, they surely didn't intend to kill him anytime soon. They had other plans.

He was sitting upright because something else had been wound around his middle and chest and passed around the chair back. Duct tape, maybe.

There was a chemical scent to the air, almost like bleach, and under it a dampness. There was something else, too. A hint of something he had smelled before, which made shivers scurry down his back and gooseflesh pebble his skin.

Through the filter of his closed eyelids, he discerned a light source of some kind in front of him. It wasn't a strong light, though. A single bulb?

Voice gave his version of a shrug. He wasn't going to be any help here.

Pilgrim could hear other voices. Outside voices. They came from beyond the walls of the room. Faint. Muffled. He opened his eyes and raised his head.

He was facing a door. From a quick scan, it was the only door in or out of the room. No windows, either. Basement room. A kerosene camping lantern sat on the floor in a corner. It gave off a dull glow but it still left an imprint on his vision after he had looked at it for a brief second. There was a second chair facing his, currently unoccupied. It matched the one he was tethered to. And it was wooden. Possibly beech.

There was little else in the room. A half-full plastic water bottle. A discarded T-shirt. A single black sock. More wire, wound tight in its reel. A scrunched old newspaper, the front page half visible: '*Climate Change as Threatening as Nuclear War, Scientists Warn: Irreversible Damag*—' The rest of the headline was cut off. And on top of the newspaper a pair of clippers, the kind you would use to cut through barbed wire or metal links.

Pilgrim zeroed in on them. They had red plastic handles, and short, very sharp scissor-blades dotted with rust.

He could still hear those distant voices. They didn't appear to be moving any closer. Gripping the edges of the chair arms, his knuckles turning white, he experimented, pressing the balls of his feet down into the floor while lifting the chair with his hands. His thigh muscles flexed hard, as did his biceps. The chair creaked. Its front legs rose off the floor by an inch or two. At that point, the stainless-steel wire nipped sharply into his ankles, despite the protection of his boots. He let the chair settle gently on all four legs again.

Eyeing the clippers, he cursed under his breath. They were too far away. The only way to get to them would be to shuffle inch by measly inch, shucking the chair closer in tiny hops. It could be done. But it would be noisy. Noise, he could deal with, but only if he would have time to cut himself free and be ready when the owners of those voices came barrelling into the room to find out what all the racket was about. And he figured it would take at least ten hops to get over there. He would need at least twenty seconds.

The voices increased in volume as they moved nearer.

The door handle turned and Nikki walked in, followed by a bigger, male version of herself. The brother, Pilgrim surmised.

'Wakey wakey!' Nikki said, her grin showing too many teeth.

Pilgrim didn't reply. He ran his eyes over the stocky man. He was a few years older than Nikki, and had the same colouring: pale eyes and a smattering of freckles dotting his untanned skin. His eyes were unflinching. The guy would make a good poker player.

Or serial killer, Voice said faintly.

He held Pilgrim's gun in one meaty fist.

'I hope you like the room,' Nikki continued. 'It's one of the finest we have. We're all about customer care and comfort here.' She laughed. It sounded like a horse's braying, too loud and affected.

Nikki moved the empty chair a little to one side and angled it so that it no longer sat straight in front of Pilgrim. She dropped down into it, a huge exhalation of breath indicating what an exhausting day she'd suffered through so far.

The brother remained standing, body centred in front of Pilgrim.

Pilgrim found their stances interesting.

He kept his eyes on the brother, matching him stare for stare, wondering if the man would be equally as impassive if Pilgrim weren't currently fastened to a chair.

I would say so. He looks nuts. Voice was stronger, closer.

'You're finally up to talking, then,' Pilgrim said to him.

You knew it wouldn't shut me up for long.

'Oh, we have a lot to talk about,' Nikki said.

'No kidding,' Pilgrim said.

She barked a laugh, sounding like a dog this time, and looked up at her brother. '*See?* I *told* you he'd be a hard-ass.'

The brother didn't flick Nikki a glance, merely kept staring at Pilgrim. Like he wanted to look inside his head, crack it open with his gaze and riffle through what lurked in there: thoughts, intentions, plans. Just stick his thick fingers in and paw his way through it all. His gaze was fucking relentless.

Pilgrim raised his brow, challenging him to speak up.

The corners of the brother's eyes tightened.

Nikki was looking back and forth between Pilgrim and her brother, a confused crease bisecting her brow.

I don't like him. At all.

Pilgrim grunted in agreement.

You should try and get control of the situation.

'How the hell am I supposed to do that?'

'Do what?' Nikki said.

Ask them what they want.

'I know what they want.'

'Who're you talking to?' she asked, a sharp edge of suspicion in her tone.

OK, what do *they want?*

'They want the girl. And my bike. Any provisions I've got. And they want me to know they've got all those things before they have their fun.'

Control. He felt Voice's equivalent of a nod. *You're probably right.*

'Oh, I'm right,' Pilgrim said.

'Like, seriously, you're one of them, aren't you?' Nikki half rose from her seat, eyeing him warily.

The smile Pilgrim gave her barely touched his lips, and yet the woman blanched, blinking nervously, her throat moving as she swallowed. She looked at her brother.

Pilgrim's voice snapped like a whip. 'Don't look at him, you piece of shit. He won't help you, not when it comes right down to it. He'll leave you bleeding like a stuck pig on the floor.'

'Shhhhh.'

The brother held an index finger to his pursed lips. 'Shhh,' he whispered, and with his other hand gently pushed his sister back down into her seat. 'You're going to wake the girl. She's asleep right now. In the honeymoon suite.'

Pilgrim kept his voice even. 'I don't know her – not even her name. I only met her today. She's no one to me.'

Voice grew quiet. He didn't know where this was going. He couldn't always read Pilgrim's intentions, the same as Pilgrim couldn't always read his.

'In fact, if you turn me loose,' Pilgrim continued, 'I'll give you a hand holding her down. She seems the scrappy sort. I bet she bites.'

What are you doing?

'She'll need at least two to handle her,' Pilgrim said, 'and I don't think your prissy-assed sister is up to it.'

'Hey!' Nikki blurted. 'Screw you!'

Pilgrim gave a small shrug, all that it was comfortable to do while wire lashed his forearms to the chair's arms. 'This is a harsh world we live in. And a harsh world calls for harsh measures. I'm willing to do whatever it takes to survive.'

Voice had gone silent again. Out of disgust with Pilgrim's suggestions, or simply confused by them, Pilgrim wasn't sure.

'Fuck you, man!' Nikki stood abruptly and turned to her

brother. 'I can help you just fine with that bitch, Russ. Don't listen to this prick. He's one of *them*. He *hears* stuff. We should be slitting his throat, not letting him talk.'

Russ considered his little sister. He blinked slowly, as if his mental processes were taking up all the power in his body, grinding everything else down to a crawl. He looked at Pilgrim, and even his words came slowly, drawling out as if he were suddenly very sleepy. 'She's trussed up as good as you are there, partner. Don't need no one to hold her down.'

Pilgrim felt a slight easing of tension in the man, a bending towards his suggestion – his gut told him so – and he pushed that final bit more, easing his way in, chipping away with a few more well-placed words. 'Yeah, but you don't want her completely tied down, do you?' he said, his voice lower, deeper, *slicker*, wanting the words to suggest themselves into the man's thoughts and not rest only in his ears. 'You want her to wriggle, fight back a little. Enough to make it fun.'

Russ blinked that slow blink again and trundled a thoughtful nod.

'*No fair, Russ*,' Nikki whined, her words breaking in. 'You *promised* it'd be my turn!'

And that was all it took to cut off any power Pilgrim had held over him.

'Oh, calm the fuck down,' Russ said to her, dragging his attention away from Pilgrim. 'You think I'm dumb? I'm not about to untie him.'

'Then what—'

'Leave the door open so he can hear,' Russ said, twitching a nasty glance Pilgrim's way. 'He'll enjoy listening to us while you do the holding down and I do the fun-making.'

Nikki laughed. It was a relieved whoosh of air, like the air expelled from a whale's blowhole. She threw her own mean look at Pilgrim, accompanied with a triumphant little smirk, but she couldn't hide the wary eye flicker she sent his fastened wrists, checking he was fully trussed up before backing out of the room.

She left the door wide open.

Pilgrim listened closely to their retreating footsteps. They went only thirteen steps and then he heard another door unlatch. The brother spoke to the room's occupant – the girl (*Lacey*, Voice reminded him, although he hadn't forgotten) – his words too low to make out. Pilgrim heard the girl's response, though.

'*Fuck off and die!*'

Pilgrim smiled. She would need to keep her nerve; the next few minutes weren't going to be pleasant ones for her.

He cocked his head towards the open door, the dull beat of his pulse counting off the seconds. He flexed his fingers a couple times, his knuckles cracking. The wood of the chair's arms creaked when he gripped it, the cords of muscles in his forearms tautening like ropes. He barely noticed the pinch of the wire digging into his wrists.

There was a scuffle from the other room, and the girl yelped. There were a few grunts and some shouted instructions from Russ, the words lost in the girl's sudden yelling.

It was all the noise Pilgrim needed. He yanked up on the arms of the chair and shoved down hard with his feet, tugging at the chair, feeling it shift a few inches over. He did it again, grunting in effort as he made the chair baby-hop closer to those clippers. He was two thirds of the way to his goal when a loud tearing sound ripped through the air. He didn't need to hear the girl's shriek to understand what was being torn away from her.

Someone whooped – most likely Nikki – and broke into gleeful laughter.

Over their exuberant sounds, Pilgrim strained harder than he dared, a jagged seam of pain crackling down the back of his skull. Pressure thumped a hard, sluggish tattoo in his temples, veins throbbing thickly under the thin tissue of skin. His arms bulged and his thighs quivered, lactic acid searing through his bunched muscles. Blood slicked his wrists, dripping down the wood and staining the grain red. He yanked himself up and sideways, his body leaning too far to the right, the chair teetering on two legs. He continued tilting, unbalanced, forcing the chair over, and crashed down, his shoulder and arm and hip taking the full brunt of the fall. His jaw clenched down on a sharp cry of pain as all his bones clacked together, the shock of impact ringing through his body, hurts flaring up in every overstressed joint. But that last push, that last rush of effort, did its job. As he landed, he scudded along on his shoulder like a ship cutting through mud to dock, his hand coming to rest mere inches from the clippers, and all it took was a few extra full-body shuffles from where he lay – his head jerking back and forth and his hips humping up from the chair's seat – first for his stretching little finger to brush the edge of the newspaper, and then for his bloodied fingers to grip on to it, crumpling it into his fist and dragging the clipper's handles close enough to claw into his hold.

Two seconds later he had twisted the clippers round and jammed the open blades between his wrist and the arm rest, slicing through the wire as easily as if it were string.

Five seconds after that he was finishing cutting loose ankle number two.

And five seconds after that, he had sprinted down the corridor and was bursting into the room.

A second kerosene lantern threw light on to the sobbing girl as she struggled on the bed underneath Russ. His pants were unfastened and halfway down his thighs. His ass was very white, with a fine fuzz of pale hair.

Nikki was at the head of the bed, her weight pressing down on the girl's arms, preventing her from fighting back, although Lacey continued to buck and twist and yell in between her sobs.

That was all Pilgrim had time to see. It was all he *needed* to see, because by then he was leaping on to the bed behind Russ and grabbing the guy's greasy hair in one fist, yanking his head back and jabbing the clippers into his exposed throat. The blades were open as they sank into Russ's neck, and Pilgrim clamped them shut, severing the windpipe, the oesophagus.

A geyser of blood erupted. More than Pilgrim was expecting. He must have jabbed deep enough to cut the carotid.

The girl turned her head away, eyes screwing shut, blood splashing over her cheek and ear. Nikki was too slow and slack-jawed with shock when she got a mouthful of her brother's blood. She scrabbled away from Pilgrim, choking and gagging, falling off the side of the bed. Her hands tore at her face in a frenzy to clear the blood away.

Pilgrim lifted Russ away from the girl, hauling him up by his hair and the waist of his loose pants, heaving him at his sister. Russ wasn't light, but he wasn't a dead weight just yet, either. He body-slammed Nikki and crushed her flat to the floor – covering her in much the same way he had covered the girl a second before – his body convulsing and shaking, his foot jack-booting against the floor, going *rat-a-tat-tat* as he tap-danced his way to hell. Nikki was mostly lost underneath Russ's bulk, only her head showing above the guy's shoulder. Her eyes were startlingly white in her blood-smeared face, her mouth flapping open and closed like a slack-jawed puppet's as she babbled a bunch of unintelligible words.

Pilgrim's mouth twisted in distaste. He stepped down off the mattress and planted his boot in the woman's face. Her head snapped back and smacked off the floor with a sickening thud.

Russ's shoe gave one last floor-tapping jerk and lay still.

A steadily expanding pool of blood grew under Nikki's head like a black halo, dark and viscous.

Pilgrim stood over them, not moving except for his chest, which rose and fell on each heavy breath. Blood dripped from his fingers, ticking on the floor faintly as if his body were trying to tick off time in the absence of anything else that could measure its passing. One-tick, two-tick, three-tick.

On the tenth tick he turned his head towards the bed. He did it in small degrees because he didn't want to see what had been done to the girl.

She had moved only to cover her chest with her arms and twist her legs together. Her shirt had been ripped in half down the middle of her torso and hung in rags to either side. Her jeans and underwear had been removed. Her legs were long and slim and shocked him with their nakedness. He looked away from them and back to her face. She had her head turned away and, he assumed, her eyes were still screwed shut.

He carefully lowered himself to sit with his back to her, the mattress sinking under his weight and tilting her towards him. He was loath to touch her – it was probably the last thing she wanted.

'Hey . . .'

Lacey, Voice whispered.

'I know her goddamn name,' he snapped.

Sorry. But Voice said it in the *sor-ree* kind of way kids did when they weren't sorry at all.

'Did they—' Hurt you, he was about to say, but he cut himself off because it was a stupid question. He lowered his head and contemplated the palms of his hands. The blood was coagulating – a mixture of his own and Russ's – clotting along the grooves and lines and calluses of his skin.

'Did he—' He bit down on his tongue hard enough to make his eyes water, then forced his jaw to relax. 'Did he manage to get inside you?'

She was silent so long he was forced to look over at her. Her head had started to turn back towards him, but she couldn't quite finish the movement. She had her fist pressed to her forehead, between her brows, her eyes were open and her lips downturned at the corners. A tear trickled out from the corner of one eye and trailed snail-like through the blood to her ear, where it was lost.

She made a guttural sound, deep in her throat, drew in a harsh breath and shook her head hard from side to side. 'No. No, but *God*, he was trying to. I could feel it *prodding* at me. He almost—' She sobbed and moved her hand from her brow to press it over her mouth. Her eyes, when she could bring herself to meet his gaze, brimmed with tears, and her words were almost unrecognisable, spoken against her hand. 'You took long enough getting in here.'

He scrubbed the back of his wrist over his mouth, quickly stopping when he realised he was probably smearing blood over himself. 'You ever want to tie someone up, use wire. It's very effective.'

She made a sound halfway between a sob and a laugh. She swiped a rough hand across her eyes, angrily rubbing her tears away. 'My grammy always said this would happen. Said it was dangerous out here and I was safest at the farmhouse. She was right.'

'Maybe. But don't think everyone's like them.' Pilgrim got tiredly to his feet and turned away from the bed, looking down at the bodies at his feet. 'These two were a bad sort. They got left alone too long and went rotten on the inside.'

He kicked Russ's foot out of his way as he went past. He headed out of the room. The girl didn't call him back, but he figured she would probably appreciate a little time to pull herself together.

He walked down the hall to the room he had been held in and collected the bottle of water and discarded T-shirt from the floor. The shirt was a little dusty, but clean enough. It had a garishly coloured print of a blue voodoo-style skull on the front, and 'Bob's Tiki Bar & Restaurant' in yellow print running along the underside of the skull's jaw. He picked up the lantern, too. When he returned to the girl, she was sitting on the end of the bed, folded arms covering her chest, legs once again clad in her jeans. She watched him approach, then dropped her eyes.

'Sorry,' she muttered.

'For what?'

She nodded at the floor.

There was a pool of vomit near her feet.

He felt a softening towards her, a tingling heat opening up in the centre of his palm, curling his fingers inwards as if they wanted to reach out to her. He didn't let them. The best thing would be for him to get her out of here. They'd already spent enough time in this place.

'Here, clean yourself up.' He handed her the bottle of water and the shirt. 'We're leaving. Get dressed.' He turned his back to give her some privacy.

For a second he didn't think she would move, but then there was the sound of the bottle cap unscrewing, a gargling, a spit. Then came a rustling of clothing. Pilgrim walked around the side of the bed and ducked down to search. It didn't take him long to find his gun, placed under the bed, far enough away from the girl in case she had somehow worked an arm free but close enough if Russ had needed it.

Not close enough, Voice said.

'I guess not,' Pilgrim murmured.

He also found her boots.

By the time he came back to the foot of the bed, the girl had cleaned most of the blood off and was dressed. The T-shirt was at least two sizes too big for her. It made her look like a ten-year-old playing dress-up.

'You OK to walk?' he asked, passing her shoes over.

She gave a short nod, glancing up at him. She bent over at the waist and pushed her feet into her boots — first her left, then her right, making Pilgrim think that was probably the order she did it in every morning after getting out of bed — and laced them up. Her fingers trembled, but she tied the laces with precise movements and didn't make a mistake.

'OK, move it.' He nodded at the door.

Glancing over her shoulder at the two bodies heaped in the corner, she opened her mouth as if about to say something. She closed it again without uttering a word and stood up. She limped her way to the door and Pilgrim followed. He didn't look back at the siblings. They wouldn't be going anywhere.

CHAPTER 10

With the lantern's help, they found their way up to the ground floor. None of the doors was locked; Nikki and Russ had never expected their captives to break free. The darkness from the basement followed them up, the night having fully settled beyond the windows they moved past, transforming the glass into blackened mirrors. The reflections of a shuffling girl and a tall, shadowed man ghosted by.

They came into the reception room and found the cat on the floor. It was laid out on its side, its chest caved in.

Pilgrim crouched down next to it and briefly rested the backs of his fingers against its neck. The fur was cool, the warmth from the animal having long seeped away.

He stepped over it, pushing out into the night and taking a deep breath as he crossed the threshold. It felt like the first full breath he had taken in a while. The night air was cool in his lungs; it smelled of earth and plants and things that were alive.

The girl appeared beside him. 'I'm sorry about your cat,' she said softly.

'It wasn't my cat.'

He saw her shrug from the corner of his eye.

'I'm sorry anyways. It seemed like a good cat.'

She met his gaze when he looked over, and held it, just like she had back at the lemonade stand.

He was the first to look away. His eyes fell on the solitary car parked in front of Room 8.

Eight could be a problematic number. Pilgrim knew this, the

same way he knew there were still four hours before the sun would rise, and that the girl weighed somewhere between 95 and 105 pounds. No more than 105, though. These were just things he knew.

'You're gonna check out that room, aren't you?' the girl asked.

'Thinking about it.'

'Is that such a good idea?'

'Probably not.'

They were silent.

'What do you suppose is in there?' she asked.

Both of them stared at the closed door of number 8. From where they stood, they could see the curtains had been drawn.

'Nothing good,' he said.

'I think I'll stay here.' The girl hugged her arms across her chest as if the chill in the air had gone bone deep.

Pilgrim nodded absently. He was finding it difficult to look away from that door – the door and the brass-coloured number 8 that hung askew from its front, almost turning it into infinity. The door had a crack running up from the bottom edge nearest the hinge; it looked like the letter Y, the way it branched off at the top. Or like a dowsing stick. Or a slingshot, like the one Nikki had used that had turned out to be a crossbow. Pilgrim's ear went hot where the arrow had nicked him – Nikki 'nicked' him, indeed – and not just hot, but *white*-hot; he expected to hear the blood sizzle and hiss like a sausage hitting a frying pan full of fat.

He realised he had raised himself up slightly on the balls of his feet and was leaning forward towards that damn room.

'Hey.'

The girl touched his arm, just above his elbow, and he blinked and felt that yawning grasp let go, and he rocked back on to his heels as the world rushed in around him.

You OK? Voice asked.

'You OK?'

He almost laughed at the unity of their questioning. He didn't feel particularly funny, though.

He looked at her, in the too-big T-shirt and bloodied jeans, and nodded. 'Yeah, sorry. I'm fine. Let's find your rifle before I get to doing anything. I'd rather have you armed than standing out here by yourself with nothing but your wits to protect you.'

'My wits are pretty sharp.'

'Not sharp enough for my peace of mind. Stay here. And yell if that door opens,' he added, already moving away.

'You had to go and say that, didn't you?' she called after him.

As it turned out, he wasn't gone for more than a couple of minutes. Their captors hadn't hidden their stuff. They most likely hadn't felt the need, not thinking one of them would end up with clippers stabbed into their throat and the other with a cracked skull. Pilgrim grabbed up his pack and, on his way out, snatched the keychain to Room 8 from its hook, pausing next to a drawer beneath the counter. A small brass key was inserted in its lock. He turned it, heard a faint click and opened the drawer. Inside were two sets of key fobs. He grabbed those, too.

There was an obvious relief in how the girl reached for her rifle when she saw it. It reminded him of a cartoon he had watched as a kid, sitting on the floor in front of the TV while a washing machine gently whirred in the background. Someone had been sitting beside him – he had seen them from the corner of his eye – but he'd been riveted by the TV, his head tilted back he was sitting so close to the screen. For some strange reason he could recall the colours of that cartoon vibrantly in his mind's eye: shocking sports-car reds, deep and profound tropical-ocean blues, greens as dazzling as a newly mown football pitch. The colour of the teddy bear, the stuffed toy the cartoon girl reached out for, was a comfortingly fuzzy tactile brown. The cartoon child had taken that bear and squeezed it tight to her chest, her face screwed up in delight.

The girl in front of Pilgrim didn't hug the gun or express such a strong emotional reunion, but Pilgrim was sure she was close to wanting to.

'Keep the gun ready,' he told her. 'I'll shout if I need you to shoot anything.' He watched her shaking fingers expertly pull the bolt back and check the weapon was loaded.

'OK,' she said, keeping it loosely cradled against her chest, just like that teddy bear.

He fished the keychain from his front pocket, clamped the plastic tag of the room key between his teeth and started walking towards the closed door. As he went, he pulled the slide back on his semi-automatic, just enough to see a round already chambered in there. He tried to be light on his feet, but his boots made a hollow *clop* each time his heel came down on the concrete.

He ducked underneath the curtained window, not wanting his silhouette to reveal his presence to anyone inside. Remaining crouched, his back flat to the wall, he plucked the key tag from his mouth and inserted the key into the lock. With a twist, the deadbolt clunked and disengaged. Leaving the key dangling, he brought his gun up ready, and shoved the door open, going in fast and low.

There were no lights in this room. With the curtains closed, there was nothing to relieve the gloom. The slab of meagre moonlight that shone in from the open door made shadowy goblins scurry for the darkness under the bed and hide in corners. He briefly considered going back for the lantern, which he'd left with the girl, but disregarded the idea. He wanted to get this done quick and get the hell out.

It took only a second to register all that information. The next second the smell hit him.

Shit.

Sweat.

The heavy iron smell of blood.

It latched on to the back of his throat, making him wish he had pulled his neckerchief up over his mouth and nose before entering.

It was a twin room. On the bed nearer the window, a body was stretched out, its arms raised above its head, presumably lashed to the headboard, legs spreadeagled and tethered to the footboard. The person's foot was the nearest body part to Pilgrim. He reached out a hand and touched the sole. It was cold.

Dead, Voice whispered.

Pilgrim didn't answer. His fingers skimmed over cool skin, searching for the pulse at the inside of the foot, by the ankle bone, which he knew wouldn't be there. He pressed the pads of his first two fingers to the spot for a count of fifteen.

Not a flutter.

Dead, Voice whispered again, a definitive note to his tone this time.

Taking his hand back, Pilgrim continued scanning the room. He could see the outline of two bedside tables, a chair in the corner nearest to him and a long chest of drawers running along the wall to his right, a small TV set on it. An open suitcase lay at the foot of the vacant bed, items messily strewn half in, half out. There were a further two doors opposite him, one to a closet, he guessed, the other leading to the bathroom.

In the end, he didn't have to choose which door to investigate first. The muffled whimper that came from behind the one on the right decided for him.

He dropped to all fours first and peered under the beds – monsters always hid there – but these ones were clear. If there had been a monster, it had already crawled out into the world.

A second noise came from behind the door on the right: a metallic clanking, followed by a quiet grunt.

It's probably another crazy sibling. Waiting with an axe.

'Quiet,' Pilgrim ordered.

He got back to his feet, his right knee popping. He silently approached the door, his boots cushioned by the thin carpeting. He watched the doorknob, imagining he could see it turning. He made a small, animalistic growl and lifted one heavy booted foot and shot it at the door, kicking it hard, popping it out of its catch. The door slammed inwards, crashing into the wall and rebounding back, but Pilgrim was already shouldering through, the gun up and ready.

He stopped in his tracks at what he saw.

'Hey! What's going on in there!'

He didn't realise he had lowered the gun until the butt bumped against the side of his thigh.

'HEY!' the girl shouted again from outside, panic edging her voice.

'Get in here!' he called back, without taking his eyes off what was in the bathtub. 'And bring the lantern!'

It took both him and the girl to manoeuvre the naked woman out of the bathtub. Nikki and Russ had done a good job of tying her up, lashing both her wrists over the top of the shower rail. They'd used the same wire they had on Pilgrim, and it had cut far more viciously into the woman's wrists than it had his. But then, she had been trussed up for longer.

The sepia glow of the lantern made the bruises on the woman's abdomen and ribs and legs appear like large black smudges, as if she were drawn with the bold swipes of a charcoal pencil. Dried and encrusted blood sheathed her wrists and forearms like black evening gloves, and her scuffed elbows had dribbled blood down to her underarms like midnight-black candle wax. The woman hissed in pain and whimpered quietly every now and then, but she didn't utter a word while they helped her step over the lip of the tub. The girl, however, didn't shut up. But her soothing patter was surprisingly welcome to Pilgrim. He had fewer words to say than even the woman.

'That's right, just a little more. Take it easy there, it's kind of slippy. Man, you're lucky the Boy Scout here wanted to check this room out, or else . . . well, never mind what else. We found you now and—' It was the girl's turn to hiss. 'Oh, man. Your poor wrists.'

It's a shame you can't kill the same people twice.

'Yeah.'

A step outside the bathroom, they all stopped. Pilgrim was on one side of the woman, gingerly holding on to one arm, and the girl was steadying her from the other. The body on the bed lay unmoving, silent, and yet it held them all in its thrall.

The woman started to tremble.

'We should get her out of here,' the girl said.

The girl was as shaken as the woman but hiding it well. He couldn't see her in the dimness, but he heard her teeth chattering.

'Do you have her?' Pilgrim asked.

'Huh?'

'Don't let her fall.' He let go of the woman and hurried over to the second bed, yanked the top blanket free and laid it over the body, covering it up. But not before he saw it was a woman in her early twenties. Her bloodshot eyes bulged up at the ceiling, and her jaw was slack, bloated tongue sticking out from between purple lips. Deep ligature marks cut into her throat.

He went back over to the girls and carefully took hold of the woman's arm again. 'Let's get outside. I'll come back for clothes.'

They walked the woman between them across the room and out of the door. For the second time that night Pilgrim inhaled a deep breath, cleaning out the stench of death from his lungs. He left the woman leaning up against the trunk of the car and went back inside for the suitcase. He made a detour to his pack on the way back and gathered his first-aid kit and a tall bottle of water and took them both to the girl, instructing her to clean the woman up and get her dressed. Giving her a job to do would help divert her attention for a short while, at least until they were out of this place.

'This your car?' he asked the woman, pulling out the two key fobs he'd found in the office drawer. He jabbed at the unlock buttons on both, but no beeping sound answered.

The woman frowned, glanced at the car she was leaning against as if to remind herself whether she owned it or not, and then silently pointed to the key fob in Pilgrim's left hand. 'Battery's dead,' she whispered. 'Need to use the key.'

The key unlocked the passenger door. He passed the fob to the girl.

'Where are you going again?' she asked, holding on to the items he had handed to her or, more accurately, *clutching* on to them.

'I'm giving the room a once-over. Then we're getting out of here. I promise.'

'OK, but can you hurry? Please?'

CHAPTER 11

Lacey watched anxiously as he went back inside. She didn't move for a tense moment, listening hard, waiting in case he shouted out to her again. While she stared at Room 8, she felt eyes on her back, coming from the motel reception.

She spun around.

No one was standing at the pane of glass watching her.

She peered towards the reception desk, skipping fast over the dead cat, but couldn't see anyone there, either. She quickly checked each corner of the parking lot, and the windows to each motel room. No one anywhere. A few hours ago she'd been desperate to see signs of other people, and now all she wished for was privacy and a decent place to hide.

She became aware of the woman standing beside her. Naked. And equally as scared, she'd bet.

'God! Sorry. I was freaking myself out again. Here' – she transferred all the items the Boy Scout had handed her to one arm and gently took hold of the woman's hand – 'let's get you dressed. You'll feel better.'

Guiding her to the passenger side of the car, Lacey pulled it open, partly using it to hide the woman's nakedness, partly to give her somewhere to sit. 'That's it. Sit down for second. Careful now.'

The woman was shaky, but she perched on the edge of the passenger seat, sitting sideways so her legs were out of the car, her feet on the ground. Lacey made quick work of cleaning the woman's cuts, not simply to limit her suffering but because

Lacey found it difficult to look at her wounds for too long. She didn't want to dwell on what Russ or Nikki had been thinking about when they hurt her, if they had laughed each time they landed a punch or kick, if they liked it when the woman cried out. She didn't want to think about the level of evil needed to do what had been done in that room, or if she'd have ended up the same way. To think about it might send her mad, might have her begging the Boy Scout to take her back home. No, she had to do this quickly, or else she'd lose the last of her courage.

She murmured apologies as she applied the hydrogen peroxide to the woman's cuts, wincing each time she flinched under her dabbing, feeling tears come to her eyes and trying very hard not to let the woman hear them in her voice as she babbled away to her, her mouth on auto-pilot, unaware of half the things popping out of it. The night was so *quiet*, and the sense of wrongness drifted all around her, dusting the air. She found herself glancing over her shoulder time after time, her skin itching. She had cleaned herself off in the basement, but she still felt dirty, contaminated. She wanted to scrub her arms and hands and everything else the siblings had touched, the same way she had after wringing her chickens' necks and plucking and chopping them up.

And still her mouth yabbered on. 'God, this is such a crappy way to meet, I know, but I'm so glad we found you. I don't come across many people, haven't really been out in the world too much, you could say. But judging from today's candidates, I'm thinking that might not be such a bad thing. That doesn't include *you*,' Lacey hastily added. She was reaching around the woman's back, helping her slide one arm and then the other into a shirt, but she paused to meet the woman's eyes. 'I don't mean you,' she repeated. 'Or the Boy Scout in there.'

Lacey crouched down to check the woman's legs for injuries. 'What I meant to say was I . . . those two gross people in the basement . . . the ones who . . .' She trailed off, an image of the two bodies down in the basement rising up, brother on top of sister, their combined blood forming a pool around them, most of it pumping from the brother's sliced neck. It had looked like a second gaping mouth, that gash, opening and closing as the guy tried to breathe. Like a fish's gill.

Something touched the top of her head and she recoiled. But it was only the woman's hand.

'It's OK.' Her voice was hushed, raspy. Her palm stroked Lacey's hair. 'It's OK . . . What is your name? You never said.'

Lacey blinked, confused, then realised she hadn't introduced herself. Heat crept into her face. 'Lacey,' she said. 'My name's Lacey.'

The woman's swollen eye squinted when she smiled. 'That's pretty.'

'It's better than my middle name. *Olive.* Can you believe it? So bad. What's your name?'

'Alex. No middle name for me.'

'Alex is pretty, too. Unless you were a man or something, then I guess it'd be handsome or strong.' That sounded stupid, so she hurried to cover it with more words. 'How long have you been here?'

Alex's smile trembled, went away. 'Three days, I think.'

A chill of horror replaced the warmth in Lacey's face. Three days. In that room. Lacey had spent ten minutes with them, a mere sliver of time when everything her grammy had tried so hard to protect had almost been ripped away, torn from her like the rind off an orange and exposing her to the world. How was this woman standing upright and talking to her? Stroking her hair in an effort to comfort? Asking her name?

'Oh my God,' Lacey whispered. 'Oh my God, I'm sorry.'

'No.' The word was firm, almost gruff in Alex's raspy voice. 'Don't be sorry. I'm glad to meet you, Lacey. You don't know how much.'

Lacey remained crouched at this woman's feet, staring up in a kind of horror-struck awe, and then stood up too quickly, stumbling a bit and laughing nervously, cutting the sound off immediately. Apologising again.

'If you help me finish getting dressed,' Alex whispered, 'I'll forgive you anything.'

As Lacey quietly helped, they touched each other maybe more than was necessary – a balancing hand here, a steadying touch there, an adjustment to help smooth out a wrinkled sleeve or turn down a collar – but to Lacey the brief touches were the only warm thing in the cold night, and she welcomed each and every one of them. She thought Alex needed them, too: the touches of someone who didn't want to hurt her.

A time or two, she noticed Alex's eyes drifting over to her motel room. She wondered if the dead woman inside was someone Alex knew, was someone she was close to.

To distract her, Lacey said, 'Here, let me look at your wrists for you.'

'Hm?' For a second, Alex seemed to have trouble tearing her gaze away from the yawning black doorway the Boy Scout had vanished through, but when she met Lacey's eyes, she blinked and focused. 'Oh. Yes. Thank you.' She allowed Lacey to take her arm, and Lacey squeezed in beside her, settling herself on the door ledge. She reached for the bottle of water.

'Where are you from, Alex?'

The woman tried to clear her throat, but it turned into a grimace. She carried on in a whisper. 'Wyoming, originally. Kind of all over since. What about you? And . . . what did you say his name was?'

'The Boy Scout? I've only known him for, like, half a day. I live just a few hours from here. He's taking me to Vicksburg. Which, I have to say, is a whole lot closer than Wyoming. Is that where you were when everything happened?' She wanted to steer the conversation back to earlier things, away from this place, but also because she wanted to hear this woman's story. 'Did things go crazy there, too?'

But Alex had drifted away again, her head turned towards the motel room, her voice low and preoccupied. 'Yeah. Yeah, craziness there, too. And then it went quiet. Deathly quiet everywhere — at least on the surface.'

CHAPTER 12

Before re-entering Room 8, Pilgrim pulled his neckerchief up and over his nose. He headed straight for the bathroom, the lantern they had left offering a welcoming glow. That welcoming aura soon vanished when he stepped into the musty, dingy little room. Green slime covered the tiles down at floor level, and smears of brown Pilgrim didn't even want to think about caked the toilet bowl and the pipes running out the back.

Above the scum-stained sink, a medicine cabinet was cracked open an inch. He swung it open the rest of the way and checked inside. He left the dirty nail-clippers alone but picked up the pill bottle. He gave it a shake. No rattling pills answered. The bottle went back on the shelf. There was nothing else of interest, other than an overturned cockroach, its legs crooked and pointed up at the ceiling. And he had read that cockroaches could survive anything.

'Guess you shouldn't believe everything you read.'

The bathroom's acoustics lent an eerie echoing quality to his voice.

He closed the cabinet and caught a glimpse of himself in the broken mirror. His left eye was splintered into fragments by a crack, spiralling outwards as though a pebble had been dropped into the mirrored surface; jagged glass ripples grew out from the epicentre of his iris. With the lower half of his face covered by faded cotton, his eyes' stare was strangely mesmerising, their depths cold and unreadable. He barely recognised them and had to drop his gaze after only a few seconds.

Voice sang in a sweetly haunting voice. Something about recognising a stranger from afar but having never been seen himself.

'One of your own?'

Purloined it from the back recesses of your noggin. Kenny Rogers? Or Dolly? Don't know which.

'Neither do I. We'll have to remain ignorant together.'

Pilgrim picked up the lantern and left the bathroom.

The body on the bed made valleys and hills of the blanket covering it. A little kid with a toy Matchbox car would have fun *vrooming* up and down that mountainous landscape.

He didn't want to, not really, but he went over to the covered body and pulled back the blanket. Even steeling himself for the blank eyes and yawning mouth didn't prepare him for it; a lesson he had learned too many times to count but one which was now compounded by this poor woman's expression. There was no dignity in death.

He wanted to close her eyes, but it was too late for that. He knew that some mortuary technicians would place a small bit of cotton ball on the eye and pull the lid down over it. That would do the trick to keep the eyes closed for when the loved ones came to visit, but Pilgrim was all out of cotton balls. What he did do was fold the pillow under the back of her neck so that her head rested higher, her chin dipping forward and her mouth closing. Holding the lantern high with one hand, he used the other to lift the blanket. She was as naked as the other woman had been. He didn't pause to study her injuries but continued searching, not looking for anything specific but feeling like he owed her something. He found it on the inside of her left wrist, partially hidden by wire and dried blood. He worked the wire loose so he could see the tattoo clearly enough to read.

Faith.

It was more likely a personal reminder to the woman, something to the effect that God was watching over her, or to have more faith in herself, or some other private message. Whatever the reason, it was as dead now as the woman herself. It served as an identifier for him, though. Faith. She wasn't a nameless stranger any more. He had seen and acknowledged her, a woman who had struggled to survive, had endured hardship and pain only to be slaughtered by two cowards. Fairness and justice had lost their place in the world. If they'd ever had a place in it to begin with.

He considered saying something, a few words of comfort, but he caught himself quickly on the sentiment. She was dead and gone and wouldn't hear a single thing he said. He freed both her wrists, covered her up again and left her where she lay.

When he stepped outside the motel for the final time, Pilgrim tipped his head back and stared up at the stars. They glinted coldly back at him. Their scattered presence, spread over the vastness of the sky, made him feel like a speck of dirt. Nothing he would ever do would impact on those stars. Nothing he would ever do would impact much past the moving of molecules around himself, a very small spherical ball of cause and effect, never stretching further than a few feet.

When he lowered his head he found the woman watching him. She was dressed and sitting sideways in the car's passenger seat, her legs in the V of the door's opening, sneakered feet resting on the ground. The girl was squeezed in next to her, the water bottle clamped between her knees. She patted at the cuts on the woman's wrists with a damp cloth.

The woman's eyes continued to watch him as he approached.

He tugged the neckerchief down. 'Does the car have gas?' he asked.

She didn't answer straight away, as if considering how wise it would be for her to offer any information. She dropped her eyes to the girl then returned her attention to him. She nodded. 'It did. Half a tank, maybe.' Her voice was husky; it cracked halfway through the 'maybe' and fell into a mere silent moving of her lips.

Screaming a lot could do that, he supposed.

'That's good,' he said, raising the lantern so the girl could see better.

Her head lifted to look up at him. 'Thanks.'

'There's some hydrogen peroxide in the first-aid kit,' he told her.

'Already used some.' She snaked a hand behind her, fishing in the footwell of the car, and came up with the hydrogen peroxide. She applied some to the cloth then went back to patting the woman's cut wrists.

The woman didn't make a peep, although she did bite down on her bottom lip, her face frowning in discomfort.

Pilgrim sank to a crouch, took a rolled-up bandage from his kit and waited for the girl to finish her administrations. He took his turn with the woman's wrist, wrapping the bandage around it a few times. He held it in place with his thumb and grabbed the adhesive tape, using his teeth to tear off a piece.

'Best get the cuts on her face, too,' he told the girl.

She got busy with them while he wrapped up the woman's other wrist. Her fingers were long and graceful, but her palms were callused and strong, the nails neat. And although her wrists were slim, they felt sturdy in his hold. He had to wonder how the two siblings had gotten the better of her.

They got the better of you.

Pilgrim frowned at that but said nothing. Voice was right. The girl had been an added distraction, yes, but he should never have assumed the situation wouldn't turn hostile, no matter how genial the person he was speaking to appeared to be. He had been lax in reading the signs, pure and simple, and he would not be caught unawares again.

He realised he was staring down at the woman's wrist, which he still held on to. The woman had certainly put up a fight –

they had physically wrecked her – and yet she was still whole, at least on the outside. He wondered if witnessing the other woman being tortured and killed had made it harder or easier. Harder because you could see first-hand what would be done to you once it was your turn, but easier because while they were busy working on her you were getting a stay of execution.

Wonder if they knew each other, Voice said.

Pilgrim glanced up into the woman's face. One cheekbone was swollen, the skin shiny and tight over the bone, making the eye above narrower. Her lip was split and her hair hung in tangles around her face. He thought she would probably be a dark blonde once she was washed up, but he couldn't be sure. Her eyes were sharp, though. Sharp with pain and anger and wariness, sharp with a whole multitude of emotions.

He studied her eyes.

They're not related, Voice noted. *But there's* something *there*.

'Yeah. Something.'

'Who are you?' the woman whispered, her voice almost giving out. 'Where did you come from?'

'Same place you did, most likely. West a ways.' He busied himself with packing away the first-aid supplies the girl had left scattered on the ground.

'He's a clam,' the girl said, a touch of admonishment in her tone. 'He won't even tell me his real name.'

'Why won't you tell Lacey your name?' the woman asked.

He sighed impatiently and straightened up, first-aid kit in one hand, the lantern in the other. 'Are you finished with her cuts?' he asked the girl.

She surprised him with a smile. It lit up her face, warmed it, made her lovely.

Pilgrim felt a muscle twitch at the corner of his left eye and wondered how much trouble he was already in, and if he still had time to extricate himself from it without causing even more.

'I don't need to know your name, Boy Scout. I like you anyways.'

Pilgrim turned on his heel and stalked away.

Voice laughed in his head.

Pilgrim did his best to ignore the girls when they started talking quietly again. He couldn't ignore Voice, though – he came from a place there was no walking away from.

He would have been tempted to leave them both right there: they had a car with gas, an open road and a weapon to keep them safe. There was little need for him to escort the girl anywhere now, deal or no deal. However, Lacey had already stuffed his pack into the car's trunk ('Saves you having to carry it,' she'd told him), and both women were sitting in the front of the car, its engine purring, waiting for him to lead the way.

There had been a brief discussion about whether to bury the dead woman's body or not, most of it conducted between him and Lacey. The woman seemed unwilling to discuss it and had only shaken her head a few times, eyes downcast. They agreed that she wouldn't need anything more from them; he had untied her and covered her with a blanket and, for him, that was sufficient. He didn't particularly want to expend energy and time digging a hole. His head hurt, and his shoulder and hip had stiffened up where he had landed on them, claws of pain digging deep into the joints at every other step. The subject of burial had quickly been dropped.

I don't know how you get yourself into these situations, Voice was musing. *This morning there was just the two of us, now we have a teenager, an assaulted woman and a deceased cat under our belts. You need to stop picking up strays.*

'Someday it'd be nice if there was just the one of me,' Pilgrim said.

Voice retreated into a sullen silence after that, and Pilgrim didn't feel one ounce of guilt for being the cause of it.

He rolled up to the car's passenger side, his bike's engine silent, and waited for the girl to wind her window down.

He ducked his head so he could address the woman behind the wheel. 'If I flash my brake lights four times in a deliberate manner, you stop the car and stay stopped till I come back to get you. Four times. Got it?'

'Four?' Lacey said. 'I just wanna make sure I understand right.' She held up four fingers in front of his face.

'*Four*,' he said, enunciating the word.

'We understand,' the woman said.

'Where we going?' the girl asked.

'Don't worry. Not to any more motels.'

He lifted the neckerchief up to forestall any further conversation and fired the bike up, loudly and deliberately revving its engine. He led them back on to the main street and towards the open highway.

Originally not wanting to travel once darkness had fallen, Pilgrim now found it a comfort, even if a cold one. He rode through the night's landscape, wanting to put miles between themselves and the motel. Because the moon was full and bright, he chose to leave the bike's headlamp off and, following his example, the car that ghosted in his wake did the same. He was confident that the road would remain illuminated well enough to navigate safely. The land was awash with a blue–white glow, as if all the colours had been leached from it, leaving an alien world in its place. Even the usual *chh-chh-chh* of insects and the howling yips of distant coyotes were absent. All was still and silent except for their engines. His shadow flitted beside him as it raced along the blacktop. And above him lay a whole other world – a world of twinkling stars that swept across their velvety backdrop as if God had dropped silver glitter into the breeze and bade the winds carry its treasure to each horizon.

The temperature had dropped along with the setting of the sun, cooling out the rocks and the blacktop and injecting a chill into the air. Pilgrim had shucked on a jacket and some riding gloves, but cold fingers of wind found their way up the jacket's sleeves and nipped in around his neck. The bike's engine kept his inner thighs and calves warm, but his ankles and feet soon began to grow numb.

He glanced over his shoulder from time to time, but the car never fell back further than a hundred yards or so. He couldn't see beyond the moon's wavering reflection gleaming off the windshield, but he knew they were in there, looking out at him in between their quiet conversation. And that comforted him, too, although he didn't dwell on the feeling. He also knew that they were feeling safer, cocooned in the warm confines of the car's cab (which had undoubtedly trapped the evening's heat), the miles stretching further and further between them and the motel's carnage. He knew it as well as he knew they were tired and sore and needed sleep, but he wouldn't stop again until he found what he was looking for.

His eyes felt full of grit. Each time he blinked he could almost hear the dry sandpaper rasp of the lid drag over his eyeball. He slowed their speed to forty when the road's centre line became two then blurred back into one. He couldn't remember when he'd last slept.

His patience rewarded him. He tapped his brakes four times, glancing back to make sure the woman was stopping as he had instructed. The car slowed and pulled half off the blacktop, the two passenger side wheels dropping into the gravelly rut that ran alongside the road. The car crunched to a stop, lopsided in its parking.

He rolled to a stop himself, planting a boot on solid ground. He pointed towards the barn he was planning on going to investigate. It was two hundred yards off the road. He couldn't see the girls inside the car, but he got a flash of their headlights to show they had seen his signal, and then the lights and engine shut off, leaving the car dark and silent.

He accelerated quickly away, choosing to keep to the road this time rather than chance going cross-country and his front wheel dropping into a critter's burrow, sending him flying over the handlebars. A dirt track angled off to his right, leading up to the structure, and he took it. He tucked his head down and covered the distance at high speed, dust kicking up behind his back tyre, a quiet thrill tingling through him at the bike's powerful torque.

The barn was a two-storey, wood-constructed outbuilding. It was in some disrepair. Before he was halfway down the dirt track Pilgrim could see the night sky straight through the roof where parts of it had caved in. There was a fenced-off corral built alongside the barn's eastern wall, most of the fence's struts nearest the dirt track lying felled on the ground like battle-worn soldiers.

The outbuilding appeared empty and abandoned, but even as Pilgrim made the observation Voice was finishing his thoughts for him.

But appearances can be deceiving, can't they?

CHAPTER 13

'What do you think he's doing?' Lacey asked quietly, watching the motorcycle's brake flame brighter, a toked-on cigarette glowing in the dark. The Boy Scout pulled to a stop outside the barn, and the red light dimmed to a burning ember.

'Checking to see if anyone's inside.'

They spoke in hushed tones, in reverence to the night and the deep, dark emptiness of the desert on all sides. Lacey was scared, although she'd never admit to it out loud. Her hands wouldn't stop trembling. She sneaked a peek at Alex's hands: the woman's fingers were looped loosely around the steering wheel. Lacey couldn't detect any trembling in them at all.

Sighing, she double-checked her door was locked then crossed her arms over her chest, tucking her fists into her armpits. She leaned forward in her seat and watched the Boy Scout's shadow detach from the bike and slip away. 'We're staying here, then?' she wondered out loud.

'Looks like it. There are a few hours left before sunrise, and we need to rest.'

The soft interior glow from the instrument panel lent Alex's face a faint greenish tinge, darkening the smudges of her bruises and opening up canyons around her eye sockets.

Alex's eyes shifted to her, and a small smile softened the sunken pits of her eyes. 'Don't worry, we can always stay in the car. The Mysterious One can sleep on the floor. This is a girls-only zone. No boys allowed.'

Lacey smiled quickly and went back to staring out the window. The Boy Scout was gone, shadow and all. The motorbike stood alone, its headlight projecting a large white circle on to the barn doors.

'Alex, why were you at the motel?'

In the heavy silence that followed, Lacey wished she could drag the words back into her mouth and swallow them. When would she learn that silence wasn't a bad thing, that it had its place, and for good reason?

Just as Lacey was about to change the subject, Alex said, 'It was my sister. She wanted to stop there.'

Lacey's head swivelled fast, her eyes widening in shock. 'That . . . that was your sister back there?'

The woman didn't say anything, only stared out through the windshield.

What if it had been Karey lying on that bed? How would Lacey feel? Distraught, lost, angry, helpless, broken, inconsolable, raging at the world. So many things, all jumbled up and locked together by one overriding emotion: devastation. She would be devastated, and she wouldn't want to talk about it to a stranger. 'I'm really sorry. I shouldn't have . . . I mean, it's none of my business.'

Alex took a deep breath. 'It's OK. I should talk about her. She deserves that much. I can't pretend like it didn't happen.' She glanced at Lacey, a quick glance that wouldn't quite meet her eyes. 'I was adopted; Sammy came along naturally a couple of years later. Not that the semantics of it make any difference. She's still my sister.' Alex looked into her lap, the curtain of her hair falling to hide her face. 'I've always looked after her, ever since I was old enough to talk. She wasn't an easy person to be around. She had . . . problems. They weren't her fault, but she could be difficult, *hurtful*. As soon as I could, I left for college; I needed to get away – my way of escaping, I guess. Left her to our parents, but they couldn't cope. Seemed like I was the only one she'd listen to. They begged me to come home, but I wouldn't. I *liked* my life, liked myself more when I wasn't around her. She was *such* hard work.' She started to cry.

Lacey reached over and touched the back of her hand. 'I'm sorry. You don't have to explain anything to me.'

'It was a *relief*. When all this happened.' Alex gestured to her injured face and, when she turned to her, Lacey could barely bring herself to look into the woman's eyes. The bleakness there was unending. 'Can you believe that? I was *relieved*. That's what a God-awful sister I am. I was glad I didn't have to find food any more or a safe place to stay, or make *all the goddamned decisions*. I just wanted it to be over. I didn't want anyone to hurt her. Never hurt her. But I was relieved when they took her away from me and I didn't have to look after her any more.' She covered her face with her hands, and the sounds that came out of her were so broken Lacey had to bite her lip.

'But you *did* look after her, Alex. All this time.'

'And see what it got her.' Alex's laugh was harsh, her words muffled behind her hands.

'It wasn't your fault. They were bad people. You didn't know they'd be there. You're lucky you're not dead, too.'

'Well, they screwed that part up. They were supposed to kill me. They promised me they would.'

'No, Alex. Don't say it like that. Your sister wouldn't want that, not ever. She'd want you here, safe with me.'

Alex roughly brushed the dampness from her cheeks. She inhaled deeply, her breath hitching on the way in.

'That's where I'm going,' Lacey told her, 'to find my sister. She's all I have left now.'

Alex slowly let out her breath and dropped her hands heavily to her lap. She glanced at Lacey and smiled so sadly it brought a spiky lump to Lacey's throat. 'You're a better sister than I am.'

Lacey tried to keep the tremor from her voice but wasn't entirely successful. 'No, I'm not. At least you were with Sammy this whole time. I haven't seen Karey for over eight years.'

It was Alex's turn to reach over. 'Oh, honey.' She squeezed her arm.

'We were really close when I was a kid,' Lacey said, the warm, enclosed space of the car feeling intimate and confessional. 'Karey's twelve years older than me, but she never minded having me around. We lost our mom when I was three, and Dad was never around much, so it was just me, Karey and Grams. I think Karey felt we had to look after each other. But she *hated* where we lived, out in the middle of nowhere. It wasn't very sophisticated. We were never in the *midst* of things, you know? Not like she wanted. She wanted to be this high-flying business exec in the city. I never understood that – why would you want to live somewhere so noisy and crowded, somewhere you couldn't even see the stars properly when you looked up? *I* sure didn't. But she hooked up with this older guy called David at university – he was nice, kind of stuffy and serious, and I really didn't see what they had in common 'cause my sister was always laughing, this great big loud laugh that rumbled up from her belly, and David would give this little smile, and when *he* laughed he made this weird, breathy sound through his nose, and they just didn't seem to match, you know?

'Anyway, she hooked up with David, got married on her nineteenth birthday, packed up, and left. Just like that. It kind of hurt, her leaving. I thought we were a team, that she wouldn't go anywhere without me. But I knew deep down she wasn't trying to hurt me, she just couldn't stay. I think she'd have gone nuts if she had. She was too big for that house. She needed to "fly the coop" as my grammy used to say.

'She moved pretty far away, too, but I'd go over and stay with her sometimes. We'd have slumber parties and all that fun stuff: paint each other's nails, braid our hair. She told me she wanted a baby but that wasn't happening as fast as she wanted it to, and each time I saw Karey after that her laugh didn't sound the same – it didn't rumble up any more but just kind of hung around her mouth and died. All her energy that used to fill up Grammy's house when she was there drained away.' Lacey paused in her telling because her chest hurt, right in the centre. She tugged her sleeve over her fist and wiped her eyes. 'My sleepovers pretty much stopped after that.'

Alex's hand had come to rest on her shoulder, but now it lifted and Lacey felt a strand of her hair gently tugged then tucked behind her ear. There were fresh tears on the woman's cheeks.

'We'd best quit or else we'll be two blubbering messes by the time the Mysterious One comes back out,' Alex said. 'He'll wonder what the heck we've been doing in here.'

'Yeah. Sob fest.' Lacey sniffed and offered the sleeve she had wiped her eyes with to Alex. 'I really am so sorry, Alex. About your sister.'

Alex wouldn't meet her eyes. She shook her head at the proffered sleeve. 'Me, too. Thank you.'

Lacey poked her hand back through her cuff and took Alex's hand, keeping hold of it as she returned her attention to the barn. The Boy Scout hadn't reappeared.

'He's been in there a while,' Lacey said.

'Not long. Just a few minutes.'

'What if he doesn't come out?'

Alex gave her fingers a reassuring squeeze. 'He will.'

'But what if he doesn't?'

'You said you only met him this afternoon?'

Lacey nodded, her eyes glued to the barn, unaware of when she'd raised her free hand to chew on her thumbnail.

Alex said gently, 'So, for all the previous years you didn't know him, he managed to take care of himself without any help from us, right?'

Lacey sent her a pointed look over her hand. 'I get what you're saying. It's just . . .' She went back to her surveillance of the barn. 'He saved me back there. He didn't have to. Could've just worked his way loose and left. He had the opportunity to – a perfect one, too – they were busy with me, wouldn't have had any idea he'd got out. But he didn't. He came back.'

She remembered the way he'd entered the room, his energy like a gathering storm, silent and deadly. He hadn't hesitated at all. It was like watching a snake strike, one animal taking out another, no feeling, no remorse. His expression hadn't altered when he'd brought the clippers down into the big guy's throat and cut him wide open. It made her feel sick, thinking about how the blood had gushed out.

'He didn't owe me anything,' Lacey murmured. 'Not a single thing.'

'And now you feel like you owe him?'

Lacey shook her head. 'No. He surprised me is all. I really thought he would've left.'

'And why do you think he didn't?'

Lacey puffed out a breath. 'I have no clue,' she admitted.

'People don't do things for no reason, Lacey.'

Lacey glanced sharply at her, but Alex's words had been gentle. 'He's a good guy. Even if he does act like a dick sometimes.'

'You barely know him.'

'I barely know *you*, but that doesn't mean I'm wrong. I know I'm young and naïve, but I'm not an idiot, Alex. I wouldn't be sitting in this car if I thought he planned on skinning us and wearing us as a party dress.'

Alex squeezed her hand, and for a second Lacey wanted to snatch it away from her. 'You're right,' Alex said. 'I'm sorry. I'm just jittery. It's . . . it's so hard to trust anyone any more.'

'You can trust *me*.'

Alex's grip tightened on her hand again, and didn't let up, as if Lacey were the only thing she had to hang on to. Lacey was suddenly glad she hadn't snatched her hand away in a fit of temper.

They both stared out through the windshield. Nothing stirred out there, not even the wind.

'He saved us both today, Alex,' Lacey said quietly, still feeling the need to defend him. 'That has to mean something.'

Lacey heard her companion take a long, deep breath. 'Yeah. I wonder what he does on his days off.'

Lacey smiled a little. 'Who knows? He must've left his cape at home.'

'Hm, along with his Lycra pants.'

Lacey snorted, and then they were both laughing, and it felt good to laugh. It eased the thread of tension that had invaded the car, eased something inside Lacey, too, her chest loosening enough for her take her first deep inhalation since leaving the motel. They sat in the warm car together, a quiet giggle breaking out every now and then, their hands still clasped, and waited for the Boy Scout to come back for them.

CHAPTER 14

Pilgrim jammed on the brakes and skidded to a stop in front of the barn's huge double doors, leaving the bike idling while he ran around the building's corner and jogged along its side. If anyone *was* inside the barn, they would surely be attracted to the noise of the engine puttering away and not hear him skirting around to the back. He pulled his handgun free and was holding it in both hands as he reached a single door at the south-west corner. It was held shut by a slab of rock that had been propped up against it. Pilgrim placed the bottom of his boot against the slab and pushed, tipping it over. The door creaked open a half-foot, beyond which he could see nothing but blackness.

Hope there aren't any rattlers in there.

'Yeah, thanks for that.'

You're welcome.

He hunkered down, his back to the wall, and cautiously poked his head through the gap, peering inside. The large, crooked hole in the barn's roof opened the space up to the moon, spotlighting the area like a stage. Other than the four stalls opposite, which he could see were empty, the rest of the building was a basic timber frame – a skeleton of wooden bones. There was no second floor, the walls going straight up into the cavernous roof space and out into the star-studded sky. There were heaps of brittle wood littering the ground where the roof's beams had landed.

He pushed the door the rest of the way open and entered the

barn. He skirted around the brightest part of the moon's spotlight, keeping to the edges of gloom, his shoulder brushing up against the barn's wall, and went to the double doors. They hadn't been opened for a while – he had to get his weight behind his shoulder before they budged. He soon had them both open and was about to climb back on his bike when he heard a car approaching. He looked up to find the girls already on their way over, turning on to the dirt track.

'I told them to stay put,' he muttered.

They're women. They do what they want.

'Well, they'll have to break that habit.'

You're outnumbered now, two to one.

'I notice you keep yourself out of these equations when it suits you.'

Yup. You've got to pick your battles in life, my friend. And it's not like I can do you much good anyhow. They'd only think you were crazy and dangerous.

'I could live with being crazy if they did what I told them.'

Pilgrim had pushed his bike out of the way by the time they reached him. He waited for the woman to pull up beside him and hunkered down to speak to her through the window.

'Might want to back her up so you can drive straight out.'

She nodded and swung the car around.

What happened to chewing them out for disobeying you?

Pilgrim stood well back as the car's reversing lights blinked on.

'I'm picking my battles,' he said.

Once the car was safely inside, Pilgrim rolled his bike in after it. As the girl and woman climbed out, each chattering away already, he scooted outside and around the back of the barn to prop the door closed with the stone again. It would serve well to keep animals out.

As he walked back around to the front, Voice spoke up again.

You need to be careful in front of Alex. You're not used to being around people. If she realises you hear me, she might not react well.

Pilgrim slowed to a stop, rubbing the back of his head, fingers kneading into the spot behind his right ear. It felt solid, whole, perfectly normal.

Appearances definitely could be deceiving.

The girls were hard at work pulling the big barn doors shut when he came around the corner. He helped them, grasping the edge of a door and tugging. He let his gaze study the empty road and landscape one last time, searching for movement in the dark or the lights of cars or flashlights shining, but saw nothing. He gave a final yank and pulled the door completely shut, closing them in.

It didn't take long to get set up. They sat in front of the car, a small campfire burning in the centre of their little circle. There was plenty of dry firewood strewn around to keep it going.

The girl had passed out some chicken from one of her meat packages, along with a few slices from a tiny, underdeveloped cucumber, and they all took turns drinking from a flask of lemonade. It was one of the finest meals Pilgrim could remember having.

'I wish we had enough water to wash up.' The girl held her greasy hands far away from her body, as if scared of contamination.

'Lick your fingers,' Pilgrim said.

'I don't see you licking yours.'

He made a show of wiping his hands on his jeans.

She wrinkled her nose. 'That's disgusting.'

'Boy Scout training. Use whatever's at hand.'

Even in the orange glow of the firelight he could see the curiosity in her eyes.

'How much training you got?' she asked.

''Bout as many years of it as you've been alive.'

The woman joined the conversation. 'You have any other useful advice?'

The firelight danced in her eyes, making the whites look reddish. Her skin appeared dusky, too, the bandages very pale next to it. She sat with her arms looped around her knees, shifting every few minutes, no doubt searching for a position in which to ease her aches and pains.

You don't have any training. You just make it up as you go along.

Pilgrim frowned, annoyed at how close to the truth Voice was. 'Don't take your boots off when you sleep,' he told the woman.

Her eyes dropped down to his boots before flickering back up to his face. 'I get that one. In case we have to make a run for it, right? Don't want to be running around barefoot.'

He nodded. 'Your feet are more useful than a weapon. It's better to run than fight most times.'

Voice scoffed. *You're so full of shit.*

'I got flat feet,' the girl said.

The woman's eyebrows went up.

'What?' the girl said. 'I do.'

'Even more reason to take good care of them,' Pilgrim told her.

'My grammy used to say I was descended from mermaids. That my feet have evolved from fins. Said I was born to be in the water.'

'And yet you lived in the middle of the desert,' he said.

'Yeah, but . . . I like taking baths.'

The woman made a soft, breathy sound, a sound Pilgrim recognised as laughter only after it had stopped. He took a swig from the flask, the lemonade tart and sweet on his tongue. There was only a little left. He reached over to pass it to the girl.

'Did you hear any news from where you've been?' the woman asked.

The girl stopped mid-sip, her face opening up with interest. She looked at him hopefully.

He sighed and took his time settling back in his seat. 'What kind of news?'

The woman shrugged a little. 'Any news.'

The firelight no longer danced in her eyes; shadows slipped across her face, hiding parts of it in turn: her eyes, her mouth, her eyes again.

Why's she want to know? Voice asked suspiciously.

'Stay away from California,' Pilgrim said.

He got the sense the woman's eyebrows lowered a fraction, but maybe it was a trick of the light. 'California? Why?'

'I was told emergency sirens went off at Diablo Canyon.'

There was a slight hesitation. 'Really?'

She wasn't expecting that, Voice said smugly.

The girl butted in. 'What's Diablo Canyon?'

'A nuclear-power plant,' the woman answered absently. 'It was a core meltdown?' she asked Pilgrim.

'Maybe.'

'My God. You think there's contamination there?'

He shrugged. 'I wouldn't like to find out.'

The deadly winds that blow east from California could travel for hundreds of miles, poisoning the lands as they go, Voice added helpfully.

No one spoke, and Pilgrim didn't share what Voice had said. He didn't know what thoughts passed through the girls' heads, but his was filled with images of deformed babies with withered stumps for arms, the entire lower parts of their bodies melted away.

The woman broke the silence. 'What about other news? Did you hear any new theories?'

'No,' he said shortly, resigned to having this same old conversation and wanting it over as quickly as possible. 'Same theories as always.'

'What kinds of theories?' the girl asked eagerly.

He stared at her over the fire, but she seemed happy to wait him out. 'You're not going to drop this, are you?'

'Nope.' A slow, crooked smile lifted one side of her mouth as if to say he ought to know better than to ask. He'd known her for less than a day, but yes, that was one thing he conceded he knew already.

'Fine.' To get it over and done with, he quickly ticked off the points on his fingers as he listed them. 'Biological attack, poisoning, after-effects of dementia vaccines, aliens, subliminal and/or psychological warfare, chemical agents in the water supply, the mystical forces of sea tides and the moon. And, my personal favourite, some kind of Rapture-type event.'

The girl's brow quirked in confusion. 'Rapture?'

'Crazy Bible stuff,' the woman said. 'When the true believers of the world ascend to heaven before the End of Days, leaving the rest of us here to perish.'

'Is this the end of days?'

'No,' Pilgrim said flatly, 'it's not. No one ascended. Everyone is still here, the dead as well as the living.'

'And it doesn't explain the voices,' the woman pointed out.

'Voices?' The girl looked back and forth between them, as if watching a tennis match. 'What are you talking about?'

Pilgrim clenched his jaw and inhaled quietly through his nose.

Count to ten, Voice advised, the words prickling with dry amusement.

'You don't know about the voices?' Alex asked, surprised.

Pilgrim couldn't miss the fear that clenched the muscles of the girl's face for a moment. She shook her head.

'She's spent the past seven years shut up in a farmhouse with her overprotective grandmother,' he explained.

The girl sent him a dirty look. 'My grammy said everyone went crazy,' she said to the woman, effectively dismissing him from the conversation. 'She told me about this one fella called Jim Jones who brainwashed all these folk in South America? Said he knew just what words to say to get inside their heads. Like he was some kind of magician or something. She said it was mass hysteria, that people can easily be led into doing the craziest of stuff. That things got out of hand.'

'There's a kernel of truth in what your grammy said,' Alex replied slowly, throwing a glance Pilgrim's way, maybe hoping he'd take over the explanation, or at least help her with it, but he remained silent. She shifted position, wincing slightly, either from his lack of response or from discomfort, he wasn't sure. 'The voices are . . . whispers, murmurings, whatever you want to call them. They were inside us. They're what talked so many people into hurting themselves and others.'

'Inside us?' the girl whispered. It was her turn to look at Pilgrim, as if searching for reassurance, but he just stared back. He didn't want to be a part of this discussion – he had little to add to it.

She turned back to the woman. 'What happens if you have one?'

'It's dangerous. For a lot of reasons.'

'What if I have one and just don't know it?'

'You should know by now. Not everyone has one. Voices don't manifest until after puberty – for some reason, younger children don't hear them. Something to do with the anatomy of the brain, maybe, I'm not sure. I don't hear anything, either, and we're lucky we don't. After everything that happened there was a lot of hatred; if you were suspected of hearing a voice you were rounded up and . . . well . . . I won't go into details. There's still a lot of fear, a lot of hate. And rightly so.'

She's not being very nice, Voice muttered. *Tarring us all with the same brush.*

'But why'd they want to hurt us?'

Pilgrim surprised himself by speaking up. 'There's no easy

explanation for that. Why did we force so many animals into extinction? There are shades of grey behind every action. Nothing is ever fully evil or fully good.'

'Voices still shouldn't be trusted,' Alex cut in.

'So, what, everyone should just continue to be paranoid and live like enemies?'

Alex didn't seem to have an answer for that.

'There's been some integration,' Pilgrim said, unsure why he was arguing the point. 'A group up in Estes Park have both hearers and non-hearers living in close proximity. There haven't been any indications of violence breaking out. They live peacefully.'

'I hadn't heard about them,' Alex said quietly, the orange firelight laying a soft sheen over her eyes. 'That's not usual, though,' she added. 'Cohabitation.'

'No,' he agreed, 'it's not usual. But things are shifting. Alliances are being made and broken and remade again. There has been a lot of movement recently.'

The woman's lips pressed into a straight, unhappy line.

'Why?' the girl asked. 'What's going on?'

'That's a good question,' Pilgrim said, stirring their campfire back to life, flames dancing higher and licking around the wood. He didn't take his eyes from the woman sitting across from him. 'Maybe the ones who've been treated like rabid dogs up until now are tired of hiding.'

Is it that simple, though? Voice asked. *There's no clear division between people who hear us and those who don't. It's not as though voice-hearers bear a brand for all to see. There are just as many people who refuse to acknowledge the voices they hear and live in fear with their secret; fewer who hear nothing at all but are our allies. It's not just a case of us versus them.*

The woman had dropped her gaze to the campfire and was staring into the flames. Her voice, husky and low, seemed to be coming from much further away than inside the barn where they sat, the night sky peeking in at them through the gaps in the roof beams. 'There were stories in the places we passed through,' she murmured. 'Of a man with dark, moth-like eyes. We were told he slips into camps and settlements at night, searching out anyone who hears a voice – even people who were never suspected of having one – and tiptoes straight up to where they lie, as if they call out to him in their sleep. He wakes them with gentle words, whispering, coaxing with slick promises, turning them against everything they love and hold dear. Then he steals them away, like some twisted Pied Piper with his flute. But not before he sets fire to the farmhouses and camps and towns where they live. Sleeping families – children and babies – all burned. And this nameless man vanishes with them into the night as if he'd never been there at all.' Her eyes met Pilgrim's, and this time the flickering shadows weren't shifting over her face, hiding parts of her features, but were trapped inside her eyes, the warm firelight unable to reach the darkness. 'There are always rumours,' she said quietly. 'I understand that. Rumours are what give life to our fears. But my sister and I saw a town burning with our own eyes. A great wall of flames that seemed to scorch the roof of the sky and turn it red. It was as though this . . . this nameless man, this Pied Piper who comes to steal people in the night, was on the road in front of us and he was setting the world on fire.'

A pop came from their own fire, a piece of wood disintegrating in a burst of red sparks, and the girl jumped.

'Where was this?' Pilgrim asked.

The woman wrapped her arms tightly around her raised knees, hugging them to her chest as if the cold were bothering her, despite the heat from the fire. 'Not far from Colorado Springs.'

North-west of here, Voice whispered.

Pilgrim grunted. 'Sounds like a tale to scare children with. Fires break out all the time.' Hadn't they seen their fair share? It took nothing at all, the merest tickle of wind, to carry an ember from one building to the next, for fires to spread quickly from house to apartment to store, each filled to the rafters with abandoned furniture and goods, masses of tinder in the waiting. A ravenous beast of flames could burst into furious life and sweep through a town in minutes; there were no emergency services to keep such destruction in check any more.

Rumours are based on fact at some point in their lives, Voice said. *We have heard of these roving groups, too, even saw one less than a week ago. How do we know the burnings aren't related to them somehow, related to this tale of a nameless man?*

'I suppose you're right,' Alex said, and for a disorienting moment Pilgrim thought she was talking to Voice. 'But I met people who'd lost their brother, cousin, friends. All disappeared. Without word or warning.'

'How long ago was this?' he asked her. 'When you saw the fire?'

'Four weeks, six at a push.'

'And this children's tale said this nameless man was looking for those who heard voices? Specifically?'

The woman nodded. 'Yes.'

Pilgrim fell into a brooding silence.

'I still don't get it,' the girl said. 'Where did these voices come from?'

A long sigh left the woman and she fidgeted slightly where she sat. Maybe she was getting as tired as he was with the conversation.

No, she's in pain. Can't you tell tell by how pinched her eyes are?

'No one knows for sure,' she replied. 'But there are plenty of theories, just like your friend here listed.'

Lacey's eyes shifted to him. 'So what do *you* think happened?'

She was all wide-eyed curiosity and ignorance, this girl, and Pilgrim felt his annoyance grow. Had her grandmother really thought she would be able to protect her for ever? All she'd achieved was to make her weak and unprepared for the world she now found herself in.

With some frustration, Pilgrim threw his piece of wood into the fire, sending a second burst of red sparks erupting upwards. 'Look, it doesn't matter what I think. No one can fix or change the past, and it's selfish of us to think we have any claim on the future. Enjoy the fact you're still alive, and be grateful for it.' He was done with being sociable for the night; all this talk of rumours and a mysterious man going around snatching Pilgrim's kind had fouled his mood. 'Enough talk. We should get some rest. It's been a long day.'

A new concern galvanised the girl into a different line of questioning. 'You're going to be here come morning, right?'

He didn't immediately answer, and his hesitation spoke volumes.

'You're looking to dump us.' It was a flat accusation.

'I didn't say that.'

'You didn't have to.'

'Things are different now there's another person here. And there's a working car.'

'I thought we had us a deal.' The girl was starting to look kind of mulish.

'We did,' he said slowly, calmly. 'But the terms have changed slightly.'

He was aware of the woman silently watching their exchange, her eyes shifting from him to the girl and back again, but now she spoke. 'I'm not here to mess up anyone's plans. I'm grateful for your help. I owe you a debt more than I could ever repay. Both of you. But me being here doesn't need to impact on anything.'

'It's not impacting, Alex,' Lacey told her. 'We saved you. You're one of us now.'

'There is no *us*,' Pilgrim stated.

The crackle and pop of the fire sounded very loud in the silence that followed.

He sighed again. 'Are you happy to go to Vicksburg?' he asked the woman.

She slid a glance to Lacey then returned it to him. 'We were headed for the East Coast before we stopped. We'd heard there were scientists out there looking to help.'

What does that *mean?* Voice said.

Pilgrim wasn't listening. She was the solution to his immediate problem, and that was all he cared about. 'Excellent. Vicksburg is east. It's decided, then. She can take you.' He pointed at the woman.

But the girl was being stubborn. 'No. *You're* supposed to take me. You have the gun.'

'You have a rifle,' he countered.

She opened her mouth to continue the debate, but he raised a hand to cut her off. 'The deal was you get a ride to Vicksburg. It was never stipulated who had to give you the ride.'

She changed tack. 'Was there somewhere you needed to go first? We could go there before we head to Vicksburg if—'

'No. There's nowhere. I just prefer being on my own.'

The girl's eyes were big, the firelight reflecting in them.

Careful now—

He lowered his voice, made it conciliatory. 'Look, let's talk more in the morning. We need to rest. We're all tired.'

He didn't wait for a reply but stood up and dusted off the seat of his pants. He went to the trunk of the car and retrieved his pack. By the time he came back and began pulling out his sleeping bag, the girls were moving, too, gathering their things together. He passed his sleeping bag to the girl, and she looked up at him.

'You sleep first. I'll keep watch.'

For a moment she looked as though she would say more, but then she dropped her eyes and nodded slowly, her shoulders slumping in a way that indicated all the fight had gone out of her.

Pilgrim left her and went to sit with his back against the barn door. From there he could hear the yipping howls of a coyote somewhere out in the darkness of the desert and then a second answering howl, closer, but not close enough to worry him. He could also keep an eye on the girls as they settled down, the low firelight sliding over them like a swarm of miniature cavorting devils. They lay near to each other, probably unconsciously, forming an L shape, their heads making the corner. They spoke for a short while, their voices low, but soon they were quiet and their breathing evened out as sleep overtook them. At the end of their bedrolls, their feet poked out; they had both kept their shoes on.

He spent the first part of his watch observing them. The soft sleep sighs, the small muscle twitches that proved, even while resting, that their bodies strived to defend themselves. He studied the peacefulness on their faces – even the woman's, whose was bruised and swollen – and soaked up these details, because it felt like he was rediscovering them. He wondered what he would say if one of the girls woke up to find him staring so intently, and these thoughts had him shifting his attention away from the dying embers of the fire and into the shadows. The shadows welcomed his eyes, and his thoughts. He wasn't rediscovering them; he had known them for a while, and they had known him.

Voice kept him company, although Pilgrim didn't ask for it.

It'll be morning soon. Then what?

Pilgrim didn't so much as grunt in response.

Seriously, what's the plan? I'm not sure I like how this Alex has been looking at us. She's not stupid. What if she's a scout or something? What if she's the one going round looking for people like us and setting fire to stuff? Maybe those two crazybirds back at the motel caught her trying to burn their place down.

Voice was being ridiculous, and Pilgrim didn't have to say it for Voice to pick up on his impatience.

You won't be so quick to dismiss my theories after she's finished stabbing us in our sleep.

He had no intention of sleeping, not for a while.

Because her story of the nameless Pied Piper worried you? Scared you might call out to him while you're snoozing and he'll creep in here and carry us away?

Pilgrim wanted to tell Voice to shut up, but he'd learned early on that engaging with him at times like this only made him worse. He'd get tired of talking soon. He always did.

And what's the deal with these scientists she mentioned? What are they up to? Experimenting, I bet. That's what they do. Experiment and cut people up and pretend like they know what they're doing.

The scientists, if there even *were* any scientists, were far to the east. Nowhere they could pose a problem for Pilgrim. Rumour and gossip, that's all this was; it's what fuelled every channel of communication they had in the absence of the internet and cellphones and TV.

Voice eventually quietened down. He would do this most nights: talk himself into silence. Pilgrim just had to wait him out. Maybe he needed the rest, same as everyone else – Pilgrim didn't know – but he welcomed the respite as a Bedouin tribesman would welcome shade after a hundred miles in relentless sun. It was the only time he felt truly alone. It was a blessed feeling – as if a pin could drop in the silent spaces of his mind, and nothing would answer.

A couple of times he stood and walked around the barn, stretching out his legs, appreciating the quiet. He stayed out of the moonlight, allowing the shadows to surround him. He rooted around in some of the rubble but found nothing of any use, and soon found himself entering the warm pool of light by the girls again, stooping to add more wood to the fire.

At one point he realised he was humming to himself under his breath. Some old tune, a song he remembered being popular in his youth, and he stopped mid-verse, the last note hanging awkwardly in the air with no place to go. He held his open palms over the fire, letting the heat burn through them, enjoying the feeling of being toasted all along his front while his back half was left cold. His night vision was being ruined, he knew, but he couldn't help but stare into those flames, watch how they licked sinuously over the burning scraps of wood, the slight draught from the cracks in the doors making the flames twitch and bend. He remembered stealing matches from his father as a child and setting light to twisted rolls of newspaper. He would stand over the bathroom sink as the paper crumbled into ash, flaking the porcelain black. The longer he stared, the red-hot embers would shift in colour, hazing into blues and greens, a kaleidoscopic colour show that mesmerised. The smell of burning aroused him. Not in a sexual sense, but it seemed to ignite some dark corner of his brain until it glowed as hot as the paper's sparking cinders.

The memory was an uncomfortable one – he didn't like thinking about the past. It served no purpose to reminisce about such things, yet he knew the recollection would continue to play at the corners of his mind as long as the fire burned.

He employed a technique he sometimes used to supress Voice, although it took a lot more effort to make it work on him and was successful only a fraction of the time. Pilgrim envisioned the memory as a scene painted on paper, then folded the painting up into neat squares and placed it inside a chest. Over that chest he ran thick iron chains, criss-crossing and wrapping them until the chest could not be reopened. Then he locked the chains with padlocks. He placed the chest that held his memories at the top of a white cliff, its ragged chalk sides so white they seemed to shine from a place deep inside the pale rock. And then he pushed the chest off the edge. In his mind's eye he watched it fall to the ocean below, watched the huge splash it made when it entered the dark depths, watched as the chest sank and continued to sink for hundreds upon hundreds of fathoms, silently dropping through the dark layers of water until it disappeared into the gathering gloom. And, even once it had disappeared from sight, he knew the chest continued to sink and would continue to sink for ever, to a place he could no longer reach, a place that could no longer reach him.

One of the girls murmured something in her sleep. Lacey's face held a frown, her mouth pulled down at the corners. She moved fretfully.

He wasn't sure why, but Pilgrim started up his humming again, a little louder this time but still low, and soon the girl settled down, her frown melting away.

He let them sleep, planning on giving them another hour before waking them so he could take his turn to rest. Somewhere in the back of his head Voice began singing his own quiet tune, something about having to escape, dying to reach someone and driving all night. But Pilgrim stopped listening almost as soon as he began.

CHAPTER 15

It took a long time for Lacey to fall asleep. With her eyes closed, she listened to the crackling fire, heard the soft breaths of Alex lying near to her, close enough to reach out and touch if she wanted. She listened for the Boy Scout, too, but she might as well be listening for a ghost for all the noise he made. She knew he was there, though, sitting without stirring, arms crossed over his quietly moving chest, his brain ticking, ticking like a pocket watch.

Mostly, she listened to herself. Inside her head she asked questions, spoke to herself, to her grammy, left each question hanging and waiting for a response, but nothing alien answered her. No voices, only her own thoughts, ordinary and expected.

Her grandmother had been old and frail, and her sanity had been a tissue-thin piece of paper separating her rational mind from the scary things hiding beyond. Sometimes that veil dropped, and her grammy would scream and gibber and fight against what she saw on the other side. Maybe a voice had been waiting for her there, the same voices Alex and the Boy Scout had spoken about.

Lacey felt herself shy away from such thoughts, and her mind instantly shifted gear and turned to what waited at the periphery. The motel. She felt the pinch of wire biting at her wrists, the itch of the over-starched bed covers under her thighs, smelled the stench of her own fear in her sweat. The shadows of Room 8 lurked behind her eyelids, Alex's sister hiding in them, lying motionless on the motel bed as if playing some cruel game of hide and seek. Inevitably, her exhausted brain transformed the body into Karey, and the image of her own sister lying dead made her heart jolt painfully.

Her fingers found an inch of skin on her underarm, and she pinched it viciously. Punishment for doubting, even for a second, that her sister was alive. Punishment, too, for her endlessly churning thoughts. She was so tired, yet they wouldn't let her rest.

The nights were cold now – did Karey have somewhere warm to sleep, somewhere safe? Had she come across people like Russ and Nikki, cruel and hateful and wanting to hurt? Was she frightened for her daughter, a tiny baby when everything happened, and now just a kid less than half Lacey's age? Addison, who was a part of Lacey because she was a part of Karey. They all had the same blood flowing through their veins, the same blood as Grammy, the same blood as Karey's mother, who'd been sick for so long, her hair falling out in chunks and cheeks so painfully hollow her face appeared haunted by the ghost of her skull, and yet she proved all her doctors wrong by refusing to die when they said she would.

Strong blood.

All of Lacey's family had it.

Two short years after her mom had passed, Lacey was five and had wandered out beyond the backyard fence to the bluebonnets. They had been so pretty, their blue heads gently bobbing as if inviting her closer (and blue was Grammy's favourite colour). She was plucking the flowers, happily humming to herself and thinking about how pleased her grammy would be when she gave them to her, when a dart of movement struck so fast she'd been unable to snatch her hand away in time.

The rattlesnake's fangs sank deep.

The pain was immediate.

Her scream must have dragged Karey away from whatever

Mills & Boon she'd been reading because before Lacey knew it her sister was there, scooping her up and running with her through the backyard and around to the car. Karey stroked Lacey's sweaty head in her lap as they sped into town and told her how silly she was to disturb such a grumpy snake, that she'd probably given it a bigger fright than it had given her. (Lacey remembered tearfully arguing this point, saying the snake was stupid and mean and that she hoped all its teeth fell out.) The pain in her hand burned like fire. A million needles stabbed into it. Black dots swam in her eyes, but she bit her lip and tried not to cry; she hadn't wanted to scare Karey.

She didn't remember much after that. Karey later told her she went into anaphylactic shock and passed out. It took four lots of anti-venom to counteract the toxins that had been injected into her system. She was in intensive care for four days. When she woke, her hand and forearm had ballooned to twice their normal size, and she had cried upon seeing them, thinking they would always be that big and people would make fun of her. It took her grandmother almost an hour to calm her down and explain that her hand would return to its usual size in a few weeks. The doctor came in and said she was a very lucky girl, but by that point her tears had dried up and all she wanted was ice cream.

Lacey got the nickname Snake Girl. But she never forgot it was Karey who did all the saving. Lacey had almost died, and surely would have if her sister hadn't acted so quickly. And *that* was why she knew Karey and Addison were OK. Karey wouldn't let anything bad happen to her daughter, just like she hadn't let anything bad happen to her. Lacey held on to that belief as tightly as her five-year-old self had held on to her big sister as Karey ran with her to the car.

She was almost asleep when she heard the soft rustle of the Boy Scout's clothing, the tiniest scratch of his boot across the grit of the floor. She sensed him rising, standing over them, his gaze dark and somehow *safe*, and then his footfalls quietly padded away.

Lacey opened her eyes and lifted her head, searching for him, but there was only darkness beyond the light of the fire. She listened for the tell-tale *sh-sh-shh* of rattlesnakes but heard nothing. She even listened for the creeping sounds of a stranger sneaking into the barn, come to snatch them away. Or, failing that, burn them to death. Inhaling through her nose, she tried to smell any hint of smoke beyond that of the campfire, but it was impossible to detect anything. She stayed in that position until her neck ached too much for her to hold it up any longer.

Lying down, she tried to stay awake, but the warmth of the fire was its own blanket, the heat a weight that settled like warm hands over her eyes and head.

Wakefulness and dreaming – there was no defining line between the two. She slept, but she didn't know it. The hands remained, except they weren't warm and lulling any more but rough and groping, shoving into her pants, up her shirt, grabbing at her, *pawing* her. She struggled and moaned, and her breaths became thicker, like they did before tears came, that horrible syrupy feeling in the back of her throat. She tried to push the violating hands away, but they were slippery as eels, evading her attempts.

And then, music. A soft, basic-note melody that slipped around those hands and up into her ears. Gentle fingers of melodies drifted over her, getting louder, solidifying, offering comfort. The hands retreated, slipped from her clothes, her body, and she slept.

CHAPTER 16

A *car!*

Pilgrim shot to his feet at Voice's words and pressed his face to the nearest crack in the barn's wall. The fire had died down to cinders, so his night vision quickly picked out the light-coloured compact car racing towards them, coming from the east. The sky there was already lighting with dawn, a slightly paler band of blue in comparison to the rest of the night sky.

The car weaved across the blacktop, passing through both lanes. It changed direction so abruptly the wheels shrieked and the car shuddered. Pilgrim thought it would skid out of control, but the driver somehow fought it back into line. In fact, the driver managed to hold it for another hundred yards before the car slewed right, the brakes squealed, the hood dipped down and the vehicle flipped. It rolled on to its roof, then to its side, metal crumping loudly and glass shattering, bouncing on to four wheels again before it went right on rolling.

Four times it rolled before the compact screeched to a stop on its roof. Pilgrim figured any occupants must be gobs of meat and bone splinters after being turned around in that metal cabin-cum-food-blender close to half a dozen times.

The noise of the crash had brought Lacey and Alex scrambling out of their bedrolls and to the wall next to him, their eyes finding their own spyholes. The silence after the crash filled his ears as if they'd been stuffed with cotton. Not even the insects buzzed.

One headlight had blown, but the other shone an insipid

yellow. It illuminated a urine glow in front of the bent-up hood. Smoke seeped out from the engine compartment. A black lead trailed from inside the car, out through the smashed back window, and snaked a few yards behind the vehicle, tapering into a long, silver aerial, glinting like a rapier on the road.

A radio, Voice whispered.

Was this part of the convoy they'd spotted? If so, what was it doing back here?

Maybe it has something to do with Alex's nameless man, Voice said craftily. *Maybe he sends out emissaries to gather his flock.*

'Stay,' Pilgrim said when he felt Lacey shift.

'But they might be—'

'*Stay.*'

He watched the vehicle closely; it had ended up not far from the dirt track leading up to the barn, maybe no more than thirty feet. He could see the passenger side, but the interior was in shadow. There was no movement.

'Maybe we should go see if they need help,' Alex said.

Pilgrim could feel her eyes on him, but he didn't look away from the wreckage. He didn't answer her, either.

What're you thinking? Voice asked him.

'Thinking we should wait.'

'Wait for what?' Alex said.

Now Pilgrim could feel them both looking at him. Voice was doing his own version of watching, poised for more questions, Pilgrim could sense it, but he was holding off for the moment.

'For that,' Pilgrim said, seeing the shadowy movement a second before the tinkle of glass passed through the night air and reached their ears.

A single figure dragged itself out of the busted passenger window. And dragging was all it could do, judging by the slow, laborious way it was doing it.

Pilgrim looked up and down the road, staring hard – there

were no signs of any other vehicles. Still, he counted to a slow twenty-one in his head, that extra one after the twenty a useful addition because, in that extra second, a car could have appeared. It didn't, so it had done its job. He straightened and motioned for the girls to step back. He pushed open one of the barn doors, only wide enough for him to slip through, and stood in the gap for a minute, studying the overturned car. The figure had stopped dragging itself, its hips and legs still inside. Now it lay still, the broken glass twinkling like scattered jewels around its bare arms.

Pilgrim felt Lacey insert herself into the gap in the door behind him, but he didn't move to allow her space to step outside.

'Hey,' she whined, bumping up against his back.

He spared her a glance, saw she had her rifle, and finally moved aside, letting her out.

'Stay behind me,' he told her.

Alex remained inside the barn, hovering awkwardly by the doors. The sight of her bruises jarred Pilgrim. The muted light from the campfire had softened them, camouflaging them in shadows and the flattering licks of firelight, but now the natural light showed them in painfully vivid detail. He needed to remember that she had better reason than most to be untrusting of strangers.

He nodded at her to stay where she was and strode away without waiting for her to speak, drawing his gun and thumbing off the safety, walking quickly but carefully, eyes skimming over the car, up and down the road, all around at the straggly bushes, and back to the car. The person hadn't moved since it had half dragged itself out into the open.

As he neared the wrecked car, Lacey having to jog to keep up with his long strides, Pilgrim lifted the gun's muzzle and aimed.

I think it's dead.

'You always think that,' Pilgrim murmured, and then, more loudly, 'I have a gun pointed at your head. Unless you want it blown off, don't make any sudden moves.'

Voice sniggered. *The dead don't move.*

Pilgrim's pace had slowed, and he ducked lower, peering into the interior of the car. It appeared empty. Closer now, he could see that the person was a boy, lying face down, skinny, his vest darkly stained with old blood. The boy's bare arms were deeply lacerated, black-ruby strings adorning the diamantes of shattered glass.

When he was no more than a car's length away, Pilgrim stopped and looked back at the girl. Her eyes were big and she was chewing on the underside of her lip, but the butt of her rifle was snugged up tight against her shoulder, and she held the gun with easy familiarity.

'Keep me covered,' he told her.

She nodded, tucking her chin in and lifting the barrel, sighting along it at the boy lying in the dirt. Pilgrim eased forward, glass crunching underfoot, his right hand keeping the gun levelled at the boy's head, his left reaching cautiously for the kid's neck. His fingers slid over warm, moist skin, pressing in at the throat, feeling for a pulse. There was a flutter.

Checking over his shoulder, making sure the girl was staying alert, he holstered his gun and leaned down to grip the kid under the arms, lifting and heaving him the rest of the way out of the car. The boy's feet dragged as Pilgrim hauled him over to a clear piece of ground, the trailing legs bent at unnatural angles, like snapped pencils. The kid had looked skinny and, lifting him up, Pilgrim discovered he weighed only a fraction more than a sack of stolen potatoes. He laid the boy down and stayed kneeling as he gripped the bloody shoulder and pulled the kid on to his back.

Lacey moaned.

Holy crap.

The boy wasn't a boy. The boy was a girl, a woman; it was hard to tell her age, but she was older than Lacey by at least a handful of years. Her hair had been hacked short, her cheeks sunken into hollows, but it was her mouth Pilgrim stared at. Raw, pulpy holes lined her gums where her teeth had been, and the dry, crusty streaks of blood over her chin and neck – in contrast to the new, shiny additions courtesy of the car crash – suggested that an amateurish tooth extraction had been performed not too long ago.

'Who *did* that to her?'

Pilgrim squinted up the road in the direction the car had come from, then up at Lacey. The sky was rapidly growing lighter; the sun would be creeping over the horizon soon. In the dawning light, Lacey's skin looked pale, almost translucent. Pilgrim thought that, if he were to look long enough, he would see the tiny blue mapping of her veins appear in her cheeks and temples, like little roads leading to her brain.

He looked up the road again, wondering what was waiting for them there.

Someone we probably don't want to meet.

The toothless girl coughed; a thick gurgling as if phlegm had caught in the back of her throat. A pained grimace crossed her face. Without opening her eyes, she held a hand up and gripped Pilgrim's wrist. It was a strong grip – he saw how her knuckles were yellow-white, the bones desperately sharp under the thin paper of her skin. Her thumb pressed into his palm.

She tried to say something, but the word was unintelligible, just a mess of wet syllables.

'What did she say?' Lacey said, kneeling down opposite him.

The girl's hand tightened on his wrist and drew his hand up to her throat. Again, she tried to talk, blood bubbling up between her lips. More rubies.

Pilgrim bent his head closer, tilting his ear towards her mouth.

The gurgle grew lower, wispier, the girl's breath becoming ragged, a pressure bearing down on her lungs. Pilgrim knew they were filling up with blood. He grew very still when she whispered a name.

Christopher? asked Voice. *What does she mean, 'Christopher'?*

He was given no time to answer because she spoke again. Another word.

'What's she saying?' Lacey asked.

'Sounded like . . . *Defender.*' Pilgrim omitted the name for now.

'Defender?'

What's going on? Do we know her? The questions were directed like arrow-bolts.

'Or maybe defend *her*,' Pilgrim added.

'We need to help her.' Lacey's face was filled with anguish. She looked at him as if he were made of magic, could mend the broken mess on the inside of the girl's body, could magic all the bad stuff out of the world. Didn't she comprehend by now that most things in this world were unfixable?

The dying girl's grip loosened on his wrist, and he felt his palm come to rest on her chest, fingers touching the hollow of her throat. He looked down. The girl's eyes were open and staring at him. The tiniest of breaths passed between her lips, but she continued to stare, her eyes dark brown pools, the whites very white. He knew she saw him. Her pupils were pinpricks latched on to his face, recognition burning in them. Her mouth moved and, although no sound came out, he saw the shape of the words on her lips.

Defend her.

Her eyes lost their focus little by little, the pupils dilating, and then she was staring right through him at the dawning sky high above their heads, as if she could see where she was going and was pleased she was leaving him and all his kind behind in the dust.

After a minute or so Pilgrim stood up. He felt staggeringly tall. The dead girl seemed like she was twenty feet below, the world elongating around him, stretching out his legs and torso, his feet rapidly shrinking away into the distance, the kid's body now the size of a sleeping baby.

Distantly, he heard Voice. *Who is she? Does she know us? She seemed to know us.*

He could feel Voice's burning desire to study the girl's face, but Pilgrim looked away. He didn't want there to be any recognition. What good would that do him? She's dead, and everything she knew was dead along with her.

I think we must know her, Voice said uncertainly.

Did they? He wasn't sure any more. There were parts of him, holes in his memory, that were great sucking chasms, and that was how he liked it. The less he remembered, the less pain his memories caused him and the less time he spent mourning for things that were beyond his reach. He didn't *want* to remember. He could almost hear the rattling of all those chains on all those chests in the dark depths of all those deep oceans. Forgetting was his gift to himself, and he wouldn't relinquish it. It was the only thing that kept him sane.

Voice roiled in exasperation. *You and your cheesecloth brain!*

Lacey remained kneeling at the girl's side. She seemed far away. Small and inconsequential. She was speaking, but the sound was muffled, like it was coming from a badly tuned-in radio. Pilgrim gripped the sides of his head and took two deep breaths.

Voice's ire dampened and shifted to concern. *You OK, compadre?*

Pilgrim grunted and dropped his hands. The dead girl's message bothered him. He didn't know how, or for what purpose, but the words she had spoken meant something. The car could have crashed ten miles up the road, on a strip of highway where there were no witnesses to hear her last words. Pilgrim knew that often a dying person would say 'please' or 'help' as their life drained away – he knew this because he had been present at a number of people's deaths – but this girl hadn't said either of those things. She had said, 'Defend her'. And 'defend her', or 'defender', somehow meant something. Something specific to him. She had found him to tell him this. Why else was she here?

She must mean Lacey, Voice said. *There's something different about her. You knew it from the start, don't pretend like you didn't. I noticed how you saw the glow in her fingers. It wasn't a mirage.*

Pilgrim refused to acknowledge what Voice was talking about.

Don't be so damn pig-headed!

Lacey heard no voice, of this Pilgrim was certain. He knew how to spot the signs, and she had none of them. But there *was* something different about her, Voice was right. She had a gulf hiding within, a space that seemed ready and waiting to be filled. It scared him, how wide open and vulnerable she was; he was scared *for* her, and he didn't know why. All he did know was that he had no interest in being anyone's protector.

Tiny Lacey, a long way down by his feet, stood up, and with that movement the world righted itself on a quick, sucking zoom, the edges shuddering out of focus.

Pilgrim blinked at her, life-size and standing before him.

'What do we do?' she asked.

'Do?'

'About her.' She nodded down at the now normal-sized dead girl.

He didn't understand her question. 'There's nothing *to* do. She's dead.'

'So we just leave her here?'

He looked down at the body again. The rubies of blood on the girl's lips had already begun to dry.

Ruby, he thought.

Ruby? Voice's feelers were creeping through his mind, tendrils whispering among his thoughts like spun cobwebs, searching, searching.

Pilgrim's eyes flinched away from the dead girl, and he shut down his train of thought.

'Let's go,' he said, turning on his heel and looking east as he started back up the dirt track.

Lacey didn't immediately follow. Pilgrim sensed she was taking an extra few seconds to gain some sort of closure, maybe apologise to the girl for not being able to help her more, apologise for the mutilations inflicted on her. But, like Pilgrim had said, she was dead, and any apologies were a salve for their own souls and not hers.

You can't hide from yourself for ever, Voice said.

He could, but that was no concern of Voice's.

Entering the barn, Pilgrim found that Alex had already packed up their gear. She was finishing kicking the fire flat before picking up her pack and, limping around the open passenger door, slinging it on to the back seat. She paused when she saw him standing there, but the pause lasted barely a second and then she was moving again, coming back to pick up Lacey's scarf.

We should get off the highway, Voice said. *It's too dangerous to be travelling on it. Not while we have the girls with us.*

The car had been going at least fifty when it flipped. And the road had been empty of any other vehicles. Which meant the girl wasn't being closely followed. And yet, even when the car lost control, she hadn't reduced her speed, hadn't tried to stop. She had been running, and whatever she had been running from had her too terrified to slow down.

Pilgrim went over to his bike and closed the latches on the panniers, getting ready to leave.

Lacey entered the barn. She stood silhouetted just inside the doorway, the rising sun flaring hot and bright behind her. Within the hour the temperature outside would be over eighty.

In another four, it'd be hitting a hundred.

In one hand, something flashed, catching the first rays of sunlight.

'What's that you have?' Alex asked.

Lacey stepped forward and lifted the item, showing it to the woman. It was some sort of small medallion threaded on to a fine silver chain.

'I found it. On the girl.'

Alex went over to her.

Pilgrim kicked his bike off its stand and leaned into the handlebars, rolling the heavy machine across the dusty floor to the barn door. He passed by Alex and Lacey. Alex held the medallion cupped in her palm. He didn't need to see the coin to know a man was depicted on it with a staff in one hand and a child on his back.

A St Christopher, Voice said, understanding dawning.

'It's a St Christopher pendant,' Alex told the girl. 'It's supposed to keep you safe when you're travelling.'

'Like a good-luck charm?'

Alex nodded and passed the necklace back. 'Exactly like a good-luck charm.'

They both flinched when Pilgrim kicked the barn door open. He wheeled his bike outside, addressing them over his shoulder. 'I'll siphon any fuel left in the wrecked car. It won't take long. We're leaving.' He slung a leg over the saddle, fired the engine to life and threw up a cloud of dust from his back tyre when he yanked on the throttle.

I thought we were getting off the highway.

'We will.'

When?

'Soon.'

How soon?

'When I'm good and ready.'

A few seconds of silence.

You're making a mistake.

Pilgrim didn't answer.

We're heading in exactly the same direction that girl back there was running from. You're asking for trouble if you keep going.

Pilgrim glanced over his shoulder. The car remained a steady truck's length behind him. Like the night before, he couldn't see the two occupants behind the windshield, but this time it was the sun glaring off the glass that hid them from view and not the silver reach of the moon. It was for the best, anyway. He'd already had his fill of the accusing glares Lacey had been throwing his way ever since they'd left the dead girl out under the sun. It's funny how she seemed fine with the idea of leaving the strangled woman trussed up in the hotel room but leaving the dead girl somehow rankled with her.

It's because it's a girl not much older than her. Could've just as easily been her back there you were leaving.

Vicksburg was another full day's driving. Longer if they left the highway; they were still three hundred miles short of crossing the border into Louisiana. Already the mix of adrenalin and lack of sleep was affecting him. A strange, tingling fatigue buzzed through his shoulders, making them weigh heavy, and he was finding it hard to focus on the road, the centre line weaving and blurring into two. Yet his heartbeat raced, a constant butterfly-fluttering at his pulse points. He knew he wouldn't be able to ride for much longer.

The sputter from his engine solved his quandary. He twisted the throttle a little, and the bike surged weakly forward but then fell back, his speed decreasing slowly until the engine gave a final handful of coughs and cut out altogether. He pulled in the clutch and coasted, the silence so unfamiliar after the constant drone of the engine that he found himself humming, a low, monotonous tone, as though he were mimicking the noise of the engine.

Pulling to the side of the road, he rolled the last few feet and stopped. He sat still, quiet. Blessedly, Voice kept his peace for once – Pilgrim just wanted to breathe and calm his heart rate; he wanted to listen to nothing for a few moments. He didn't even let the sound of a car door opening behind him disturb his meditation.

'Everything OK?' A smoky huskiness still roughened the woman's voice, but in a day or two it would be back to normal. Possibly the only part of her that ever would be.

He rubbed at the tight muscles in his neck. Moving stiffly, he climbed off the bike and came to stand next to her. A pull tugged at him, a tightness in the bottom of his stomach that wouldn't ease. It wanted him to turn his head and look up the road, wanted him to sniff the air as if he were some kind of animal scenting its quarry. Instead, he stood very still and stared at his bike. It ticked and pinged as it settled. The tank was covered in dust, the bodywork dented and cracked, and the chain was starting to rust. He was going to miss it. And at that thought he knew he would be leaving it behind whether he liked it or not; there were three of them now, and he couldn't take their fuel from them.

He pulled his neckerchief down off his face. 'I'll ride with you for a while,' he said.

They set to work unloading his bike.

Alex didn't look up as she helped empty his panniers. 'Lacey said the girl back there'd had all her teeth pulled out.'

He grunted softly.

'Why would anyone do that?'

'Not because they're the tooth fairy, that's for sure.' He went to the car and loaded everything into the trunk.

Alex remained crouched beside his bike. Whatever she was doing, she wasn't making any move to get up. He sighed and traipsed back over to her.

She looked past him to the car, and presumably to the girl

who sat in it, before raising her eyes to him. 'We don't want to cross paths with whoever did that.'

He nodded, his decision now made. 'I agree.' He'd had the notion to travel along this road until he came across someone who could tell him what had happened to the dead girl, and why she was whispering mysterious words to strangers. If he'd been alone he would have surely continued on such a path – his disapprobation still ran hot under his skin – but Voice had been right: to do so while these two girls tagged along would be reckless.

'We need to get that girl to Vicksburg and her family,' Alex said.

He knew nothing about any business of family, but he said, 'Again, I agree.'

'That should be our main concern.'

'Yes.'

Alex stood, levering her way up with a quiet groan and a hand braced on one knee. She stared him straight in the eye. 'You know, I can't work you out at all.'

He flicked a fly away from his face. 'No one's asking you to.'

She was quiet. Her eyes narrowed slightly, but Pilgrim detected a faint softening at the corners of her mouth. 'I don't know what's happened to you. I don't know whether there's anything other than just *you* in that stubborn head of yours, and I won't ask. I don't expect you'd tell me, anyway, and I don't expect I'd like the answer even if you did. But I do get the impression you don't have a whole hell of a lot in this world. Except for maybe that junker over there.' She jabbed her chin at his bike, but he didn't look away from her, even though her use of the word 'junker' was unfair and offended him a little. He wasn't sure what point she was trying to make with all this.

'What I will tell you is that I don't have much in this world, either,' she continued. 'Not any more. All I do have is in that car. Do we understand each other?'

Her car was important to her, and it should be. Any means of transportation was a valuable commodity, and she should do everything in her power to retain it.

I'm not sure that's what she meant— Voice began.

'I understand,' Pilgrim told her.

'Good. We should get going, then. Unless you like standing out here catching flies?' She raised her eyebrows, but her non-sequitur confused him. She ended any further conversation by walking past him and going back to the car.

Pilgrim stood for a while longer, giving his bike a last fond look, and then followed her. The cable and long, rapier-thin antenna that had trailed from the crashed car had connected to a mobile CB radio fastened to the dash. He had liberated both and transferred everything to Alex's car, mounting the aerial to the roof with its magnetic base. The power plug had slotted neatly into the cigarette lighter. He'd left Lacey fiddling with the dials, roaming through the crackling channels for transmissions. He hadn't told her what he was specifically looking for – she no doubt thought he wanted her to use it so they could stay away from whoever had hurt the dead girl; any information it might tell them could be useful. The radio's casing had taken a beating in the crash, the plastic cracked and part of its insides showing, so Pilgrim didn't hold out much hope of it receiving anything. The static had sounded decidedly garbled when he left the girl fooling with it.

He rechecked the antenna on the car's roof – its base didn't budge – and opened the back door. Lacey turned around to look at him as he slid into the back seat. She was wearing the baby-fly sunglasses again. He glimpsed a glint of metal at her throat. The St Christopher.

'You're well and truly stuck with us now,' she said, smirking.

He couldn't help but smile. It was a weary smile, and it felt strange on his face, as if a mask of sand would crack free from his skin and fall into his lap. The tugging sensation in his gut seemed to lessen now that he was sitting in the car.

'Who knows, maybe you'll get to *like* having us around.' Lacey arched an eyebrow, almost challenging him to reply, and turned back to the CB. The crackling grew louder for a moment.

'Heard anything?' he asked her.

'Thought I did at one point, but then got nothing but *shhffhhht*.' She added a few crackles and whistles for effect.

'You tried the channels I told you to?'

'9, 10, 14, 19, and . . . um—'

'21,' he said. CB channels for emergencies, highway traffic and regional road news from the old days.

'Right. 21. Tried them all. *Nada*.'

'Go back to 15, and leave it there.' That was the channel the radio had been tuned to when he'd first switched it on. Presumably, the channel the dead girl had been monitoring.

'Gotcha,' Lacey said.

Pilgrim settled back as Alex pulled on to the road and smoothly accelerated. He didn't look at his bike as they went by; he had left different parts of himself everywhere he'd been. Pretty soon all he'd have left were the boots on his feet and the sole ability to place one in front of the other until there were no more steps to take. Perhaps then he'd give himself the luxury of looking back.

'You should get some sleep,' Alex said, her eyes meeting his in the rear-view mirror.

He eased lower into the seat, his eyes heavy-lidded, the cushion softening and opening up to meet him. 'Get off the highway at the next off-ramp,' he said. 'And don't stop for anybody.' He sank down, down into the seat's foamy embrace, until he was encased on all sides, as if lying in a plush, slumberous coffin.

CHAPTER 17

Pilgrim slept deeply. He didn't dream. (Dreams were for people who still believed there were safe places left in the world.) There were flashes of images in the dark, though. Memories that were lodged in the back of his skull, hidden in the vast oceans of his mind and supposedly safeguarded in locked chests. Occasionally, they slipped free from their bindings, not even chains able to hold them.

In one he saw a naked man strung up by his neck, swaying high overhead at the end of a rope tied to a telephone pole. A piece of cardboard strapped to his chest read 'He Hears' in trembling black marker. He had one shoe on. A black-and-white wingtip. A scattering of kids gathered beneath him, the eldest no older than eight, throwing rocks and empty cans as if he were a dangling human piñata who would spill his contents if only they could strike him in the right spot.

In the next image, Pilgrim saw three adults hunkered around a campfire, a ragtag group of dirt and bones and scraps of clothes, their eyes white in their ash-streaked faces. A small dog was being spit-roasted over the open flames. They hadn't bothered to skin it or remove its collar. The animal was alight in several places, the smell of burning fur musky and offensive. When they saw Pilgrim, they stood and yelled and waved angrily at him to get away. He didn't recognise any of the words they used – they had lost the ability to verbalise their frantic sentiments. They were more animal than the poor mongrel that was being cooked.

The last image wasn't a memory. Or at least not one he

remembered. He stood in the middle of what used to be a town, but now its landscape was moon-like with craters and cracked streets and sidewalks on all different levels, as if God himself had shifted the tectonic plates beneath the Earth to create steps, some leading up into heaven, others down into the bowels of hell. All the buildings had been levelled. There were no people. Pilgrim was the first man to stand in the town since it had been destroyed and would probably be the last. This place was the definition of desolation. Nothing lived here any more. And yet the sky was alive with red, pulsing static, bursting with electricity every few seconds, a low drone buzzing from its depths as though invisible power lines ran hot above his head. With each burst of fizzing electricity, the hairs lifted on his arms and the droning caught on crackling sounds, almost like words. The longer he looked up at that shifting, red-static sky, the more he thought he could understand it, thought the sky was speaking to him. It said, 'Thanatos' and 'Listen' and 'Slaughter' and 'Death', and the words made his blood fizz with static, too, so that it ran hot and fearful under his skin.

Pilgrim opened his eyes, and he was in the back seat of the car, looking at the napes of Alex's and Lacey's necks. There was no hypnopompic transition for him: he was simply asleep and then awake.

The girls were talking again. All they seemed to do was talk. Beneath it, the low-volume static from the CB radio provided a cushion of white noise.

It's what women do, talk. That and make men feel inferior. Voice hovered nearby as if he'd been waiting for Pilgrim to awaken.

Pilgrim wanted to tell him about the last part of his dream, about the red, pulsing sky and the words it had spoken to him, but something stayed his tongue. It had left him with a vague feeling of apprehension, and he didn't want Voice picking up on it.

He directed his attention out of the window, at the position of the fat molten ball in the sky. He hadn't been asleep for much more than an hour. He was glad to see they had followed his instructions and left the highway behind. They were now driving through an abandoned town, very different from the one he had awoken from. Broken windows, broken doors, rusting cars without wheels, overgrown grass and straggly bushes, caved-in roofs, collapsed garage porticos. The sign for a one-screen picture house they passed read 'N W SH W NG – M AX: (R)'.

The inside of the car was stuffy and hot. It made him groggy. He stayed slumped where he was and listened to them talk.

'I'm pretty sure it's the next right,' Lacey was saying. There was a rustle of paper as she lifted the map up and folded it in half, and folded it in half again, laying it back in her lap, her head bowing over it.

'Just tell me when to turn,' Alex told her.

'You'll really like Vicksburg, Alex. My sister lives in this really big house, so there'll be plenty of room for you.'

She's got a sister, Voice said in a musing kind of way.

Pilgrim studied the side of Lacey's face when she reached over to pick up the CB's handset. The arm of her sunglasses hid her eye, but her profile was all soft, clean curves. There was a tiny bump at the bridge of her nose, as if she had broken it falling off her swing set, or if a goat she milked had butted her while she pulled at its teats, or maybe she had slipped while getting out of the tub after taking one of the baths she so loved.

Don't, Voice warned.

'That'd be nice,' Alex said. 'We should see how your sister feels about it first, though. She might not want strangers in her house.'

A few clicks came from the CB as the girl keyed the mic on and off, on and off.

'Oh, Karey won't mind – she likes having visitors. You'll get to try her scones. She makes the *best* scones, I swear.' The static cut off as she keyed the mic on. 'You all hear that? Who out there wants scones? Chocolate orange scones, strawberry and white chocolate scones, and plain old raisin ones. She's not so great at baking apple pies,' she said in a more conversational tone, 'but her scones are to die for. Here's S. Levee Street coming up.'

Alex took the turning on the right. The radio crackled and Pilgrim's ears perked up, but no answer came through.

'I used to make the most awesome cookies,' Alex said. 'I loved my kitchen. It was the tiniest kitchen in the world – think postage-stamp size, that's how small. But I could reach everything from standing in the one spot. It was wonderful.'

'My sister's kitchen is pretty big. And old. It's got cast-iron stoves and stuff.'

Alex's next question sounded tentative. 'Do you think she knows you're coming?'

Lacey turned to look out of the passenger window. Her voice was bright and loose, but Pilgrim heard the forced cheer injected into it. The radio went silent again, the static shutting off, as if it, too, wanted to better hear the girl's words.

'She should, yep. I waited such a long while. 'Cause, you know, I wasn't sure if she'd be coming, and Grammy said we needed to worry about our lot, and my sister was more than capable of looking out for hers. She has David and Addison – that's my niece, did I tell you about her? I'm an aunt.' Lacey laughed, as if that was the wildest thing ever. 'My sister finally got pregnant after a bunch of times trying. My grams said Addison was a miracle baby. Karey had her a couple months before everything went nuts, so I haven't even met her yet. That's awful, isn't it? That I haven't met my own niece? But my grammy said it wasn't safe to, you know, go travelling across two whole states. She tried the one time, after I hounded and hounded her to. It didn't go so well. And Grammy's eyesight got pretty bad – she couldn't hardly see anything by the end . . .' The girl trailed off, but then caught herself, and the full-wattage of her brightness came back. 'So after Grammy passed, I thought I'd make my own way there.'

'Wow. So your niece would be seven now?' Alex asked.

'Yep. Almost eight.'

'And how long has it been since your grammy passed away?' Alex asked gently.

Lacey made a low, humming noise while she thought about it and went back to clicking the mic's transmission button. 'Guess it must've been . . . three months ago? Yeah, about three months.' She tried to sound offhand about it, but Pilgrim would bet the girl knew exactly how long it had been, probably to the day.

'So that's when you set up the lemonade stand you told me about?' Alex said.

'Not straight away. I wasn't sure what I'd do, to be honest.' *Click-click-click.* 'I mean, Grammy had gotten pretty forgetful, and I tried talking to her, but it didn't help much. Had to figure stuff out on my own.' A static-silenced *click.* 'We don't get hardly any traffic passing through, but I reckoned someone would come by eventually. Took a chance on it being someone who'd help. And it wasn't like I didn't have my toad sticker.'

'Toad sticker?'

'My grammy's old paring knife.'

Pilgrim had listened enough; he straightened up, groaning as he stretched out the kinks in his back. He said, 'You'd planned on sticking me, then, if I hadn't paid my way?' He was slightly irked, in retrospect, that he had allowed her on to the back of his bike without first checking her over for weapons. She could have easily slid that toad sticker of hers between his ribs if she'd so desired, and he wouldn't have been able to stop her.

Lacey had started in her seat when he spoke, but now she swivelled around, hooking her arm over the seat back so she could face him. 'I'd planned on sticking you if you'd gone and tried to git me, yep.'

Git ya. Voice cackled.

'Lucky I was happy with just the lemonade.'

Lacey smirked at him. 'Right. Or else you'd be full of holes, like in the cartoons when someone gets punctured and they take a drink and it all pours out of the wounds like a human fountain. I remember those.'

Pincushion Pilgrim.

'Feel better?' Alex asked him. 'You weren't asleep long.'

'Feel fine.' He twisted his neck, heard it crack, and opened and closed his left hand, pins and needles prickling through it.

Lacey scrubbed at her nose with her fist, then said, 'You hungry? I was just telling Alex about my sister's scones—'

'Chocolate orange, strawberry and white chocolate, and plain old raisin. I heard.'

'You dirty possum,' she said, but she was grinning when she said it.

'I wasn't playing dead.'

She lost some of her smile, the last bits hanging around as if undecided where to go.

'Opossums play dead to deter predators,' he said, explaining the difference. 'I was asleep.'

Her smile had disappeared. The radio static fell ominously silent again. 'I wouldn't know. I've never seen a real-life one.'

'And probably won't. Most likely they've all been caught and eaten, or else gone back into the wild—'

'From the map,' Alex said, interrupting, 'we worked out we're just south of Fort Worth. So only about six hours away from Vicksburg.'

'Good,' Pilgrim said, nodding. 'That's good.' He turned to Lacey. 'You're going to Vicksburg because you think your sister is there?'

Pilgrim—

Lacey frowned, suspicion sharpening her words. 'Yeah, why?'

'You understand the chances of finding her alive are slim.'

Pilgrim. There was a definite reprimand to Voice's tone this time.

'Hey, now,' Alex said at the same time, glancing back at him. 'We should see first before making any assumptions.'

'False hope is dangerous,' he told her. 'You know as well as I do that the odds aren't good.'

'You don't know anything,' Lacey said, staring hard at him, her eyes kind of squinty. Pilgrim wasn't sure why she was angry; he was discussing the realities of the situation, that was all. 'You think you do because you've been out there more than I have. But you don't.'

'I didn't say I did,' he said, frowning now. 'But if that's the only reason you want to go to Vicksburg, then you need to rethink—'

Alex interrupted again. 'We'll hope for the best, and see what we find. OK? There's nothing wrong with that.' In the rear-view mirror, her eyes bored into his, effectively silencing him.

Lacey shot him her own last look and turned around, slumping in her seat and crossing her arms. The mic shuttered a bunch of fast clicks as the girl depressed the button in quick succession, cutting into the radio's static.

That clicking is getting really annoying.

'The more you click that or hold the mic button down, the less likely we'll hear any transmissions.'

The girl huffed, and the clicking stopped. A soft wash of white noise settled throughout the car.

Pilgrim scratched the side of his face.

Teenagers, Voice said, as if that explained everything. *Don't worry about it. We had a sister once, too. You remember her? Had the same curly hair as—*

'Not now,' Pilgrim said.

Alex sent him another frowning look through the rear-view mirror, but he paid it no mind.

Not now, not now. It's always 'not now' with you. Never want to listen.

'Can I see the map?' he asked, reaching one hand between the front seats and leaving it hanging there, waiting patiently until Lacey sighed loudly and slapped the map into his open palm.

'Thank you,' he said.

She made no response.

He found the stretch of highway where the car had crashed, then traced the path of the dead girl's flight with his finger, his eyes scanning the names of each town and city, waiting for the word 'Defend' to jump out at him. But it didn't. There was no mention of 'Defend', 'Defender', 'Defending' or any other form of that root word anywhere in a hundred-mile radius. Pilgrim laid the map down and used the pads of his thumb and middle finger to rub his eyes.

Look!

A green sign swept past, pointing to a road on the left.

'Stop.' Pilgrim twisted in his seat, his eyes fixed on the sign as though it might pop out of existence if he let it out of sight.

The library was a small building, only a single storey high. Its roof was brown tiles, its bricks beige and weathered. Elmer the Patchwork Elephant had been painted on one of the front-facing windows, but he was missing his head, the pane broken clean in half. The door had been pulled off its hinges, so now there was only a doorway and an open invitation, which Pilgrim felt sure the librarians of old would have been happy about. Everyone was welcome at the library, after all.

'What're we doing here?' Lacey asked, stepping out into the heat of the mid-morning sun.

Pilgrim had thought the fresh air outside would feel better than the baking stuffiness of the car, but he was wrong.

Baked like one of Lacey's sister's scones.

Pilgrim slid his sunglasses on and surveyed the parking lot. The concrete was faded and cracked. So were the sidewalks. The rear of five properties overlooked the car park, and he checked the windows of each house, but no one was watching and he felt no eyes on him. His ears were picking up on something, though. More a vibration than a noise. A faint buzz in the concrete beneath his feet. A generator, possibly. That could mean people. But they were choosing not to show themselves, and that suited Pilgrim.

'Looking for some books,' he said, and swung his door shut. He made a show of taking out his gun, releasing its magazine and checking it, before slotting it back into place.

'Yeah, I got that. But what books?'

Pilgrim almost smiled when the girl lifted her rifle, unconsciously following his example and checking over the weapon in exactly the way he would have asked her to if she hadn't done it of her own accord.

'I'll show you when I find them,' he told her.

She trailed after him to the back of the car, where he popped open the trunk and lifted his pack out, slinging it on to his back. Lacey and Alex followed his example, taking all their belongings with them. Alex locked the car. Pilgrim didn't say that, if anyone wanted it, they'd bust it open in ten seconds flat and be gone before they had time to come back.

'Why does *everything* have to be a mystery with you, man? Can't you just tell me which books?'

He looked down at Lacey. Her sunglasses continued to hide her eyes, but he could tell by the way her brows were scrunched up that she was scowling at him.

'You'd rather be told than to see for yourself?' he asked, genuinely surprised.

'Yes.'

He looked at Alex, and she shrugged, smiling slightly. He

noticed she'd taken a tyre iron from the car and slid it under her belt.

He turned back to the girl. 'I don't know yet. I'll know when I see them.' And he walked around her and headed for the library's entrance, doing a third and final scan of the surrounding area as he went.

There was a moment's silence, and then: 'You're kidding me, right? You don't even *know* what books you're looking for?' He heard her tramp up behind him.

Pilgrim stopped in the doorway. The mustiness of old books wafted out to greet him, and he inhaled deeply. 'They used to think making books digital – making *everything* digital – was the future. But where are those things now? Lost, that's where.' He didn't turn to her as he spoke. 'Books are real. They're all about feeling them in your hands. Leafing through their pages. Smelling the ink. You'll know it when you have the right one.' Gun held ready, he stepped inside. 'And stay alert,' he added. 'We don't know who's hanging around.'

The sun became smoky as it filtered through the windows, its yellow beams alive with floating dust motes. Pilgrim tugged his neckerchief up over his mouth and nose, feeling the motes tickle the back of his throat when he breathed in. He slipped off his sunglasses with his free hand and walked deeper into the lobby.

The room opened up, the issue and returns desk to his right, and a long table stretching out before him, dark wooden shelves lining the walls to each side. On his left, a gap in the shelving made way for a wide staircase that led down to basement level and a faded grey sign informed him that the children's library was downstairs. The shelves were all empty of books, occupied instead by dust bunnies and dead insects.

Is this such a good time to be stopping for reading material? Especially if there could be teeth-extracting crazy people around?

'It's always a good time.'

Lacey stepped up beside him. 'What's always a good time?'

'To broaden our minds,' he replied.

'Right.' She frowned doubtfully at him.

Ahead, stacks of lateral-facing shelving ran six deep before opening up into a reading area populated with coffee tables and study carrels. An L-shaped staircase led up to a mezzanine level, which more directional signs revealed had once housed the non-fiction section; it formed a balcony over the reading area below.

'So where are all the books at?'

He ran his eyes over the emptiness, looking for the door he wanted. 'A lot have been burned,' he told her absently. 'They make good fuel for fires.' Wandering alongside the table, left hand trailing across its smooth top, fingers unconsciously following the wood's grain, he spotted the door marked 'Staff Only'.

Jackpot, Voice said.

'Jackpot,' Pilgrim agreed.

He expected the door to be locked, but the knob turned easily and the door pushed silently inward. It was like looking into the bottom of a sinkhole; his eyes were unable to latch on to anything in the complete absence of light. He reached into the side pocket of his pack and took out a flashlight. The beam stabbed into the darkness, cleaving it open and bathing everything in harsh white. Stepping slowly inside, listening for movement, he swept the flashlight back and forth, picking out a desk and a chair, two filing cabinets with all the drawers gaping open, a cork board with curling notices pinned to it, and an overturned metal waste basket. On the far wall, another door beckoned. It was also unlocked. When he opened it, a chilly breath of air washed over him, as if the room beyond had exhaled after a long slumber, and with it came an even stronger stench of mustiness and mildew.

Six rolling stacks took up most of the space. The middle bay was rolled open and, when Pilgrim glanced into it, he saw each shelf was filled with books. Hundreds of them.

Well, whaddya know. You've struck gold, Pilgrim, ol' boy.

He holstered his gun and slipped into the bay, being careful to step over the stacks' runners, and caressed the spines of the books, his eyes scanning their titles. He pulled out a slim paperback copy of Ira Levin's *Rosemary's Baby* and flicked through the yellowed pages. The book felt good in his hands. He unslung his pack and tucked the paperback inside.

He went back to running his fingertips over the books' spines, pausing here and there to feel the slightly upraised or indented font of the lettering.

You can't carry them all.

'Five,' Pilgrim said. 'I can carry five.'

Fine. But be quick about it.

CHAPTER 18

Lacey almost followed the Boy Scout into the back room, but he didn't spare her a glance, too busy searching for his precious books to care if she was there or not. Forget him if he wants to go searching for some mysterious *you'll know it when you feel it* book. She had better things to do than trail after him like some hungry chick waiting for its feed.

She stood next to the long, empty table, watching the light from his flashlight bob about in the darkened stockroom. She glanced down at where her hand rested on the dusty tabletop, her fingers having matched and run along the same tracks the Boy Scout's had made through the dirt. She drew her hand back, irritably rubbing the grime off on her jeans.

Alex touched her elbow. 'He doesn't mean it. His people skills just need some improving.'

'No kidding,' she muttered.

Alex hooked her arm through Lacey's and tugged. 'Come on, let's go find our own books. He can come get us later.'

Lacey let Alex draw her away. They wandered over to the stairs, the light growing fainter the further they walked from the library's entranceway. On the wall, its detail lost in the dimness, a six-foot-tall painted bunny greeted them at the top of the stairs. Lacey pulled out two candles from her pack and held them steady while Alex lit them. They followed the bunny downward into the dark, holding on to the bannister as they went, a new painting of the rabbit, mid-hop, spaced every five steps or so. The candlelight threw their shadows back on to the walls, the bunny coming alive in the wavering flames, jumping and bouncing along with them.

The children's library was a cave of gloom. They kept to the right when they reached the bottom, running their hands along the shelves to orientate themselves.

Alex stopped, and Lacey almost bumped into the back of her. 'Wow, look at this.' In front of Alex, a large green-bodied caterpillar hung from the ceiling. Alex poked it with a finger and it swung away on its wire. It came back and she caught it in one hand.

'It looks like it's been eating chillies,' Lacey said.

Alex laughed softly. 'It's the Hungry Caterpillar – it'll eat anything.'

Lacey stared at the thing, not getting the reference. 'OK?'

Alex looked at her as if she'd sprouted her own caterpillar out of her eye socket. 'Good Lord, you've never heard of the Hungry Caterpillar?'

For some reason, Alex's surprise at her lack of knowledge annoyed Lacey. 'No. I'm sorry my grandma wasn't a library user and didn't read to me much. I was, like, nine when everyone decided to throw themselves off bridges and in front of trains and kill each other and stuff. I never got the chance to read widely.'

Alex let go of the caterpillar, and it swayed gently on its wire. 'I'm sorry. I was reliving my childhood there for a second. I didn't mean to imply you should know it just because I do.'

Lacey's irritation vanished instantly. 'God, I'm sorry, Alex. I'm just being a shit. Ignore me, OK? What kind of book is it?'

Alex smiled, but it was melancholic, distant. 'A children's picture book. Our nanny used to read it to us when we were little.'

'Not your parents?'

'They weren't the bedtime-story type.' Her smile became tinged with bitterness.

'They're gone, too? Your folks, I mean.'

Alex reached for the caterpillar again and cupped it in one palm, stroking her thumb across its body. 'Same thing happened to them as to most everyone else. My mother was a little more imaginative about it, though – she did the whole Sylvia Plath thing. Always did have a flair for the dramatics, did dear old Mom.'

Sylvia Plath was another reference Lacey didn't understand, but she wasn't about to ask for an explanation. She wanted to say again that she was sorry, but she was so sick of those words. Sick to death of them. They tasted hollow and dusty in her mouth.

'You think we could find the Hungry Caterpillar book in here?' she asked instead. 'I'd really like to read it.'

CHAPTER 19

To save on weight, Pilgrim was picking out three more slim paperbacks – Vonnegut's *Cat's Cradle*, Wyndham's *Day of the Triffids* and Matheson's *I Am Legend* – when he realised it had been too quiet for too long.

He swung the flashlight towards the open door.

No one stood there.

At the rare discovery of all these untouched volumes, he had momentarily forgotten the girl and the woman, but now the silence screamed at him in their absence. Even the faint vibration in the ground had disappeared. He quickly slid a fifth book off the shelf, not bothering to glance at its title, and stuffed it into his pack. He made his way out of the stacks, slinging the pack on to his shoulders, and went back through the outer office and into the library proper.

They weren't waiting for him out there, either. Only silence and dust greeted him. He stood motionless and listened.

Maybe they—

'Shhh.'

He heard nothing. He considered calling to them but decided against it. There was no reason to call attention to himself if he didn't need to.

It doesn't feel safe here, Voice whispered. *Not for us, and not for them. Trouble always seems to find us.*

Pilgrim's eyes were drawn to the open doorway. He could see the parking lot from where he stood, and for a second he envisaged striding out of the library, not looking back as he brushed past Alex's car and carried on walking. The girl would be upset to find him gone, he knew, but he wouldn't have to face her wounded expression or the sad betrayal in her eyes because he'd be two miles up the road and placing more distance between them with every step.

I thought you wanted to help them, Voice said.

Pilgrim saw the woman's eyes in the rear-view mirror again, except now, standing in this empty library with nothing but the weight of the pack on his back and the weight of Voice in his head, he thought he understood what she'd been trying to tell him: This is all she has. Don't take it from her.

We might even get some scones out of it, Voice added.

'You know as well as I do her sister is dead.' But his tone lacked bite. He was staring at the trails his fingers had made in the dust on the tabletop. Next to them he saw a smaller set where the girl had run her fingers along the surface, criss-crossing over his own.

He wasn't a heartless bastard, after all. Not completely.

'I guess I did tell her I'd get her there,' he said quietly.

You did.

'And it won't take long.'

It won't.

Pilgrim moved off, his head down as he studied the scuffs of footprints in the dusty carpeting.

Just so you know, for a guy who's always complaining about wanting to be alone, you play Papa Bear very well.

'If you've got nothing useful to say,' Pilgrim told him, 'do us both a favour and don't say anything at all.'

Like a child needing to have the last word, Voice added, *You're as cranky as a bear, too.*

Shaking his head, Pilgrim flicked on his flashlight and headed down into the basement, where Winnie the Pooh, Elmer the headless Elephant and the Gruffalo waited for him in the dark.

★

The children's library was a low-ceilinged, sprawling area the size of the whole adult fiction and non-fiction lending library put together. The dark gave it an eerie, claustrophobic feel, despite its open-plan design. With the child-sized, dark wooden shelving and floor-level kinder boxes, there were plenty of places for someone to hide. Pilgrim took out his gun, keeping its muzzle pointed at kneecap level.

The bookcases nearest to the stairs were empty but, as he moved deeper into the maze, books began to appear, some fallen over, others collapsed in a pile in a domino effect, the odd one still standing upright as if placed on display by the librarian only that morning in order to catch the eye of an excitable child. Obviously, the chore of carrying these books up the stairs had been too tiresome an enterprise for the book thieves, who had limited their efforts mainly to the ground floor above.

At the end of many aisles, homemade creatures or animals had been hung or exhibited, each one designed to capture the imagination of young visitors. They captured the imagination of older visitors, too, and Pilgrim gave the grotesquely long-legged spider a wide berth as he reached the end of one particular aisle, the arachnid's papier-mâché body as big as his head. Far too easily he could imagine the spider unfreezing and stretching its spindly legs before quickly scuttling towards him with an unexpected burst of speed. He hurriedly walked past.

Hidden under the stairs, an arched doorway drew his attention, a soft glow of candlelight dancing over the alcove room's walls. There he found the girl standing in front of a tree. Alex sat in a beanbag chair with a book open on her lap, a candle on a shelf above her left shoulder, its wax base melted into the wood. She glanced up at him when he appeared, a faint smile of greeting there and then gone. He nodded to her and looked over at the tree with which the girl was so entranced.

Looking closer, he could see it was made of card and paper painted brown and stuck in long strips to imitate bark. The leaves themselves were cardboard dressed with green tissue paper.

Lacey reached out and laid her hand flat against the imitation bark, head tilted back to gaze up into the tree's canopy. In the branches, two colourful birds sat silent and watchful.

'Someone made all this,' the girl said in a whisper.

Pilgrim stepped closer and, unable to resist, holstered his gun and rested his own palm on the trunk. It was rough to the touch but not cold.

Like bark, Voice said.

'Yeah,' he murmured.

'Must've took hours and hours. Isn't that amazing?' Lacey looked over at him. Her eyes shone in the low, flickering light from the candle. 'That somebody took so long to create something like this, just so kids could look at it and play under it.' She turned back to the tree, her hand stroking the bark as if it could feel her caress.

Pilgrim glanced up into the branches and found a stuffed bird staring down at him, its black button eyes unblinking. A dead sentinel for long-dead children.

Listen, Voice whispered.

Faintly, Pilgrim heard voices. Real, outside voices.

Lacey must have noticed his head swing around, the sudden stillness in his stance. 'What is it?' she asked him.

'Something upstairs,' he said. 'Wait here.'

Alex was already on her feet, the book she had been reading hanging down by her side. There was a green snake on its cover. She asked a question with her eyes.

'Get ready to move,' he told her, and left them, turning his flashlight off, finding his way back to the stairs, the voices coming a little louder as he began to ascend.

At least three of them. Maybe more.

Pilgrim stopped halfway up, high enough for him to tune the voices into actual words, but the speakers were still out of sight.

'. . . we gonna do, Jeb?'

'We're gonna see what the hell these folk are doing here. Why they're transmitting shit on our CB channel and why the fuck they're driving around these parts.'

I told you trouble has a way of finding us, Voice whispered.

'But the signal we was followin' shut off. How'd we know if they're the same folks?'

'They have an antenna on the fucking roof of their car and a CB unit inside it. The hood's still hot. It's a safe fucking bet it's the same people, you moron. Now, we search this place till they turn up and hope to Christ they've seen her.'

A third voice joined in. 'Boss wants Red back. So we look till we find her.'

The first voice spoke again, sounding miserable. 'She won't let us find her. Not after what got done to her. She don't wanta be found.'

There was a meaty slap followed by a yelp.

'For chrissakes, stop moaning like a fucking bitch.'

The whiny one whined some more. 'You don't gotta hit me, Jeb. Jeez.'

'Then shut the fuck up and go check out the rooms through there. Bill, take the downstairs. Holler if you see anything.'

Pilgrim retreated, silently retracing his steps back to the alcove room. He motioned for Alex to blow out the candle, and then drew her and the girl close. The darkness was impenetrable for the moment, but he knew his eyes would quickly adjust.

'There are three of them,' he whispered, voice barely audible. 'One's heading down here. We keep quiet and we keep together. No shooting unless there's no choice.'

They were huddled so close together he could feel the tension vibrating off them, the burning heat of their anxiety. Already the girl's breathing was fast and shallow.

It's not going to work, Voice said.

He was right. The girl was practically hyperventilating. They would just get in the way, or make a noise and draw the man to them, but either way they'd all end up dead, and that wouldn't do.

'Never mind,' Pilgrim whispered quickly. 'Stay here. Keep the gun on the doorway. Shoot anyone who appears – don't worry about the noise.'

'But what about you?' Alex whispered.

Murder in the dark? Voice asked, a grim glee to his words.

'Murder in the dark,' Pilgrim replied.

CHAPTER 20

He shucked off his pack and left it beside the tree, then slipped out into the dark of the children's library. The bright beam of a flashlight bounced down the stairs as the man – Bill, he had been called – headed down to them.

Leaving his gun holstered, Pilgrim slid a knife out of the sheath at the small of his back. Keeping low, he ghosted behind the nearest shelving, ducking down and passing under the hanging papier-mâché spider just as the man stepped into view.

Bill's footsteps stopped while he surveyed the library, the flashlight's beam arcing over Pilgrim's head in a long sweep.

The guy whistled under his breath as he started down the aisle directly in front of the staircase, two aisles from where Pilgrim crouched. A pool of light marked his progress under the shelves. Pilgrim waited for a few seconds and then slid back under the spider, went two aisles over and glanced down the walkway. The man was a black silhouette with his back to him, his head swivelling left and right in slow panning motions, the flashlight coming up every couple of strides to direct the beam over the tops of the bookcases and punch holes in the gloom. He was armed with a shotgun, which was propped, barrels up, against his shoulder. Bill reached the end of the aisle and turned right.

You'll have to make a move soon. The yahoos upstairs will be finishing their search and heading down here next.

Pilgrim straightened up just enough to watch Bill from over the top of the shelves. The man was heading towards the kinder box section where wooden tubs littered the floor and cover was scant. Pilgrim ducked back down and hurried stealthily along the aisle. He could hear his own boots skimming across the carpet with a soft *whisk-whisk-whisk*.

Bill stopped whistling.

Pilgrim froze, heart thudding. There was a faint pool of light filtering under the bookcase by his feet, but that wasn't enough to pinpoint Bill's location.

He heard you.

'What the . . .' Bill's voice trailed off, and then he was moving again. Faster. His footsteps quick.

Pilgrim chanced lifting his head and saw the man marching back towards the stairs where he had started, heading for the alcove room.

Go!

Pilgrim stayed low and darted back the way he had come, his boots making louder whisking sounds as he ran, half bent over, the noise hopefully lost in Bill's own hurrying footfalls.

He must've seen them.

Pilgrim didn't care; he had to stop Bill before he stepped into that archway, or else Lacey would shoot, and the sound of the shot would bring the other two running. He came low and fast around the corner and almost fell as he tried to stop. Bill had halted at the end of his aisle and was poking at the hanging papier-mâché spider with the barrels of his shotgun, chuckling wheezily.

'Damn thing,' the man said, amused.

By sheer luck, Bill wasn't facing in Pilgrim's direction. But all it would take was for him to turn and it would be game over. He was also directly looking at the arched entrance to the alcove.

Retreat or advance?

Pilgrim advanced. He sacrificed speed for stealth this time, carefully placing one boot in front of the other, going as fast as he dared. His eyes never left Bill, even when the man knocked the spider on to the floor and stomped on it, the carapace crunching loudly, just like it would if it were a real spider. Bill kicked the flattened arachnid, and it sailed off into the dark, disappearing through the archway. From inside the room came a surprised cry, quickly muffled but not quickly enough.

'The fuck?' Bill said. He went after the spider, shotgun coming up. He was less than twenty-five feet away from the doorway, and closing.

Pilgrim stalked him like a shadow, coming up fast from behind, but he knew it wouldn't be fast enough to stop the man before he made the room's archway and Lacey pulled the trigger, so Pilgrim spoke before he was even within reaching distance, said, 'Hey, Bill,' in a low voice, saw him flinch and swing around, the gun barrels swinging with him, the two black nostrils getting ready to spit out fire and death. Pilgrim expected to hear the deafening *clap-bang* of the gun going off, the horrendous *CRACK* of the cartridge igniting that would undoubtedly alert Bill's pals, but Pilgrim was still stepping forward, still advancing, and he grabbed the barrels as they came around and yanked on them hard, hearing Bill grunt and the dry snap of his finger as the bone broke, trapped in the trigger guard.

Pilgrim pulled the shotgun away from Bill and brought up his other hand, the one still holding the knife, and punched it into Bill's gut, right under his ribs, punched it in deep and felt the hot gush of blood spill over his hand, scalding, almost painful. Bill dropped the flashlight, and it hit the carpet at their feet and spun, a disco light strobing and flashing before it bumped up against Pilgrim's boot and stopped, its beam pointing back through the archway, where Alex stood with tyre iron in hand, and Lacey beside her, the girl sighting at them down the barrel of her .22. But she wouldn't need to shoot anyone because Bill, his eyes wide and staring into Pilgrim's face, collapsed to his knees – a slow, lazy drop, as if he were proposing marriage and wanted to take his time over it, his rough hands holding on to

Pilgrim's hand, which still held the knife that was imbedded deep in his guts. He fell away, his hands sliding from around Pilgrim's, and curled on to his side, a soft releasing of breath leaving him in an endlessly long sigh. And then it stopped, and he lay still, and breathed no more.

Pilgrim wasn't still; he cleaned his blade off on the guy's shirt and put it away. He picked up the flashlight and headed for the girls. They parted to let him through, and he swept past them to collect his pack from beside the tree, telling them to gather their things. Ten seconds later, he was leading them back across the children's library, winding through the kinder boxes to the south-east corner, the flashlight picking out the emergency exit. Behind them, from upstairs, someone called down to Bill.

Of course, Bill didn't reply.

Pilgrim didn't pause or look back but depressed the lever of the door and pushed outside into the blinding sun.

They ran up a flight of concrete stairs and skirted the outside of the library to the front, where Pilgrim stopped to peer around the corner. Their car was parked where they had left it. Next to it was a Frankensteinian jeep bristling with antennas, the headlights and grille missing, the rear portion of its roof ripped off, leaving the back loading compartment open to the elements. Its passenger door stood wide, waiting for its occupants to mosey on outside and climb back in. There were no signs of Jeb or Whiny.

What about Sneezy and Dopey?

'You're really not helping,' Pilgrim muttered. He turned back to the girls, handing the shotgun to Alex as he talked. 'I'll get in the car first and open your doors – Lacey in front, Alex in back. All the bags go with Alex on the rear seat. Get in, but *don't* slam your doors. Once you're in, get down as low as you can, on the floor if you can manage it. And don't get up until I say so. Ready?' It didn't matter if they weren't, but he waited for a response. Lacey chewed on the inside of her cheek so hard Pilgrim felt sure she would chew right through her face, but she barely hesitated before giving a nod. Alex's bruises were stark against her ashen skin, but she nodded without any hesitation at all. She gave him the car keys.

Tough gals.

'Tough enough,' Pilgrim said. 'Let's go.'

Drawing his handgun, he jogged out into the open, his eyes not straying from the entrance to the library. Key ready in his hand, he inserted it into the driver's door, opened it and reached into the back to unlock the rear for Alex. She slipped in and was already reaching for their packs before Pilgrim had even finished taking his off. He slid into the driver's seat, hissing as his back hit the blisteringly hot upholstery, and leaned over to unlock the passenger door. Behind him, the rear door clicked quietly shut. Lacey hurried around the front of the car, and Pilgrim inserted the key into the ignition, getting ready to start the engine as soon as her backside hit the seat.

Lacey cried out as a huge black Rottweiler leapt at her from the rear bay of the jeep. She fell against the side of the car, the dog viciously pulled up short by a chain fastened to its collar, tethered to something in the bed of the vehicle. It barked savagely at the girl, deep, loud barks that smacked the ears. The animal strained to get to the girl, its muscles bunching under its sleek coat as it struggled to pull itself free, its muzzle snarled back to reveal sharp yellow teeth.

'Get in!' Pilgrim twisted the key, the engine cranking over but not firing up.

Lacey scrabbled at the door, fumbling the handle, and Alex reached over the seat to push it open, shouting her name.

The engine turned over and over, and Pilgrim feared he would snap the key he was twisting it so hard. The car roared to life just as the man who must be Jeb burst out of the library's front door, Whiny right on his heels. They were like two bearded scarecrows dressed in plaid and dirty denim, all arms and legs and heads too big for their bodies.

Pilgrim thrust the car into reverse.

Jeb's gun came up.

'*DOWN!*' Pilgrim roared.

The girls flattened themselves and two gunshots cracked in quick succession, holes punching through the windshield to Pilgrim's right, spiders' webs fracturing the glass. One bullet slammed into Lacey's headrest and the second zipped past to thud into the back seat. Pilgrim floored the pedal and the car peeled backwards, leaving two strips of rubber on the concrete. He spun the wheel hard and the car swung on a wide skid, tyres shrilling. He slammed it into drive and the car leapt forward from its haunches.

No more gunshots came.

He glanced over his shoulder and saw the men run for the jeep, slamming into it, the engine gunning.

Should've disabled their car, Voice said.

Pilgrim bit back his irritation. He'd thought about it but hadn't wanted to waste the time. He'd known it would only take a few short minutes for the men to discover their dead friend down in the children's library.

Lacey's crawled up from the footwell of the passenger seat and looked out the back window.

'Did you see that?' she asked breathlessly.

Pilgrim took the exit of the parking lot too fast, clipping the kerb opposite before straightening up and stamping on the accelerator. The speedo needle rose steadily.

He heard the squeal of wheels as the pickup came after them.

'It had "Defender" on the back of it,' said Lacey.

He chanced a glance at her.

'I saw it. I swear.'

He believed her. 'Think you can shoot at them?'

She looked back out of the window. The jeep was about a hundred yards behind and closing. 'I can try,' she said.

Good girl.

'Try,' Pilgrim told her.

She squirmed over the headrest of her seat, Alex grabbing hold of her and helping pull at the girl until she fell sprawling into the back.

'Hold on. Corner.' Pilgrim feathered the brakes, shaving off as little speed as possible, and took the corner at over thirty, everything in the car – their packs, the girls, any item not bolted down – sliding to the left. The suspension creaked, the car shuddered, and Pilgrim had to clamp on to the steering wheel so hard to keep on course his forearms hurt. Then they were clear and he saw, no more than a mile away, the ramp leading back on to the highway. He mashed the gas pedal to the floor.

Behind them, the jeep shot around the corner, skidding across the entire length of the road and almost colliding into a half-collapsed traffic light. It had already gained twenty yards on them.

They'll be on us before we hit the highway.

'Lacey?' he asked.

'*Lacey?*' Alex called to the girl.

'*Nearly there!*' Lacey yelled back, her voice far away.

He glanced in the rear-view mirror and saw her half hanging out of the rear side window, her and her rifle sticking out so that her head and shoulders were visible only through his side mirror. Alex was holding on to her around the waist while the girl sighted the jeep.

He touched the brakes again, slowing them and allowing the jeep to gain another precious few yards.

I hope you know what you're doing—

The rifle went off, the sharp crack shockingly loud in the confines of the car. A second shot went off as Pilgrim hit the on-ramp to the highway. He watched in the mirror in quick glances and saw she had scored two hits out of two: the windshield directly where the driver sat was fractured with bullet holes. The jeep swerved off the road, tyres kicking up clouds of dust, the rear end fishtailing wildly. Alex pulled the girl back inside the car and they both watched as the pickup skidded to a stop. The two girls laughed. Alex threw an arm around Lacey's shoulders and hugged her.

Pilgrim didn't laugh – the driver's door sprung open and Jeb jumped out, his gun up and pointing at them. A metallic pinging *thunked* all along the car's rear fender, and then the impossible happened. So many times Pilgrim had read how difficult it was to hit a moving wheel. To blow it out. But he felt the back end of the car jump up, felt the steering wheel shimmy between his palms as the car slithered out of control. He fought to keep it on the road. A terrible grating noise came from the rear wing, the rubber of the destroyed wheel having already stripped free from its rim.

A lead weight pulled at the steering wheel, dragging it to the left. He tried to wrench it back in line but overcompensated, and in the space of a single day he watched a second car flip, this time witnessing it from the inside. The world revolved unnaturally around him. The car slammed on to its side. The engine screamed as the power train continued to drive the back wheels but failed to gain traction. Metal screeched and buckled, glass exploded as windows shattered. Cries came from the back seat. The car tilted again and rolled on to its roof. Pilgrim's head connected first with a strut, then with the ceiling, and everything blinked out, the TV in his mind shutting off, and the next thing he knew he was outside, lying on his back, the boiling sun beating into his eyes.

A kick to his ribs had him coming fully awake. He instinctively tucked up into a ball and wrapped his arms around the lancing pain.

That's cracked at least two, Voice said.

Pilgrim would have told him to shut up if he'd had the breath.

'Fucker killed Bill,' a familiar voice said from above him, followed by another kick, this one connecting with his kidneys.

'Leave him alone!'

Pilgrim spat out blood and dust and looked up to see the second auburn-headed guy, Whiny, cuff Lacey around the back of the head to quieten her down.

Pilgrim went to get up, but a boot stomped down between his shoulders and mashed him back to the ground.

'Stay the fuck down,' Jeb told him.

He didn't. He shoved at the earth, levering himself up again. Jeb's boot caught him in the face. It took two more kicks before Pilgrim dropped.

'Bastard doesn't know when to quit.'

'*NO!*' Lacey cried. '*Stop it!*'

Pilgrim lay on his stomach, his head throbbing sickly, his lower back alive with dancing pain. Hooked barbs jabbed into his side. He slid his hand down over his hip, patting for his gun in its holster. It was gone.

We've been in some tight spots before, compadre, but I don't know how you're getting us out of this one.

'"Stop it"?' Jeb asked the girl. 'Stop what? Me hurting this piece of shit right here?' He kicked Pilgrim in the leg, the toe of his boot jabbing deep into the muscle of his thigh.

'*Yes!* Stop it! Please!' She struggled to pull free, but Whiny had a wiry look about him, and no amount of squirming could break his grip.

Jeb cupped a hand around his ear in a parody of deafness. 'Sorry, can't hear you.' He booted Pilgrim in the ribs again.

Groaning, Pilgrim curled on to his side, using the movement as cover as he went for the hidden sheath at the small of his back. Fifteen feet away, Alex lay similarly on her side, near to the crashed car. It had landed on all four wheels again, although

Pilgrim didn't recall when that had happened. Alex's eyes were open and she was looking at him. She gave a minute shake of her head, but Pilgrim wasn't sure what she was trying to say – don't make a move on them? Don't make a move on them *yet*? Was she telling him to give up, and to just let it go?

His shaking fingers found the handle of the knife.

And what're you going to do with that? These boys have guns.

'Shuddup,' he managed, the words a broken mumble, his mouth not working. He turned his attention to Jeb and squinted at his boots, his vision blurring for a moment, fastening his eyes on the frayed, grimy cuffs of the guy's jeans.

'What's that now?' Jeb said. 'You telling *me* to shut up?' His mouth was puckered in what Pilgrim assumed was an expression of intense dislike, the bristles of his beard twisted up on one side. It made him look retarded. 'How about you shut *your* fucking pie-hole, dipshit.' And he reached down and gripped the collar of Pilgrim's shirt, yanking him up on to his knees.

Pilgrim bit back a cry as all his pains flared white-hot. Sweat broke out on his brow. But Jeb was close enough now and Pilgrim pulled out his knife and stabbed it into the guy's stomach. He'd wanted to get him dead centre, like he had with Bill, but Pilgrim's head was swimming and he'd misjudged, getting him more in the side, under the guy's ribs. It was good enough, though, because Jeb shrieked like a woman and released Pilgrim's collar. Pilgrim wrenched the blade out, went to punch it back in, but everything was moving too slowly, the world winding down to a crawl, his hand and Jeb's arm moving through an invisible gelatinous liquid. Pilgrim's vision cleared as he watched the revolver come slowly, slowly, up, almost to point-blank range by the time it was aimed at his head. Jeb's dirty-nailed finger tightened around the trigger. Pilgrim knew the gun was a Smith & Wesson Chief's Special, which held .38 calibre cartridges, and that .38 cartridges travelled upwards of six hundred feet per second. Once the bullet left the three-inch barrel, it would hit him approximately .0035 seconds later. Faster than he could blink. He knew all this the same way he knew he was about to die.

It's empty. He emptied the gun into the side of our car.

But Pilgrim knew it wasn't. He'd counted two shots fired at the library, and a further three had slammed into the fender of their car, one of which blew out the tyre. That left one. And one was all it would take.

No, it's empty, Voice said again, but he sounded uncertain.

Time sped back up, the gun kicking in Jeb's hands, the shot blasting out a wash of desert heat, a flame licking out of the muzzle, beautiful in its fiery red. It was the last beautiful thing Pilgrim would see before the bullet slammed into his head and Voice fled into the darkness.

PART TWO

The Girl Who
Heard Voices

CHAPTER 1

Lacey screamed. She couldn't hear the scream, but she knew she must be screaming because her mouth was open and she could feel the vibrations of the sound rip up through her chest. Her throat hurt.

It's not real, she thought. No no no, not real.

Oh, it's real all right.

The way his head had snapped to the side, the gun too close, firing right into it. The way he'd dropped to the ground, heavy and limp.

NO.

And the horrible bearded man stepped over him and tried to fire more bullets into his back, even though he was down and not moving.

Not moving!

But the gun made a dry clicking noise again and again and again.

'Leave him alone!' she screamed, and this time she could hear herself. She wrenched away from the smelly ginger-haired man holding on to her – he stank of tuna fish, stale sweat and unwashed hair, and Lacey had thought she would puke all over him when he'd first grabbed her – and ran at the one who'd shot her friend, shoving him away hard enough to make him stumble and drop on to his butt.

'Fuckin' *bitch*,' he spat.

She didn't want to look down, didn't want to see what had been done to him, what the bullet had shred into and destroyed, but she couldn't help herself, she had to look, just in case—

In case what? a small voice asked.

—in case! In case! But all she could manage was a quick glance because, *God*, there was so much blood, and she suddenly felt hot and woozy, like she had that one time she'd taken a scalding-hot bath while she'd been on her monthlies, and when she'd stepped out of the water the world had gone all psychedelic and trippy, and she'd woken up naked and slumped against the bathroom wall with her grammy bent over her, fanning her with an old copy of *Better Homes and Gardens*.

She didn't want to pass out again so she looked away from the Boy Scout fast, and clapped a hand over her mouth to stop the strange moaning sound coming out of her.

'Jeb!' The smelly man rushed over to the one she'd pushed on to his butt.

'He stabbed me, Pose.' The bearded man said it in a musing kind of way, as if he couldn't quite believe what had happened. He held up his bloody hands to show his friend. 'I'm bleeding all over the fucking place.'

Lacey heard her name and turned to find Alex trying to get up, one hand on the wrecked car for balance. She hurried over and tucked herself under the woman's arm, helping her to her feet. Alex shuddered in long, shivering waves. Lacey noticed blood over the side of her neck and more staining the shoulder of her shirt.

'I'm OK,' Alex said, her arm tightening around Lacey's shoulders. 'I'm not hurt.'

'Alex. Alex, they shot him.' Her breath stuck in her throat and she pressed her face into the woman's hot neck, drawing in deep breaths.

Alex held her tight, her shivers diminishing, little by little. It made Lacey aware of her own trembling.

'For fuck's sake, Posy, stop gawping at him and give me a fucking hand.'

Lacey lifted her head out of Alex's shoulder. The smelly man – Posy? – stood gazing down at the Boy Scout where he lay crumpled in a broken heap. But at Jeb's words Posy scrambled to help his friend up, the wounded man cursing and gasping. She felt a surge of satisfaction at seeing the sopping, bloody mess of his shirt. The Boy Scout had got him good.

'What the fuck you staring at?'

She started and met the man's eyes. They were dark and mean and filled with pain – but seeing him suffer gave her a fierce kind of pleasure. The words came before she realised she'd even opened her mouth. 'I'm staring at you bleeding to death,' she said.

His face went purple and he lifted his gun and aimed it at her. It shook as if his hand were palsied. 'I'll fucking shoot you, too, you cock-sucking little cunt.'

His gun's definitely empty, that small voice said.

'Your gun's empty,' she told him calmly. *Too* calmly. It weirded her out.

Alex murmured her name, and the arm around Lacey's shoulders tightened.

'Oh yeah?' Jeb's voice shook. 'Is that fucking right?' He fumbled at the gun, opening its cylinder, and emptied the shell casings on to the ground. From his back pocket he brought out a handful of fresh ammo and started shakily loading the brass cartridges into the chambers. He slammed the cylinder closed and cocked the hammer. 'It's not fucking empty now, is it, you smart-mouthed bitch?'

'Jeb . . .' Posy said timidly.

Jeb turned on him. '*What?*'

'Boss wouldn't want us to kill no gals.'

'I fucking *know* that. What, you think I'm an idiot?'

'No, Jeb . . .' he said slowly.

'Then shut the hell up and get that dead piece of shit in the back of the jeep already.'

'But he's tall, Jeb. Don't think I can pick him up by my—'

'Then get them to help you!' Jeb waved his cocked gun at Lacey and Alex again. '*Fuck*. Do I have to think of *everything*?'

Posy nodded like an obedient dog, handed his shotgun to the wounded man and bent down and attempted to lift the Boy Scout under the arms. He didn't get very far.

'*You*.' Jeb thrust his gun at Alex. 'Get over there and help. Come on, *come on*, move it!'

Alex let Lacey go, her hand giving her shoulder a last squeeze, and joined Posy, leaning down to take hold of the Boy Scout's dusty boots. Even between the two of them they got maybe three yards before the dead man slipped from their grip and ended up in the dirt again. Lacey gritted her teeth. She couldn't look at him; to look at him would crack the fragile shell she had hastily erected around herself. One glimpse of him lying face down and she would fold inward, crumpling around the pain in her middle. She felt like she'd been booted in the stomach, right in the tender spot under her breastbone, her insides bruised from pelvis to heart.

Jeb watched her, and she in turn watched him, her gaze flicking down every now and then to where he was pressing his arm over his wound. He looked pale. The blood staining his top was dark and wet.

She breathed through her nose in hard little pants. That's it, she thought. Keep on bleeding, you bastard. Bleed it all out.

The third time they dropped the Boy Scout, Jeb exploded. 'Fuck's sake! Just leave him! I don't have time for this shit! Get their stuff and get 'em in the jeep.'

Posy trailed back and forth, transferring their packs into the back of the jeep. The big black dog back there trailed back and forth along with him, its chain chinking and its snout digging into the packs, snuffling around in them. Posy came to Jeb for his shotgun and kept it aimed at Alex and Lacey as Jeb limped around to the driver's side and painfully climbed into the back seat. In the open V of the passenger rear door, Lacey looked in at him. His lank hair hung over his forehead in greasy strands, obscuring his eyes; his unkempt beard hid the rest of his face. What little skin she could see was pasty and damp. She didn't want to get in there with him; it was like being cornered with a dying animal. A dying, *armed* animal.

'Get in,' he ordered, his gun on her.

Lacey climbed into the jeep, sliding her butt over to give Alex room. The door slammed shut after Alex, and Posy went around the front to the driver's door. Lacey pressed as close to Alex as she could, away from Jeb and the unhealthy heat emanating from him, but once Posy was behind the wheel Jeb leaned nearer, pressing his unwashed body up against her, and jabbed the barrel of his gun into her side. He dug it into the soft flesh under her ribs and she cried out and tried to bend away from him, but she had nowhere to go.

'Try 'n' pull anything and I'll gut-shoot you where you sit,' he said coldly. 'In these close quarters, the bullet'll pass right through you and into your lady friend there. Two birdies with one shot.'

Posy let out a shrill guffaw of laughter.

'*Drive*, Pose. I need the Doc.'

Exactly *like the Seven Dwarfs*.

Evil ones, she thought.

Posy pulled back on to the highway's slip road, steering carefully around the overturned car as if the act of driving were a complicated task for him, and the jeep steadily gained speed as they came up to joining I20. The shot-out windshield and missing rear part of the roof were a godsend: within seconds the wind rushed noisily through the cabin, dispersing much of the stink and heat that had built up.

Lacey twisted round, biting back another cry when Jeb dug the barrel into her side again, but she didn't care. After not wanting to look, now she *had* to.

You shouldn't look back. Looking back does no good.

She looked anyway, until the dusty pile of clothes that was the Boy Scout was out of sight and there was nothing but empty road stretching out behind them.

CHAPTER 2

'How come you were on our channel?'

The bleeding man's dark, bleary eyes bored into Lacey's as if his glare could drill the answer straight out of her. Maybe it could in normal circumstances, but she had no clue what he was talking about.

'On the fucking *CB radio*,' he growled. 'What were you doing transmitting on our channel?'

Alex's arm, already wrapped around Lacey, pulled her in closer. 'We were going through all the channels,' Alex answered. 'Curious to see if anyone would answer, that's all.'

'Where'd you get the unit from?' There was a tight suspicion in Jeb's pain-filled eyes.

Don't tell him anything.

But again Alex answered before Lacey could open her mouth. 'We picked it up a couple weeks back.'

Lacey didn't know why Alex had lied but was glad she had.

She's not stupid. Look at him, he's a murderer.

Jeb grunted, hazily glaring for a moment longer before slumping back with a sharp, hissing sigh.

'Where are you taking us?' Alex asked.

'To see the Boss,' Posy said from up front. Closed up in the cab with him, Lacey could see the adolescent pockmarks in Posy's cheeks, his wispy, gingerish beard growing in patches and not doing much to hide them.

'Shut up,' Jeb told him, but the words lacked force. He sounded drugged, sleepy. His head drooped a little where he sat,

171

and the gun didn't jab quite so painfully into Lacey's side any more.

She glanced into his lap and saw that his blood had seeped down into the denim; a dark, spreading stain across his crotch.

He spotted her looking. 'Keep your fucking eyes off me.'

She went back to looking out through the windshield. A single tear fell from her eye, on the side Jeb couldn't see. She silently wiped it away.

'Who's the Boss?' Alex asked. She had leaned forward a little so she could direct her questions at Posy.

'He's the daddy to our family. The father to our flock. The—'

'One more word passes your lips,' Jeb told him, 'and I'll tell the Boss it was you who wasn't watching Red properly when she got out.'

Posy shut his mouth.

'Who's Red?' Alex asked the bleeding man.

'Some other troublesome bitch. Who knew the world was so fucking full of you?' He laughed. It wasn't an amused sound.

A sign went past. 'Williamstown – 4 Miles'.

'You'll have *all* the answers you want soon enough – and wish you didn't, I bet.' Jeb wheezed another laugh. His head drooped lower, his chin touching his chest.

Lacey shifted slightly, leaning away from Jeb and rocking into Alex. She felt the woman look at her but didn't turn to meet her gaze; she was too busy glancing down at the gun nudged up against her side.

I wouldn't go for it, that voice warned. *At least not yet.*

Over the last few minutes Lacey hadn't paid too much attention to the internalisation of her thoughts. Mainly because everything had happened so fast, and also because she suspected she was in shock. She had been too distracted to concentrate properly on anything. Now she had the time to listen more closely she was beginning to realise these weren't normal thoughts. Not normal at all. For starters, it wasn't *her* voice she was hearing.

Who says it's not your voice?

She went cold. She squeezed her eyes shut. No no no, please don't let this be happening to me. I can't cope with this happening to me now. Please.

It's happening. But it's OK. You don't need to be scared.

She opened her eyes and looked at Alex.

The woman raised her eyebrows at her.

I think it's happening, Alex, she thought at her. I'm hearing them. Help me.

Alex didn't answer, of course. She wasn't psychic.

You're not crazy, the voice said. *At least, no more than you already were.*

'*No*,' she moaned, despair knotting inside her.

Jeb's head came up a notch when she spoke, but it bobbed back to his chest again within a few seconds. The gun shifted a little more, no longer digging into her side but pointing towards the dash.

I know you're scared, but you don't have to be. I'm not going to hurt you, I promise. Now, it's easier to keep your thoughts separate if you speak them aloud, but it's less suspicious if we can talk in here. And it'd be much *safer to avoid suspicion.*

She glanced around at the others again, her heart thrumming in her throat, but no one seemed to be aware that she had a voice talking at her that no one else could hear. Posy was focused entirely on his driving; Jeb was mumbling something under his breath, his eyes closed, and twitching every now and then like a dog does when it dreams of running and killing rabbits; one of Alex's arms remained wrapped around Lacey's shoulders, the warmth and weight of it a comfort, while the long, slim fingers of her other hand nervously picked at a loose thread on her jeans. She stared out of the side window, her thoughts a million miles away.

Lacey shook her head. She wasn't going to engage with this thing in her head. That way lay madness. Frequently, at the end, she had caught her grammy talking to herself, mumbling to people who weren't there, flapping a hand next to her head as if trying to bat away an annoying insect. Lacey had always believed it was a genetic thing and, though she was only sixteen years old, she might have even considered that dementia was getting an early start on her, its fingertips grazing, searching out a better grip for later on. But not any more. It was a *voice*, exactly like Alex had described. It was the same thing that had caused everyone to lose their minds and kill themselves.

You're not losing your mind. Trust me.

Lacey closed her eyes, didn't like the darkness behind her lids and quickly opened them again. What if it made her do something crazy?

Panic raced up her spine at the thought. She didn't want to hurt anyone!

Calm down. You have all the control in this. I can't make you do anything you don't want to.

So far it was only talking. She didn't feel any anger or evil intent from it. But that didn't mean she should trust what it said.

Just try and clear your mind. Please. If only for a moment. We need to talk.

If she spoke to it she could ask where it had come from, what it wanted from her. Her grammy always said that ignorance often led to fear. You had to understand something before you could gauge whether it was worth being afraid of or not. And if she didn't like what it said, well, she could deal with that when it happened, right? One step at a time.

Just concentrate on thinking about nothing. It'll help.

Taking a deep breath, she stared at the pebbled plastic of the dash and, before she knew it, it began to blur. She panicked and lost concentration. Her mouth was so dry it was practically impossible to work up any moisture. She swallowed painfully.

You're doing really well. Keep breathing. Think of your mind as a blank slate, a black chalkboard waiting for words to appear on it.

She wished it would stop talking. A creeping fog seeped in from all sides, the brightness of the outside world dimming at the edges, like it did when she was on the verge of being asleep. Sounds and smells grew faint. The same fog slipped into her ears and nostrils.

Good. Very good, it said in a soothing voice.

She directed her thought deeply inwards, imagining her head as a bottomless, black well, the words jagged and jittering and boldly white with her fear, floating down into the dark.

– What do you want? Who are you?

She waited, but there was no answer, and again she considered the possibility that her mind was already lost.

I'm just a voice. I'm not here to harm you.

She jolted when the car bounced over a rock, and her concentration fled, the noise of the world rushing back in – the blowing wind, the racing engine, the jangle of the heavy chain in the rear as the dog moved around – all of it assaulting her senses.

She clamped her eyes closed and tried to shut it out. It took her a full minute to quieten her thoughts.

– But where did you come from?

The reply came quicker this time. *Where does life come from? It just comes into being. Not here, and then suddenly there. Poof, like magic.*

– What? You're telling me you're magic?

If I can't be explained by science, then I must be magic, right? But we're getting off topic.

That wasn't an explanation, and she was beginning to think she was being talked down to, like she was some stupid kid. She bit down on her anger.

– So *why* are you here?

It seems I need to be somewhere. *There wasn't much time to deliberate all the pros and cons. I had limited choices.*

– But what *are* you? What do you *want*?

Want? I don't want anything. I'm as surprised by all this as you are. I've never heard of anything like this happening before. You shouldn't tell these people about any of this, Lacey. It'd put you in danger. You must listen to me.

It knew her name! Fear and frustration pounded thickly through her temples. In fact, a whole mess of emotions was building up inside her, a ball of pressure in her chest that was rising up to her throat.

Are you going to cry? The voice sounded appalled at the possibility. Then Lacey had to wonder how a disembodied voice could project the feeling of being appalled through to her, but she was feeling it, all right, and it was another emotion on top of all the other emotions already engulfing her. There was too much going on in her head and, honestly, having just her own thoughts in there was more than enough, but now she had hers and this *other's* and her feelings were shooting off all over the place like an out-of-control garden sprinkler.

'I'm not gonna cry, you asshole,' she said, but angry tears were already flooding her eyes.

'What?' Jeb's head came up. His eyes were bloodshot and glassy when he looked at her.

Shhhhh, the voice reprimanded

'*Fuck you*,' she hissed.

Jeb's eyes cleared and his brow came down. 'The fuck you say?' He straightened up, wincing at the movement, and re-adjusted his grip on the gun. 'Better watch your mouth, girl.'

What a hypocrite!

Lacey could feel the disgust lacing those three words, coating her mind in a slimy muck. She couldn't tell where that disgust ended and her own feelings began. It all jumbled together and she was talking again before contemplating how wise it was to share her thoughts out loud. 'You're telling *me* to watch *my* mouth?' she said, her face feeling hot and swollen. 'You haven't stopped cussing since you first spoke to us.'

Jeb appeared lost for words for a moment. Then he was moving, the gun whipping up too fast for Lacey to react. It lashed the side of her head, a glancing blow that cut sharply through her mixed-up thoughts, slashing them down to just one: PAIN. She clamped a hand over her brow, felt the hot dribble of blood already running from the gash the gun had opened up.

Alex turned, her arm protectively hooking Lacey in closer while her other hand came up, palm held out to Jeb. She told him to put the gun down, to back off, they'd be quiet, they'd behave, there was no need to hit anyone, please. Lacey didn't see anything else; she sat with her head down and her face held in her hands. Alex gathered her in, murmured soft words into her ear, but every muscle in the woman's body was quivering and Lacey could feel the hard gallop of her heart in her breast.

The rest of the journey was made in silence.

Even the voice kept its peace.

Jeb impatiently gave Posy directions – he couldn't seem to remember where they were going. They had hit Williamstown a few minutes earlier, and Posy took a random number of lefts and rights, winding them deeper into the crumbling, grey buildings, diverting on to different streets when they met barricades made up of shells of burnt-out cars and weary-looking police roadblocks. The rubble of downed apartment buildings blocked sidewalks, spreading out into the middle of the street like spilled cookie crumbs.

A couple of times Lacey thought she spied a flash of movement up in the second or third levels of buildings, but when she looked again there was no one. She figured it must simply be another thing her mind was making up. May as well get used to being crazy. She was sure it was a slippery slope from here on in.

Although Lacey wasn't familiar with being in cities, she

remembered what the Boy Scout had told her. They were dangerous, he'd said. They were full of merciless scavengers and people who didn't have a civilised thought left in their heads. In other words, stay the hell out. Alex must have heard similar warnings, because as they moved nearer and nearer to the main streets tension gradually stiffened through her until Lacey felt like she was being held by a contraption of steel cables.

Lacey kept her gaze off the sidewalks nearest the taller buildings. It was as if flooding measures had been called into effect, sandbags piled high in barricading moats around the ground floors. Except they weren't sandbags. Even knowing she shouldn't look, she couldn't keep her eyes from the piles of mummified bodies heaped at the buildings' bases. Jumpers had rained out of the skies back then, and not a single Supergirl or Iron Man among them. They must have hit the ground with such grisly thuds. A digger, its yellow paint faded to curdled buttermilk, sat frozen with its bucket halfway raised, human limbs hanging like noodles between the tines of its fork. Nearby, a dump truck was already filled to the brim with dried-up, shrivelled corpses. Attempts had been made to remove the bodies, but time wasn't on anyone's side. Had the men who drove these vehicles chosen to join the dead after they began work to clear them up? Had the voices been whispering to them the whole time, chipping away at their defences until they broke and succumbed? Is that what would happen to her?

Lacey shivered and dropped her gaze to the footwell, exactly like she had all those years ago in her grammy's station wagon. She searched out Alex's hand and gripped on to it, anchoring herself to the woman, hoping she would keep her grounded and sane. Alex instantly curled her fingers around Lacey's hand in return.

Their vehicle turned on to a narrow backstreet, tall tenements on either side blotting out the hazy afternoon sun. It was a dead-end. Lacey shifted in Alex's hold, sitting up a little straighter, looking around and wondering where they were being taken. The jeep had almost reached the end when Posy picked up the CB mic.

'Defender-One, Defender-One on the ten-four. Roger 'n' out.'

After a few seconds of crackling, an irritated voice came back to them. 'Posy? Who the hell let you on the radio again?'

'Copy that, tin dog. We're a go for dockin'.'

A sea of confused static, followed by: 'You mean you want us to open the door?'

'Roger, Roger.'

A shout went up and a large corrugated-metal door began rolling upwards in jerks. A gap appeared at the bottom. Posy steered the jeep towards the opening, waiting until the rolling door had reached the roof before driving through. As soon as they cleared the door, the mechanism reversed direction and the door clattered shut behind them with a clanking finality that made Lacey's teeth clench.

The man who had opened the rolling door ambled over to them. He looked like a copy of Jeb and Posy: too thin, eyes hollow sinkholes in his bearded face. This guy was older, though, with long streaks of grey running through his bristles and at his temples.

'What's up, fellas?' he drawled, pulling Jeb's door open and looking in at them.

Lacey could hardly tell what he'd said; the words were so mushed up in his mouth it was like he was trying to chew on them rather than speak them.

'Need me the Doc, Lou,' Jeb moaned, agitatedly shifting in his seat.

Lou glanced down at the blood saturating the front of Jeb's shirt and stepped out of the way as Posy opened his door and slid out from behind the wheel. Posy went to the rear of the jeep, a few clanks coming from behind as he untethered the dog.

Lou nodded and drawled, 'I'd say you were right about that,

brother.' He made it sound like *brudda*. 'Hold up. I'll go and fetch him.' He slanted her and Alex a curiously dead-eyed look, then turned and ambled away again, mounting five concrete steps up to the loading dock and disappearing through a set of swinging doors. Lacey figured they were in a loading area at the rear of a mall; the space was big enough to accommodate three large trucks while they delivered their goods on to trolleys and forklifts that would run up and down the main concrete docking platform. Three lots of swinging doors led off from the platform, only the middle set having been used so far.

A few more people had appeared, shuffling closer as Jeb ushered Lacey and Alex out of the back seat. Lacey put her back to the jeep's side panel as a woman broke off from the new group and approached. It was hard to tell her age, but her skin was lined and webbed with wrinkles. She wore a ratty purple shawl over her bony shoulders, held in place by her equally bony fingers. The knuckles were knotted and sore-looking, arthritis freezing them into hooked claws.

Jeb still loosely held his gun, and he used it to dismissively wave the woman away. 'Don't you fucking touch them, you old bitch.'

The woman's voice was as aged and crooked as her joints. 'Ah, don't be a sourpuss. We just want us a little feel.' She shuffled a couple more feet and lifted one thin arm. The loose, papery skin hung like a dead turkey wattle below the hag's upper arm, and it wobbled as she drew closer to Lacey.

Lacey leaned away from her, revulsion twisting her mouth. If the hag touched her she was afraid she'd scream: it felt locked up just behind her tonsils, a buzzing panic so close to the surface her pores shivered with it.

'Touch me and I'll break your arm,' she whispered.

The hag's eyes narrowed into glittering slits. In a split second she transformed from a frail old woman, albeit a scary one, into a menacing, evil-spitting witch.

Oh shit, I've done it now, Lacey thought dimly, all her bravado evaporating as swiftly as it had come. She's gonna put a hex on me and I'll drop dead.

The middle set of swinging doors, through which Lou had disappeared, swung back outwards, and a smooth-shaven man came through. He appeared cleaner than the others, his clothes neater, and he wore an unusual rounded hat pushed to the back of his head, the kind Lacey had seen in old black-and-white photographs and her grams had told her were called bowlers. He carried a small brown leather doctor's bag. His pale green eyes skimmed over her and Alex and came to rest on Jeb. His lips thinned in disapproval.

'What happened?' he asked. He spoke quietly, but the room had become hushed when he'd entered, all talk seeming to die down in preparation for his words.

'Some fucker stabbed me, Doc,' Jeb told him.

As Doc stepped past her to inspect Jeb's injuries, Lacey caught the scent of menthol, cool and fresh. Grammy's clothes had always held a hint of peppermint (from where, Lacey didn't know), and the man's aroma spiked her nostrils and sent such a rush of homesickness through her she *hurt* with it. She would give anything to be back home, sat in her grammy's armchair, one of their photo albums open in her lap and that fusty odour of dust and old things enclosing her like a familiar, well-worn blanket. She didn't care that she would be all alone in that big, rambling farmhouse, didn't care that the creaks and howling wind at night would keep her awake in her cold bed, didn't even care that there would be a pit of gnawing hunger in her stomach that forced her to lie curled in a ball, holding on to it to make it stop hurting. She would rather that than be here with these people.

But you'd have never met the Boy Scout, she told herself. Never have met Alex.

Yeah, and look how that turned out: the Boy Scout shot in

the head and Alex stuck here with me, as far away from my sister and niece as I've ever been, and waiting for God knows what other nastiness to happen, nastiness that I don't even want to think about. Never anything good, though. Never good.

Right in that instant, Lacey *hated* the world. Wished with all her heart it were gone. And failing that, wished that she herself were gone from it.

No, the voice said sternly. *Don't think that. Not ever.*

A low, guttural growl made her stiffen. She found the dog staring up at her, its head fat and ugly, its sharp teeth bared. Posy gave its chain a harsh yank, and the mutt licked its chops and quietened down.

Jeb hissed in pain. The Doc had pulled up his shirt and was bent over him, his long, slim-fingered hands moving deftly.

'Pose, take them up to the Boss,' a sweating Jeb said between gasps. 'Tell him what happened to Bill. And that we couldn't find Red but we brought these two to make up for it.'

Posy nodded fast. 'Sure, Jeb, sure.'

Lacey took a last, long look at Jeb, the man glaring back at her, his brown, chipped teeth gritted behind his beard. She wanted to ingrain him in her memory, how his eyes were sunken into his face, the skin bruised in half-moon crescents beneath them, make sure she remembered how he looked right this second – like a dead man walking – because she was sure the Boy Scout had killed him. Jeb just didn't know it yet.

CHAPTER 3

Posy led them through whitewashed corridors, Lou bringing up the rear.

He's checking out your ass.

When Lacey turned, sure enough, Lou was staring at her butt. He didn't even pretend to be embarrassed or guilty that she'd caught him at it, either. All he did was stare at her with his wet, dead-fish eyes. After a moment she dropped her gaze and turned away, calling him a 'Pervert' under her breath, not quite brave enough to say it loud enough for him to hear.

Posy whistled as he walked, checking back on them every so often, smiling cheerfully through his patchy beard as if they were all off on a picnic together. The chain that linked Posy to his dog jangled and tinkled like sleigh bells. The dog's claws clicked on the shiny floor as it trotted just ahead of him.

Lacey had reached for Alex's hand again as soon as they'd left the loading area. The woman's cold fingers had closed over hers, holding on tightly. Now Alex drew her closer and ducked her head, pitching her voice low so only Lacey could hear.

'Leave the talking to me.'

Lacey nodded. She had no real desire to talk to these people, especially not to anyone who was in charge of them. She'd rather fade into the background and pretend like she wasn't here.

Good luck with that.

She had been ignoring the voice for a while now, hoping it might go away. You didn't talk to your crazy, not if you didn't want it talking back. And, like Grammy used to say, 'Ignore something for long enough and it'll slink away like a skunk in the night.'

I'm not a skunk.

'You're worse than one,' she muttered.

Hah! Made you talk!

She clamped her lips together, dismayed that it had managed to manipulate her into speaking.

Takes a lot of practice to shut me out. It sounded almost smug. *Pilgrim was a master at it, and even he struggled.*

The voice lapsed into a heavy, brooding silence, all smoky, grey clouds that swirled morosely in and around her thoughts. She wanted to ask who or what a pilgrim was, but she wouldn't break her silence, not even if it killed her.

They came to a concrete stairwell and went up four flights. There, Lou stayed by the heavy fire-door, and Posy carried on down the corridor, gesturing for them to follow. He'd become chattier the closer they came to their destination. It was a nervous chatter, which in turn made Lacey nervous. Her palm began to sweat in Alex's grip.

'Oh man, Boss is gonna be happy with you two. Yessir. He likes him some fresh meat. 'Specially when it's pretty.'

He'd turned around to talk to them, walking backwards and not looking where he was going. He trod on the Rottweiler's paw and the dog gave a high-pitched yelp, and Posy stumbled and cursed, dancing around it. He dropped the chain. Sensing its freedom, the dog darted off, pounding away up the corridor, its jangling chain snaking behind it.

'*Shit!*' Posy ran after the dog. 'Princess, come back!'

Princess? *You gotta be kidding me.*

Lacey was thinking the same thing but stubbornly cut the thought off before the new presence in her head registered it.

'*Posy.*'

It was like Posy ran into a wall. The dog continued its escape, unpursued, the chain clanking and scraping along the floor as it disappeared around the corner. Posy stood stock still, his shoulders hunched up around his ears.

The call came again. '*Posy.* Come here. I want to talk to you.' The drawl was slow, with a timbre deep enough to cause vibrations.

Posy turned, uncertainty and fear at war on his face. You could see the tensed hesitancy in his posture, as if he wanted to turn tail and run in the same direction as his dog, but then he came unstuck and retraced his steps, stopping outside an open doorway.

'Hi, Boss!' Posy said, too brightly.

'You found her?'

Posy's fingers clutched bone-white on to the door jamb.

'Hmm, not exactly,' he admitted.

There was a long pause. Lacey exchanged a look with Alex and could see deep concern in the older woman's eyes. Lacey felt it, too, a threat hanging unspoken in the air, a brewing storm readying itself to erupt.

'But . . . but we found somethin' else,' Posy offered tentatively.

'Is that so? Show me.'

'Yes. Yessir, right away.' Posy looked back at them, his eyes big and desperate. He waved at them to come closer. 'C'mere, yes yes, come come. I'll show you, Boss. You'll like it, I *swear.*'

Lacey didn't move, her feet suddenly glued to the linoleum flooring, but Alex was already starting forward, tugging on her hand to follow. Lacey gave a last look behind her, back to the end of the corridor, where Lou stood watching them, unmoving, like a reptilian guard dog, and Lacey decided right then and there she would rather have Princess barking and growling at her than this man's dead-eyed stare.

What I'd *really* prefer, she thought, is to have my rifle.

Gonna shoot your way out like Butch Cassidy?

She didn't know who that was – all she meant was she'd feel

much better with a gun. Or with the Boy Scout. But thinking of him made something come unstuck inside her and a warm, traitorous pressure rise up her throat and lodge behind her eyes, so she quickly adjusted her thoughts.

Posy stood back and ushered them into the room, waving his arm in a waterwheel motion, eager to get them inside. The hot, muggy air hit her as soon as she stepped through the doorway. They were four storeys up, yet all the windows remained closed, each one a full sheet of glass that extended floor to ceiling and offered an expansive view of the city below. It was a ruined city, crumbling from the top down like one of Karey's awful apple pies, bits dropping off at the edges. It was still beautiful, though, especially when lit in the drowsy afternoon sun, shadows stretching lazily across streets to slink up walls and doorways. From a distance, the graffitied paintwork and murals looked like prehistoric cave paintings.

The same soft light decorated the room's walls in melted butter. The rest of the room was uninteresting: a cracked leather armchair in front of a low coffee table, both empty. The view filled up the rest of the space.

The man who Posy had referred to as the Boss stood in one corner, arms folded, leaning casually up against a window. He didn't turn to look at them when they entered but continued to gaze out over the city.

A king surveying his kingdom, the voice said.

Lacey didn't think he looked like any king she'd ever seen, although she admitted to not having seen many. This man looked like one of the rednecks she'd seen in a movie one time. She shouldn't have watched it, she knew it even as the first ten minutes played out, but she had begged and begged Karey to let her sit with her until her sister had finally caved in. It felt exciting and dangerous staying up after Grams had gone to bed, snuggled up in the dark with the TV's volume turned right down and Grammy's knitted blanket wrapped around their shoulders.

Lacey hid behind it when the movie became too scary, but neither the blanket nor the reassuring presence of her big sister could stop the awful pig-like squeals of the rednecks' victim following after her. Even now, after all these years, she could still hear them.

The redneck in front of her was tall and broad-shouldered. His strong jaw was covered in silver-flecked dark stubble, and his long, lean legs appeared as strong as tree trunks. More lumberjack than redneck, then. There was something else that set him apart from the rednecks in the movie, and Lacey's throat began to ache when she realised what it was. This man reminded her of the Boy Scout. Not in colouring or facial similarity, or even in physical size, but there was something in his stillness, in his ease with himself, that echoed the characteristics of her dead friend.

'Boss?' Posy said.

The Boss's head turned. He tipped it to one side, as if he were listening to something far off in the distance, but it lasted only for the next second and then he was focused on Lacey and Alex, his eyes taking stock, roving over them, up and down, stopping at places in between, even pausing to study their feet, before coming back to their faces.

'Names?' he asked.

Lacey opened her mouth but quickly closed it again when Alex spoke up. She had already forgotten her agreement to stay silent and let her do the talking.

'I'm Alexandra. This is Lacey.'

His eyes rested on Lacey's face for a long moment. Then he spoke to Alex again. 'You don't look like family.'

'No, we're not,' Alex said.

'Lovers?'

'No.'

'Friends, then,' he said.

'Yes. We're friends.'

'Can never have too many friends,' he said, the corners of his eyes crinkling in an entirely too-pleasant way. The deepness of his voice sent a sonic vibration humming through Lacey's chest. It warmed her like a nip of her grammy's sherry used to.

I don't like him, the voice said.

Neither did Lacey, but she didn't share that with the voice.

'Friends, yes, Boss,' Posy said happily. 'Friends are good.'

The Boss pushed away from the window and strolled slowly towards them, his eyes dark and knowing. He hadn't once acknowledged Posy's presence, and he didn't glance in his direction now as he stopped behind the armchair, his big hands resting on its back. He casually leaned forward, his gaze fixed on Alex.

'Where is Red, Posy?' His attention flicked to Lacey, then returned to Alex. The small smile he wore was amiable enough.

Posy smiled nervously at Lacey, then looked back at the tall man. 'Boss?'

'I sent you out to find her. Where is she?'

'Hmm . . . no sign, Boss. We looked all over. Up and down, crossways and underways. No sign nowhere.'

The leather creaked in the man's grip. 'Where're Jebediah and William?'

'Jeb's downstairs. Doc's lookin' at him. He got hisself stabbed.'

'By who?' He raised his brows at Lacey and Alex. 'By you?'

Lacey shook her head.

'No,' Alex answered.

'Bill's deader'n shit,' Posy said sadly.

For the first time, the Boss turned to look at Posy. The young man grew still, his nervous jittering disappearing as soon as taller man's eyes found him.

'Who?' was all the Boss said.

'Some tall fella. He was with them.' Posy jerked his thumb at Lacey and Alex. 'Jeb shot 'im in the head.'

'He's dead?'

'Yessir.'

'He's killed Jeb, too,' Lacey said.

Alex squeezed her hand hard enough to make her bones grind painfully together.

The tall man turned to her. He smiled, all charm and warmth. 'Has he now? This man was your friend, too, I take it?' he asked.

'We knew him, yes,' Alex answered, unsuccessfully trying to redirect the man's attention back to her. Already, Lacey regretted speaking up.

'It would seem Jeb paid him back in kind, shooting him in the head and all,' the Boss told Lacey.

Her face grew hot, a throbbing sensation in the back of her skull making her eyes pulse in their sockets.

Keep it together, girl. Don't let him get to you.

The tall man's eyes crinkled even more, the attractive wrinkles emanating outwards like starbursts. 'He *was* your friend, I can tell. And that's OK – friends come and go. It's in their nature to be transient. But he's dead now, and I' – he leaned further over the armchair, pitching his voice lower so that he was speaking directly to her – '*I* can be your new friend.'

'I don't want any more friends, thank you,' said Lacey.

The tall man laughed, the boom of his amusement bouncing off the walls. Lacey half expected to see plaster fall from the ceiling.

He grinned broadly around at the others, even clapped his hands together, seemingly delighted by Lacey's reply. 'She doesn't want any more friends, she says.' He laughed again.

Posy laughed, too, but you could tell he didn't see what was so funny. He brightened immediately when the Boss came over to him and slung a beefy arm around his gawky shoulders.

'I like this one,' he told Posy, still grinning at Lacey. 'You did good. I forgive you for not finding Red. I have others still out looking for her. They will bring her back.'

Posy smiled real wide. 'Yeah, Boss. Yeah, they'll find her, I bet.'

'Have these two been checked for—' The big man whistled and twirled a finger above his ear.

Lacey's heart stopped. She even imagined she could feel the something in her head, that new space at the back from where the voice sparked and spoke to her, grow perfectly still, as if it were suddenly paying very close attention.

'No, Boss. Not yet.'

The tall man slapped Posy on the back, hard enough to make him jolt forward. 'There'll be time enough for that later. Go see how Jebediah is doing and report back to me.'

'Sure, Boss, sure. I'll go see.' Posy eagerly bobbed his head, walking backwards again, still grinning and nodding as he went through the door.

Lacey listened to his running footsteps scamper up the corridor.

'He's a fool, but he has his uses.' The Boss smiled apologetically. 'Forgive me, I haven't introduced myself. Charles Dumont.' He made a mocking half-bow to them. 'A fancy name for a country bumpkin, I suppose you're thinking, but my great-grandpappy was French and my great-grandma French-Peruvian. I'm afraid my claim to civility starts and ends there. I'm a New Orleans boy born and bred, although such divisions of birthplace are fairly redundant these days.' He had an odd way of speaking, his drawl slow and considered, his vocabulary a lot more sophisticated than that of the rednecks in the movie Lacey had watched.

He's not everything he appears. Quelle surprise.

'Mr Dumont, could you tell us what you want?' Alex asked.

Charles Dumont pursed his lips. 'What I want?'

'Yes. What do you want from us?'

All amusement and charm dropped from his face. 'Alexandra, allow me to be blunt with you. I want and will take everything from you I damn well please.'

Dumont went straight back to smiling once he'd said it, but

the dead calmness of his words spun round and round like a top in Lacey's head.

Everything he damn well pleases.

He'll get it, too.

– You need to help us.

There was a second's stunned silence. *Who, me?*

– Yes, you! Who else do I have talking to me inside my head?

I don't know. You weren't speaking to me a minute ago.

– Well, I am now! Can you help us or not?

I don't know . . . Maybe. But we have to be careful. I'm not sure what these people are looking for, but if it's voice-hearers they want, maybe we could— The voice meandered off into unintelligible mutterings.

– Could what? What are you talking about?

Lacey exhaled hard and fast through her nostrils, trying to keep hold of her patience, and it wasn't until she noticed Dumont watching her that she realised this internal conversation was playing out on her face.

'Sorry,' she said.

He looked curiously at her.

'I get distracted sometimes,' she explained.

'Distractions can be dangerous,' he said. 'Especially when it's important you pay attention.'

'I'm sorry,' she said again.

'I think Alexandra and I need to have a private conversation. I'd like you to wait down the hall with Louis.'

Lacey looked up at Alex and held fast to her hand. 'No,' she said.

'It's OK,' Alex said, but she looked scared. 'It won't take long.'

Dumont had gone to the door. He called for Lou.

'Alex—' Lacey began.

'Shhh, it'll be OK,' she whispered. Stepping in front of her, Alex cupped the back of her sweaty neck. 'We're just going to talk, work something out. Everything's going to be fine.' She tried to smile, but it was a poor effort.

Lacey's heart hammered. She felt panic rise like an electric current, starting in her stomach and trickling up to her throat, bathing it with an unpleasant metallic taste.

Alex stroked the back of her head.

'I wish I had my rifle,' Lacey said miserably.

Alex's smile was sad. 'Me, too, honey. Me, too.' She glanced over Lacey's shoulder, smile wilting. She took her by the shoulders and looked her square in the eyes. 'Don't worry about me. I'm tougher than I look.'

Lacey wanted desperately to believe her.

Look what she's been through already, the voice reasoned. *She's a survivor if ever I saw one.*

Dumont came back in, Lou behind him. He ordered the man to take Lacey out of the room, and Lou took hold of her arm just above her elbow. His grip bit into her flesh as though his fingers were made of bone and nail and dead things. He tugged her away from Alex.

'Alex!'

Alex looked more scared for Lacey than she did for herself. 'Shhh, it's OK, baby. Don't fight them.'

Lacey tried to snatch her arm out of Lou's grip, desperate to go back to Alex, but Lou wrapped both arms around her waist and physically lifted her off the ground. She yelled and kicked and threatened vicious bodily harm, but he was surprisingly strong for a skeleton.

The last thing she saw before the door slammed shut was Dumont, all amiability gone, a dark excitement in his eyes, and this time he looked *exactly* like those horrible rednecks who hurt the poor, pig-squealing man in the movie. And, behind him, Lacey's last friend in the whole, entire world stood alone in the centre of the room, the setting sun painting the left side of her face, highlighting the bruises that hadn't had time to heal.

CHAPTER 4

Lou carried her to the end of the corridor and out into the stairwell. She had stopped yelling by the time he had kicked open the fire-door, but she was still trying to wrestle herself free from his hold. He threw her into the corner. Her elbow glanced painfully off the guard rail, her shoulder thudding into the concrete wall. She turned and put her back in the corner, staying down, and glared at him.

'Stay put,' he said.

'Fuck you, Grandpa.'

He wheezed a laugh, his beard twitching up at the corners of his mouth, but said nothing more.

She hunkered there, her elbow throbbing and her hand tingling horribly, and wished Lou dead. Wished he would drop dead right where he stood, a clogged artery sending his heart into cramping spasm, or a clot in his brain firing off spastic jolts through his limbs, making his eyelids flutter madly while the rest of his brain imploded.

You're a mean little thing, aren't you?

She folded her arms over her knees, hid her face in them and gave into the tears. She made sure not to make any noise, not wanting to give Lou the satisfaction of hearing or seeing her cry. In the darkness of her folded arms she couldn't stop the replay of sounds her brain had recorded: Alex's pained whimpers in the bathroom each time the Boy Scout unwound another strip of wire from her bleeding wrists, the little gasps when either of them accidentally touched one of her many bruises, the way

Alex had whispered her name that first time, one eye narrowed because of her swollen cheekbone, her voice roughened from screaming. Only now the sounds were superimposed over the room Lacey had just been in, and it was Dumont standing over Alex, with the backdrop of the broken city behind him. He towered over her like an adult would a cowering child.

You should stop this, the voice said. *It does no good.*

Her grammy would say the same. And hadn't the Boy Scout told her that not all people were bad, and he would know, wouldn't he? He would know better than anyone.

She made a gigantic effort to push the awfulness away, and in its place she saw the Boy Scout walking towards their car, his motorcycle empty of gas and leaning on its stand behind him. The faint smile he'd given her when he'd climbed into the back seat and she'd told him that he was stuck with them now – it was such a small thing, that smile, but she'd seen it, and it had made her happy because maybe it meant he didn't mind that so much, being stuck with her. And now he was dead. And Alex would be dead soon, too, or worse. Lacey hiccupped on a sob and clamped her teeth together so hard she was afraid her jaw might crack.

The voice came again, even softer this time. *I'm sorry.*

– No you're not! she thought furiously.

I am sorry*, Lacey.*

– You said you could *help* us.

I said I could 'maybe' help, it said carefully.

'Then help already!' she said out loud.

Lou grunted, but Lacey didn't look up.

Shhh. OK.

She did look up this time, the smallest flame of hope stirring within her breast. If it helped her, helped Alex, she wouldn't care if hearing voices meant she was crazy. 'OK?' she asked.

Yes. OK. Now stop talking. You're drawing attention to us.

'OK what?' Lou said to her through a mouthful of teeth and beard.

'Nothing,' she said. 'I'm not talking to you.'

The one they call Doc will be coming up the stairs soon. When he gets here, you need to tell him that Dumont is messing with Alex.

– The guy in the hat? Why? What'll that do?

Just say it.

'Then who're you talking to?' Lou asked suspiciously.

'No one. Fuck off.'

Lacey!

Lou's bushy eyebrows lowered and joined in the middle but, before he could answer, a door opened and closed somewhere below them, echoing in the stairwell. Two sets of footsteps began to ascend.

Lou stepped over to the railing and peered down. 'Ho, down there!' he called.

'Lou! We're comin' up!' It was Posy.

A few seconds later, the wispy-bearded man loped around the corner and bounded up the final flight, his thin chest heaving from the effort. Behind him came Doc, his hat sat on the back of his head, his stride more graceful, his eyes already looking upwards at Lou, then sliding over to find her sitting in the corner.

'Charles wanted an update on Jeb,' he told Lou in that quiet voice of his.

'Yup. He says you should go ahead and leave the information with me,' Lou said.

Doc glanced over at Lacey again, his striking green eyes considering and sharply intelligent. Without saying a word to her, he nodded to Lou and gave him the update. Jeb was stitched up, but the next few hours were critical. Jeb's injury was severe; he was unlikely to recover. He'd lost a lot of blood.

Lou said he would pass it all on, and once again the man in the hat looked over at Lacey.

Say it now. Quickly.

195

Doc turned to go, and Posy hastily scooted out of his way.

Say it!

Doc had already jogged down three steps.

'He's-got-my-friend-Alex-in-that-room-with-him!' The words ran together in Lacey's rush to get them out.

Tell him he's messing with her.

'He's *messing* with her!'

Posy made a low, nervous, humming sound.

All she could see was the back of the man's hat, black and perfectly oval. Slowly, his head turned and he looked at her again.

She was breathing hard, her panic so real it felt like a live thing fluttering inside her heart, her throat, her ears.

Doc looked away from her and down at the ground in front of him, at what Lacey wasn't sure, the steps maybe, or his own feet, and for a long second she thought he would continue on his way without another word, just carry on down the stairs and turn the corner without looking back, and she would be left on the landing with the old, bearded, empty-eyed man, nothing to do but sit and wait and imagine all the horrifying things happening to her friend. But then he turned on the spot and came up to the top of the stairs and quietly asked Lou to open the fire-door. Lou didn't immediately move to obey. He looked over at Lacey, his eyes narrowed, his beard twisted into a sneer. He mumbled something that sounded like 'Little bitch', but he didn't say another word as he moved out of the way, pulling the door open as he did.

'Oh, boy,' Posy breathed, bouncing on his heels as he looked between Lou and Doc.

Doc disappeared into the corridor. Lou and Posy went next, and Lacey jumped up, hobbling after them, nearly falling, her feet lumps of tingling needle-pricks as blood rushed back into them. She stumbled through the door, the heavy mechanism clunking shut at her heels.

Doc had already reached the closed door by the time she caught up with them. Posy was at the rear, and he glanced back at her, excitement shining in his eyes. Doc didn't knock but swung the door open and strode inside, Lou right behind him, already apologising for the intrusion.

All Lacey could see was Alex. She was practically sitting on the floor, her back against Dumont's leg. Her shirt had been torn open and the skin of her breasts and stomach was pale except for the ruddy smudges of old bruises. A belt had been wrapped around her neck and she was strung up by it, the end of the leather wrapped in Dumont's fist. He held up most of her weight by that single tether, her butt a few inches off the ground. Already her eyes had rolled up, only their whites showing. Her tongue lolled out of her mouth. The belt dug into her neck, red, angry skin rucked up above it. Her face had turned purple.

Lacey tried to push past the bodies in her way, but it was like trying to push past stone pillars. Shouts rose and accusations were thrown around, Dumont's booming roar overriding them all, but Lacey wasn't listening; she dropped to her hands and scurried past legs and feet, moving quickly. Reaching Alex, she batted at Dumont's hand, clawed at it, punched him in the thigh, screaming at him to let go. The choking sound Alex was making was awful, but what was worse was when she stopped making the noise altogether.

Lacey closed her teeth on Dumont's hand and bit. Hard.

The man yelled. His hand sprung open. Alex dropped to the floor.

Dumont backhanded Lacey and she fell backwards, landing on her butt, catching herself on both hands. She tasted blood but pushed herself up and went to Alex, her shaking hands scrabbling at the woman's neck, struggling to loosen the too-tight leather band biting into her throat.

The prong in the buckle! Move the prong!

Lacey heard and dug the metal prong out of the leather, and

the belt loosened. She ripped it off Alex's neck and threw it aside.

Alex didn't draw breath.

'No no no no,' Lacey moaned.

She slapped her.

The woman's head rolled to one side.

'Alex!' she screamed, and slapped her harder, palm stinging painfully off her cheek.

Alex jerked and sucked in a huge breath, her eyes snapping open. She lurched upwards, instinctively fighting Lacey off, but Lacey grabbed hold of her hands and said her name over and over again until the tension left the woman's body and recognition entered her eyes. Then they widened. Alex tried to say something, but already it was too late. Hands grabbed Lacey from behind, and for the second time she was dragged, kicking and howling, away from her friend. The door slammed shut between them, Alex lost behind it, and a scream erupted from Lacey's throat that stripped her insides bare. And when it died away nothing was left but air and bones and hopelessness.

CHAPTER 5

They locked her in a freezer.

Thankfully, there was no power, so it wasn't cold. Someone had peeled away the insulation rubber from around the door, so a thin strip of light came through. Not enough to illuminate the room by much, or help Lacey's dark-adjusted eyes; she could barely make out the empty metal shelves and a few dangling hooks hanging from the ceiling. (The shelves she investigated mostly through touch.)

She had spent some time banging her fists against the door, yelling to be let out and shouting for Alex. Distant calls answered her, but none came from her friend, and neither she nor they could understand what the other was yelling. Her throat began to hurt after twenty minutes so she stopped. She went around the room again, but there was nothing of any use. All the hooks seemed well attached to the eyelets bolted to the ceiling, and she wasn't tall enough to try to work the housings free.

Eventually, she sat down, legs crossed in a lotus position, and just stared at the box of light shining around the doorframe. She tongued at the cut on the inside of her lip. It had stopped bleeding, but the jagged soreness of it was comforting somehow. She carried on until the taste of copper filled her mouth.

Occasionally, she would see the shadowy impressions of feet walk past at floor level, the light in the freezer room dimming for an instant, and she would call out, but she got no response.

'So. Your plan worked out great.' She said it with a mean

sarcasm she was unwilling to temper. She saw no reason not to speak out loud to the voice any more. She didn't give a flying hoot if people thought she was crazy.

Its presence, an unfurling jasmine blossom, bloomed in the back corner of her head. *You're both still alive, aren't you?*

'For the time being, maybe. I don't even know where they took her.' She didn't need to explain who she meant.

She's not far.

Lacey took a deep breath and opened her mouth.

Further away than those other people you were yelling at.

Lacey closed her mouth and was quiet for a while. She shifted a little, her butt starting to ache from sitting on the hard floor for so long. Finally, she asked, 'How did you know all that stuff? From before? How do you know where Alex is?'

Maybe it's you who knows it.

'I don't know it. How could I know it? I'm not any kind of mind reader.'

You don't know what you are. Just like I don't know what I am. We don't know how your brain works, how it's wired, how it can be used. How am I here, for example, talking to you?

'How should I know?' she muttered. 'For all I know, I'm just imagining all this, just like Grammy imagined stuff. Now she's passed it on to me and it's my turn to suffer.'

You're not imagining me. You'll come to see that in time.

'Prove it.'

There are lots of things that are unprovable, Lacey. Even things you think of as defined and finite. Maybe time itself doesn't run like you think it does, like a piece of string from one point to the next, with past and present and future all marked along it. Maybe time is space, surrounding us like air. Maybe we can know what will *happen or might* happen *as well as what is happening and what has just passed. I'm beginning to think it's all something that can be learned.*

Lacey pressed her fingers to her temples, these ideas new and very big, the space inside her head feeling way too small to fit them all in. She wasn't sure she liked this 'we' business it kept talking about, either.

Everything is fluid. Nothing is guaranteed. We're in constant flux. The only thing we do know is that we know nothing.

'But you knew that Doc person would come up the stairs.'

It was one possibility, yes.

'And you knew what to say to him.'

I thought it might get a reaction, yes.

'But that's like predicting the future.'

No, it's just being observant.

'Observant? That still doesn't explain *how* you knew those things.'

You want a clear explanation?

'Yes.'

OK. It was magic.

'God, you're *such* a shit.'

It giggled, or at least that's what it felt like to her, like froth bubbling up and bursting in a succession of tiny, gleeful pops. It was a weird sensation.

The catch on the freezer door disengaged, and the heavy door swung open. A glare of light hit her in the face and Lacey turned her head aside, lifting a hand to block it out.

'Can you lower that?' she asked, squinting.

The flashlight's beam lowered, and Lacey blinked past the black spots in her vision to find Posy standing in the opening. He set a stool down and sat on it. He didn't speak but looked down at his feet and shuffled nervously. To Lacey, he appeared shy. She hadn't forgotten the slap he'd given her around the back of the head, though.

'What do you want?' she said, not attempting to be nice.

He cleared his throat, then made that strange, low, humming sound. 'Hmm . . . these yours?'

For the first time, she noticed he carried something else. When he held them up, she recognised a handful of paperbacks.

'No. Where did you get them?'

'Your pack.'

Lacey shook her head, her eyes going back to the books. 'Not mine, no.' She knew whose they were. The Boy Scout had found the books he was looking for. She wanted to scoot across the floor and snatch them out of Posy's hand, hunker covetously over them and page through each one, greedily reading every word.

'You can read?' Posy asked, looking hopefully at her.

She didn't answer but held out her hand for him to pass the books over, holding her breath, hoping he couldn't see how desperately she wanted them. When he did, she placed them carefully in her lap and looked at each one in turn. She took her time rubbing her thumb down the spine of each book, fanning the pages, a soft draught of musty air tickling her nose. For a moment tears filled her eyes, making reading the titles and authors impossible. She pressed one book to her nose and breathed in. A droplet of moisture splashed on to the back cover. She sniffed and wiped it dry with her sleeve.

'Can't you?' she asked.

He shook his head. 'Jus' my name. Can write it, too. Never learned to read good, though. Mama said I had me a slow start, and I'm still catchin' up. Wasn't breathing when I popped out of her.'

'Um, wow,' she said, unsure how to respond to that.

'Yep. I'm special.' He tapped a finger to his head, looking proud. 'Been told so.'

'Special how?'

'Special different.'

He's 'special', all right, the voice said, not kindly.

'You hear a voice?' she asked, curiosity nibbling at her.

The guy's brow dropped into a scowl. 'No. I don't hear nothin'.' He seemed disappointed by the fact.

Lacey wanted to tell him he could have hers if he wanted.

Hey, the voice complained.

'*Do* you read?' he asked again.

'Never did much as a kid,' she admitted. 'I wasn't very good at sitting still for long. Preferred making mud kitchens and slug farms. My grams liked reading her gardening magazines, though, and my sister was obsessed with romance novels. So yeah, I can read.' She held up the books he'd given her. 'Did you want me to read one to you?'

Posy nodded fast, his frown melting away and a smile so happy spreading across his face it hurt her to look at him. This man may not have pulled the trigger, but he had helped kill her friend, and now he sat here pretending like nothing had happened. The stool was barely able to contain his gangly legs and eagerness.

'You want to trade, then?' she asked.

'Trade?' His happiness momentarily paused, his face twisted quizzically, his lack of understanding stamped all over it.

'Right. Trade. I'll read to you if you take me to see my friend.'

Posy stood up, came forward and snatched the books out of her hands. He grabbed up his stool and stepped outside, swinging the freezer door shut.

Lacey shot to her feet and was at the door as soon as the catch locked. Her hands shook, panic squeezing them into balls. 'Wait! I'm sorry, I didn't mean it! I'll read to you!'

Nothing.

She pressed her forehead to the cool surface of the door. 'Posy, I'm sorry, OK? Just come back in and I'll read to you. Please.'

Lacey stared at the floor, the strip of light broken up by two shadowy lumps where Posy's feet stood on the other side.

He's an idiot.

'Posy?'

He didn't answer.

'Posy, I know you're there. I can see your feet under the door.'

The latch unlocked and Lacey stood back as the door swung open.

His eyes were solemn, his mouth a straight line hidden in his reddish-brown, tufty beard. For the first time, Lacey realised he wasn't all that much older than her, no more than nineteen or twenty.

'No more tradin'?' he asked her suspiciously.

'No, no more talk of trading. Just story time. Word of honour.' She held her hand up, palm outwards, to show she meant it.

He came back in, and she retreated to give him room, lowering herself on to the floor while he took his seat again. He leaned forward to hand her a book. Lacey took it, a fine tremble to her hand, and brushed a tender palm over the cover. Then she turned the pages reverently until she reached the first one full of writing.

Using her finger to keep her place, she glanced up. 'Ready?' She waited for Posy's nod before she cleared her throat and began. '*Something Wicked This Way Comes*. A Prologue . . .'

She paused her reading at Chapter 14.

'Do you think I could have some water?'

Posy blinked slowly at her. He was swimming back up to her after being submerged in an ocean of imaginary lands. 'Water?' he asked dully.

'Yeah. My throat is dry.'

'Hmm . . . OK, wait. I'll get some.' He jumped up and hurried out, pushing the heavy door shut behind him until it *clunk*ed closed.

He'd left his stool. Lacey stared at it, the three legs looking like an alien's tripod machine, backlit by the strip of light running along the bottom of the doorframe. The long shadows of its legs crawled across the space between them, reaching out to her.

It'd be heavy, she thought. She could wait for Posy to come back. Wait for him to open the door and step inside, bring the stool down on his head with all her might. Brain him. Then run.

An image of the Boy Scout lying face down in the dust, dark blood pooling around his head, flashed into her mind, and she shook her head, muttering a '*No!*' to herself. A 'no' to what she wasn't sure.

Before she had decided on a course of action, Posy was back, struggling to pull the door open while holding a bowl of water.

It's like you're his pet, giving you a saucer to drink out of.

Shut up, she thought.

Posy cupped the bowl in both hands and offered it to her. She nodded and smiled her thanks and took the bowl, bringing it to her lips. She sipped cautiously at first, testing the lukewarm water, but it tasted fine, if a little stale. Filling her mouth, she swilled the tepid water around her teeth and gums and swallowed it down. She rested the bowl in her lap on top of the upside-down book, which was still open at the page she'd been reading from.

'Is Posy your real name?'

He'd been biting at his dirty nails while he watched her drink. Now he spat out a piece and shook his head. 'I jus' like flowers.'

'Which are your favourite?' She took another small sip.

'I like the li'l white ones with the yellow middles.'

'Daisies?'

He nodded and moved on to his next nail. Is that what she looked like when she gnawed on her nails? She really had to quit. It was pretty disgusting.

She swirled the water around in her bowl. 'Mine are lantana. Have you heard of them? They're poisonous to most animals, including us, but birds can eat their berries. I like that. That they can be two things at once: poison or food, depending on who you are.'

He kept on biting.

'But I get the Posy thing, I think,' she went on. 'Daisy's too girly a name, right?'

As if Posy isn't.

Posy grunted and spat out another bit of nail. 'You gonna read some more?'

Lacey nodded slowly. 'In a minute. I need to finish my water.' She swirled the bowl some more and lifted it, casually pausing before taking a sip. 'Posy, what are they going to do with us?' She drank, watching him over the bowl's lip.

He had stopped biting his nails, his hand poised in front of his mouth. He met her eyes for a split second and then dropped his gaze to the ground. He shrugged. 'Doc put you in here. Freezers make good lock-ups, he said.'

'So you've captured other people, too? What's happened to them?'

Posy lowered his hand and glanced over his shoulder, leaning back to see if anyone was near enough to overhear. He looked back at her and lowered his voice. 'Don't always get to see. Sometimes they stay, sometimes they jus' up 'n' disappear.'

'Disappear where?'

He shrugged again. 'Sometimes they get moved. Other times killed, I guess. Sometimes eaten. That's Dolores – says she gets tole to eat 'em. She's a crazy old bitch.' That last bit was said as though he was repeating something he'd overheard one time.

The skin on the back of Lacey's neck went ice-cold. A fist reached right inside her and grabbed hold of her guts, squeezing them tight, and for a second she thought she would puke up the water she had just drunk.

'If I disappear,' she told him, 'I won't be able to read to you any more.'

'I know,' he said sadly. 'Can't find Princess neither.'

Lacey placed the empty bowl beside her. 'I can help you look for her.'

He didn't seem convinced.

'This one time my grammy lost her reading glasses, and I remembered she'd been repotting some fruit plants in the yard. So I went out and took a look around, and you know what she'd done? She'd buried them in a pot of soil. Right at the bottom. Maybe she was trying to grow a spectacle tree – who knows? Point is, I'm real good at finding stuff.'

Posy had gone back to staring at his knees. 'I'm not s'posed to let you out. I'd get in trouble again.'

Like with Red?

'Is that what happened with Red?' Lacey asked softly. 'You helped her get free and she ran away?'

He looked up at her sharply. 'It was an *accident*. I jus' left for a *second* to go get her food. She couldn't eat prop'ly no more, see. When I got back she'd up 'n' disappeared, like some of the others do, 'cept not the *usual* disappeared – this one was a *bad* disappeared. Boss wasn't happy. He liked her to tell him 'bout the stuff in her head.' Posy wrapped his arms around his middle and rocked on his stool, the flashlight's beam rocking back and forth with him, the swinging light making Lacey nauseous.

Stuff in her head? Ask him what—

But Lacey was already talking. 'She must've been real scared to run away like that.'

'Flitting Man scared her but good. Scared everyone good.' Posy stopped rocking and peered closely at her. 'I shouldn' talk to you no more. I'll get in trouble.'

'It's OK, I won't tell anyone. This can be our little secret. Just the two of us.'

What's the Flitting Man?

'Red is good,' Posy said. 'She was good to me. Didn't hafta be nice, but she was. It wasn't right what got done to her.'

'What got done to her, Posy? What scared her so bad?'

His eyes narrowed and he went back to chewing his nails, mumbling from behind his hand, all the while watching her. 'She tole Boss someone was comin'. Someone with death in his eyes. That she'd met him afore, long ago in the desert, and that his job was to put the pieces t'gether so that people like the Boss and Doc and the Flitting Man ain't got no hold no more. She wasn't tellin' him to warn him. No, sir. She was tellin' him like Jeb tells me sometimes when he's took my blanket. The one with the patches. Took it away and hid it, and won't tell me where. Like that. Like she *liked* knowin' 'bout what was comin'. Red is good,' he said, nodding firmly. 'The Boss ain't. Flitting Man is worse. But Red is good, and she didn't like neither of those two. Not one bit. It was my job to watch her, keep her safe. She liked me. Said she wanted me to stay close, away from Doc. She wasn't allowed out, see. She was too precious to be let out.'

As what he'd said sank in, the skin over Posy's cheekbones tautened, and fear widened his eyes. He stood up, knocking the stool over with a clatter, and went out of the door to check the corridor both ways. He came back to her, speaking fast. 'Enough talk. Talked too much. I need to go now.' He picked up the stool.

Lacey scrambled to her feet. 'Wait! At least let me help look for your dog.'

'No. Talkin's done.' Posy stepped out of the room, and before she could lift a hand or protest against it he slammed the door closed, shutting her in the dark.

Lacey called after him, but there were no shadowy feet standing outside the door this time. He had gone. In a fit of temper, she threw the book across the room and heard it thump against the wall. A second later it hit the floor with a smack. She immediately went after it, sorry she had thrown something that had belonged to the Boy Scout, and cradled the book in her hands, smoothing out the creases and bends in the cover. Carrying it back over to the door, she lay down on her belly, holding the book in the dim swathe of light creeping in from under it.

She read the back cover, her lips moving, forming the words silently. She imagined the Boy Scout's eyes running over the same lines, the words entering her brain in the same way they'd entered his, until they had both absorbed the exact same knowledge. She shared that with him now; neither time nor space could take it away. He felt closer to her in that moment while she read then re-read the back cover, lying on the floor, alone in the dark, her eyes growing tired, the words muddling together.

You're not alone.

'Suppose not,' she whispered, laying her head down. She closed her eyes and let her thoughts drift. 'I'm a crazy girl with my own doohickey in her head for company.'

It's actually quite pleasant in here. Very clear. Like being surrounded by polished glass. No annoying holes – everything unbroken and smooth and whole.

'That's nice.' Sleep thickened her voice, made her slur. 'What should I call you, anyway? Doohickey doesn't sound right. And are you a he? You sound like a he . . .'

You can call me Voice. I don't mind that so much. Voice suits me just fine.

CHAPTER 6

She didn't know how long she slept, but when she awoke she was cold and stiff and still lying on the floor, her head near the door and resting on top of the paperback. She levered herself up to a sitting position. Her stomach gurgled so loudly she pressed both palms to it in surprise.

'Man, I'm so hungry I could eat a girly-named dog.' She said it to no one but herself but waited for a reply.

None came. Voice remained quiet. Lacey wondered if he slept like she did. Or maybe the crazy in her head had decided to vacate the premises.

'Maybe,' she whispered, 'they already ate the dog . . .' She refused to continue that line of thought, though, locking it away before her imagination could taunt her further with it.

Pushing at the ground, she rose carefully to her feet and did some half-hearted stretches: fingertips to toes, hands on hips and swivelling her upper body in hip pivots. She even did some jumping jacks at the end, hoping the exercise would warm her up. In fact, she did feel marginally better by the time she went back to the door and pressed her ear to it.

'Hey! Anybody out there?'

She hammered on the door.

'Are you planning on starving me to death! *Heeey!*'

Nothing. She stepped back and kicked, slamming the bottom of her shoe into the freezer door, putting her full weight behind the blow. It didn't move.

'This is ridiculous,' she said. She limped round in a small

circle. Her foot hurt from the kick, like when you jump down from a too-high wall and your soles slap the floor in a concrete belly-flop.

Foot-flop, she thought, and laughed.

She wished she hadn't kicked the door so hard.

When she heard approaching footsteps, Lacey stopped walking. She expected to see Posy when the door opened, but the clean-shaven man, the one with the funny-looking bowler hat, stood there instead. Doc. The smell of menthol came with him, but this time there was something underneath the mintiness that didn't smell quite so fresh or so nice. His clear green eyes were unreadable as he looked at her.

'Do you have breakfast?' Lacey asked him.

He said nothing, only turned away and walked out of sight, leaving the door open. Lacey didn't immediately follow. What if it was a trap? He could be testing to see if she'd try to make a run for it. She bit at the inside of her cheek and edged forward. She picked up the paperback, which she'd left on the floor, and, holding it to her chest, peered around the door. The man was ten feet away, half turned towards her, waiting. Lacey looked the other way, the long expanse of corridor empty and inviting.

'I wouldn't think about running,' the man called Doc said quietly. 'There are twenty people in this part of the building. Without me, they'd mistake you for a threat.' Again, without waiting for her, he turned and continued along the corridor.

After a moment, Lacey tucked the book safely under the waistband of her jeans and followed. 'Where's my friend? Is she OK?'

No answer.

'Where are you taking me?' she asked.

'I want to show you something,' he said, without looking back.

'Show me what?'

'You'll see.'

'What is it with people not wanting to straight up tell me stuff? What if I told you I wasn't moving another step until you told me what it is?' She halted in the middle of the corridor and folded her arms.

He stopped, too, and half turned to her again. His fine eyebrows were raised slightly, nearly disappearing under the brim of his hat, whether in surprise or puzzlement she wasn't quite sure.

'I would say that would be a very foolish thing to do,' he said evenly.

He met her eyes for a long moment, and Lacey felt a cold, needle-sharp sensation open up in her belly. Fear. She wasn't sure why – there was no unfriendliness in the man's stare, no pent-up tension, the kind that often came before violence – but she was convinced that he somehow knew exactly what she was thinking, could read her like a book, and that he found her amusing in the same way a bug expert would find a tiny insect amusing as he poked at it beneath his magnifying glass.

'You will come?'

He said it in such a way that Lacey wasn't sure if he meant it as a question or a statement of fact. The sentence was ambiguous in its meaning, much like the man himself.

She nodded mutely.

The briefest lifting of his lips signalled a smile, and then he turned to lead the way once more.

Lacey lost track of the turns and the number of corridors they walked along, but at last the behatted man led her into a room. Before she took one step inside, the smell hit her: old meat, dried blood, hot faeces. A single bed sat in the corner, and on it was Jeb, his head turned away from them.

Doc's watchful eyes rested on her as he went to a spare chair set up against the back wall and took a seat.

Without conscious thought, Lacey took the final steps needed to bring her to Jeb's bedside. The closer she approached, the chillier she became. It was as though waves of coldness were radiating from the man, bleeding down from his bed and into the floor at her feet, soaking through her shoes and crawling up her legs, injecting themselves directly into her marrow. Jeb's pallor was so white she could see the purplish, web-like capillaries beneath his skin. His breathing was laboured and shallow.

'He's lost too much blood.'

Lacey looked over when Doc spoke. The man had neatly crossed one leg over his knee and was sitting naturally straight-backed.

'This is what you wanted to show me?' she asked.

'Not quite. Almost.'

When she looked back down at Jeb, the man's bloodshot eyes were open and staring up at her.

'*You*,' he whispered hoarsely, his white lips dry and cracked. 'You fucking whore, you *killed* me.'

Lacey shook her head quickly, guilt slamming into her stomach like a fist. '*No*. No, it was *your* fault. You should have let us go. Why couldn't you just leave us alone? We'd done nothing to you.'

'The talking fucking maggots will eat out your brain. Eat through your dirty-bitch brain, will make you *rot* for what you done to me. Rot like your fucking friend. I hope the coyotes picked his body clean, dragged his fucking entrails along the road like a skip-rope. Where are all the skip-ropes gone? Been fucking burned or used for nooses. Nooses . . . Jesus Christ, why am I so fucking *cold*? *Doc?*'

Doc stood up and entered the dying man's field of vision.

'Doc! Help me, Doc, *please*. God, it *hurts*.' Jeb shivered so hard the bed rattled against the wall. He tried to clutch the bedclothes closer about him, but his hands patted over the covers, rubbery fingers unable to grasp anything. He started to cry, broken sobs that left him on heaving shudders, but no tears leaked from the corners of his eyes. His face had collapsed in on itself, all lines and broken, brown teeth and bristling hair.

'I can't help you any more, Jebediah,' Doc said. 'Only your own God can help you now.'

'*Fuck my God!*' Jeb screamed. '*And fuck yours, too!*' He glared at Lacey with such seething hatred it knocked her back a step. Spittle flecked his beard. He clawed a hand at her. '*I'll fucking kill you! I'll KILL you, you fucking bitch! Send you to hell with all those fucking maggots in your brain!*' His eyes bulged out of his head and he convulsed. He fell back on the bed, his teeth clacking shut. He made horrible gurgling noises as he shuddered, air ticking dryly in his throat. His arms curled into his chest, waving around like an insect's mandibles, hands hooked in like claws.

'What's happening?' Tears unwillingly came to Lacey's eyes. Her heart thudded so hard all she could hear was the drumbeat of it all around her, as if she were trapped inside a womb. She wanted to run away and keep running until all she could hear were her slapping feet and her rushing breath, until the blood rocketed through her veins like machine-gun bullets, but she was unable to move, just as Jeb was unable to stop what was happening to him.

'His organs are failing,' Doc said.

Jeb started to babble. 'Please please *please*. I'm sorry, Doc, I'm *sorry*! Please fucking help me, *please*! *IsweartofuckingGodI'msorry!*'

'I'm sorry you got yourself stabbed,' Doc said, although he didn't sound very sorry.

Jeb's eyes rolled in their sockets, rolled around to pin Lacey in place. There was still rage and hatred there, yes, but mostly there was terror. A pitiful terror. His lips had rolled back, his rotting teeth had clenched, and his white lips were bleeding from being bitten.

Lacey stood rooted to the spot until the last of Jeb's shudders died away and the man expired with a long, rattling breath. His hands remained frozen in claws at his chest. His glassy eyes stayed fixed on her face. He looked shrunken and wretched, as if death had sucked every last ounce of moisture from him. What was left was just an emaciated carcass.

Lacey breathed hard, as if she'd been sprinting.

Death had laid a pall over the room. Lacey could feel it like a cloying presence, stoppering up her ears and mouth and throat until she thought she would choke.

Into the silence, Doc spoke. '*That* is what I wanted to show you.'

Lacey was led back to her prison. She didn't remember a single step. The door was locked, and she was left alone in the darkness, but she was unaware of either the loneliness or the lack of light. She sat and stared and clutched the paperback in both hands. She was vaguely aware of Voice trying to talk to her, to draw her out of the deep, dark place she'd withdrawn to, but she remained unwilling or unable to engage.

Food was finally brought – some cold porridge-type gruel – and she ate it automatically without tasting it. She drank from the bowl, which had been refilled. Then she curled into a ball, the book at her centre. She slept fitfully, her dreams filled with clawing, insectile hands, and maggots stuffed in her mouth, crawling their way up into her brain, where they wriggled and writhed. Later, she saw her loved ones, all lined up in a row, each one bleeding from gaping wounds in their bellies: her grammy, Alex, Karey, the niece she had never met (who was small and faceless), even the Boy Scout. He looked upon her with pity, his hands cupped under the river of red pouring from his stomach, and asked in sad tones why she wasn't helping the people she loved.

She woke up crying.

She lay there, and hours passed. Sometimes she listened to Voice, sometimes she didn't. He asked her questions about her sister, about what she thought her niece would be like. She didn't answer any of them.

Posy came and tried to get her to read some more, but he left again when she failed to acknowledge his presence.

I thought you wanted Jeb dead.

It was these words that poked a small hole in the numb shield she had built around herself.

'No,' she whispered, swallowing past the soreness in her throat. 'Not like that.'

Dead is dead, no matter how it happens.

'Shut up,' she whispered, closing her eyes as if, in the closing of them, she could shut Voice away, too.

He inflicted much worse on the people he came across.

'I want Alex,' she said. A hot, scalding tear burned its way down her temple and dripped into the shell of her ear.

Don't be a baby.

'I want my grams.' More tears followed the first.

For the first time, Voice sounded irritable. *Don't go all soft on me now. Where's your backbone?*

'Don't have one,' she muttered.

Well, find it. This isn't the time to show weakness.

She rolled over on to her other side, putting her back to the door. 'Just leave me alone.'

It wouldn't help you if I—

'Leave me alone!'

Voice hovered for a second longer and then left, the back of Lacey's head gaping emptily. She immediately missed his presence, but she clamped down on the feeling almost as soon as it came.

What would her grammy think of her, sulking around like this? Lacey caught her breath on a sob because she *knew* what her grammy would think, and that she wouldn't have stood for it. She would have dragged her up by the elbow by now, wagging her work-gnarled finger in her face, telling her to buck her ideas up Missy, 'cause no one likes a cry-baby, that nothing gets done by moping around and feeling sorry for yourself, and there's always plenty to do and plenty to *plan* on doing when there was more time to do it.

'But why would he want to show me that, Grammy?' she whispered.

She didn't expect an answer, and she didn't get one.

'I don't understand why he would take me in there just to watch him die.'

Lacey was almost overwhelmed by images again, of how Jeb had convulsed and cried out, of how he'd glared at her right until his last breath rattled out of his dying lungs. Lacey sat up in one quick movement but kept her head down, holding steadfast on to the image of her grammy, of the hand-knitted blanket she would wrap around their shoulders and the wide, scratched wedding band on her ring finger, of her callused hands, strong and capable, but equally good at unknotting tangles in hair or coaxing out splinters. The picture of her grams was far stronger than the picture of the dead man, and Lacey rubbed at her eyes to ingrain that image into her head, rubbed and rubbed until dancing phosphenes floated on the black backdrop of her eyelids. She smiled. 'Fancies,' her grandmother had called them. They were there to remind you that, even in the dark, there was always something to be found.

'I love you, Grams,' Lacey whispered. 'I wish you were here with me.'

She slid a hand under her collar and found the St Christopher medallion. It was hot to the touch, and only grew hotter the longer she held it. Out of the darkness, where the fancies floated and the spirit of her grammy still lived, a thought developed in Lacey's mind, flimsy at first, but quickly growing into something solid and tangible.

She opened her eyes.

'Voice? Voice, I need to talk to you.'

Lacey released the St Christopher and touched her hot fingertips to the spot behind her right ear. Voice half appeared, like a striking flint in the dark, not fully there but no longer gone, either. He was a 'fancy' of his own kind.

'Voice, I think I have an idea.'

Reluctantly drawn out, Voice asked, *What kind of idea?*

CHAPTER 7

Dumont stood on the docking-bay platform, overseeing the loading of the vehicles. There were two pickups, three cars and a Winnebago in the concreted area, people scurrying around them, busy with packing gear into trunks and truck beds. Away from all the activity, two boys, no older than ten, crouched near the back wall, taking turns flipping coins. The next thing Lacey knew, the older boy had shoved the smaller boy over, a mean push that knocked him sprawling, his handful of change scattering in a glittering arc. The little guy popped right back up and jumped on his attacker. He pounded on the bigger boy with fists and elbows until a woman hurried over and dragged him off, giving him a smack around the head for his trouble. The older boy, the one who'd started the fight, remained curled up in a ball. No one went over to check on him.

Lacey returned her attention to the activity by the vehicles and tried to ignore Lou, who was standing close behind her. Too close. She could feel his body heat seeping out of him.

'What's going on?' she asked Dumont. There were more people than she remembered seeing earlier. Easily over thirty. There was a group of six loitering over by the Winnebago, standing listlessly, mostly staring at the floor. A few appeared to be speaking, but not to each other; no one looked up or even acknowledged the person beside them. Four more, three men and a woman, sat on the floor with their backs resting against the RV, their hands tied in front of them. They looked sullen and defeated and watched the goings-on around them with hostile eyes. The man in the middle sported a black eye and a fat lip, and the front of his once-white shirt was stained with streaks of what could have been dirt but Lacey suspected was blood.

Dumont cocked an eyebrow at her. His wide shoulders stretched the material of his shirt. 'We're making preparations to leave.'

'Leave to go where?'

'My, you're a nosy mite, aren't you?' Dumont went back to watching his people. 'It's time we headed for new pastures. We've picked this place dry. No more useful folk to round up in these parts.'

He's taking people, Voice whispered. *Just like in those stories.*

'Do you tie folk up when they're not useful?' she asked.

Dumont called down to a man called Terence who was examining a pickup's rear tyre. Had he collected the car jack from someone called Stevie, Dumont wanted to know. Terence assured him that he had.

Lacey didn't think Dumont had heard her question and was opening her mouth to re-ask it when he said, 'No. Those people down there will be useful at some point. They're just not ready to join our cause yet. But they will.'

'What cause?'

'I don't think you're ready yet, either, my dear. All in good time. Posy!'

Lacey spotted Posy down among the others, carrying what looked like the Boy Scout's pack and heaving it into the back of a truck. He stopped at Dumont's shout and looked up.

'I've been told you've been on the radios again.'

Posy dropped his head and shuffled where he stood. Literally, shuffled where he stood like a fat kid caught with his finger half scooped in a jar of peanut butter.

'You're not to touch them again. Understand? Touch them, I break your hand. And maybe even the arm attached to it.'

Posy muttered to his feet.

'He can't hear you, dick for brains!' Lou shouted from behind Lacey, making her heart seize and her shoulders tense up.

Posy didn't lift his head, but he did raise his voice. 'I won't, Boss. No more radios for me, Boss.'

Dumont nodded, satisfied. 'Good boy. Carry on.'

Next to the pickup Posy went back to loading up was the jeep that had brought her here. And there was that word again, in tidy silver lettering on its rear panel. 'DEFENDER'. Lacey's hand crept to the hem of her shirt, reaching under it, her fingertips briefly touching the paperback book she had shoved into her waistband, trying to draw courage from it.

'Red,' Lacey said.

Dumont didn't move, not to look around at her nor even to acknowledge he had heard her speak.

But he's listening, all right, Voice said.

'I know where she is,' Lacey said.

This time Dumont turned all the way round to face her. She recalled how his arms had bulged with muscle while he lifted Alex off the floor by her neck. She remembered how the veins had stood out on his forehead, his face dark from exertion, his eyes alive with excitement.

'And I'm to believe this why?' he asked.

'I can prove it to you. But first we talk terms.'

He broke into a bright smile. 'Oh, I do like you. You're very entertaining. You know, Doc told me you didn't take Jebediah's death very well, even though you had wished him dead. Even though you seemed quite satisfied by the fact he was near to death's door the last time we spoke. But it's hard to watch someone die, isn't it? Even someone you don't like. *Especially* someone you don't like. Just imagine how it would feel watching someone you *do* like slowly die. Now that's a new experience altogether.'

Lacey breathed heavily through her nose, fighting to keep

her face impassive, trying very hard to look him steadily in the eye and not show any sign of weakness, exactly like Voice had told her, when in fact all she wanted to do was curl into a ball at his feet like that kid down there had after he was attacked.

'I'll show you where she is,' she said. 'All you have to do is let Alex go. And when I've led you to her, you let *me* go.'

'You think Red is worth two people I already have in my possession?'

Yes.

'Yes,' she said, hoping Voice was right.

Dumont rubbed his chin, smiling, exchanging looks with Lou. 'How do you plan on proving to me you know where she is?' he asked her.

Lacey didn't answer, she simply reached to the nape of her neck, unclasped the St Christopher pendant and held it out by its chain. The silver coin spun in the air, catching the light every now and then and flashing it into Dumont's eyes. He stared at it as if she had hypnotised him, not even blinking when the flicker of light blinded him.

'I could just torture her whereabouts out of you,' he said, almost too quietly for her to hear, still staring intently at the pendant.

Lacey pooled the St Christopher and chain into her shaking hand, hiding it inside her fist. 'Sure, you could do that. But it'd be wasting time. And she wasn't in such good shape last time I saw her.'

Voice gave a surprised guffaw inside her head. *No, she certainly wasn't.*

'Here are *my* terms,' Dumont said, stepping closer to her, his large hand closing around her fist, where she held the pendant. 'You lead two of my men to Red. When she is found, *you* are released. And when Red is returned to me, Alexandra is released.'

She felt completely trapped by him. He loomed over her, his

dark head bent so he could look directly into her face, his warm hand enveloping hers, his grip strong but not painfully so.

'How can I trust you'll let Alex go and not just kill her?' Lacey asked, her voice barely above a whisper, amazed she had managed to find it at all.

You're doing good, girl. Just keep it together a little longer.

'Why would I kill her?' Dumont said, seemingly surprised by such a question. 'She's far more entertaining to me alive.'

'That doesn't prove to me you'll let her go.'

'Come with me,' he instructed.

He towed her after him, pulling her along by the hand clasped around her fist. She stumbled to keep up as he led her down the concrete steps and into the crowd of busy people loading up the cars. Dumont called over his shoulder to Lou, telling him to bring the woman.

Reaching the back of a pickup, Dumont ordered Posy and another man to stop what they were doing and unload its bed. Posy kept slanting them curious looks as he lifted out the Boy Scout's pack, along with a few other bundles.

'What's goin' on, Boss?' Posy asked once the bed had been cleared.

'Go get the chain for the door, boy. Be ready to open it.'

Posy set down the last bundle and wandered over to the chain pulley, all the while sending confused looks over his shoulder at Lacey.

On the concrete docking platform, the middle door swung open and Alex was shoved through. She almost fell but caught herself with one hand on the floor.

'Alex!'

The relief that washed over Alex's face at seeing Lacey was visible even from fifty yards away. She looked awful, though. The welt and bruises around her neck covered the entirety of her throat in darkly mottled purples and blues. Lacey's vision blurred with tears as she ripped free from Dumont's hold and ran. Alex had reached the bottom of the concrete steps when Lacey hit her, arms going around her and hugging her tightly.

Alex gasped, flinching a little, her voice clenched with pain and barely above a whisper. 'Not so hard, baby. You're squeezing the life out of me.'

'Sorry.' Lacey loosened her hold a little.

'What's going on?' Alex whispered in her ear.

Lacey felt the woman rub at her back, right between her shoulder blades, and she almost burst out crying. 'I told him I know where Red is.'

'Who?'

'*Red*. The girl he's looking for.'

Alex didn't say anything.

'It's the girl we saw crash her car, Alex. The one I took the necklace from.'

Alex held Lacey's shoulders and gently pushed her back far enough to meet her eyes. 'You're sure?'

Lacey nodded fast, not sure how long they'd have before Dumont separated them. 'I showed it to him. It's hers. He wants me to take his men to her. Then he'll let me go.'

Already Alex was nodding. 'That's good. Go with them. Do whatever it takes, just get away as soon as you can. Don't get all the way back there if you don't have to.'

'He said he'll release you, too. When they bring Red back. He promised.' Her voice cracked on that last word and tears filled her eyes again because she knew how ridiculous that sounded, how unlikely a man like Dumont would be to keep his word.

'That's great, honey,' Alex whispered as firmly as she could with a voice that was damaged and broken. 'Don't worry about me. I'll be fine.'

'You always say that,' Lacey accused, the tears spilling over. 'And then you end up getting strangled or something.'

Alex gave her a pained smile. 'My intention is always to be fine, though. That's the main thing.'

'Enough!' Dumont was suddenly there. He snatched up Lacey's wrist and pulled her away from Alex. 'Louis, you're going. Pick someone else to go with you. Now.'

Lou didn't argue but went to a stoop-backed man stood over by the Winnebago's rear bumper and exchanged a few words with him. Both men came back over to them.

'Take her.' Dumont shoved Lacey at them, and she stumbled into their arms, wrenching away from them as soon as she regained her balance. 'When she's led you to Red, and you're sure it's her, let her go. You hear me? You release her, alive and well, and come back here. If you hurt her, I'll rip out your spines. We clear?'

Lou and the stoop-backed man nodded.

Dumont looked to Lacey. 'Good enough?'

She let the question hang inside her head, waiting for Voice, needing him to make the decision for her even if he was all in her imagination, because already an unbearable guilt was festering, growing inside her.

It's good enough, Voice said. *There might be a way to come back for her.*

She looked over at Alex, and the woman nodded to her again. A resolute nod; nothing weak in how she stood there and met Lacey's eyes.

Lacey turned to Dumont and said, 'Remember what you promised.'

Dumont threw a hand up. 'Posy! Open the door!'

With a clatter, the rolling door began to crank upwards, a bright strip of sunlight widening on the concrete as it rose.

The two men grabbed her.

'Alex!' Lacey struggled as they forced her into the front of the truck. 'No! Wait! ALEX!'

She continued to fight them until Lou climbed in beside her, behind the wheel, and punched her in the ear. She slumped in the seat away from him, holding the side of her head, her ear already swelling, hot and painful. A big boom clanged through the cab, and she flinched as the truck rocked on its suspension. Dumont stepped back from Lou's door, a large, distended bulge on its inner panel where he'd kicked it.

Lou held up a hand in apology. 'Apologies, Boss. Won't happen again.'

'See that it doesn't.'

When Dumont turned away, Lou sent Lacey a sly grin.

Posy had finished opening the roller shutter. It took two attempts for Lou to shut his dented door, but when he had he started the engine. Lacey twisted in her seat as the truck pulled forward, watching as Alex moved further away from her. Dumont came to stand at her side, one hand lifting to rest on the woman's shoulder.

Lacey held on to Alex's eyes, wouldn't look away, right up until Lou drove the truck out into the sunlight and Alex disappeared from view, and even then Lacey continued to stare out of the rear window as the roller door clattered down in a fast, noisy descent.

It was the only thing you could do, Voice said. *At least one of you has a better chance of getting out of this alive now.*

'What about Alex's chances?' she whispered.

Voice didn't answer.

For once, Lacey didn't have anything to say, either. She twisted back around in her seat and stared unseeingly at the glove compartment.

It's not such bad odds. Two and a half survivors out of three.

It took her a second to catch up.

'Two and a half? What're you talking about?'

Lou took out a hand-held walkie-talkie and spoke into it. 'Heads up, Jacky. Boss wants to roll out in thirty minutes.' He leaned forward and looked up at the roof of a neighbouring building, and Lacey saw a man step to its edge. He waved down at them. The guy replied that he was on his way, his voice sounding tinny through the radio's small speaker. Because she was busy listening to all this, Lacey completely missed what Voice said.

'What?' she said, not caring that she was speaking aloud.

Two and a half out of three isn't so bad. You're *still kicking. And I'm pretty sure the Boy Scout is. And it's not like Alex is out of the picture yet, either. She's the half*, he added helpfully.

Lacey's heart reared up in her chest, punching her breastbone.

'Say that bit again. About the Boy Scout.' She was having difficulty catching her breath.

I saaaid, Voice repeated in an exaggerated way, *that the Boy Scout isn't entirely dead. At least, he wasn't the last time we saw him.*

THE PART
BETWEEN PARTS
The Man Who
Was Lazarus

CHAPTER 1

Pilgrim wished he were dead. If it would mean the abominable hacking pain in his head would disappear, then he would gladly offer himself up to whoever the hell was in charge of hell these days and dance a merry jig to gain their favour. Anything – *anything* – to make it stop.

He had been cold for a long time, but the cold meant nothing in comparison to the molten agony flowing up his neck into his skull. It was like someone had chopped his head clean off and replaced it with the searing ball of the sun. Although shivers racked his frame and made his teeth chatter, his head flared hot with rancid pain, throbbing in sync with his too-fast heartbeat.

At some point he had managed to roll on to his back, and then the second fiery sun in the sky jabbed hot pokers into his eyes.

He lay there for what felt like months with the pain, and when he finally did manage to lift one hand to probe at the back of his head, his fingers found a pulpy gouge behind his right ear. Bone shifted sickly underneath his gentle pressing, and pain exploded like a nebula. He flinched rigid and cried out, a high, piercing cry like that of a wounded animal. Then blessed darkness claimed him once more.

When he awoke, and found he still wasn't dead, he groaned miserably. The sound didn't last long, though, because his throat wasn't a throat any more – it was a long strip of broken glass. Swallowing was impossible and breathing was difficult. Air whistled down his windpipe.

He eventually became tired of the pain and the inability to breathe properly and his burning need for water. So he sat up.

He regretted it immediately. A stabbing sensation pierced his side, and he clamped a hand over his ribs. He dry-heaved, and that small, convulsive, peristaltic movement set his head to thumping in sickly waves. He waited and, when it passed, the pain became a fraction more tolerable.

He somehow found himself standing, weaving and blinking in the sun. He squinted at the wrecked car in front of him. Blinked again, because his left eye didn't seem to be focusing properly. His right eye was still good, and he used that to study the broken glass, the blood, the tyreless wheel rim. That should mean something to him, he knew, but his scrambled brain wouldn't let him grasp on to the what or the how or the why. And it hurt to think too hard, so he let it go. He stumbled over to the wheel tracks in the soft dirt at the edge of the road. Knew there had been a second vehicle here. That meant something, too.

He needed water. That was his first concern. Now that he was standing up, his wanting to die had shifted down the list a place or two. He gazed back towards town. It was within walking distance. He squinted far up the road, turned around and squinted the other way. The horizon greeted him in both directions with nothing moving between him and it.

He paused on his way back to the car and bent to collect something from the ground. He almost fell flat on his face when the world tilted like a carnival mirror around him. Straightening up carefully, he breathed slowly, letting the pain recede, rhythmically flexing his fingers around the rock he'd found. It was heavy, as big as a baby's head. A good size.

He brushed the glass off the driver's seat before getting in, placing the rock on the passenger seat beside him. Holding his left hand in front of his face, he noted the palsied tremor, the dried blood. He couldn't still his hand's trembling, so he lowered it again and began to search. He found a crumpled map in the footwell and, on the back seat, a dark red scarf with tassels. The slinky material slipped between his fingers, the tassels tickling. When he held it up, the red fabric was so thin he could see the road right through it. It turned the whole world blood-red. He fashioned it into a bandana and tied it over his head, not tightening it too much when the back of his skull protested. The map he folded and slid into a pocket. He checked his other pockets and found a scratched-up Zippo, which worked, a penknife and a roll of string. With nothing left to check, he passed his fingers over the ignition and was surprised to find the key there. Closing his eyes, he twisted the key and the engine fired to life on the first try.

'Potjack,' he muttered.

Turning the rattling car around, the wheel rim juddering and screeching along the asphalt, Pilgrim headed back into town.

He gripped the rock in his stronger right hand as he went from house to house. It wasn't much of a weapon, but it'd do its job if anyone chose to ambush him. Upon entering each house, he spent five minutes on the threshold, listening, not moving until he was satisfied his was the only presence. And even then he felt edgy, watched. He wasn't sure if this was a normal emotion for him, but either way he didn't like it.

In the third house he found an almost-empty bottle of bleach in the upstairs closet. In the fifth, he found water in the cistern in the en-suite bathroom. He added a few drops of the bleach to it and drank it all, the taste metallic and harsh. In the eighth house, he found a bottle of aspirin in a first-aid box hidden under a workbench in the garage, and filled an old saucepan with the remainder of the water in the hot-water tank. It almost filled the pan. He drank half in one go and chewed on four of the painkillers. He left the house.

Turning a street corner, he glimpsed a figure dart past on his left. Pilgrim's head snapped around, his arm coming up, brandishing the baby's-head-sized rock, ready to slam it down on his attacker. He immediately regretted the movement as pain engulfed his head and neck and shoulder. All that greeted him was a deserted street, some sad, droopy-looking trees and two rows of perfectly matching overgrown front yards. Groaning quietly, he lowered the rock, feeling awkward and foolish. More emotions that didn't sit well with him.

Weeds and vines spewed out of the sidewalk drains, leading down into the sewers, but, though technically alive, they and nothing else on the street moved. He briefly pressed his palm over his left eye. It felt hot and tender to the touch.

. He stood for a while, giving the figure a chance to reappear, and while he did more swirls of dark blood drifted past the damaged vision in his left eye. He sighed. He couldn't even trust his own eyesight any more.

He went back to his search. In five out of the next eight houses he found bodies. Thankfully, he hadn't needed to add to them by caving anyone's skull in. Many were strung up with makeshift nooses, two had self-inflicted gunshot wounds, a family of four was in a garage, slumped in the seats of their Nissan people carrier, a pipe running in from the silent car's exhaust to the back window. And the last body he found had, quite creatively, taped a plastic bag over its head. The bag had Mickey Mouse on the front, his black, circular ears perfectly covering the corpse's eyes.

For many people, their deaths had been a private affair, undertaken in the safe confines of their homes or in secluded spots. Those who acted on impulse, or lacked sufficient time to plan, had had no qualms about taking their lives, or anyone else's, in public.

As Pilgrim wandered from house to house, he didn't look too closely at the framed photographs of smiling family members on mantelpieces and side tables, didn't look at the stuffed toys arranged on the window seats in the pink- or yellow- or purple-painted bedrooms, or the empty cots with soft baby blankets lying disturbed and covered in dust. He didn't want to see the happy faces of the dead people whose homes he was ransacking.

He found himself standing on a front driveway, the half-filled saucepan held in front of him, not knowing how or when he had come outside. He was staring at a crack in the blacktop, a weed poking up like a frilly, green handkerchief. His eyes shifted to the pan he held. He frowned. He was missing something, and it took him a moment to realise he'd lost his rock somewhere. He quickly glanced around, checking for any more darting figures, but he remained alone. His worry abated a little. He tilted his head back to regard the endless blue sky. Everything was so quiet. Unnaturally so. It didn't feel right.

'Hello?' he said.

There was no reply.

His sense of disquietude was broken by a large, ear-popping yawn. Exhausted, he went inside and found his rock on the dining-room table where he now remembered leaving it. He lay down on the first couch he came across, placed the saucepan of water carefully beside him and fell asleep with the rock balanced on his stomach.

When he opened his eyes, it was still light outside and he knew where he had to go. He took three more aspirin, finished the water and was leaving the house when a soft creak came from upstairs, followed by the closing click of a door.

He stood for a moment, one foot in, one foot out of the house, and cocked his head to listen. There were no further sounds, and yet he knew someone was up there. Had been in the house the whole time, creeping around him while he slept. The thought should have troubled him, should have set off alarm bells, but it did neither of those things. Leaving the front door open, he retraced his steps to the foot of the stairs.

There was a strong pull on him to leave, to *move*, but something held him back. He set the rock on the second step and started climbing.

He didn't bother with three of the closed doors on the landing but went straight to the fourth. Gripping the handle in his weak left hand, he turned it and pushed.

The first thing he noticed was the body of a child on the bed. The arms and legs were stubby, disproportioned. Its mop of coarse hair spilled across the dusty pillow. No, not a body, but a child's life-size doll. It lay partially hidden beneath a pink bedspread.

The second thing he noticed was the boy huddled in the corner. The boy was very much alive. He stared at Pilgrim with big dark eyes.

The third and final thing Pilgrim noticed was the knife the boy held. It wasn't pointed at him threateningly but pressed to the boy's own wrist; it had cut into the skin. A thin dribble of blood wound its way under his forearm and dripped red dots on to the grey carpeting.

Pilgrim stayed in the doorway. He gazed at that thin line of blood and said, 'Thanatos.'

The boy frowned, a vulnerable quirk to his brow that spoke more of his uncertainty than of any fear.

Pilgrim frowned, too, not sure where the word had come from. 'Don't,' he told the boy. 'Don't do that.' It took a lot of concentration to get those three words out; it was like trying to speak around a mouthful of stones.

The boy's wrist was dented inward by how hard he was pressing. The knife trembled in his grip.

Pilgrim had to consciously move his tongue around his mouth to form syllables. 'What's your name?'

Slowly, from side to side, the boy's head shook.

'No names? OK. You . . . live here?'

Again, a shake of the head.

Pilgrim worked the mechanics of his mouth, forcing his jaw open and closed. 'Man of few words.' He nodded in understanding.

The boy's expressive eyes took on a curious cast. 'What has happened to you?' He had a strange, lilting way of speaking, almost musical, not native.

Pilgrim took a couple of careful steps into the room and crouched down, putting himself and the boy on the same level. He stayed near the foot of the bed, leaving a good six feet between them, and used the bedstead to lean against. He was grateful for the support. 'I lost something . . . important. Now I need to find it again.' Pilgrim waved a hand next to his head, frustrated at the damned obstructions inside it. 'I'm having trouble . . . finding my words today.'

'Where did you last see it?'

Pilgrim flicked a look at the knife. Detected a slight lessening in the pressure of the blade. 'I think at the—' He struggled with the word, couldn't find it, said instead: 'the building with books'.

'The library?'

'Yes. The library.'

'You should go back. See if it is still there.'

Pilgrim nodded. 'That was the plan.'

The boy regarded him earnestly. 'You know the thing you have lost?'

He hadn't, but as soon as the question was asked the answer was waiting for him. 'A girl.'

'She is related to you?'

'No. Just a girl.'

'But she needs you?'

'Yes.' Pilgrim asked a question of his own. 'How old are you?'

'I am thirteen. How old are you?'

Pilgrim cracked a smile. 'Too old to remember.'

A small smile visited the corners of the boy's mouth, then solemnness stole over his face again. He lifted the knife's tip from his wrist. 'Sometimes . . . sometimes it is good to talk to another person. It can be lonely.'

Pilgrim nodded. 'It can. But sometimes it can also be peaceful.'

'Yes. Sometimes.'

Pilgrim glanced down at the knife, which the boy now held loosely in his lap. 'You have parents?' he asked cautiously. 'Family?'

'Yes. They are dead.'

The way he said it held such finality.

'You're here alone, then?' Pilgrim glanced around the bedroom, although he already knew it was empty except for him, the boy and the limp-limbed doll on the bed.

'Not fully alone, no,' the boy replied, and Pilgrim sharply returned his attention to him, but the boy only added: 'I am here, speaking with you.'

Pilgrim made a soft noise of agreement but remained unsure as to whether the boy had meant something more. A snake of suspicion curled restlessly inside him, and he was at a loss to explain why.

The boy nodded to him, a formal bob of his head. 'I will be OK. Thank you. See?' He waggled the knife and placed it beside him on the carpet, that wisp of a smile coming and going again. 'No more bad thoughts.'

Pilgrim was unconvinced. The boy had appeared to be on the brink of slitting his wrists when he first entered the room. It felt wrong to leave him in this empty house with the bodies of so many old suicides littered around, all reminders that maybe escaping into death was better than the existence in which they currently lived.

Pilgrim felt that tugging sensation again, that urge to move riding his limbs, nudging at him to stand and go back downstairs and out into the daylight. *Too much time is passing*, that tugging said. *More time than you have.*

He held out his empty hand to the boy. 'Would you come with me? At least as far as the' – he grasped hold of the word before it could slide away from him again – 'the library.'

The boy's dark eyes dropped to his open hand, then lifted to his face. There was a trace of something sparkling in their brown depths.

'Hari,' the boy said quietly.

Pilgrim frowned. 'Hari?'

'Yes. Hari. That is my name.'

CHAPTER 2

Pilgrim drove the juddering car to the library, his teeth gritted against the squeal of the metal rim against asphalt, the sound driving jagged pieces of glass into his head. On each street, he inspected every house – the eyes of their windows, the mouths of their doorways, the fabric of their exteriors – in search of any recent signs of activity. He might as well have been searching for life on Mars. The town appeared completely abandoned except for him and the boy, but there had to be people somewhere. This town was the perfect size: not big enough to warrant undesirables travelling here to scavenge but sizeable enough to offer decent comforts and amenities. Yet, there were no signs of life.

Between Pilgrim's increasingly perturbed sweeps, his eyes drifted over to his passenger.

Hari sat beside him, his arms wrapped around the hemp satchel in his lap, gazing silently out of the passenger window. Before leaving the bedroom, the knife had disappeared inside the bag and the boy had taken out two rice cakes, giving one to him. Pilgrim had eaten it ravenously while the boy watched wide-eyed. Hari had then offered him the other half of his own rice cake, and Pilgrim had eaten that, too.

'Were you heading somewhere?' Pilgrim asked, his question pulling the boy's attention away from a yard they were passing, a rusted mower sitting in the middle of a tangle of grass.

Hari nodded, a single bob of his head, as if this were his default affirmative setting. 'There is a place. By the sea.'

Pilgrim remained quiet, waiting the boy out, and after a few more seconds Hari said, 'It is a secret place. An Inn. Hidden away.'

'And you've been there before, to this . . . Inn?' The more Pilgrim talked, the easier the words came, his lips and the muscle of his tongue no longer resisting his every attempt to wrestle them into line.

The boy looked thoughtful. 'No. But I have read about it.'

Pilgrim took a left turn, using his right hand to do most of the steering. His body automatically guided the car, and Pilgrim let it, trusting his instincts. He made another alert study of the street as they came on to it. The library parking lot was coming up on their right.

'And you trust whoever wrote about it?' he asked, glancing over at the boy.

'Yes.' The boy rubbed his fingertips over his lips, glancing at Pilgrim from the corner of his eye as if afraid to make direct eye contact. 'I was also told about the red skies. Do you know of them?'

Pilgrim's heart flipped in his chest – only a small blip – as if his body knew *exactly* what the boy spoke of but his brain was unwilling to make the connection. A second contraction lanced through the back of his head as if warning him against asking questions. He winced through the pain. 'No. I don't think so. What are they?'

'It is said that, if you see them, then you will not easily forget.'

Pilgrim had forgotten many things, but who was he to argue? He wanted to tell the boy he was being too cryptic, but his tongue rebelled at the word and outright refused to shape it. Instead, he said, 'You're not being very clear, Hari.' He swung into a parking space in front of the library's main entrance and stopped. The clunking engine fell silent.

'Many things are unclear to me also,' the boy said quietly, his expression serious. 'But there is no place here for me. So I will go there, and see what I find.'

Pilgrim sat for a long moment, staring out of the windshield at the open entranceway to the library, watching in fascination as a faint, fuzzy ring of blackness pulsed around the doorway. It throbbed in sync with his pains, his left eye narrowing as it intensified in bursts. His wrists rested casually over the steering wheel, though he felt anything but casual. He could feel the boy's eyes on him. What was he to do with him? He had nothing to offer, no food, no protection; only a ride.

'Hari, I think it will be dangerous where I'm going. I'll take you as far as I can, but that's all I can offer.'

A nod. 'This girl you are looking for?'

Hari's expressive eyes were so darkly reflective that Pilgrim could see a shiny version of himself staring back at him, distorted, larger than life. It was disconcerting, having Hari's eyes swallow him up so completely.

'This girl is very lucky to have a friend such as you.'

Entering the library, Pilgrim left Hari in the foyer and headed downstairs, flipping his Zippo open on the way and thumbing it alight. With the trembling flame guiding him, he found the dead man.

Everything was floating back up, appearing slowly through the murky waters of his mind. Upon seeing the dead man, Pilgrim remembered the papier-mâché spider and how the man had kicked it into the alcove room. Raising his head and squinting closed his blurred left eye, Pilgrim looked towards the dark opening to the room hiding under the stairs. The room pulled at him like a physical hand tugging on his shirt.

Crossing the threshold, his gaze fell on the beanbag. There was a depression in it and a picture book lay open on the floor. He knelt beside the chair and, spying an accumulation of wax congealed on a shelf just above it, sat his burning Zippo in the spot. He rested his palm on the seat of the beanbag, the material coarse to the touch, the impression of a person still indented into the polystyrene balls. The woman had sat here. He could see her in the wavering light of the flame, her dark blonde hair, her bruised face and her mostly-shadowed eyes; eyes that seemed to watch him, probing at his soul as if trying to pick it apart.

What was her name?

He knew it. He *knew* he knew it.

But it wouldn't come.

Frustrated, he held on to his sore ribs with one hand and swivelled around and sat in the chair, the soft rustle of the polystyrene a strangely furtive noise.

That's when he saw the tree. It grew tall in the corner of the room, cloaked in shadows. The hidden birds in the branches watched him with black eyes. Its colours were concealed by the darkness, and yet he knew the leaves were a diaphanous tissue green and the bark was painted an abrasive brown. He could feel the roughness of it under his palm.

The tip of his tongue touched the edges of his front teeth. Retreated again. Crept back to feel out a shape. An L.

'Lacey,' he whispered.

And another name. Almost the same shape on his tongue.

Alex.

'Yes. Alex.'

He felt a hot splash on his hand but, when he looked down, the only blood there was streaked and dried a crusty brown. He heard the gunshot, felt the percussive gust of hot air in his hair, but the burst of pain never came; his head only throbbed with a liquid thickness, irritating the backs of his eyes. The tree before him seemed to pulse and ripple, a static white light flashing around its edges.

He closed his eyes and breathed deeply through his nose, waiting for the sensation to pass. When he felt steadier, he climbed out of the beanbag chair and left the room. He went to the dead man and checked his pockets, found a tin of self-rolled cigarettes, a box of matches, a battered wallet that held nothing but two creased photographs (both of a pretty brunette who smiled timidly at the camera) and a handwritten letter, the ink so fuzzy and indistinct that Pilgrim had difficulty reading it. He set the wallet and its contents aside. Under the man's leg cuff, he found a sheath strapped to his calf with a bowie knife inside. Pilgrim took it and strapped it to his own leg.

With nothing left to pilfer, Pilgrim climbed out of the children's library.

Hari was gone when he stepped into the bright, open space of the library foyer. Pilgrim unfolded the map from the car and laid it out flat on the floor. He found the road he had been travelling on when he'd met the girl, could easily trace the path they had taken, but he couldn't read the names of the towns and cities in between – the words wriggled like tiny black maggots and the more he tried to focus on them the more they writhed. He cupped a hand over his left eye and used his good one to read, but it was no use. He folded the map back up and sat for a while in the slanting sun that shone in from the doorless entryway, waiting for Hari to show up. The library doorway framed the car and the parking lot, the cloudless, blue sky above it and his dusty boots in isolation. It would have made a perfect portrait of his life: there wasn't much to see.

He sat there for too long, the world too quiet around him. Finally, he stood painfully and went outside.

'Did you find anything?' The boy was sitting on the wall beside the doorway, his feet dangling a full ten inches above the ground.

'Yes,' Pilgrim said. 'But dead men tell no tales.'

Hari frowned gravely at that.

Pilgrim became aware of a strange humming beneath his feet, a faint buzzing in his soles and ankle bones. 'You feel that?' he asked.

'The vibration? Yes. There are generators running beneath the town. They must have electricity down there.'

'"They"?' Pilgrim studied the boy, from his dark hair right down to his battered, dangling tennis shoes.

'Yes. The people here are not welcoming to strangers, though. Not even to a lone boy.'

With a cupped hand, Pilgrim shaded his sensitive eyes and examined the surrounding buildings, but there was nothing to see that hadn't already been seen. Perhaps his eyesight hadn't failed him earlier, after all, when that darting figure had vanished so quickly from sight.

'They're very good at hiding,' Pilgrim commented, impressed by their ingenuity. No wonder he hadn't spotted any signs of life above ground. If you wanted the amenities of a town but didn't want to be discovered by passers-by, then going underground made perfect sense.

'Yes. But then, so are many people. They must have heard the tales. It has made them extra wary.'

'Tales?'

'Of a man. Who takes people from their homes. He comes for those who hear beyond what you or I can hear. And he ties them up into sacks and carries them away in the night. You have not heard this tale?' Hari asked, his head tipped to one side.

'I . . . No, I don't think so.' But that wasn't entirely true, was it? Hari's tale touched on something familiar, like a bedtime story once told to him long time ago by his mother.

'It is said he is travelling the world to find his people. And when he is finished, the red skies will come.'

The nearest sewer grate, thirty yards away across the parking lot, was set flush to the street, the kerb cut out to accommodate a cast-iron storm drain. Hidden in the darkness, anyone could be staring straight back at him, even a man who stalked the night looking for his people.

'Where did you hear these tales?' he murmured.

The boy shrugged unhelpfully. 'All over.' He hopped down from the wall. 'Where must we go now?' he asked.

It took some effort for Pilgrim to drag his eyes away from the inky depths of that storm drain and all the things it might hide: real and imaginary men alike. There was one more item on his shopping list before they could leave, and it didn't involve crawling down into the sewers to find it.

He found it on his way out of town. Between the twinges in his side and the feebleness of his left hand (and his wary monitoring of the nearby sewer grates), it took him thirty minutes to change the ruined wheel rim on the car and replace it with a half-deflated wheel he took from an abandoned Datsun. He lost count of the times the tyre iron clanged to the ground. Each time, Hari wordlessly picked it up and handed it back to him.

When Pilgrim finished, he celebrated by lighting one of the dead man's rolled-up cigarettes, slowly sucking on it until the stub singed his fingers. He offered one to the boy, but Hari only smiled shyly and shook his head.

On his way to the driver's door, Pilgrim gave the new wheel a kick. It wouldn't hold up for long, but it would do for a while. A direction was set in his head. East. In the absence of having anywhere else to go, he knew he must head east. The same direction as the sea and the boy's secret place.

Another word rang in his head. 'Ruby'. This one he didn't understand. However, it felt significant somehow, so he said it a few times to himself while he drove, interspersing it with the names Lacey and Alex until it began to sound like a mantra. Lacey, Alex, Ruby. Lacey, Alex, Ruby. Sometimes he would mix it up and say Alex, Ruby, Lacey, or Ruby, Lacey, Alex. His tongue tangled over the names many times.

Suddenly, he said, 'Defend her.' He didn't know what that meant, either.

He received a few odd looks from Hari while he talked aloud to himself, but the boy remained silent, maybe understanding that Pilgrim was working through his churned-up thoughts and memories and that asking any questions might distract him from them.

As Pilgrim hit the highway, he glanced west, maybe out of habit – checking both lanes for traffic – or maybe it was something more. Whatever the reason, in the distance, and rapidly growing smaller, he spotted a vehicle driving away from him. It was too far to see what kind of car it was, or anything else in detail.

'Another car,' Hari whispered. The boy turned to look at him questioningly.

Pilgrim frowned and momentarily wondered about the vehicle, but he knew it wasn't the direction they wanted, that he'd been that way before and that there was nothing back there waiting for him. He took the turn eastward.

Stop.

It was his own voice he heard in his head. It was strangely flat, as if the sound had been deadened by padded walls. Still, it had an authority to it.

Stop the car.

Pilgrim pulled up. After a moment, he swivelled in his seat and looked back through the rear window. He frowned into the distance, but there was nothing there, only a long, open road. Whatever vehicle had been back there was long gone.

'Ruby,' he said. Then: 'Lacey.'

'Which is the girl you are looking for?' Hari asked, eyeing him curiously.

'Lacey,' he replied.

Pilgrim lit another cigarette and left it hanging at the corner of his mouth, the smoke trickling up into his bad eye. Still, he continued to stare.

'Shit,' he said, and sighed through his nose, two plumes of smoke jetting out.

He spun the wheel and turned the car around, facing back the way he had come. He looked at Hari.

'This is the end of the road?' the boy said.

Pilgrim sucked on the cigarette and blew out another long, smoke-filled sigh. Through his missing window, he flicked ash on to the road. 'I'm sorry. It's much sooner than I expected.'

'That's all right. Sometimes we must trust ourselves, yes? Sometimes we must go back so that we may go forward.' The boy held out his right hand, and Pilgrim half smiled, clamped the cigarette between his lips again and reached out to grip it. It felt slight in his hold, but Hari gave his hand a firm up–down pump.

'You'll be OK?' Pilgrim asked.

'Of course! I wish you the very of best luck,' the boy said, in his lilting, musical accent.

'You, too, Hari. Maybe I'll see you down the road a ways.'

The boy smiled down at his hemp satchel. 'Maybe,' he said shyly. He climbed out and shut the door with a gentle, considerate *clunk*. Then he stood back to give the car plenty of room to pull away.

Pilgrim watched in the rear-view mirror as the thin figure of the boy shrank smaller and smaller. It took six full seconds for the clouds of dust to obscure Hari and turn him ghostly and insubstantial. As if he'd never been there at all.

CHAPTER 3

Lacey was in pain. A constant ache in her back and hips and the outsides of her arms that fused her muscles together in an acid-drenched mass. She'd spent so much time holding her limbs against her body, away from the men to either side of her, that the strain had taken its toll. All she wanted to do was relax in her seat. But she wouldn't. Not while she could withstand the pain.

Occasionally, the truck's wheels ran over something in the road that caused the vehicle to sway, rocking Lacey from side to side, nudging her up against either Lou or Rink. She'd jerk away as if burned, holding herself stiff and separate from them.

You're stubborn as a mule.

The pain made it hard to focus her thoughts, but talking to Voice was a distraction, ineffective though it was.

– I don't care. I'm not touching them.

You won't catch cooties and die.

– I'm. Not. Touching. Them.

Fine, but you're not the only one who has to live with the discomfort, you know.

– Tell me again about the Boy Scout.

Voice sighed, a whistling that tickled the inside of her ear. *I told you three times already. The last time I saw him, he was still alive. Which was the last time* you *saw him, back at the roadside.*

– But that was then. We left him bleeding with a gunshot wound to the head. Anything could have happened since then.

The awful twangy music on the truck's stereo ended, and

Rink leaned forward to fiddle with the controls. Lacey shifted away from him when his arm brushed her shoulder. The music had been another thing she had been trying to drown out. All they seemed to sing about was love, loneliness and home-sickness. It reminded her that, with every song played, the distance she had covered on her way to Vicksburg was slowly being cancelled out. Her sister and niece were like stars in the night sky, shining strongly above the horizon, but no matter how hard or fast she ran towards them, they stayed agonisingly out of reach.

Rink removed the ejected CD. 'What should I put on now, Lou?'

'Don't care. Just don't crank it up too loud.'

Rink opened the glove compartment and went fishing in the crap in there, coming out with another disc. He slid it in, and after a few seconds of ticking silence, the opening of some guitar-heavy rock song came on. She wished it was a Beatles CD.

Lacey glanced out of the windows, but nothing had changed; it was the same old deserty expanse of land, broken up by random scenic turn-offs which seemed only to want to draw tourists' attention to even *more* unchanging desert scenery.

'You better be right about this, girl,' Lou mumbled through his beard.

'I am,' she said shortly.

'You fooled the Boss, but you don't fool me any. You're a wily one.'

She didn't reply.

'Better watch your step.'

A minimum of words had passed between the three of them since they had started out, but now he wanted to chat? Fine. She'd chat. 'Where was everyone headed to when we left?' The walkie-talkie had fallen silent after leaving the city, and no useful information had been relayed before Lou had clipped it to his belt, where it had been ever since.

Rink began to answer, but Lou spoke over him. 'That's on a need-to-know basis. And you don't need to know.'

Rink laughed. 'It's class-*y*-fied.' He began tapping his fingers on the dash, using it like a drum kit. His tempo was all off.

Another annoyance.

'Is Red classified, too?' Lacey asked. 'I mean, Dumont sure is expending a lot of manpower getting her back.' The way Lou looked at her made her think that maybe chatting wasn't one of her brighter ideas. 'It's inconveniencing you guys, though, right? Wouldn't you rather be back with everyone else than stuck out here with me?'

'Keep talking, missy,' Lou told her quietly, 'and you'll wish you weren't stuck out here with us neither.'

'It's 'cause Red's different,' Rink said. 'She's worth any ten of us. And that's not just Dumont talking. If we don't find her, we're all up shit creek. We want her back just as much as he does.'

'Enough!' Lou snapped gruffly. 'Listen to your damn music and keep your yaps shut. Both of you.'

Chat time hadn't lasted very long. Lacey sighed and folded her arms across her chest, attempting to ease some of the ache in them. It helped. For maybe a minute. She decided to try meditation and closed her eyes. That lasted for maybe two.

– I wish Red hadn't, you know, crashed and stuff. I would've liked to talk to her properly.

Me, too. She sounds very intriguing.

– I wonder what they mean by all this 'she's different' stuff.

I wonder, too. I doubt these boys will tell us.

Lacey unfolded her arms and reached under her collar. The St Christopher was warm, like it always was. She rubbed the design, picturing it in her mind: the child, the staff, the curving waves of the water St Christopher waded through. There must be a Bible story behind it, but she didn't know what it was.

Maybe the child was Jesus, and St Christopher had only one leg – hence the staff – and he was hobbling his way through the water because baby Jesus couldn't swim and he wanted to get back to his donkey on the other side.

There's no donkey in the original Bible story. Sorry to disappoint.

She refolded her arms and crossed her legs at the ankle. Much better.

– How long have you been around for, Voice?

What do you mean?

– How long have you been here? As in *existed*?

Memories are funny things. They're not entirely reliable. I think I've been around a while, but I'm not sure I perceive time the same as you do.

Lacey felt a shiver of apprehension. Had he been hiding in her all that time and she'd never known?

No. Not with you.

– With who?

Doesn't really matter. I'm here now.

– It matters to *me*. What if you were in someone horrible? That's gotta rub off at some point. Transference, and all that.

It wasn't anyone horrible. Cantankerous, maybe, but not horrible. You have to understand: this shouldn't have happened. Voices don't leap from person to person. It's not possible.

– It must be. You did it.

Yes, but I don't know how. And it's important you don't tell anyone it's happened, either.

– Why not?

She could feel Voice's frustration percolating, close to boiling over.

Because I said so. Please, just take my word for it. Right now, we have more pressing matters to discuss.

– What's to discuss? I'm blocked in on both sides. I guess I could try and grab the wheel and yank it, but I'm not wearing a safety belt. If we crash, I'll get flung out through the windshield.

Are you even really a he? I think of you as a he now, but you never actually said.

He ignored her question. *So you've been looking for ways out. That's good. What else have you noticed?*

– I'll tell you what I've noticed if you answer me one question.

Voice's frustration bubbled for a few seconds longer, but then it simmered down. *Fine. Deal.*

– Why are you here? In me, I mean. And why now?

Technically, that's two questions. But fine, I'll answer. I'm in you because I had a split second to make a choice, and it was between you or someone who was stupid. It wasn't a hard decision. And it's happened now for the same reason you're stuck in this truck heading back the way you've come and away from your sister. Circumstances and events don't always play out like we expect them to. We can't always control what happens.

He had answered and yet not answered. Not really. She formed more questions in her mind but, before she could direct them inward, he said, *We had a deal, Lacey. You've obviously been taught the importance of keeping your word. Now honour our agreement.*

She huffed a long sigh and answered.

– Lou's got his gun down the side of the door nearest him. Way out of my reach. And Rink has his tucked in the side of his belt. I could make a grab for it but, chances are, I won't get very far. And if I did somehow get it, knowing my luck, it'll go off and punch a hole clean through me.

OK. So we wait.

– Yeah, guess so.

On the stereo, the rock song crescendoed in a barrage of manic drumming and wailing guitars. Rink attempted to keep up on the dash with his finger-drumsticks. Lacey's concentration wavered until the song ended and a new one with a quieter melody came on.

– Going back to the whole 'why the hell are you here?'

thing. Does that mean you know where you came from? Like, originally?

It was Voice's turn to sigh. She had to rub the tickle of it away from the back of her ear. *Why are you so interested in this?*

– *Why?* Because you're taking up space in my head, that's why. Why *wouldn't* I be interested?

You don't even know what happened seven years ago.

– You're right, I don't. My grammy either didn't understand what happened or lied to me about it. And no one seems to want to talk about it much.

Because most people are still scared. They talk around the subject because they don't understand it. They think, if they ignore us, we'll go away.

– Us? You mean you? The voices?

Yes. Voices helped kill a lot of people.

– But how?

How would you kill someone if you were in their head?

Lacey thought about it and then shrugged.

– I'd just tell them to, I guess.

Exactly. They got told to do it, although not in the way you're thinking. It was much more insidious than that. Think about it: we know so many of your weaknesses. They're all right here inside your heads. You hide them from the world, even from yourselves, but you can't hide them from us. It probably took nothing at all to pull up those thoughts of inadequacy and failure and worthlessness and power them into self-destructive acts.

– How, though? Like, give me an example or something.

Of course, you want an example. Fine. OK. So there's a guy called Ted, right? Ted's married with three kids. He works for a big law firm in LA, and was put in charge of this high-profile case between some A-list actor and a male escort who claimed he had – well, it doesn't matter what he claimed. Ted lost the case over some stupid bit of evidence he'd overlooked. Cost the company bundles of money, damaged their reputation; it was a sorry situation all round. Ted got spectacularly canned for it. But still, every morning, he kisses his wife goodbye, leaves for work and comes home ten hours later to eat dinner with his family. Except Ted isn't going to work, he's going to a casino, playing craps and poker and blackjack, trying to win enough money so he won't have to tell his wife he's lost his job. Worse still, while researching the A-lister vs Escort Boy case he found out a dark little secret about himself, one that's been whispering to him from the shadows ever since, and he finds himself on the same streets the male escort worked on, handing over what little cash he has left to some sixteen-year-old boy who'll get on his knees in front of Ted's zipper in some seedy alleyway, because Ted can't afford a motel room and can't bring himself to do it in the family car.

Lacey listened with growing unease, wanting to tell Voice to stop, to quit, she'd heard enough, but somehow she wasn't able to utter a word.

So when that small voice starts to whisper to Ted that he should kill himself, it's not yelling, 'Kill yourself, faggot!' it's telling him he's a truly awful husband and father. Just terrible. Imagine what will happen when they find out what disgusting things he's been doing in all those alleys, and they will find out. It's just a matter of time. Imagine the shame. They'd be better off without him. He knows that, right? At least they'd have the insurance money. At least you can give them that, Ted. Oh wait, you have horrible debts now, too, don't you? What a pathetic waste of space you are. You know what would be best? To take your family with you — that way they won't have to suffer the humiliation of all the things you've done. Won't have to be homeless on the street when the house is taken away and your bank accounts closed. You don't want to die alone, either, do you? You want your family with you. Wouldn't that solve everything? Wouldn't that be just perfect? What are you waiting for, Ted? You failed at everything in your life, even at being a man, but you can make up for it now. Do something right for the first time in your miserable life. Go ahead, it'll all be OK. You can do it.

Lacey was silent. She didn't even feel the cramped pain in her cricked neck and sore shoulders any more.

Two days of a voice whispering that into his ear and Ted is sitting on his bed, sobbing as he loads his shotgun, waiting for his eldest to come home from school.

– Jesus–

Everyone has triggers, Lacey. And I imagine they only increased tenfold when the deaths started, because everyone could see how easy it was. They could see a way out. *Sometimes, I think everyone wants an excuse to jump ship and let everything go. It'd be so easy, wouldn't it? To give up. All this struggle and strife – gone. You could finally rest and stop worrying. All you'd need is a little push.*

Something clutched inside Lacey, a lump of despair, black and malignant, pressing up against the hollow of her throat, and her mind finally unlocked and she was able to say:

– Stop. Please stop.

I'm sorry. But you see how simple it must've been?

– Yes . . . Did . . . did you kill Ted?

No! Of course not! Ted isn't real. Well, someone like Ted was real, but I never knew him. Anyway, I wouldn't do that. I'm not like the others who did those things. They're different to me. I've been here much longer, with someone who accepted me . . . Well, mostly accepted me. Kind of.

– But why? Why did all that happen?

Now, that's the million-dollar question, isn't it?

– You don't know?

Instead of answering, Voice said, *Hey, I think we're stopping.*

A second later, Lou hit the brakes.

CHAPTER 4

Keeping the car at a steady fifty, the wind whistling through the shattered windows, it took the better part of thirty minutes before Pilgrim caught sight of the vehicle. He didn't try to catch it up but sat back and kept his distance. His thoughts remained with the boy standing alone at the roadside, one thin arm raised in farewell. Claws of guilt gripped at him. It was an unusual feeling, almost like hunger, scratching at him from the inside. Also like hunger, the feeling, he found, could be put aside when necessary.

The world was all sky, the road he and the unknown car travelled on merely the smallest belt of land, insignificant and unchanging in comparison to the infinity of the skies reigning above. It was awash with a watercolour of neon pinks, tangerines and indigos, its never-ending palette altering with every passing mile.

Red sky at night, shepherd's delight.

He couldn't recall the second part of that idiom, but he assumed it didn't end well.

Every now and then, he would glance down at the fuel gauge but, generally, he didn't look away from the car in front. It was a mere speck on the horizon, but there was little else to distract him – not a road-side lemonade stand in sight – so he didn't worry about losing track of it. The longer he drove, the longer he spent thinking, and the longer he spent thinking, the more he probed at the chasm of space at the back of his head. Something about following the car nudged at him, a finger poking at his broken brain, encouraging him to remember.

Poke.

Poke.

Poke.

The sky above him lightened, the dusk rolling rapidly in reverse, clouds dispersing as if by magic to reveal a perfect, steam-rollered blue sky. A heady smell of hops caught in his nostrils. A black cat stared at him from the roadside. As if framed in place, the whole image began to jitter, shaking so fast the animal blurred at the edges and three identical black cats superimposed themselves over the first: one sitting, one standing, one doing neither of those things. And then the shuddering stopped and the cat was strolling away from him, tail lifted high in a question mark. There was another shaking jitter and the walking cat became a sitting cat, lazily licking itself in a strip of sunlight on the top step of a wooden porch. The scene jittered again: the cat was standing. It juddered until it blurred: now sitting. Standing, sitting, standing, then licking its paw, the cat flicked from one to the next at incredible speed until one cat became all cats in all positions at all times. And then it stopped. And the black cat was lying on its side. Silent. Motionless. No more jittering or shuddering or blurring. Its ribcage was crushed, stomped flat beneath someone's boot, and this final image seemed to hold great meaning for Pilgrim: the cat, who was free to stand or sit or do whatever the hell its tiny heart desired, would always end up like this; stamped on by something bigger and more powerful than itself.

With a thunderous rushing, the clouds blew back in over Pilgrim's head, but now they were blood-red, dark and bloated and filling up the sky. They began to jitter and shake, just like the cat had, dark veins of dangerous light flickering from inside, except they weren't clouds any more but vast, pulsing organs, purple and angry, and readying to explode.

And then they did, fire bursting from the sky in all directions.

A sky of flames roared down on the Earth, a flash flood of immense heat and shrieking red.

Pilgrim gasped and blinked and was back in the car. It had drifted, the wheels rumbling off the edge of the road, skirting into the dirt. He pulled the car back on to smooth blacktop, and released his death-grip on the steering wheel. The real sky had turned to dusk. In the rear-view mirror, a few stars scattered over the darkening horizon.

Pilgrim passed a shaking hand over his face. For the first time in a long while, he was entirely alone with his thoughts, and he wished to God he weren't. When he had awoken at the roadside, back when he had wished for death, the silence had confused him. But as his most recent memories came back to him, in disjointed images and tattered flashes of sound or sensation or smell, each one hit and knitted together and jarred something else loose. Something that was achingly absent.

'Voice?'

There was no reply.

He answered himself in a whisper. 'He's not here.'

Pilgrim's fingers crept to the back of the scarf, where his hair was stiff with blood. He didn't touch the wound again, remembering the weird sponginess of the bone back there. It made his stomach twitch uncomfortably just thinking about it.

Of course, he had known Voice was gone. There had been something intrinsically missing since he'd woken up at the side of the road with the appalling pain in his head. The world was too quiet. There had been no annoying commentaries or unwanted advice. The distraction of meeting the boy, of having him to talk to, had hidden Voice's absence, but now the emptiness resounded. He was surprised by how much the realisation that Voice had disappeared angered him.

Had the head wound killed Voice? Previous trauma to the head had resulted in Voice falling quiet for a time, but never for long. Maybe he had retreated to a locked part of Pilgrim's mind from which he was unable to break free, and was forever trapped? Was there someplace voices went, dispersing into the ether like sparks flying from a dying fire and fading into the dark? Or had Voice simply ceased to exist, the electricity that had sparked his existence sputtering in a last effort to survive before finally fizzling out?

All Pilgrim knew was that his mind felt like a church, hauntingly empty, with every pew sitting unoccupied and the cold marble tombs lying silent and still underfoot. His thoughts echoed, solitary and alone.

Dead or gone, it amounted to the same thing. Pilgrim was Voiceless. He suspected that his anger disguised a far deeper feeling of loss, but there was a dark wonder, too. He hadn't known voices *could* be lost.

The car ahead stopped.

Pilgrim pulled over, staying a fair distance away, and had to really squint to be able to make out two people climbing out of what he now saw was a pickup truck and cross to the other side of the road to look at something. The sun was setting, but the day's residual heat had baked into the road and a heat haze shimmered up from its surface, obscuring the truck and its two occupants behind an undulating, underwater-like wall. It wasn't until one of them went back to lower the truck's rear panel that Pilgrim realised what was happening.

They had pulled out a long, thin plank and were pushing his motorcycle into the truck bed. The bike had run out of fuel, but Pilgrim had left the key in the ignition, and it was in good running order. It was ripe for the picking.

His hands tightened around the steering wheel, his left noticeably weaker. He flexed the fingers of that hand while he waited for the truck to pull back on to the road. He knew where their next stop would be, but he was done with following like some lost lamb. He floored the gas pedal, and the car jumped forward. He was taking a calculated risk, but all he had was a knife, and they would both be armed.

'Lacey,' he said.

He came up fast, the engine revving worryingly high, the wind howling like a lost soul, shivering through the car. A high-pitched squeal came from somewhere under his feet.

The two men must now be aware of his presence, but the truck stayed glued to its lane, its speed barely changing. This suited Pilgrim. He wasn't ready for a confrontation. Not yet. From rear bumper to front bumper, they were no more than twenty yards apart. Pilgrim could see the man in the passenger seat twisting around to look at him through the rear window.

Pilgrim had the peculiar urge to lift his hand and wave, but he didn't, he veered the car left into the outside lane and started to overtake. The engine screamed. The wind noise rose in an angry whine, vibrating through the chassis. As the nose of the car grew level with the truck's front door, Pilgrim glimpsed the bearded profile of the driver. He was older, grey-streaked, with a crooked beak of a nose. Pilgrim didn't know him. As the two vehicles came level, he lost view of the higher truck's cab. Then he was past, and still accelerating. Pilgrim veered back into the right-hand lane and watched the truck in his rear-view mirror. The two men were talking animatedly to each other, but that wasn't what caught Pilgrim's attention: the girl who was sitting between them did. She stared back at him, looking like she'd seen a ghost.

A ghost, he thought and smiled. He felt like a ghost, hollow and vague and not really there.

Maintaining his faster speed, Pilgrim left them in his dust, hoping they wouldn't deviate from their mission and deem him worthy of chasing down. He kept one eye on the truck and another on the road ahead, but they didn't grow in his mirror and, in ten minutes, as the truck grew steadily smaller, he finally lost sight of them.

An hour later, the barn came into view. It sat like a tornado survivor on the horizon, its roof caved in, panels missing from its sides. Pilgrim spotted the black rubber strips in the road where the girl's car had lost control before flipping, and he had a superstitious moment when he didn't want his own wheels to pass over them, but by the time the thought had come and gone, his tyres had passed over the marks without incident.

He didn't expect the body to be there – would have thought animals or human scavengers had dragged it away by now – but she still lay where he had left her. She was on her back, her eyes closed, arms by her sides as if she were taking a nap. He stopped the car, got out and stood over her, his shadow falling across her face. She was smaller than he remembered, somehow younger, like a little lost girl, which he supposed she was. He felt drawn nearer, gazing so intently at her face that he could see every pore, the cracks in her lips, could count every one of her eyelashes. He saw her alive, tall for her age, and too thin – she bowed in the middle as if her bones were hollow and the weight of her head too much, because there was a lot going on up top, Pilgrim knew: there were so many thoughts and designs that they flashed out of her like shooting stars in a firework display, bursting above her head and lighting her up in a multitude of colours – blue and green and purple and—

'Ruby,' he murmured, and the sound pulled him out of her, brought him back to himself, and all he saw was a colourless girl, dead on the ground. A girl he'd met before, when her smile was wholly beautiful and her eyes glimmered with intelligence. He didn't know how, or when, but he had known her. Ruby. How else could he know her smile? He didn't have the imagination, nor his damaged mind the capability, to conjure up images he hadn't before seen. At least, he didn't think so. He longed to ask Voice – he had access to what was left of Pilgrim's memories, defective though they were, and even some Pilgrim wished were gone – but now that he was willing to accept his help, Voice wasn't there to offer it. Not any more.

Pilgrim glanced up the road, but there was no sign of the truck yet. It wouldn't stay that way for long. He carefully, even tenderly, picked the girl up, ignoring the sharp, piercing stab in his ribs. A smell came with her, a whiff of decomposition, but it wasn't offensive, and again Pilgrim was struck by how unaffected her body was after having been left outside for so long. He found it equally as strange as her body having been undisturbed by animals, but there was no time to ponder further on it. She lay unnaturally stiff in his arms, as if she had been frozen in place, and yet she was warm to the touch. It unsettled Pilgrim to feel her so warm, but he knew it was just a surface temperature, the body having been stretched out in the sun all day. He placed her in the trunk.

He came back and made a few marks in the dirt around where she had lain, crawling and shuffling tracks that headed in the direction of the barn, and then he got behind the wheel and drove up to the front of the barn, backing the car quickly inside and closing the big double doors.

Through a missing slat in the barn wall, Pilgrim watched the truck approach through the heat haze and pull to a stop behind the overturned car. The two men climbed out and stubbed around in the dirt, talked some, even poked inside the upside-down car. Eventually, they looked up at the barn. The hunched man nodded at something the older man said and started up the track, kicking at a brick every now and then on his way. He had a hitch to his gait to match his lopsidedness, as if one leg were shorter than the other. He carried a rifle similar to Lacey's.

'Maybe it *is* Lacey's,' he said to himself – or maybe he only thought it. He wasn't sure any more. He felt unbalanced and incomplete without Voice. Some might even say crazy.

Pilgrim backed away from his spyhole, retreating to the rear of the barn and quietly crouching behind a stall wall. He slid his stolen knife from its sheath at his ankle and pressed his face to the scratchy wood, his good eye finding a second knothole to spy through.

The hunched man heaved open the barn door and came in rifle first. Seeing the car, he swung the gun back and forth, thrusting it into every corner.

'You'd best come out,' the hunched man called into the dust motes, the dying sun's rays slanting through the barn in golden beams, hazy around their edges, spotlighting the floor in a patchy pattern.

Pilgrim watched the man slouch forward and touch the car's hood. It would be warm, he knew. He also knew when the man noticed the lifted trunk lid because his head came up and he glanced about himself as if expecting someone to be sneaking up on him. The man cautiously stepped around the open driver's door, shoving his gun inside as he checked it was clear, then shuffled to the rear of the car and looked in the trunk. The man straightened up – as much as his hunched back would allow – and Pilgrim felt the waves of astonishment coming off him as he gazed down at the dead girl. Pilgrim was already moving, even as the man's eyes fell on the body, even as the man gasped quietly. By then, Pilgrim was close enough to hear the breathed word that came out of him.

'*Red.*'

Pilgrim stepped up behind the hunched man and brought the point of his blade up under the man's chin, pricking into the soft, vulnerable skin there. Pilgrim felt him stiffen.

'Don't speak,' Pilgrim whispered. 'Pass the rifle back with your left hand. Nice and slow.'

The man didn't move, so Pilgrim pricked him hard enough to draw blood.

'*Now.*'

The man slowly offered the gun and, without removing the

blade from his throat, Pilgrim accepted it. He almost dropped the thing, the gun too heavy to hold in his left hand. He rested the rifle's stock on the ground.

Something's wrong with you. It was the same voice he'd heard before, the one that had told him to stop the car. It sounded like him but it held an authority, a self-awareness, that made Pilgrim pause.

'Nothing's wrong,' Pilgrim replied.

That bullet must've caused brain damage.

'No more brain damage than usual.'

'It's not me you're talking to, is it?' The man's voice trembled; Pilgrim could feel it vibrate through the blade he held at his throat.

Pilgrim's lip twitched at the irony. In the absence of Voice he was answering his own thoughts. Old habits die hard, it seemed. 'Yes, I'm talking to you,' he told the man. 'We're going to move to the barn door. And when we get there you're going to call to your . . .' He stopped, unable to think of the word he wanted. '. . . to that other guy waiting out there, and tell him you found her and that he's to come take a look.'

'Did you kill her?'

Say yes.

'No. Now move.' Pilgrim stepped back and swung the rifle up, shoving the muzzle between the man's shoulder blades. With the gun, he guided his captive around the car and to the front of the barn, where he jabbed him hard again. 'Open the door wide enough so he can see you, but not all the way.'

Crouching again and staying out of sight, Pilgrim leaned after the man as the door creaked open. Pilgrim pulled the gun up against his shoulder, grabbed the back of the man's belt so he couldn't run off and slid the knife up between his legs, letting the point prick the guy's balls.

The man gasped. 'W—wait! I'm like you! I . . . hear a voice. I'm sure I do.'

'Goody for you. Now, just as I told you now. Unless you want me to make you a soprano.'

'You could join us!' the man rushed out. 'If you hear, the Boss'll take you in. No questions asked.'

'That's nice, but I don't play well with others. Now *call*.' To speed things along, Pilgrim pricked his balls again, harder.

'*Lou!*' the man yelled, his voice coming out high, as if the castration had already been performed.

Pilgrim couldn't see anything, crouched down behind the door as he was, but he imagined the older man turning to look towards the barn. 'That's a good boy,' he murmured. 'Keep going.'

'Lou, I found her! She's here! Come take a look!'

Pilgrim tugged him back inside before he could reveal anything else, pulling on his belt and making him walk backwards. He slid the knife away, picking up the rifle with his good right hand and standing up. Safely away from the door, Pilgrim dragged the guy around to face him, swinging the heavy stock of the gun in the opposite direction, letting both meet in the middle. They connected with a loud *thonk*, as though Pilgrim had whacked a coconut instead of a human head. The man's eyes rolled up, and he dropped to the floor. But he wasn't out. He moaned feebly.

Hit him again, he was told.

Pilgrim lifted the gun straight up and, as if he were digging a grave with a shovel, chopped the stock down on the man's head.

The moaning cut off.

The pickup truck was approaching, the noise of its engine getting louder. Pilgrim grabbed the man's feet and dragged him out of the way of the barn's doors. Taking the rifle with him, he went back to the barn door, spying through a hole as the truck's engine cut off and the grey-bearded man (*Lou*, his voice supplied for him) jumped down from the cab. He looked older, but he moved with a sinuous ease that belied his age. Pilgrim checked the rifle, making sure there was an unfired cartridge in the breach. He slid the bolt home.

Pilgrim breathed heavily. Sweat trickled out from under the scarf wrapped around his forehead and dripped from his jaw. He felt light-headed and floaty, and he had to place his feet carefully, each step feeling like it was falling through the ground, an unexpected drop that made his stomach lurch.

Keep it together, old man. Almost done.

When he looked again, Lou had dragged the girl out of the truck and was holding on to her wrist. In his right hand, he held a sawn-off shotgun.

He'll cut you in half with that, that small voice warned.

'Only if he fires it,' Pilgrim said.

Pilgrim didn't look too closely at the girl. He didn't dare. He had to focus.

Lou was holding the gun casually down by the side of his leg.

Taking a deep breath, steadying his heart rate, needing to still the shaking in his limbs, Pilgrim kicked the door open, the stock of the rifle locked in good and tight against his shoulder, but already his left arm was trembling too much, the barrel stuttering as he sighted down it at the grey-haired man. Pilgrim didn't shout, didn't tell the man to lay his weapon down, but squeezed off a shot and felt straight away that his weak hand had failed him, the barrel kicking up too far, the bullet flying high.

Lou had released the girl and was lifting the shotgun even as Pilgrim slid another cartridge into the rifle's breach. Before he could fire it, both shotgun barrels burst with flame and Lou's gun *boomed*.

PART THREE

The Girl Who Was Found
and
The Man Who Was Lost

CHAPTER 1

'What's he doing now?' Lou said as the beige car accelerated to pull level with them.

Lacey leaned forward, but all she could see was its roof and a very small part of the empty passenger seat. The colour was very familiar, though, and her heart contracted, then swelled to twice its size before expelling all its blood back into her system. Her head throbbed.

'Oh my God,' she whispered.

Be careful, Voice told her. *Hope can be dangerous.*

She knew that; she didn't need to be told.

The car pulled in front of them and drifted back into their lane. It was Alex's car, Lacey knew it. It *had* to be. She still couldn't fully see the driver, could only make out the vague shape of him sitting in the driver's seat, but whoever it was, he was tall.

'Shouldn't we go after him?' Rink said.

Lou didn't answer. He was hunched over the steering wheel, eyes fixed on the rear of the car. For a dreadful moment, Lacey thought he would say yes, but he slowly eased back in the seat, his tension uncoiling.

He shook his head. 'No. We stick to the plan. We find the girl and get back.'

'But he might have stuff we need,' Rink said.

'Unless he's got the keys to the world's biggest hoard of fresh food and canned goods, I don't give a flying fuck what stuff he might or might not have.'

'I just mean maybe we should—'

'I said *no*.'

They had only detoured from their plan once, when they'd spotted the Boy Scout's bike and decided to stop and bring it along. She was thankful for its presence and found herself turning around to glance at it every now and then. It made her think of the miles she had spent sitting on the back of it, holding on to the waist of the strangely reserved man, when she'd still thought it would be an easy task to travel the seven hundred miles from the west side of Texas all the way to Mississippi and her sister's home. She had been an idiot. She knew nothing of the world, and the world knew nothing of her. And now she understood with a painful clarity that her ignorance had brought a whole mess of trouble and suffering down on those she cared most about.

Voice started to sing.

Woes are found and evil's sown in a troubled town.
It's easy to cry there, easy to run, and even more easy to say that
*   you're done.*
In a troubled town, where all looks grey, night follows night and never
*   follows day.*

The rest faded into the background as Lacey's thoughts shifted away from Voice. She had never felt so far away from anything and everybody she knew. She watched the back of that beige car dwindle into the distance and cursed herself for being a sucker who was so quick to hope. How could he know she would be heading back this way? He *couldn't*, that was how. It would be impossible for him to know.

Voice stopped singing and said, *And yet, when you have discarded all impossibilities, however improbable the answer you are left with is, it must be the truth.*

– It could just be another man who'd found Alex's car, and

took it. Just like these jackasses have taken the motorbike they happened to find.

That's . . . probably a more likely answer.

Lacey sighed and Voice went back to singing. A different song this time. The lyrics were haunting and, as Lacey listened, tears filled her eyes and melded the road and sky into one.

Lazarus rises, Lazarus falls, Lazarus listens whenever he's called,
He has no coffin, no dirt, no door,
Only two boots and the sand on the floor.
He may be dead, but he's not yet done,
He's risen again with the dawning sun.

'You're the most depressing thing in all the world,' Lacey said.

Lou looked at her, but she didn't turn her head and continued to stare out through the windshield. Thankfully, he kept his silence, and it stayed that way until Lacey lifted her hand and pointed out the barn.

'There,' she said.

'I see it,' Lou mumbled.

'See the overturned car, too? That's hers.'

'You never said she'd gone and wrecked the car.' Lou began to slow the truck, glancing over his shoulder as he cut across the left-hand lane, the wheels juddering and crunching over the gravel at the side of the road. He stopped ten yards away from the upside-down rear bumper.

His sins are forgiven, and he's arisen, Voice sang. *Long live the prince of bedlam.*

'Shut *up*,' Lacey said impatiently.

Lou turned to her, his dead eyes staring.

He's like a snake, she thought. And no amount of anti-venom would prevent his poison from spreading. His bite would be deadly.

'Time for you to talk, you sneak-mouthed brat.' The words drawled out of Lou's old-man mouth. 'You've dragged us all the way out here, so now you tell us where the fuck she is.'

'She was right there the last time I saw her.' Lacey pointed at the empty patch of glass-flecked ground next to the missing side window. 'I swear. She was lying there, all her teeth pulled out of her head. It was horrible. Who would *do* that to her?'

Lou and Rink shared a look. Lou jerked his head at the younger man. 'Let's take a look. You,' he told her, 'don't move an inch. You move it, I slice it off.'

They both climbed out, taking their guns with them, but Lacey didn't look away from the keys Lou had left in the ignition. Before he closed the door, Lou leaned back in, plucked the keys out and pocketed them, giving them a pat through the front of his jeans.

'You won't be needin' them any time soon.' He gave her a mean little smile.

'Shithead,' she muttered as soon as he'd shut the dented door – it took him three attempts to get it to catch.

She watched as they poked around in the wreckage. She could see the long scuff marks in the dirt where a coyote had probably dragged Red away. It made her feel sick, thinking of how it must have torn at her with its teeth and claws. She swallowed thickly, averting her eyes from the darkened dirt where the girl had bled.

> *The sun boils down and the bugs alight.*
> *They nibble and chew in feastly delight.*
> *Nothing is left but skin and bone;*
> *When all life's gone, the creepy-crawlies roam—*

'God, what is it with song time all of a sudden?' she said angrily. 'Give it a rest already.'

He paid her no mind.

Bite and suck, drain us all dry.
Snacking on us till we've all gone and died.

Lacey began humming loudly to herself to drown him out.
Voice stopped singing. *What's that?*

'You're not the only one who can sing, you know.'
But what is it? I like it.

'"Dear Prudence." By the Beatles. Have you heard of them?'
. . . No.

She continued humming her second-favourite Beatles tune
while Voice listened, and watched the two men talk, their
mouths moving with no audible sound coming out. 'We should
have buried her,' Lacey said.

Dirt's too hard. And what would you have dug the grave with?
Spoons?

'It would've made them work for their prize at least.'

Rink set off up the track towards the barn, the toes of his
right boot turned inwards slightly, as if God hadn't screwed
his leg on properly. What with his stoop-backed posture, Lacey
suddenly felt sorry for him. Maybe he hadn't wanted to join
Dumont and his gang but it was the only way he could survive in
a world where hunchbacked, gimpy men mostly ended up dead.

I love how your brain works.

Lacey paid no attention to Voice and slid over the seat to
move behind the wheel. She cranked down the window, feeling
a breath of warm air brush over her sweaty brow. She stared at
the barn. The wooden outbuilding looked imposing somehow,
even with its roof caved in and gaps in its sidings. Lacey couldn't
remember the name of it, but there was a human condition that
caused people to see faces in everyday items. Grammy had told
her about it once, about how someone thought they'd seen the
face of Jesus in a grilled cheese sandwich (someone else believed
it, too, because they bought it for $28,000), and how car
designers used it to design the nose of vehicles, knowing they

had to make their sports cars look aggressive, with angry eyes (headlights) and mouths (grilles), to appeal to male buyers. Now she could see the face in the barn's fascia: its huge mouth of double doors waiting to eat anyone foolish enough to come too close, and the two smaller hatches on its second level – once used to store hay in the loft space – wooden eyes that watched its prey approach.

Rink reached the door and pulled it open, and the barn readied itself to eat.

'If we don't find the girl, you don't get to go nowhere.'

Lacey stared at the dirt track leading up to the barn, studying the wheel ruts in it, not looking at Lou as he leaned up against the truck's fender next to the driver's door.

'In fact, if we don't find her, I'm sure the Boss won't mind if me 'n' Rink punish you for all your black-tongued lying.'

'Just try it, and you'll end up like Jeb.'

Lou moved faster than she thought possible, his hand a striking viper, fingers gripping her lower face, painfully digging her cheeks into her teeth.

'You and your sassy mouth,' he whispered, breath hot and rank in her face. 'Is it even you doing all the talking? I bet it isn't. I bet it's some black-tongued thing hiding behind those pretty peepers, telling you what to say.'

Lacey couldn't help her eyes from widening a little.

'Don't you get how this all works yet?' he said. 'We do whatever we want with little pieces of ass like you, don't matter what you got hiding inside. We fuck you till you're dry and eat the rest. Roast you up while you're still alive so we can hear you scream as your juices cook.' He squeezed her face tighter, his fingernails gouging into her skin. 'You're nothing but a walking meat puppet to me.'

She didn't breathe, didn't move. Surely he was just trying to scare her. They wouldn't really do those things to her. Maybe to Princess, but not to her.

Voice didn't answer, but she felt that his silence revealed more than it hid.

'*Lou!*'

Lou's fingers released her, and Lacey immediately scooted away from the window and out of his reach. She rubbed at her stinging face. She could feel dents where his fingernails had dug into her skin.

'Lou, I found her! She's here! Come take a look!'

Lacey didn't take her eyes off Lou as he climbed in, but slid her butt all the way back over the seat to press up against the passenger door, as far away from him as she could get. Lou didn't spare her a glance. He drove them up the track, cut the engine and snaked a hand around her wrist. She whimpered as he pulled her out of the truck after him. She tried to wrench her arm away, but all he did was yank on her harder. She cried out, almost twisting on to her knees to ease the cruel pressure on her creaking wrist.

Pilgrim, Voice whispered. Lacey thought she heard astonishment in his tone, but her head was a pressure cooker filled with her gasping breaths so she couldn't be sure.

The barn's mouth opened and a tall, scarlet-headed man came out, rifle pointed at them. It went off, and Lacey ducked instinctively, surprised when Lou released her wrist. She fell into his legs and wrapped her arms around his knees, dragging him off balance. The *boom* of the shotgun slapped her ears, knocking her deaf. The rifle fired again, the shot muffled in the ringing in her head. Half tangled in Lou's legs, Lacey heard a funny, smacking thud and felt the man jerk. Then he was falling, his knee clipping her chin, her teeth nipping the edge of her tongue. Tears flooded her eyes. When she swallowed, she tasted blood.

Lou's shotgun landed a few feet away.

Lou landed on his back.

She scrabbled away from him, going for the gun, fumbling it into her hold and pumping another round into the chamber, spinning to face the man who was dealing out all the death. She froze, breathing hard through her mouth.

The Boy Scout stared back at her.

Pilgrim, Voice breathed, and this time there was no mistaking his wonder.

CHAPTER 2

*B*OOOOM!

The dirt in front of Pilgrim's boots burst in a spray of grit, pellet-like bits pelting his legs, but this time his left hand was locked steady around the stock – he wouldn't miss twice.

Pilgrim had watched the girl fall into the man's legs, sending him stumbling, and realised it was the only thing that had saved his life, the shotgun's buckshot hitting the ground in front of him. Pilgrim squeezed off his second shot, and this time it flew straight and true, the bullet smacking the older man on the right side of his chest, shoving him sideways and back, the shotgun flying out of his hands. He dropped, sprawling on his back, Lacey landing in an untidy heap at the man's feet.

Pilgrim chambered a third cartridge, still moving forward, surprised by how quickly the girl scurried to the side and snatched up the shotgun, spinning to face and point it at him.

'Pilgrim?' she said.

He was surprised – but then she'd always had the power to surprise him – but he had no time for it now and skirted around her and leaned over the downed man, giving him a prod in the chest with the rifle's barrel. Blood was blooming in a large circle on the right side of his shirt, spreading rapidly like an ink spill. His breathing came fast and choppy.

'I think you killed him,' Lacey said. She spat blood on to the floor.

Pilgrim nodded, inclined to agree with her, watching the

man's chest stutter erratically. He lowered the gun. His left hand was trembling badly now.

'You're wearing my scarf.'

He lifted his shaking fingers, brushing them over his brow, having forgotten all about the scarf he'd tied around his head. He tried for a shrug and felt his right shoulder hop up and down. 'It's a good colour. Suits my complexion.'

'Hm, yeah. I hate to tell you this, but your complexion is looking pretty crappy.'

For the first time, he looked at her – *properly* looked at her – and there were colours shooting off her like little sparking embers. They crackled around her head and shoulders and arms, much like the tree down in the children's library had crackled with energy, except this was a fiery red. It worried him, those sparks – they seemed angry, as if they were trying to convey something and he was being too dense to understand.

He forced a smile. 'Probably because I got shot in the head.'

She got to her feet, swatting dust off her clothes as she did, and came right up to him, tipping her head back so she could meet his eyes. Holding on to the shotgun, she reached up with her free hand and rested her palm along his cheek. It was warm and dry and softer than he'd expected. His left hand twitched, an involuntary spasm, as if it wanted to lift and hold her palm to his face. He clenched it into a fist until the impulse passed.

'The white of your eye is all bloody.'

Dizziness swept over him, and he closed his eyes. The world spun around him, and he stood at its dark epicentre, imagining invisible roots sprouting up around his boots and winding around his calves, tethering him fast to the rotating Earth. He waited for the spinning to stop.

Lacey's hand disappeared from his cheek, and he opened his eyes to find her staring strangely at him, her head shaking slowly. The red sparks had stopped jumping off her body. He was glad.

You're dehydrated.

Was that his own thought? It had sounded like his own. Even though it had come out of nowhere. Maybe he *was* dehydrated.

'How are you even here?' she said, so quietly he had to strain to hear her.

'Magic,' he said, and saw surprise flash across her face. He licked at his dry, cracked lips. 'Do you have any water?'

Her expression opened up again. 'God, sorry. Yes. In the truck. Wait here, I'll go get it.' She hurried away from him.

Pilgrim glanced back down at the dying man at his feet, but dying had turned into dead. The man's face was slack, his mouth agape, the soft muscle of his tongue a pale slug lying within. The blood was already drying in the sun to a hard carapace, moulding to his unmoving chest.

Pilgrim felt nothing. The man had undoubtedly been the protagonist of his own story, the centre of his small universe, and everyone around him bit players, but now his life story had reached its violent denouement. Pilgrim wondered if the guy had ever seen it playing it out this way. Probably not. Men like him always thought they would live for ever, preying on those weaker than them, taking everything they wanted and giving nothing back. Maybe he had been the main guy in his story, the one man who ruled his world, but to Pilgrim he was just another dead man in a long line of dead men. Still he felt nothing.

Pilgrim traipsed over to the barn, wanting to be back in the shade, the sinking sun burning into the nape of his neck.

'There's a little food, too!' Lacey called from inside the truck.

Pilgrim rested his back against the warm wood and slid down into a seated position, resting the rifle crossways over his lap.

The girl jumped down from the cab and came to him, holding a large bottle of water and what looked like two soup cans.

'Peaches,' she said, smiling.

He must have looked blank, because she shook the can at

him, its contents sloshing. 'Canned peaches. It's like nectar, I swear.'

His stomach clutched painfully, its emptiness almost caving in on itself. She passed him the water first and sat down cross-legged, angled at ninety degrees to him.

He sipped the water, not wanting to overfill his belly, and passed it back to her, exchanging it for the peaches. He felt her watching him as he struggled to hold the can in his left hand and open it with his right.

'Want me to do it?'

He passed it wordlessly back and stared at the track, looked up and down the road, too, but they were all alone, could be the only two people left alive in the world right then, for all he knew. It was a pleasant feeling, just to sit and let his weary bones rest, to think he had reached an ending – just him and the girl and the empty world. The sky was turning crimson in the west, a hidden cauldron sending streaks up into the sky, a great big furnace pumping out heat beyond the horizon.

'It's nice here,' he said.

'Huh?' Lacey glanced up, almost finished levering the lid off. She looked around, not appearing to see any of the beauty he did. 'I guess so. Where did you put the girl?'

It took him a moment to grasp who she was talking about. 'She's in the—' Again the word escaped him, so he said: 'In the space at back of the car.'

He accepted the can from her, careful not to spill any of the juice. The sweet scent of the peaches reached his nose and saliva flooded his mouth, quickly followed by a wave of nausea.

Lacey was staring at him again.

'You put her in the *trunk*?'

Pilgrim took a sip of the juice. It was very sweet, and very good. After the first rebellious spasm of his stomach it settled down, and he drank half the can.

'What about Rink? Where's he?'

He had a segment of soft, tender fruit in his mouth and couldn't answer.

'The stooped, gimpy guy,' she said. 'The one who went in there looking for her.' Lacey nodded at the barn.

'He's sleeping.' Pilgrim popped two segments of peach into his mouth and chewed slowly, rapturously, savouring the delicate, slippery texture on his tongue, the burst of flavour.

'We need to talk to him. He needs to tell us where Alex is.'

Pilgrim stopped chewing and swallowed. Watching her from the corner of his good eye, he licked each of his fingers and tilted the can up to his mouth, drinking down the last two fingers of juice.

Lacey carried on talking. 'They were packing up to leave when I left. Planning on heading somewhere new. Lou and Rink wouldn't tell me where. We can't leave her.'

Pilgrim said nothing.

There's that sneaky 'we', his own voice whispered, wanting to add its thoughts to the conversation. *If it's not 'we', it's 'us'. We're being set up as a family unit.*

'How many were there?' he asked, trying to appear non-committal while his aching brain turned over, the broken cogs squealing as they *click-clack*ed into rickety motion.

'Many what?'

'People.'

'Oh. Not so many. Like, maybe thirty or so.'

'Did any of them—' He struggled to think of the word. 'Did any seem to be there . . . against their will?'

She looked at him closely for a moment. 'You don't just mean me and Alex.'

'No. Was there anyone else?' The gimpy-footed man had said the Boss would welcome Pilgrim, no questions asked. And Hari had told him about the man who came at night to steal people. People who 'hear beyond what you or I can'. Bedtime

281

ghost stories didn't scare Pilgrim, but all of this was starting to make a disturbing amount of sense.

Lacey chewed on the inside of her cheek, her gaze drifting away from him and along the dirt track. 'I saw four others tied up,' she said, returning her gaze to him. 'Just as I was about to leave. And there were others who called out to me while I was locked in the freezer. They might've been the same people, though.'

'But that was all you saw? Just four?'

'There was a handful of people who were kind of out of it. Like, muttering to themselves, staring.' The girl shrugged. 'Out of it. They weren't tied up or anything, though.'

'Women? Men?'

'Both.'

He was quiet a moment as he rubbed the length of his finger around the inside circumference of the can, sucking the last bit of juice from it. 'Interesting,' he said quietly.

'What's interesting?'

'That they're keeping people prisoner.'

'I guess so.'

'And Alex is normal.'

She squinted at him. 'Normal?'

Did she realise she was repeating everything he said? 'Right. She doesn't hear a voice.'

The girl blanched and blinked. 'Oh. Right.'

'I heard a story about a man taking people. People who hear voices.'

'Like the story Alex told us?'

Pilgrim must have looked baffled, because she took pity on him and explained. 'She said she'd heard about this Pied Piper guy. He'd sneak into places when everyone was asleep and whisper in folks' ears – ones who heard stuff, anyway – and then take them away. He'd burn up everyone else. You don't remember?'

Was that why Hari's story had seemed so familiar? Alex had already told it to him? 'People with voices, that's what she said?'

The girl nodded and fell silent, looking down at the bottle of water in her lap. She unscrewed the cap, lifted it with both hands and took a few of sips. The bottle shook in her hands.

'"Let us go then, you and I,/ When the evening is spread out against the sky/ Like a patient etherised upon a table."'

Her eyes swivelled back to him. She lowered the bottle.

'It's a poem,' he told her. 'From a book. You remember those things I showed you? Books?'

Her lip curled in a half-hearted smirk. 'I remember. Is there more of it?'

He nodded.

'Will you tell me?'

He stared out at the road, considering, not answering straight away. He cleared his throat. '"Do I dare to eat a peach?"' He tipped up the can and gazed into its empty bottom. '"I shall wear white flannel trousers, and walk upon the beach./ I have heard the mermaids singing, each to each./ I do not think that they will sing to me."'

She seemed to wait for him to carry on. When he didn't, she said, 'Is that how it ends? It's sad.'

'No. There's a little more.' He glanced at her, resting the can on his thigh, and when she met his eyes, her own wide and expectant, he finished the poem for her. '"We have lingered in the chambers of the sea/ By sea-girls wreathed with seaweed red and brown/ Till human voices wake us, and we drown."'

She was looking at him as though she had never seen him before, as if he had unexpectedly sprung his own magical merman tail, its scales all shiny and blue. It seemed he could surprise her, too, on occasion.

'It's beautiful,' she said.

'Bleak but beautiful,' he agreed.

'What's it called?'

'You know, I don't remember.'

A smile spread across her face. It was lovely. And, this time, Voice wasn't around to warn him against its pull.

'You remember a whole chunk but you can't remember the title. That's funny.' She reached around her back and brought out something flat and rectangular. She held it out to him.

Surprised, he took the book from her and rubbed his thumb over the title, the white letters jumbled and wriggling around, no matter how many times he smoothed them over. He felt an almost-unbearable sense of loss.

'You've been reading it?' he asked.

'A little.'

He passed it back to her, and she accepted it slowly. 'You keep it,' he told her. 'It needs newer eyes than mine.'

Shifting the empty peach can from his leg, he placed it upside down against the barn wall and started to get up. It was a long and painful process. Lacey jumped to her feet and hovered near to him, as if to catch him in case he toppled over.

Once up, he took a moment to catch his breath. He knew the girl was worried – it was in every line of her face, in the darkened cast of her watchful eyes – but she didn't ask if he needed help, for which he was grateful.

'Come on. Let's go see if Goldilocks is awake.'

He wasn't. He was still out cold.

Pilgrim tied Rink's hands and ankles and then forced himself to go back outside. It wouldn't be wise to keep a fresh corpse so close to their camp. The smell of blood would draw animals.

They hadn't come for the dead girl.

He couldn't explain that. It was an anomaly. But he didn't think it would happen twice. So he dragged the body to the truck, and Lacey helped him lift it into the back. He drove to the road and went a half-mile up the highway before dumping the body in the brush. When he came back he parked the truck inside the barn, out of sight.

Exhausted, Pilgrim sat while the girl collected wood for the fire. Desert nights became cold very quickly once the sun had set. She chattered away as she worked, telling him everything that had happened since he had been left for dead. They used the makings of the old campfire, setting up in the same place they had before, but Pilgrim felt the wrongness of the scene, and Lacey quietened in her chattering once the fire was lit. There were three people here once again, but they weren't the *right* three. Alex was missing.

Pilgrim attempted to wake the man a few times, but there was no response.

I hit him too hard, he thought to himself.

He'd been unsure of the strength in his left hand so had struck the man with extra force to make sure it was an incapacitating blow. Now he was concerned he had hit hard enough to crack his skull.

Head injuries can be troublesome, said that new little voice.

Pilgrim breathed a laugh. 'They sure can.'

As he came back to sit by the fire, he saw that Lacey had the book open and was reading. He sat down quietly, not wanting to disturb her, but she looked up at him anyway and closed the paperback.

'Words are important, aren't they?' she said.

He tried to settle himself comfortably, but he quickly came to realise it was a futile task, so he became still and looked over at her. She was waiting for his answer, such a look of earnestness on her face that he was momentarily discomfited by it. The firelight flicked over her skin, shadows coming and going on the contours of her face, but her eyes remained bright.

Because she had asked with such seriousness, he considered his answer carefully before giving it. 'Words *should* be important. They're all we have now. They're who we are.'

She nodded and seemed satisfied with his answer. She stared into the fire for a while, thinking, and eventually looked back up. There was a timidity in the way she regarded him that he hadn't seen from her before.

'Your family,' she said. 'What happened to them?'

He returned her stare. He could tell his gaze made her uncomfortable. It wasn't his intention to make her fidget, but her question had thrown him.

'There are things I don't like to remember,' he said. This wasn't the whole truth; there were many things he *couldn't* remember. Not fully. He was well practised in casting them over that white cliff and down into the deep, dark fathoms of the ocean. What remained of his memories was patchy, or lost completely. More still had vanished with the shot he'd taken to his head. There were parts to him he could no longer even remember forgetting.

Lacey said, 'I get that. But you don't forget your family.'

'No,' he agreed, 'you don't completely forget them. But you bury them. In more ways than one.'

She frowned, unhappy with *this* answer.

He gave her what he could. 'I had a sister. She was younger than me.' And he made the effort to picture her, sitting next to him on the floor, both of them so close to the TV set their heads were tilted back at the exact same angle. Her hair fell in ringlets, soft curls that bounced when she giggled; her giggle was like feathers on his soul, tickling out a smile even when he was in the foulest of moods. The colourful cartoon played out in front of their eyes – the shocking racing-car reds, the vivid ocean blues, the fuzzy tactile brown of the teddy bear the little cartoon girl reached for and hugged tight to her chest – while the washing machine rumbled quietly in the background, their mother busy doing the laundry.

'What happened to her?'

For once, he disregarded the warning bells set off by his

instinct for self-preservation and consciously cast his memory back, reaching down into that inky pit at the rear of his mind, but not far (it hurt his head to delve *too* far). He came up blank. It should have concerned him, his lack of recall, but instead he was relieved. 'I don't remember.'

'How can you not remember your sister?'

'Practice.'

'That's sad. Does that mean you'll forget me, too, some day?'

'Memories last for as long as they need to. Then they pass on, like everything does. That's the way it should be.'

Her frown became exasperated. 'That's not a proper answer.'

He half smiled, and even that small movement hurt. 'Yes it is.'

'I won't ever forget my sister.'

'Because you feel you still need her,' he said quietly.

'I'll always need my family.' The girl seemed angry with the direction the conversation had taken, and she went back to fire-gazing, her expression stony.

Pilgrim closed his eyes, the canvas of his eyelids painted red with the backdrop of flames. He didn't know how long he sat like that before the girl's voice came again.

'What do we do if we can't wake him?'

It was a struggle to open his eyes. 'If he's not awake by morning——' He left the rest unsaid.

'We can't leave her,' she told him. 'Alex, I mean. You didn't see what Dumont did to her. He was——' Pilgrim watched the shadows on her throat move as she swallowed. 'He *likes* hurting people.'

There was a tight band around his head, and it pulsed in tandem with his heart. His head hurt, but it was a dull ache, a constant pressure on the backs of his eyes and in his temples, a swollen throbbing behind his ear.

'I don't think the walkie-talkie will work unless we're close to them. All the transmissions quit after we got out of town.'

The radio sat by her side, switched off for now to conserve its battery. She had rushed back outside after they'd checked on Rink, dropping to her knees beside the dead man and shoving at his shoulder, rolling him far enough to unclip the hand-held radio from his belt. It had been undamaged in the dead man's fall, which was uncharacteristically lucky. Their luck hadn't amounted to much so far.

Unable to abide the pressure any more, Pilgrim pushed the scarf up off his brow and removed it. His neck felt like a twig trying to hold up a boulder.

'You need to rest,' Lacey said.

It was becoming hard to focus. Sitting beyond the fire, Lacey was a reddish blur in his failing sight, flames spitting and sparking all around her. It scared him to see her like that, burning, sitting in silence while she was steadily consumed.

He shifted to lie down and must have made a noise because, the next thing he knew, Lacey was beside him, her arm encircling his shoulders, supporting his weight as he lowered himself to his side. She had found a blanket from somewhere, and he felt it settle over him, warm and oddly protective, like armour. Or perhaps it was the girl. For the first time in a great many moons, he didn't worry about going to sleep unguarded.

He heard her whisper to him as he closed his eyes, her words sinking into his head like blocks of carved wood, lodging behind his throbbing eyes and in the base of his skull, engraving themselves into the bone back there.

'You remember what you said to me, at the motel that first night?' she whispered. 'Right after you saved me. You said those people were a bad sort, but not everyone I meet would be like them. That I should try to remember there are good people in the world. Do you remember saying that?'

He murmured something, maybe an affirmative to her question, maybe just a meaningless sound; it didn't matter. The girl continued her whispering.

'It's like, for Alex, all she's ever had are the bad sort. People hurting her, taking away the ones she loves, treating her like she's nothing. But she's not nothing to me. Just like you're not. She's as much my family as my sister and my niece. Do you understand?'

Her lips were almost touching the shell of his ear, the words burning gently now, a warm, scarring brand.

'Do you understand?' she whispered again. 'She's my family, and I'm not ever going to forget her.'

CHAPTER 3

Lacey didn't sleep. She sat next to the Boy Scout, one hand resting on his booted foot, and stared into the fire. Occasionally, she added wood to the dying flames. Her eyes were dry as tinder, as if every last tear had been wrung out of her and all that was left were hard gristle and dry resolve.

She looked at him every now and then while he slept. He looked peaceful, the strong line of his body relaxed. It was only when he was awake and in his movements that she saw how he hurt, how he held his body in a stiff, precise way, saw how his left eye squinted slightly when he regarded her, its sclera stained almost entirely red. It made his eye look alien, the iris a dark island surrounded by a sea of blood. She had noticed the trembling in his left hand as he tried to open the peaches but now, as he rested, the trembling ceased. Asleep, he looked whole again.

Maybe he *is* magic, she thought.

Maybe we all are, Voice said.

'Most people would be dead if they got shot in the head,' she said.

I suspect the bullet ricocheted off his skull. It's a dense one.

'You know him.' It wasn't a question. 'You called him Pilgrim.'

It'd be best if you didn't call him that.

'Why not?'

Because he wouldn't like how you'd come to know it.

'What does that mean?'

But Voice didn't answer. His words, like a song, had reached their end, the needle on the record sailing over a sea of crackling silence. Lacey knew the needle would reset itself and start anew at some point, but not until Voice was ready.

She wanted to get up and check on Rink, wanted to go collect the book she had left on the other side of the fire, but she didn't want to break her connection to the Boy Scout. Her hand on his boot. His boot under her hand. He had found her, she didn't know how, and deliberately hadn't asked, and now she felt that, if she let go, something terrible would happen. She realised she was being ridiculous, but that didn't change how she felt. In the end, she compromised. Thirty seconds. That was how long she'd give herself. Thirty seconds to get up, get the book, check Rink and come back again. That was a safe amount of time.

Still, she hesitated.

'Quit being stupid,' she told herself.

She released the Boy Scout's boot, stood up and started the count – one thousand, two thousand, three thousand – and went to Rink first, bent over him and felt for a pulse. Couldn't find one and had to press her fingers all along the side of his throat, searching it out. Ten thousand, eleven thousand, twelve, got to eighteen, starting to panic and think maybe he was actually dead before she felt the slow throb. She rolled back his eyelid. He didn't move. She slapped his cheek, said his name. Nothing. Twenty-two thousand. She jumped up and dashed to the book, scooping it up and promptly dropping it in her haste – twenty-six thousand – snatched it up again and turned to leap over the fire, stumbling on landing. Twenty-nine. She dropped on to her butt and stuck out her hand.

'Thirty,' she said, breathless, and gently patted the Boy Scout's foot.

She didn't remember falling asleep, but she woke up to find the Boy Scout gone, the blanket she had placed around him now covering her. Beside her head, the paperback lay face down and fanned open to the page she had read up to before closing her eyes. The morning – a harsher light compared to dusk – gilded the barn in long, slanting beams.

She could smell gasoline. A curl of panic flowered in her gut, and she sat up, the blanket falling off. Rink was still laid out on his side – if he had moved during the night, it hadn't been by much.

A clanging slam made her flinch, and she reached for the shotgun beside her. The Boy Scout came out from between the two vehicles, wiping his hands on the seat of his pants. He stopped when he saw her with the gun and put his hands up in mock-submission.

She lowered the gun and pushed the rest of the blanket aside. 'What're you *doing*?' She said it accusingly, making an inelegant struggle out of getting up. 'You scared me half to death.'

'We're about ready to go,' he said, unapologetic.

She kicked the blanket aside and stood watching him as he collected the rifle that was leaning up against the side of the pickup and brought it to her.

He took the shotgun out of her hands and handed her the rifle in its place. 'You're better with a rifle.'

He walked off without another word and went to Rink. He bent over him, reaching down to his own boot and sliding out a knife.

Lacey's stomach gave a funny lurch. 'Wait!'

But all the Boy Scout did was cut the man's ankles free. He sent her a look as if to reprimand her for even considering that he would slice an unarmed man's throat while he lay unconscious.

'We'll take him with us. Help me lift him.'

Lacey saw the truck's rear panel already lowered and ready. As she walked past, she glanced into it. The motorcycle was there, lying on its side, and another body – smaller and slight – had been tucked up against the back of the cab under the rear window. Lacey's red scarf had been laid over the face and tied in place.

Lacey crouched down and picked up Rink's boots while the Boy Scout grabbed him under the arms. They heaved him up and awkwardly shuffled their way to the truck. Lacey hiked up the man's legs when he began to slip, clamping his boots to each hip. He was *heavy*.

'We're taking Red, too?' she asked, huffing for breath.

'Red?' The Boy Scout had a grimace of pain on his face. Sweat beaded on his forehead.

'The girl.'

Reaching the back panel, Lacey held on to Rink's legs as the Boy Scout hauled him bodily into the bed. He landed with a muffled thump. Lacey winced, thankful that the man was already out cold. The Boy Scout helped her swing Rink's legs in after him and then lifted up the panel and locked it into place. He leaned against the back of the truck, wiping the back of his wrist across his brow.

'Her name's Red?' he asked.

'Yeah. Like the colour.'

'Like ruby.'

'I guess so, sure.'

Almost too low for her to hear, he murmured, 'Always the colours.' He straightened and walked around her, heading for the driver's side. Over his shoulder, he said, 'Get anything else you want to take. Five minutes and we're gone.'

In her head, Voice whispered: *Red-Ruby, Ruby-Red*.

A half-mile up the road, a flock of black birds wheeled in the sky. The Boy Scout didn't remark on them, but Lacey wound down her window and leaned out to watch. There weren't many – less than a dozen in total – but they were big and looked almost prehistoric the way they spread their wings wide, using the thermals to glide in lazy, graceful circles. Every few seconds, one or two would break rank and drop low, flapping among the brush, their low squawks coming in over the engine noise as they fought over whatever was down there. The sounds were unnerving, especially the desperate flapping of their wings, beating against each other.

'Turkey vultures,' the Boy Scout said.

She nodded. They were another survivor of this world, clinging to life. Humans, rats, coyotes, vultures. It said a lot. She wondered why they were still here, when so many of her own kind weren't.

They're sometimes called carrion crows, too, Voice said.

'Carrion?' she said.

The Boy Scout nodded. 'They can always find dead things to eat.'

Dead things. Like bodies. Lacey looked away from the birds and cranked her window up.

She dozed for a while, her head nodding with the gentle rolls and undulations of the road. She didn't think of anything, and she didn't dream of anything: she was just a girl dozing in a car on her way to somewhere that wasn't here. The sun was a warm presence in the cab with her. It was a blanket that cradled her in every crease of her body, comforting and real. She had left the window open a crack, and a gentle breeze blew in to ruffle the hair at the nape of her neck, a whisper of fingers caressing her. In her half-awake, half-asleep mind, she wished they could drive like this for ever on an endless highway with the sun constantly shining and a warmth that welcomed you no matter who you were or where you'd been.

Inevitably, something changed. The engine noise droned to a lower pitch, and Lacey frowned, her eyes closed. When the car pulled to a stop she reluctantly raised her head, her neck stiff, and forced her heavy eyelids to lift. She looked all around, but the road was empty in both directions. She turned to the Boy Scout and found him looking at her. His left, blood-red eye was hard to meet, although it wasn't his fault it freaked her out. She half expected a nictitating membrane to flick over it, a translucent film there and gone again in a reptilian blink.

'You know how to drive?' he asked.

She glanced down at the steering wheel, down further into the footwell at the pedals, and back to the controls. She shrugged. 'You just point it and go, right? It doesn't look like rocket science.'

'It's not, but we'll see. Slide over behind the wheel.'

He got out of the truck, and Lacey slid over the seat into the warm spot he'd vacated and placed her hands on the wheel. It felt very large, like it belonged on a ship rather than in a truck. She reached for the rear-view mirror and began adjusting it. The Boy Scout came into view. He had stopped at the back of the truck and was undoing the rear panel, folding it down. The truck rocked as he leaned in to check on Rink, and Lacey moved on to the side mirror, rolling down the window to fiddle with that, too, nudging it back and forth into place. She had both hands wrapped around it when she saw a reflected Boy Scout jump down from the back. The van rocked some more as he pulled Rink out of the truck, the man's body landing heavily on the ground with a sickening, boneless *thud* that made Lacey's breath stop. The Boy Scout dragged him a few feet away from the road and paused there, bent over. He glanced up, and their eyes met in the mirror. It must not have lasted long, that look, but time seemed to stretch out around it.

Lacey was the first to look away.

She sat facing forward, her hands in her lap, and didn't move when the Boy Scout climbed into the passenger seat a few moments later and closed the door.

They didn't speak. The bright sun still shone through the windshield, and the cab was still cosy hot, but Lacey wasn't warmed by it any more.

'Let's start off with the gear shift,' the Boy Scout said.

He leaned over and showed her how to move the steering-column-mounted shifter to D for Drive and R for Reverse. The positions showed up on the dashboard panel right under the speedo as she ran through the different gears. He explained that, out of both foot pedals, the most important one was the larger one on the left. They had to shift the seat forward for her to reach, but, once she was settled, he had her hold the brake pedal down and start the engine. Her hand tightened on the steering wheel when it roared to life.

The Boy Scout told her to release the parking brake.

She'd forgotten which one that was.

The higher pedal, Voice said, *up on the left. That's it.*

'You're in Drive?' the Boy Scout asked.

The D, Voice told her.

She glanced down at the indicator. P was highlighted, so she pulled the lever towards her and moved it down until D was marked. She nodded, nerves tingling through her middle.

'OK, let the brake pedal out. You'll feel her start to go. Move your foot over to the gas and press on it gently.'

Geeently.

A thrill of excitement shot through her when the truck rolled forward, and she forgot all about her nerves as she skimmed her right foot off the brake pedal and on to the gas, pressing it down. The truck lurched forward, and she lifted her foot immediately. The truck lurched again, slowing down.

'It's fine. Try again. No jerky movements. Press down *lightly* on the gas.'

There's nothing to hit out here. Don't worry.

She controlled her foot better this time, pressing it down in small increments. The truck built up speed. She flicked her eyes down very fast to the speedometer.

'I'm doing twenty!'

Woo! We're flying!

The Boy Scout said, 'OK, let's go a little faster.'

By the time she hit forty, she was giggling and had all but forgotten about the dead man they had left in their wake.

CHAPTER 4

At first, Pilgrim didn't know if he were dreaming or awake. He heard voices, or rather one voice. A one-sided conversation.

'I wish you would just give me a straight answer . . . No . . . Because you told me not to . . . Yes, I realise that, but it's not like—' The girl exhaled, a frustrated sound. 'OK,' she muttered. 'Never mind.'

Pilgrim kept his head down, his chin resting on his chest, his arms folded. The truck's tyres hummed underneath him, a constant droning that wanted to lull him back to sleep. He resisted the temptation.

'Man, you're as bossy as Grammy . . . She was, but that didn't mean she wasn't bossy—' She made a soft *huff* of laughter. 'You didn't know her . . . Doesn't matter, they're *my* memories, not yours. You weren't even there . . . Ha! *No.*'

'Who're you talking to?' Pilgrim said. He hadn't lifted his head, but he'd opened his eyes in time to see the girl stiffen when he spoke.

'W–what?'

He yawned as he sat up, rolling out his shoulders and twisting his neck until it cracked. 'I said, who're you talking to?'

'No one.' She stared through the windshield, perched close to the wheel, her hands set at the ten-to-two position.

'Sounded like you were talking to someone,' he said.

She gave another soft laugh, but it didn't sound quite as

natural as the one before it. 'There's no one but you and me in here, compadre.'

Pilgrim narrowed his eyes at her. 'Compadre'. She had never called him that before. 'That's right. There isn't.'

Lacey glanced over at him, met his eyes and quickly returned her attention to the road. 'I was just talking to myself. I do that sometimes. You know, working stuff out in my head. It helps.'

She's lying, that new voice whispered.

Maybe she was, and maybe she wasn't. Still, his damn curiosity, so active in recent days, had been piqued again.

'I talk to myself, too, sometimes,' he said, watching her.

She made another noise, less like laughter and more like a breathy snort. 'No you don't. You barely talk. It's like trying to get words out of a rock.'

He frowned. Scratched his jaw. 'I speak plenty.'

She smirked. 'Sure you do.'

'I'm just not used to—' He made a grasping motion with his hand, as if trying to pluck the word out of the air.

People?

'People?' Lacey said.

He lowered his hand and nodded. 'Yes. People.'

'You like to be on your own.'

He thought about this and, although it wasn't altogether true, he said, 'Yes. It's easier.' He began to wonder how and when he had lost control of this conversation.

'But it's lonely, too. Being by yourself.'

Pilgrim didn't answer – technically, she hadn't posed a question. The mention of loneliness made him think of the boy he had left behind. Pilgrim had looked for Hari at the spot at the side of the road, but there was no sign of him, as if the boy had been a figment of his damaged mind, now vanished over a cliff edge and fallen into nothingness. Whatever Hari's provenance, the boy had found another way to continue his journey, one that Pilgrim had no power over.

Hari had said he got lonely sometimes, and Pilgrim had replied that loneliness could also be peaceful. Now, looking over at the girl and appreciating how the sun bathed her in its golden light, how it bleached the fine hairs on her arms, how the lowered sun visor stamped a strip of shade across her face from mid-nose up, he thought that maybe peace could be found not only in solitude but also in company.

'When my grammy was gone,' the girl said, 'that old farmhouse seemed about three times bigger than usual. I used to wander around the rooms, going in and out, shifting the furniture a little – just by an inch or so – lining it up with the dents in the rugs. Then, the next day, I'd go around again, shifting it all back. I rattled around that house like a lost ball-bearing. You know those puzzle games?' She looked over at him. 'The ones where there's these little holes you have to get the balls into, and you tilt the puzzle and have to be real precise and careful to get those little balls to drop into each slot, holding them there while you fit the next one in?'

He nodded. He knew the kind of game she meant.

'Well, I felt like one of those balls. Rolling around and around, looking for the place I was supposed to slot into, never able to settle. I realised I had no place any more. Not now Grammy was gone. So I said to myself, "Lace, if you stay here all by yourself, you'll die here. You'll die alone and no one will ever know you were even alive in the first place." And that was . . . well, I didn't like thinking about that.'

She had gone back to looking out through the windshield, but her gaze seemed to be miles away from the road in front of them. Pilgrim guessed it was all the way back in that farmhouse, in the backyard where he had found her kneeling by the well.

'To die alone in that place without anyone ever knowing or caring. Like my life wasn't worth anything. I couldn't see the point in that, you know?' She said it quietly, as if not expecting a reply.

They lapsed into silence – well, Lacey lapsed into silence, and Pilgrim remained quiet. He found himself staring out of the side window as the desert swept past, but he barely saw it. He was left with his own thoughts bouncing around his head, whizzing back and forth with no real place to go, much like those ball-bearings in the puzzle Lacey had described. It was unsettling, having nothing to anchor them down with.

They drove past turn-offs, towns beginning to appear, scattered in the distance. More and more highway businesses rolled by: automotive forecourts (boasting lots filled with once-new RVs and trailers, now faded and resting on deflated tyres and rusting trailer jacks), mattress stores, fast-food developments that housed six or seven different chains, every last one of them empty of visitors.

'Tell me—' He cleared his throat when the words came out gravelly and too quiet. 'Tell me something about Alex.'

He felt Lacey look at him, but he didn't take his eyes from the huge billboard sign approaching. The words were inde-cipherable to him, but the picture of the pretty woman lying on a fluffy pillow, a soft smile on her face while she slept, drew his gaze and held it captive.

'Like what?' she asked.

'Anything. Doesn't matter.'

Why do you want to know? he was asked. It sounded like him, this voice – mature, male – but it wasn't altogether him. Something was off: maybe in the accent, maybe in the preciseness of its diction. The questions and comments came without intro-spection or pre-thought, as if a smaller, separate version of himself were sitting inside his head, observing everything.

You never wanted to know about her before.

Well, he wanted to know now, that was all. He felt no need to explain it to himself, or find the exact motivation behind the request.

From the corner of his eye, Lacey shrugged.

'She draws. Pencil drawings, mostly. She had pads full of them, she said, hundreds and hundreds of sketches she'd done, but she lost them all. Said it's surprising how hard it is to come by good pencils and paper any more. She misses it, though.'

'You didn't see any?'

She glanced at him, eyebrows raised. 'Of her drawings? No. But she has the most amazing hands. You never noticed them?'

Pilgrim shook his head but, even as he shook it, he realised he was lying. There had been bandages, lantern light, and yes, there they were, outside the motel with Alex sitting in the passenger seat of her car, twisted to the side so her feet rested on the ground. Lacey was squeezed in next to her, perched on the door lip. He had been wrapping Alex's injured wrists and had noticed the strength in her fingers, the calluses on her hands. He'd wondered how those people at the motel had gotten the best of her, as if her predicament had been a singularity in this woman's history, and yet here she was again, gotten the best of. Pilgrim thought that maybe her bad fortune was brought about by her continued attempts to protect others.

Lacey said, 'They're, like, really slim, and her fingers are long. They're so graceful. I bet her drawings are really beautiful. I'd love to see one.' She said it so wistfully that Pilgrim started to wish for it, too. He couldn't recall when he'd last taken the time to appreciate a hand-drawn piece of art.

He was interrupted in his thoughts by Lacey holding her hand up in front of her face, her tone changing to one of distaste as she turned her hand over to study it. 'Mine are nasty. I have stubby fingers. Look.' She thrust her hand out to him.

Her fingers weren't stubby, her hands were just small, the digits short and blunt-fingered.

'You bite your nails,' he noted.

'I know.' She sighed and put her hand back on the wheel. 'It's a bad habit. Grammy told me it's worse than licking a toilet seat.'

He laughed, the sound rusty and unnatural to his ears. 'Why the hell would you want to lick a toilet seat?'

She smiled at him, a look in her eye as if to say he'd surprised her again. 'I wouldn't. Obviously, I'd rather eat my own fingernails.'

'Yum.'

'Shut up. Did you ever notice how the initials for Boy Scout are BS?' Her smile became a grin. 'BS is short for *Bullsh*—'

'I know what it's short for,' he said. 'Fortunately, for me, it's not my real name.'

It was an opening for her to ask him what his name actually was, and the old Lacey would have jumped at the chance. This Lacey, however, bit her lip and kept her thoughts to herself. The silence stretched out so long it passed from the heavy, artificial stage and became comfortable once more, settling around Pilgrim like a welcome friend. He didn't intend to doze again, but soon his head began to nod, his eyelids droop more heavily. The sounds of the engine and the wheels lifted away.

He was standing before a white-fronted hotel, three storeys high, its wrap-around porch fenced with white railings, the balcony above supported by tall, white columns. It was very impressive in a scaled-down sense, like a small town's attempt at big-city grandeur. The hotel was surrounded by rich garden beds and blooming flowers, a long, lush lawn that ran from the back porch steps all the way down to a rocky shoreline and, beyond that, out to the ocean. The waters stretched as far as the eye could see, the cobalt blue of the sea seamlessly meeting the celeste blue of the sky.

The sea held on to him, called to him, as if sirens floated beneath the cold surface, gazing upwards, hungrily waiting for the next man to stray too near. He could hear their breathing in the waves and on the breeze, whispering through the swaying grasses. On the back porch, a set of wind chimes stirred, emitting a fairy-bell tintinnabulation.

'*The sea.*'

He opened his eyes at the sound of his own voice. He wasn't sure he'd spoken it aloud until Lacey said, 'The sea?' She glanced over at him.

He sat up, rubbed a wrist over his eyes.

'You said something about the sea,' the girl said.

'I don't remember.' And he didn't, not really. Already, the image of sea and shoreline and grass and porch and white-columned hotel was fading. 'I must have been dreaming.'

Lacey looked at him a moment longer, but they were passing a sign and her head turned to read it. She jabbed her thumb back as it swept by.

'Williamstown,' she said. 'We're nearly there.'

Pilgrim stayed quiet as Lacey drove them deeper into the maze of residential houses, which soon turned into an urbanised centre filled with blocks of run-down stores and collapsing tenements. He held the shotgun in his lap, leaning forward in his seat, his eyes continuously roaming, picking out every over-turned car, every shaded area where someone could be hiding in a doorway or on top of a fire escape or behind a fence, wall, or tipped-over dumpster, checking out every vantage point where a potential attacker might be watching from. It was a mistake being here, he knew. Too many places for ambushes, for traps to be pulled, for disturbed people to run at you with nothing but destruction in their heads. Cities were places scavengers were most likely to converge, with so much ample shelter and the opportunity to rummage for supplies. It drew the mentally ill like flies; they recognised their old lives in the restaurant districts, the shopping malls, the abandoned theatres, the familiar block-by-block geography, and they drew a cold comfort from it.

Lacey had switched on the walkie-talkie, but other than a loud, shrill electronic whistle that had made them both jump, there had been nothing but cricket-like clicks and the odd *whoosh* of voiceless static.

They stayed far away from the columns of black smoke that billowed up from the skyline before them, not wanting to get near to any fires still ravaging the buildings and cutting off access to streets. On four separate occasions, different figures appeared and drifted out to stand in the middle of the road or on a side-walk, staring at them as they drove through. Sometimes these figures were alone, sometimes they numbered five or more. Each time, Pilgrim instructed Lacey to take a turn. He half expected them to give chase, but none did. They only stood and watched.

Pilgrim's eyes passed over the heaped bodies without pause; they resembled a ridge of sediment the winds had pushed up against the taller buildings as an extra support for their founda-tions. Vehicles had been driven at speed into their concrete walls, front ends crumpled like concertinas, airbags deployed and deflated. Papyrus-skinned bodies in tattered clothes slumped in the front seats with their seatbelts unclasped. Oblivion at 60mph. An overturned ambulance, maybe on its way to help the crash victims, rested upside down on its roof, rear doors flung open, a confetti of disused medical supplies rotting in the gutter.

A short while later, someone dashed across the street far ahead of them, the flash of movement so swift it darted out of sight before Pilgrim could clearly identify it as man, woman or child. He worried the people they had seen were setting a trap for them but, after driving a further ten minutes, and with no further sightings, his suspicions died down a little.

'This is it,' Lacey whispered.

He wasn't sure if she had picked up on his wariness, or if she herself felt the danger of being in such a place, but she seemed jumpy, her eyes flitting back and forth, unable to rest. She steered the truck into a narrow street, hemmed in on both sides by tall apartment blocks. She pulled to a stop at the end, the street curving to the left and dead-ending in four black, squat posts. The vast siding of a mall-type building rose before them. Only a red service door and a large corrugated roller shutter broke its expanse.

'Stay in the truck,' he said. 'Keep the engine running.'

He got out, shut the door on her protests and walked over to the red service door, trying not to wince every time his right foot came down and pain shot through his ribs. He kept his finger curled around the shotgun's trigger, his head swivelling left and right. He ran his palm over the smooth door; it lay flush against its frame. The lock was a heavy-duty one. When he pulled on the handle, the door didn't budge. He moved back from it, lifted the shotgun and hammered the stock off the door in three hard raps that echoed in the empty street. He stepped back, shouldered the shotgun and waited.

He slowly counted to ninety-five, the digits of his birthdate added together, missing a few numbers in between when his brain refused to supply them.

No one answered his knock.

He went over to the roller shutter and studied it. Along the bottom ran a strip of black rubber, presumably to cushion the metal when it hit the ground. Resting the shotgun against the wall, Pilgrim crouched and dug his fingers under the rubber runner, scraping his knuckles until he had a grip. He heaved upwards, his pains flashing white-hot, the back of his skull splitting straight down the middle and a blade slicing deep into his side. The roller shutter lifted, though, and a small gap appeared at his feet. Grunting, he let the door go and it clattered shut. He waved Lacey over with the truck.

Within two minutes, the roller shutter was high enough for Lacey to edge the truck forward so Pilgrim could rest the shutter on its hood.

Someone could come in behind us if we leave it open.

He knew that, but he'd much rather have a clear escape route than be held up trying to operate the shutter mechanisms if they had to beat a hasty retreat.

They left the truck wedging the roller shutter open and ducked under it. Even as they stepped inside, a storage container crashed on to its side off to their right, and a man fell out, sprawling across the floor, a clinking of glass bottles rolling after him. He lurched to his feet, shoes skating on a carpet of rotting food packets and inches-thick muck, and made a run for it. Pilgrim heard Lacey gasp, but he was already giving chase. The man had one foot on the bottom step leading up to the loading dock when Pilgrim's hand snagged the scruff of his neck and a sharp yank dropped him at Pilgrim's feet, the pleas already running together in their rush to get out.

'Don't hurt me! Please God, don't hurt me!'

'*Stay down!*' Pilgrim snapped, wincing at his creaking ribs as the man twisted on his knees and looked up at him beseechingly, hands held high to show they were empty.

'I don't have anything!'

Pilgrim could see that. The man's face was half encrusted with dried blood, as if one hand had been raised in defence when he was splashed with gore. An eye-wateringly strong stench of alcohol came off him, as if the fumes were seeping from his pores.

'We just want some answers,' Pilgrim said.

Lacey had joined them. She held the rifle loosely, but Pilgrim didn't miss how it was pointed at the man's chest, her finger a breath away from the trigger.

The collar gripped in Pilgrim's hand tugged fast with the man's eager nodding. 'Yes! Answers! I can do that!'

Pilgrim looked him over: old blood, torn clothes, days-old beard, bloodshot eyes. Underneath the alcohol fumes, he reeked of sweat and death and cough syrup. 'Whose blood is that?'

The man's stubbly face crumpled, and Pilgrim clenched his jaw while the man broke down. It took to the count of thirty before the guy gained enough control to force the words out of his gibbering mouth. 'My . . . my friend's. Our building, it caught fire. They got us when we came out. They s–slit his throat right in front of me. Jesus, there was so much b–b–*blood*.'

Pilgrim released the guy's collar and let him slump over as he sobbed into his hands. As the man wept, Pilgrim glanced at Lacey. The rifle had drooped and was now aimed at a spot in front of the crying man's knees. Her mouth was downturned at the corners. Pilgrim didn't like looking at him – he had the lame, scared vibe of a wounded animal left alone to die. He preferred to avert his eyes while the snot and tears leaked out of him.

A number of creeper vines had snaked in through the dry-wall panels and hung down like garlands, their leaves vibrantly green next to the grey drabness of concrete. Places had a feel to them. Lacey's house had felt lived in, worn, full of memories. The motel owned by the deviant-minded siblings had felt impersonal and somehow misaligned. The library had a welcoming, cultured vibe. This place felt vacant and sterile; not sterile in the sense it had been scrubbed clean, because the leftover trash of people living here was everywhere – there were overturned metal barrels which had served as cooking fires and sources of warmth and light, there were empty boxes and cans of food and crumpled bottles, there were even discarded clothes and dirty blankets – but sterile as in empty of life. No one else was here. No one alive, anyway.

'This place is empty,' Pilgrim said when the man finally quietened down a little.

A wet sniff, then: 'They left already.'

'What's your name?' Lacey asked.

'Jack. Jack Hancock.'

'Do you know where they went, Jack?'

The man didn't lift his gaze, his head weaving a little as if he couldn't quite hold it steady. 'No,' he mumbled. 'Wish I did.'

'No good will to come from following these people,' Pilgrim told him, suspecting he was telling Lacey, too. 'They're dangerous.'

'They killed my friend.' For the first time, something other than defeat and insobriety coloured the man's words. 'They . . . they can't just *do* that.'

'Of course they can. Don't be naïve.'

The bloodied man scowled up at him so hard some of the dried blood on his face cracked and flaked off, and for a second Pilgrim wondered if there was a little fight left in him, after all.

Before he could do anything stupid, Lacey stepped closer, drawing the man's attention. 'Jack, you should get away from here. We saw people on our way in, and they didn't look friendly. You understand what I mean?'

He scowled at her for a moment, too, but then all the anger seemed to drain out of him and he slumped where he knelt, his expression becoming bleary and lost. 'Yeah,' he mumbled. 'Yeah, I know what you mean.'

'Here.' Lacey slid a hand under his elbow and helped him get clumsily up. 'OK?' she asked once he was on his feet, hunched over and breathing heavily. Pilgrim hoped he wouldn't throw up.

The man nodded, keeping his head down.

'Your friend wouldn't want you getting hurt,' Lacey said quietly.

'Yeah,' he mumbled again. 'Yeah—' he stumbled away from them, heading for the shutter door. He didn't look back as he bent and shuffled underneath it, and they watched until his feet disappeared. They listened to his footfalls recede until they disappeared, too.

Lacey whispered, 'Jack be nimble, Jack be quick.'

'Jack'll get his ass burned on a candlestick,' Pilgrim finished.

'Hey' – Lacey frowned at him – 'don't be a dick.'

Pilgrim took the rebuke and walked over to the storage

dumpster Jack had tumbled out of. Using the barrels of the shotgun, he poked around in the bits of clothing and crap in there, but there was nothing of any use.

'Do you know where they kept her?' he asked Lacey.

She shook her head. She wouldn't look at him but swivelled this way and that as she scanned the loading area.

'What about the room where you first saw Dumont?'

'Maybe,' she murmured.

He peered closer at her and realised she was very close to crying.

He frowned. 'What's wrong?'

Her lips trembled, but she didn't answer him.

'Look, I'm sorry for saying Jack would get his ass burned.'

'It's not that.' It took two more attempts before she could get the words out, and when she did, they came out sounding hopeless and lost. 'I don't know how we're going to find her. There's nothing *here*.' She clamped her bottom lip between her teeth, her mouth turning traitor on her again, softening as tears welled.

She glanced away from him, an almost-guilty shifting of her eyes, as if his witnessing her tears were a shameful thing.

He continued to frown at her, puzzled. He didn't like seeing her upset, but he wasn't sure what he should say. There was a high possibility they *wouldn't* find Alex. With no clues other than a direction in which she was likely to be headed, Pilgrim didn't know how they would go about finding one solitary woman. And even if they *did* find the group responsible for taking her, there was no guarantee she would still be alive.

'We'll find these people,' he heard himself say, not sure where the words were coming from. 'We won't give up. We'll look until there's nowhere else we *can* look.'

'What will they do if they find out she doesn't hear anything? They're looking for people with voices, right? That's what you said. What if they slit her throat like they did Jack's friend?'

He *had* said that, and now he wished he hadn't. In all honestly, he didn't know what these people wanted. He'd merely been speaking out loud. 'It'll be OK,' he said. 'She's attractive.' He winced when he said that, but there was no hiding from the truth. 'They'll keep her around, at least for a while.'

The girl nodded, her head down, and then she did a peculiar thing. She stepped forward and put her arms around him. He had to move the shotgun quickly out of the way or else she'd have hugged that, too.

Pilgrim stood still, his side complaining at her hold. He was aware of his heart beating and wondered if it sounded loud to her with her ear rested over it. Her tears, warm and wet, soaked through his shirt. He could feel the hard length of the rifle she held pressed along his back and hoped she had taken her finger off its trigger; otherwise, he might end up with a second gunshot wound to his head.

He patted her on the back. He hoped it made her feel better.

Eventually, she eased away from him. He didn't know how long she had hugged him for but wished he'd counted so that he'd have a number.

'Done?' he asked.

She wiped her nose on her sleeve and shook her head at him, a slight eye-roll accompanying it. '*Yes*, I'm done. We can go now.'

'Good.' He turned away from her and headed for the swinging service doors.

CHAPTER 5

As she followed behind him, Lacey made sure to keep her rifle's barrels pointed away from the Boy Scout and down at the ground; she was jittery and didn't want to shoot him in the leg accidentally.

She directed him on which way to go, taking her cues from Voice's guidance, because she'd forgotten most of it. As they took a left and a right, and then another right, Voice lectured her on the importance of being observant and vigilant at all times, but she pretended not to hear him, mainly because she thought he was being unfair. She'd had a lot on her mind at the time.

They climbed up the four flights of stairs before reaching a fire door she recognised, wedged open by a small block of wood. She pointed the Boy Scout through it and they walked along the silent corridor, their footsteps echoing.

He limped slightly, and she hung back to examine him while he walked, worried that his injuries were worse than either of them wanted to admit. When she'd hugged him, she'd been alarmed by how much heat his body gave off. It was like hugging a furnace. But his heart had beat steadily and solidly in her ear. And she trusted his heart.

The door to the room where she'd first met Dumont stood open. Inside, the city lay before them in a panoramic view of collapsing ruin. This time it held no beauty, there was no buttery sun to soften its rough, crumbling edges, no warm, orange brushstrokes to paint it in a kinder light – now all she saw was a dying, leprous civilisation far past any possibility of rescue. A new addition had been spray-painted on to the middle pane of the floor-to-ceiling windows, a large black outline of a man's head in profile. In its centre was a spiral, like that of a snail shell, winding round itself. It gave Lacey double vision the more she tried to follow the spiralling coil.

'I've seen something like that before . . .' she said.

The Boy Scout was silent as he stared up at the messy design. Thin dribbles of paint had slid down the length of the glass. He reached out and ran a finger across the spray-painted face, clearing a line through the place where its mouth should be.

'On a billboard, not long after leaving my house,' she continued. 'A painted spiral. You probably don't remember.'

He shook his head and turned away from the window. He went about scouring the rest of the room, but there was nothing else to find. Lacey tore her eyes from the black-headed outline and its vortexing mind and sat down in the leather armchair, the seat creaking under her weight. She slowly leaned back, laying the rifle over her thighs. She reached under her collar and rubbed the St Christopher between finger and thumb. It was warm from her skin and the more she rubbed it, the hotter it became.

What's going on, Red? she thought. What the hell would you do if you were here?

Run in the opposite direction, Voice replied.

Lacey closed her eyes. Other than his reappearance to direct her through the corridors, Voice had been suspiciously quiet ever since the Boy Scout had found her. She had tried questioning him, but Voice simply reminded her not to use the name Pilgrim, that the name would only cause trouble, and that some things weren't for her to know yet. The 'yet' made her hopeful. Maybe Voice would stop being secretive soon and just tell her.

She rubbed the medallion. A soothing, rhythmic smoothing of her thumb.

– But what would she do if she *couldn't* run in the opposite direction?

Then I imagine she would stand still until a better solution presented itself.

'You're no help at all,' she breathed, eyes still closed.

There's nothing wrong with standing still. Movement is overrated.

– We can't just sit here and do nothing! Alex *needs* us.

Au contraire, mon cœur, *if you sit still, maybe you'll be able to hear the way forward.*

– *Hear* the way forward? What the hell are you talking about?

Shhhh.

She hated being shushed. *Hated* it. She scowled and swore, a string of curse words that would have resulted in Grammy getting out the bar of soap and scrubbing her tongue with it until she gagged, even though her grams hadn't been averse to cussing herself at times.

'Shhhh,' the Boy Scout said.

Her eyes flashed open. '*Seriously? You're* shushing me now, too?'

He cast her a brief, enquiring glance, but then he went back to listening, his head dipped slightly towards the open door. He appeared so attentive that Lacey found herself holding her breath and listening hard, as well.

Then she heard it. It was very faint, but she definitely heard it.

'A dog,' she whispered.

The Boy Scout walked out into the corridor and stopped to listen again.

It could have almost been mistaken for the wind, the howling high-pitched and faint, rising and falling in waves. They followed the noise and as they got closer, and the howls became louder, the sound gained nuances of pain and misery. It got to the point where Lacey wanted to cover her ears to block it out.

'Maybe we shouldn't be trying to find it,' she said.

But the Boy Scout didn't answer. He paused on the landing of a concrete stairwell, the howling swirling around them, directionless and haunting.

Lacey shivered.

A ghost dog.

The Boy Scout headed downwards, trotting down the steps so she had to hurry to catch up. Two flights and he stopped, crossed the landing and swung the door inward. The howling notched up a few decibels.

Lacey nearly jumped out of her skin when a loud, piercing whistle sounded right in front of her.

'*Jesus!*' she gasped. 'What're you *doing*?'

The Boy Scout lowered his fingers from his mouth and the whistling stopped.

The dog's baying had stopped, too. Then a harsh, grating bark took its place, a barrage of echoing retorts that went on and on and on, one after another.

'I recognise that bark,' she said reluctantly.

From the stairwell's landing, they walked the length of the main corridor and turned into a hallway that branched off it. Three quarters of the way down that corridor, they found Princess shut up in a room. Lacey stayed back as the Boy Scout went to look through the narrow glass panel in the door. Spotting him, the dog threw itself at the door, the whole panel shaking in its frame as the barks ratcheted up in volume. Over and over, the dog crashed into the door, desperate to break out, its claws scrabbling at the floor at the door's base, trying to dig a way out to them.

Not only did Lacey recognise the dog's bark, she also recognised the corridor. Another reason she had backed up against the nearest wall, unwilling to step any closer.

Princess didn't get turned into a burger, after all, Voice said.

The Boy Scout appeared oblivious to the thuds and bangs of the dog throwing itself at the barrier between them; he continued to stare through the glass panel at the room beyond. Lacey could imagine what he was staring at, but she didn't expect what he said next.

'There's something written on the wall in there.' His head turned, his eyes coming to rest on her face.

'*What?*' she said, not sure she had heard him correctly.

'Words. Written on the wall. Above the bed.'

The way he was looking at her and the way he said 'bed', his tone flat, inflection non-existent, brought all manner of emotions tumbling through her. Guilt, fear, horror, anger. She didn't want to look inside that room. The brassy taste of panic coated the back of her tongue.

'What's it say?' she whispered.

The Boy Scout shook his head and stepped back from the door, the dog rebounding off the other side, the sound of their voices sending it wild so they had to speak louder to be heard over the barking.

'Come read it,' he said.

'Is *he* in there?'

It was so hard to read him; his eyes were entirely unfathomable as he gazed back at her. 'The man I stabbed? Yes. I think it's him.'

'I don't want to see him.' She realised she was holding the rifle so tight her forearms ached. She made herself loosen her grip.

Easy now, Voice murmured.

'You don't need to look at him,' the Boy Scout said. 'Look above him, at the wall.'

She didn't move forward. She could feel her heart pounding at the base of her throat, her pulse thudding through her temples. 'Why can't you just tell me what it says?'

'Because I can't.'

Her panic exploded. 'But *why*! I don't want to look at him! I had to watch him die and *I don't want to see him*!'

'I can't read,' he said.

'Yes you can!'

He looked unhappy. 'Not any more. Letters won't stay still. They wriggle around like worms. The head wound must have caused it.'

Her chest heaved from her outburst. She stood there, her back jammed up against the wall, and stared at him. The Boy Scout looked back at her calmly.

'You can't read at all?' she asked.

'Believe me, I wouldn't make you look in there if I didn't have to.'

Panic, although quashed for the moment, stirred in her chest again, tightening through her lungs and making it hard to breathe. 'What do you mean? What's in there?' She was scared of the answer.

'The dog's been in there a while. It must've got hungry.'

Lacey squeezed her eyes shut, turning away from him *and* the room to press her brow against the cool wall. But closing her eyes only made it worse, because Jeb was waiting for her in the dark: his staring eyes, his sunken cheeks, the spittle in his beard, the clawed hands that had spastically drawn up to his chest. Except now there were ragged chunks ripped out of him, raw gaping wounds, and body parts chewed off, his entrails hanging down the side of the bed like a rope of sausages.

She moaned and opened her eyes. Stared hard at the blurry no-space somewhere behind the wall in front of her face.

She felt the Boy Scout hovering near her shoulder, although she hadn't heard him approach. She rolled her eyes to the right, looking at him without turning her head.

He said, 'Keep your eyes on the wall. Don't look down from it.'

'Yeah, right,' she muttered. 'Easy for you to say.'

He gently took hold of her elbow, and she let him steer her

316

away from the wall and lead her the few steps down the hall. Those few steps weren't enough – she would have gladly walked the circumference of the planet first.

Princess had stopped barking. Now she snuffled at the bottom of the door, as if she could smell fresh meat, and whined and gruffed and snarled. She started frantically clawing at the gap again.

She wants dessert.

Lacey made an angry noise, one she hoped the Boy Scout would interpret as a way of attempting to bolster her courage, and which Voice would translate as a wordless version of 'shut up'. Neither of them responded, so she figured it had hit both its marks.

'Use your hand. Hold it so you can't see. Like this.' The Boy Scout laid the flat of his palm over the bottom half of the glass, effectively shielding her from any view below it.

'Keep your hand there,' she whispered. 'Don't move it.' She gripped his wrist, just in case he decided to ignore her wishes and lift it away. His skin was as warm as the rest of his body – *too* warm – but it was good to hold on to him. Just while she did this.

She leaned forward, bringing her face closer to the glass. The door shook when Princess crashed into it, and Lacey flinched, gasping, her heart pinballing in her chest.

'It's OK,' the Boy Scout said. 'It can't get out.'

'Princess,' she told him shakily.

'What?'

'The dog. Her name is Princess.'

'OK. Princess, then.'

'It's a girl dog.'

'I figured. You're stalling.'

'I *know*, I know . . .' Taking a deep, steadying breath, Lacey leaned in the final few inches, looked over his blocking hand and peered hesitantly into the room. 'Oh my God,' she whispered.

'What do you see?'

'My name. Someone's written my name on the wall.'

'Is that all?'

'No . . . it says, "Hello Lacey. RIP Alexandra. Resting place here," and then there's an arrow pointing downwards.' She moved her head back and looked up at the Boy Scout. 'But it's pointing down under your hand, to the bed, and I can't look.'

The Boy Scout told her to step back. When she had moved, he stepped into her place and looked inside. 'It's pointing to a folded piece of paper in his hand,' he said.

'No . . . no way. We're not going in there.' She shook her head, even though he wasn't looking at her.

'We don't have much choice.'

'Are you shitting me? There's a rabid dog in there. Whatever sick little note he's left for us, it's not worth getting our asses chewed off for.'

'It could help us find Alex.'

She stared at him and for the briefest, blackest moment she disliked him intensely for pointing that out. Pointing it out and making her realise that they would have to go into that room despite everything screaming at her not to. She immediately felt a crushing guilt, and she dropped her gaze from him and stared at his dusty boots.

'You don't have to go in,' he told her, and that just made her feel worse.

'No,' she said, and hoped he couldn't hear the trembling in her voice. 'Tell me what you need me to do.'

CHAPTER 6

Pilgrim knew he would have to be fast.

He had given his shotgun to the girl: it was better for close range and would cause far more damage than the rifle. It wasn't the dog's fault they needed access to the room, and he didn't want the girl using the shotgun unless it was necessary, but if she had to, she couldn't hesitate. He explained what else he wanted from her, and she nodded, a jerky up–down motion of her head. She held the gun in a firm grip. He knew she was scared, but she wouldn't run. Pilgrim couldn't help but respect her for that.

He gripped the door handle. The dog hadn't stopped barking or growling or whining since they had entered these corridors, but now it went quiet. Disconcertingly so. When Pilgrim leaned in closer to the glass panel, he found the dog staring up at him with its black, shiny eyes, its muzzle wrinkled back to silently reveal its sharp, bloodstained canines.

'Ready?' he asked the girl.

'No, but do it anyway.'

Pilgrim was empty-handed, the rifle leaning up against the wall, his knife still in its sheath. He rattled the door handle to get the dog's attention, and it reared up on to its hind legs and planted its paws on the door. Its head was nearly level with his. Its teeth snapped at the glass, mere inches away from Pilgrim's face, leaving drool streaked on the panel. With each hot, doggy breath, the window steamed up. Princess's rabid glare challenged him to open the door. A low, ominous growl rumbled from her chest.

'There's a good Princess,' he murmured. 'Be a good girl now. Play nice.'

He unlatched the door and opened it an inch. The dog immediately jumped down and tried to jam its broad head into the gap. Its teeth snapped at him, strings of reddish saliva drooling from its jaws. It snarled and barked and wriggled, trying to force its way out. It was amazingly strong, its slabs of muscle bunching and flexing under the sleek, black coat, and Pilgrim had to struggle to hold the door closed, the dog's snout already nudging through.

He counted off in his head.

– One –

He grabbed hold of the door jamb, the dog's weight forcing itself into the growing gap and pulling him off balance.

– Two –

The snout was all the way through now, the dog's head jammed in the opening, shoulders too wide to fit. Pilgrim could feel his weaker hand losing its grip.

– *Three* –

He lifted his knee, bringing his foot high – just as the dog wedged its shoulders through and crouched down to leap – braced himself and stamped his boot down hard and fast on top of the dog's head.

Princess let out a bleating yelp and dropped to the floor, legs buckling. Despite being dazed, she immediately tried to get back up. Pilgrim stamped his boot down again, the contact satisfyingly solid, and the dog collapsed, a long whine sighing from it. It didn't try to get up again.

'Get the other door,' he said to Lacey, but she had already hopped across the corridor and was pushing it open for him.

Pilgrim didn't pause to worry if the dog would rear up and sink its teeth into him but kicked the door wider and grabbed the Rottweiler by the scruff of the neck and yanked on the creature, sliding it across the shiny floor. He grunted at the effort it took to drag the dog's weight across the hall and into the room opposite. Princess growled and rolled its head under his hold, its teeth snapping, but it was a sluggish attempt and not one that put him in any danger of being bitten.

When he released the dog's neck, the animal heaved upwards, trying to get its legs under it, gathering its balance and struggling to its feet. It had managed to stand when Pilgrim slipped out of the room, and Lacey swung the door shut, the latch barely catching when Princess slammed into the other side, the dog's guttural barking taking up again.

The dog threw itself against the door with a particularly vicious thud. It yelped and momentarily stopped its attacks, but it soon started up again.

'Can't keep a good dog down,' Lacey said, but despite her attempt at humour, the corners of her eyes were pinched, and neither of them could ignore the awful stench leaking out of the room they had just cleared.

'I'll get the note,' he told her. 'Watch the dog doesn't get out.'

He couldn't pretend not to notice the utter relief that washed over her face, but he didn't hang around to see what emotion followed it. He tugged the neckerchief up over his nose and entered the room. He breathed through his mouth, but that just made the stench of rotten meat and excrement coat his tongue, and he was hacking before he could stop himself. He lifted the edge of his neckerchief and spat on the floor.

'You OK?' Lacey called.

'Yeah. Give me a minute.' He clamped his hand over his mouth and nose and used that as an extra barrier to breathe through. It helped, a little.

The man, whose name Pilgrim couldn't remember – or what was left of him – lay on the bed.

He's seen better days, that new, separate part of him said.

Pilgrim grunted and held his breath as he stepped closer. He didn't linger too much on the state of the dead man. He had seen his fair share of half-eaten corpses and was familiar with most of the organs of the human body, in all their states of putridity. He did take a moment to look into the dead man's clouded eyes. A lot can be told from a person's eyes, he believed, and this man's, although milky and vague, still held a hint of hatred that not even death could erase. Pilgrim remembered those eyes narrowed on him as the man brought the gun up to his head, remembered the hard glint of satisfaction as he squeezed the trigger. This man had taken pleasure in dealing out pain and death, and now it had come back on him threefold.

Life's a whore, then you die.

'Life's a sadist.'

Maybe it's karma.

'I don't believe in karma.'

I don't think you believe in anything. You're a nihilist.

'I'm not, I—' but he stopped, realising it was foolish to argue with himself.

No less foolish than when you argued with Voice.

He wanted to explain that the only reason he was talking to this part of himself was because he still acutely felt the loss of Voice. It felt natural for him to converse with himself. But that didn't mean he wanted to start an internal debate about it.

He closed off these thoughts and looked at the dead man's hand. The fingers curled around the note so Pilgrim had to prise them open in order to remove it. He didn't bother looking at the man again and left the room, pulling the door tightly shut behind him. He ushered Lacey further up the corridor, away from the lingering stink and the barking dog, and handed her the note.

He watched her eyes skip over the words, shifting down the page, line by line, then go back to the top and scan through it again. He waited patiently for her to read it aloud. When she did, she had to pause a few times to steady her voice.

Dear Lacey, if by some small chance you have found your way back to our mutual deceased friend, I commend your tenacity. There was something special about you, though, so I would be little surprised if you did succeed in recovering this little love letter. I must tell you, your friend Alexandra is enchanting. She keeps me constantly entertained. I know she misses you terribly — she cries out for you sometimes when I've hurt her particularly badly. It breaks my heart to hear it. So, being a generous man, I have decided to share with you our next destination (honestly, to see you again would be a pleasure. Maybe this time we can be friends!). Head east to the Great River Road and follow it south a ways on Route 61. I'm told you can't miss it — a steamboat hotel and casino, which sounds delightful, don't you think? I very much hope to see you there.

Yours sincerely, Charles Dumont.

PS There may yet be a happy ending to all this. Bring Red, if Louis and Rink don't already have her, and we'll talk.

Finished, Lacey neatly folded the letter back up and slowly ran her pinched fingers down each seam.

Pilgrim said, 'Lucky we brought the dead girl along with us.'

Lacey slipped the paper into her pocket, not looking at him as she spoke. 'I don't think he meant "bring her body".'

Pilgrim went to retrieve the rifle he'd left leaning against the wall. 'He didn't specify. She can still be used as . . .' He used the pretence of checking the gun over as he searched for the word he wanted. '. . . as leverage.'

Lacey still had her head down when he came back to her. He waited, but she didn't look up. 'Alex is alive. It says so in the letter.'

'I know.'

'Then we should go while we still have light.'

She nodded, but something was bothering her. He waited a moment longer, but when nothing was forthcoming he took out the map and spread it flat against the wall. He asked her to show him where Route 61 ran. Her finger traced a north-to-south line that followed the Mississippi River from Wyoming, Minnesota, all the way down to New Orleans, Louisiana.

Her finger floated back up and paused at the S-bend in the river, where the Mississippi snaked at its most easterly point. It was a quarter of the way down the Mississippi–Louisiana border.

'I'm pretty sure I know what steamboat casino he's talking about,' she said. 'My sister took me there one time. Here' – her finger tapped on a city directly north of the area she'd pointed out – 'is where my sister and niece live. And here is the casino.' Her finger moved down again, drifting south for maybe ten miles out of the city.

Pilgrim followed the route they would be travelling with his eyes, heading east from where they were, trailing down to rest at her fingertip. 'So you're saying he could be going through Vicksburg to get to this casino?'

She nodded. Now he understood why she'd grown so quiet.

'If he's only passing through, there won't be any danger to your sister or niece.' He didn't know that for a fact, but Vicksburg was a city, not a small town. In effect, Lacey's sister and niece were tiny needles in a haystack made up of thirty-five square miles. If they were alive, the chances of Dumont coming across them were very small indeed. He tried to reassure her again, but the girl had fallen into an uncommunicative silence and, with nothing left to say, Pilgrim refolded the map and led her back the way they had come, corkscrewing to the bottom of the stairwell and coming out at ground level. They were heading for the swinging service doors that led out into the loading bay, his hand out and ready to push through, when he was brought to a stop.

Lacey walked into the back of him, a small sound of surprise coming from her.

'What—'

He chopped his hand down to silence her, never taking his eyes off those red doors. He tapped his ear and then pointed, indicating she should listen.

He didn't know why he had stopped. He had heard nothing, and there was nothing out of place in the corridor. But those two swinging doors held his gaze like a fishing line hooked through his eyeballs. They reeled him in and he felt impelled to lean towards them. The doors seemed to pulse, the red deepening in colour, the edges fuzzing and throbbing as if they were the chamber doors to a beating heart, and he squinted his left eye closed because his blurred vision, combined with the doors' throbbing, made him feel sick.

The crack of a gunshot rent the air and Pilgrim ducked, even as a hole splintered through the right-hand door, the bullet passing through with a splatter of blood, trickles of wine-coloured gore already starting to dribble down and pool on the floor.

Pilgrim blinked, and the door was smooth and unmarked again, no signs of bullet damage and no trickling blood. They had also stopped pulsing – they were ordinary service doors once more.

His head ached abominably.

'You think Jack came back?' Lacey whispered behind him. 'I can't hear anything.'

His left hand was trembling badly. He balled it into a fist and pressed it against his thigh, keeping it out of sight.

'It's nothing,' he said. 'My mistake.'

Nevertheless, he was cautious in how he pushed through the swinging doors, and only when he found nobody waiting for them on the other side and they had climbed back into the cab of the truck did he uncurl his finger from the gun's trigger.

Leaving town was a far quicker enterprise than entering it. Pilgrim drove while Lacey sat in the passenger seat and stared out of the side window. She hadn't spoken more than a handful of words in the past twenty miles. He was loath to break the silence; it didn't feel like a morose one, merely a contemplative stillness. Maybe she needed the quiet to sort out her thoughts.

Or maybe she's busy talking inside her head. This new part of him was beginning to sound just as annoying as Voice.

Pilgrim felt his hands reflexively tighten on the steering wheel. He had recognised the signs straight away; (he was, after all, well versed in them himself): the unfocused look to her eyes while she was inwardly thinking, the talking to herself, the randomness of some of the things she said, like calling him compadre – something that only Voice had ever done. He didn't understand it, though, couldn't begin to work out how Voice had jumped from him into her.

Or maybe it's her own Voice.

If it were her own Voice, how would she have known his name? She had said 'Pilgrim' at the barn when she'd seen him. It would be impossible to know that without having being told. In fact, as far as he could recall, she was the first person to have ever spoken the name out loud to him.

Maybe voices communicate between each other.

This made Pilgrim pause. Could that be possible? Could there be some interconnecting cognitive network that ran from person to person? That seemed entirely too implausible. Sure, there were people who heard voices, but the voices were self-contained, locked up inside heads, exactly like his Voice had been locked up inside his.

Except for when Voice had jumped into the girl—

Isn't hearing a voice and conversing with it for years implausible, too?

'No, it just makes me crazy.'

He didn't realise he'd spoken out loud until he felt the girl's eyes on him. She had the same enquiring look in her eyes that he was sure had been in his a time or two over the past twenty-four hours.

326

He said, 'Just arguing with the voice in my head.'

Her brows came down in a small frown, and the inquisitive look turned to one of suspicion. 'You talk to voices?'

He had to be careful. 'Just the one.'

'You never mentioned this before.'

'It's not something you talk about.'

'What does it say to you?'

'Contradictory things, mostly.'

That's because you're so often wrong.

'Is it your own voice, or more like a stranger's?' she asked.

He had looked back to the road to correct the truck's slight drift, but now he glanced back to her, his own curiosity kicking up a gear. 'These days, it's more my own,' he answered. He and Voice had shared similar intonations in the pronunciation of certain words, but Voice was very different in his views and ideas to Pilgrim. They often disagreed. Pilgrim wasn't sure if it had always been that way, or if the development of Voice had been a slow evolution, one so incremental he hadn't noticed it happening. He tried to remember a time when he hadn't had some sort of back-and-forth dialogue going on with Voice inside his head but couldn't come up with an answer, and a serrated blade of pain reminded him that it wasn't prudent to be thinking so hard or so deeply on such matters.

Lacey's attention had drifted like the truck, her gaze focused somewhere in the space down by her feet. Her frown had tightened and she shook her head slightly, as if to herself. 'Mine used to be my own,' she murmured.

He glanced at her a few more times after that, but she didn't say anything more. She went back to gazing out of the window.

'What does yours say?' he finally asked.

She shrugged. 'Different stuff. It knows things I don't, though.' She threw a quick glance at him, probably to see his reaction. 'That makes no sense, does it?'

He tightened his grip on the steering wheel because all he

wanted to do was pull over, turn to face her and peer into her eyes to see if Voice lurked behind them. But he *knew* Voice, knew him inside out, and he wondered if Voice had even told the girl where he'd jumped from. Pilgrim doubted it. If the girl knew, she'd be talking his ear off, asking questions, offering theories and guesses on what it all meant. She didn't know. Not yet. And Pilgrim was *glad* she didn't. He was surprised by how violated he felt, how vulnerable, knowing that Voice was now inside someone else's head, with all the minutiae he had amassed over the years spent living inside him. All that intimate knowledge. But Voice also knew that keeping his own existence secret would be safest for the girl, and to do that the girl had to believe that telling Pilgrim wouldn't be wise, either. In effect, the act of keeping Voice a secret from everyone prevented the girl ever finding out who Voice had jumped from.

Pilgrim answered her absently. 'Your mind is a tricky place. The subconscious picks up on a lot that you don't consciously register.'

The girl made a soft noise and slumped down in her seat, head twisting back to the side window, posture throwing up a barrier against further discussion. Which was fine with Pilgrim. She had said more than enough.

In honesty, he was pleased to know Voice was alive and had vacated his head for somewhere younger and brighter. He had believed Voice had died or fled deeper into his mind, never to resurface. It had struck a nerve, Voice's desertion, and the anger it generated hid a much deeper sense of abandonment, a feeling that Pilgrim didn't want to analyse too closely. He now suspected Voice had simply left for a more viable host, suspected it may have been an instantaneous decision, made in the split second the bullet struck Pilgrim's skull. Pilgrim marvelled at it. Wouldn't have believed it even possible if he hadn't seen the evidence of it.

He would have liked to discuss the phenomenon with Voice,

even with Lacey, but he sensed that overloading the girl with such notions would seriously undermine her coping mechanisms. Already her anxiety levels were high (as shown by her spontaneous hugging, crying and near-hyperventilation in the face of the dog and the half-eaten man). On top of that, she had begun biting her nails as soon as she slid into the passenger seat. Her hopes for finding her sister alive must now be tenuous at best; she had seen more of the world in these past few days than she had in the previous seven years.

No, it would be best to keep these thoughts to himself. There would be time to discuss them later, when her stress levels had evened out.

'You should keep this to yourself,' Pilgrim told her. 'About hearing a voice. It's dangerous to talk about them.'

'Yeah,' she said, the reflection of her eyes meeting his in her side window. 'That's what he told me, too.'

They would reach Vicksburg by sundown, and Pilgrim stopped only once for a restroom break. The further east they went, the lusher the land became. The dying yellow grass grew greener, and the low-lying bushes flashed by in verdant bursts, soon to be joined by more and more trees: silvery ash, pale-boned sycamore, the winged elm and the rough-barked hickory. Pilgrim hadn't realised how much he had missed seeing such displays of healthy growth, had become so accustomed to the emptiness of the deserts that he now found it hard to tear his eyes away from the sides of the roads where all this vegetation flourished.

He had often thought of this world as a veil. That he and every lost soul who wandered it were merely wraiths, and that the abandoned cities they haunted, and all the open plains in between, were superimposed over the real world, a world bustling with life, the cities loud and forever in motion, the honks of horns and the shouts of hot-dog vendors and the rumbling of a thousand wheels all travelling in a starburst of directions. The reality he lived in was a dying veneer laid over the old, vibrant one.

Pilgrim drifted through this world, barely causing a ripple, his presence unnoticed and, most days, unneeded. He was good at being a ghost. Sometimes he thought it was what he'd been born for.

As the sun started its slow descent towards the horizon at their backs, the truck's shadow stretched out, much like its own wraith. Pilgrim looked down at the fuel gauge and knew they would be chugging on fumes by the time they hit Vicksburg's outskirts. He knew it wouldn't get them to Lacey's sister's house, the same way he knew that driving through the town's streets this time would attract unwanted attention and lead to Bad Things. He didn't know how he knew this, but intuition was all he had, and to ignore it would be foolish. They would walk the final miles and worry about finding a ride later.

A sign approached, and Pilgrim asked what it said.

Vicksburg was ten miles away, Lacey told him.

The trees became a continuous barricade that flanked the highway and made it impossible to see anything but rolling grey road. Spanish moss began to appear in the trees, first only in thin weaves, but soon it thickened and weighed down the boughs as though a million industrious spiders had spun their webs, uncaring of how they smothered the drooping branches. Knitted gossamer strands blew in the wind. It was a haunting sight to see all those trees so overwhelmed by the thread-like interweaving plant, but it was merely a sign of nature, of one species staking its claim over another in the absence of anything to prevent it.

'My grams wasn't well when she died,' Lacey said.

Pilgrim glanced over at her, her words unexpected after the long silence, but she kept her face turned away so he couldn't read her expression. He waited for her to continue. When she didn't, he asked, 'What happened to her?'

Her shoulder hopped up and down in a small shrug. 'She didn't know who I was some days. Other days, it was like she was sixteen again, giggling like a kid. Those were the best. She was happy when she was sixteen. She met Grandpa the day after her birthday, and they were married by the time she turned nineteen. Just like Mama. Just like Karey. I guess that means I've got three more years to find my one true love. If I want to keep up the family tradition, that is.' He saw the corner of her mouth lift in a smile, but it was more an automatic twitch than one that was felt.

He listened to the low thrum of the wheels, the odd tick of stones and gravel pinging off the truck's undercarriage. 'It must have been hard, looking after her,' he said at last.

Again that shrug. 'Yeah, sometimes. But she looked after me for twelve years, so it was no big deal.' She paused, her lips twisting as she chewed on the inside of her cheek. 'One night I woke up to find her standing over me. She had a knife in her hand. It took me an hour to talk her into handing it over to me. I thought she was going to kill me. Thing is' – she slid her gaze over to him for the first time since she had begun talking – 'I think she heard things. I caught her talking to herself sometimes, arguing, mostly. Another time, I found her hidden in the cupboard under the stairs. She'd stuffed herself into this tiny space: you should have seen it – *I'd* have struggled to fit in there. I spent ages searching for her, calling out, thinking she'd some-how wandered off. But she never answered me. Never made a peep. I only found her by accident. She was all scrunched up, her head twisted at this weird angle, and she stared up at me with this look of utter terror on her face. I think she was hiding because she was scared of what she might do.'

'Do? You mean hurt you?'

She dropped her eyes and turned away again, as if the power of speech had left her.

Pilgrim stopped the truck. He turned in his seat and pulled Lacey around by her shoulders to face him. 'Do you trust me?'

The girl looked deep into his eyes. She nodded.

'Good. You're not going crazy,' he told her. 'I swear to you.'

Her eyes welled with tears. 'Are you sure?'

'*Yes*,' he stressed. 'I'm absolutely sure. Hearing a voice isn't always a bad thing.'

'My grammy killed herself,' she whispered. 'I found her. In bed. She'd stuffed her bedsheet down her throat.' The tears spilled over. 'Why would she *do* that?'

He squeezed her shoulders; they felt narrow and fragile beneath his hands. 'I don't know. No one knows what goes on inside a person's head. But she'd have never hurt you. She loved you. And she did a fine job of raising you.'

The girl nodded, bit her lip. A tear dropped from her jaw. 'She did. She was the bravest woman ever. Like my sister. Like Alex.'

Pilgrim ran his finger under her chin, catching a second tear before it could fall. 'Like you,' he said. 'Now, enough with the tears. They make me uncomfortable.'

'I know,' she murmured, and smiled, just a little.

Five minutes later and five miles further down the road, Lacey said, 'You think my niece will like me?'

He blinked, tried hard to keep the frown from his face. 'Why wouldn't she?'

'I don't know. It's hard to make a connection with someone you've never met before.'

'You seem to do OK. Look at you and Alex.'

'It's not the same. Alex is older.'

He didn't see what difference that made, but said, 'I think she'll just be happy to have someone who cares about her.' He didn't mention the low probability of finding her niece alive; he was learning not to share all his thoughts, even without having

Alex staring daggers at him. He was pleased that not all his memories were completely lost to him.

'Yeah,' Lacey said quietly. 'Yeah, you're right. I just . . . I really want her to like me.'

'She will. If I can like you, anyone can.'

She smirked, and reached over to punch him in the shoulder. 'Asshole.'

Seven miles later, after crossing the mighty Mississippi River and just as they reached the town's cemetery, the truck began to cough. And two miles after that, the engine died.

CHAPTER 7

O ver eight years had passed since Lacey last stepped foot in Vicksburg. Karey had been seven months pregnant with Addison at the time and, to put it bluntly, she had been puking an awful lot in those final few months before Lacey's niece was born. Not the standard morning-sickness levels of vomit, either. It was acute nausea and pernicious upchucking (Lacey loved the word 'pernicious'), and it had gotten to the stage where Karey was having to stick an IV tube in her arm every day to combat dehydration and lack of nutrients and to pump herself full of electrolytes. Grammy worried that Karey wasn't taking the bed rest the doctor had ordered, so they had come and stayed for two weeks until Karey felt better. Anyway, eight years was a long time between visits, and a lot had changed.

The Boy Scout had lifted Red out of the pickup bed, and Lacey gathered together everything else. There wasn't much left to loot from Lou's truck: half a bottle of water, the last two cans of food – one chicken soup, the other alphabet spaghetti – a flashlight, a multi-tool, the walkie-talkie, the shotgun and the rifle, and a handful of extra ammunition for each. That was the grand total of their worldly belongings, other than the clothes on their backs. She tried the radio. It bleeped twice at her when she turned it on.

'The battery's dying,' the Boy Scout told her. 'Best keep it off for now.'

She switched it back off and watched as he popped the truck's hood and leaned inside. 'What're you doing?'

'Pass me the multi-tool.' He held a hand out behind him without raising his head.

She fished it out of her pocket and laid it across his palm, peering over his shoulder while he unfastened the truck's battery and lifted it out.

'What's that for?'

'A fully charged battery is the beating heart of a vehicle. We'll need another set of wheels soon if we're going to get to Alex.'

The mere mention of Alex's name made Lacey's chest tighten a little, right over her heart. Too much time had passed since she'd last seen her, and every extra minute spent removing truck batteries or walking to her sister's house or finding another useable car could be another hour Alex suffered at the hands of Dumont. An image of Alex flashed into Lacey's mind, the bruises and cuts and the pain marked across her body, and how she'd looked when Dumont was throttling her with his belt, face dark purple, eyes bulging, tongue sticking out. Lacey bit her lip hard enough to reopen the cut on the inside of it, the iron taste of blood sharp and sickly. She passed a shaking hand over her hot eyes.

We're coming, Alex, she thought fiercely. Just hold on, we're coming for you.

They left the truck's hood propped open, and Lacey gave the vehicle a last affectionate pat on its fender – she had spent a goodly number of hours in that cab, and it had taken her safely away from Dumont and back into the care of the Boy Scout. Both things she was grateful for.

Lacey had taken the map when the Boy Scout offered it and had plotted a route to Karey's street, staying away from the main roads as much as possible, sticking close to the river. They had about three miles to walk, which should take a little over an hour.

It'll take longer with him having to lug Ruby-Red and that battery around.

But, like the Boy Scout said, and despite how much Lacey didn't like using the poor girl's body, it was still leverage, and they might need her. Besides, Lacey figured Red would be happy to be useful in any way that might help gain an advantage over Dumont.

So they walked, Lacey in the lead, the Boy Scout bringing up the rear, with Red slung over his shoulder. To the west Lacey could see the light of the setting sun flicker over the Mississippi as if pirates had scattered gold doubloons across its surface. She felt exposed being out in the open and spent a lot of time looking over her shoulder, looking up into the darkened windows of the warehouses they passed, looking up and down alleyways, expecting to hear a shout go up and a pack of wild-eyed and slavering cannibals to charge them, spilling out of the mouths of those same alleyways, whooping and hollering and chasing them down. They were in a warehouse district, though, where the old railway tracks ran parallel to the river, and there wasn't much around except a huge, once-white grain-storage silo with 'BUNGE' on its side and rusting poles and strands of wiring stretching across the road from building to post to building, as if someone had decorated for Christmas but forgotten to add tinsel and lights to all the cabling.

The river was a massively wide stretch of water to the west that had doubled in size since the last time she had been here. There were numerous signs of flooding. Far in the distance, along the river's banks, she could see submerged piers and shipping docks, only the odd mooring post sticking high out over the water, while the rest of the decking rotted below. The railway yards lay feet deep in murky water, the long-disused tracks visible only as a much darker, double-lined ruler mark beneath the river's surface.

As they came nearer to the brown-and-white brick train station, they stopped to stare at the classic old building, its Grecian-pillared countenance looking kind of ridiculous stranded up to its knees in the middle of a flood field.

'I'm guessing the next train is delayed,' Lacey said.

Toot toot! All aboard the Floodline Express! Tickets free. Inflatable armbands ten dollars.

She laughed. Couldn't help it. It was funny.

The Boy Scout raised his eyebrows at her, and she quickly swallowed the laughter. She studied the map for a moment then told him Karey's house lay a few miles inland.

The rest of Vicksburg sat on a bluff, safe from the rising flood-line. The drainage ditches, wooden levee gates and berms had valiantly held back most of the overflowing water, but even from here Lacey could see the cantilever lattice bridge, where freight trains had once crossed the Mississippi, and how close the waterline was to spilling over it.

Further along, after walking the gentle incline of the street for about a mile, the scene opened up again, allowing a better view of the near banks of the Mississippi. Lacey stood silently as the Boy Scout stopped beside her.

There were hundreds of cars, some wedged together as many as five deep, lining the banks. They had all been driven into the water, nose first and en masse. Some vehicles had been swept away, occupants inside, while others had become grounded or packed too tightly for the river's tide to pull them out.

The cars were now rusted and flaking apart, as much rotting skeletons as the people who'd once driven them.

'Why do you think they did it?' she asked quietly, staring down at all those cars. 'My grammy said it was like when Princess Diana died in Britain. Did you hear about that? You'd be old enough to, I reckon. She said thousands of people lined the streets, crying and wailing like it was their own mother who'd been killed. But it was just some woman they'd never even met. They only knew her through TV interviews and newspapers articles. Grammy said they all went crazy, as if some contagious disease had swept through everyone, except it was made up of hysteria and senselessness.' Lacey shook her head; it was so disturbing to think that people could be affected so easily and in such vast numbers. 'Her story about what happened here would change whenever I asked. Mostly, she said gas or chemicals did it. That they'd been released in the big cities by terrorists. That was her favourite one – that terrorists did it – but she'd tell me anything to stop me bugging her with questions, I think, to stop me wanting to go anywhere near other people who could hurt me. She worried about me a lot.'

'She was right to worry,' the Boy Scout said.

'She never mentioned any voices, though,' she murmured. 'Why do *you* think they did it?' she asked again.

He didn't answer straight away, and when she looked at him she found him staring not at the river, with its collection of rotting metal carcasses, but at the sky high above their heads.

'We had our chance,' he said, so quietly Lacey didn't think he was even talking to her. 'I think our time was up, and we were the only ones who didn't realise it.'

She frowned, confused. 'But we're still here. How can our time have been up?'

His eyes left the sky, falling back to Earth to where she stood. He gave a small, tired smile. 'We always have been slow to catch on.'

At the next junction, Lacey put their backs to the river and led them east, the sidewalk ascending in a steeper incline. A few raindrops spattered on the map with a muted *rap-rap-rap*. She glanced up at the darkening sky, could see the twinkling stars where rainclouds had left the heavens clear in ragged patches.

A raindrop got her slap-bang in the eye. She squeezed it shut and rubbed it with a fist and turned to look back at the Boy Scout. 'Can you believe it? As soon as we're out of the truck, it decides to rain.'

He didn't appear all that troubled by the chance of a

downpour. All he said was 'Let's hurry. It's not safe being outside.'

She led them up to the top of the street and took a right. Within fifteen minutes they were deep in a residential area. They saw only two living things other than themselves, the first a mangy-looking dog, its fur so thin Lacey could see the pink skin beneath; it trotted across a street that bisected the one they travelled on and paused when it sensed their presence, its shining eyes regarding them silently for a few seconds, the fading light reflecting like lamps in its pupils, and then it turned away and continued on, disappearing around the corner of a single-storey, white-and-yellow clapboard house. The second living thing was a man, or what had once been a man. Now he was a sack of skin and sharp bones, of hunger and desperation. His eyes were lamps, too, but they didn't shine with an inward luminescence like the dog's but with a wild glow that made Lacey think he would leap on them if they'd been closer. Leap on them and start tearing at their faces with his teeth.

All three of them (four, if you counted Red) stood still and watched each other, not one word passing between them. And then the man made a strange growling noise in the back of his throat and gave an angry shake of his head, more a tic than any sort of human gesture. The man hit himself in the temple, a sharp blow with the heel of his hand, and dismissed them by turning away and stepping into the shadows of a doorway, the darkness reaching out to hide him.

A dangerous animal, Voice said quietly.

Lacey didn't think he was referring to the dog.

The Boy Scout gently nudged her from behind, wordlessly urging her to move on. Now that she was so near, for reasons she didn't want to think about too closely, she wanted to dawdle a little longer, even at the risk of having her face gnawed off by a hunger-ravaged wild man.

Ten minutes later, the murmuring of approaching voices had

them halting in their tracks. The Boy Scout hissed at her to get off the sidewalk, and she hurried into the nearest yard, hunkering down behind a strand of tall, white-flowered bushes. Hydrangea, she thought, and had the vague notion her grammy would be proud of her for knowing that. A light, sweet scent came from the flowers.

As the Boy Scout crouched awkwardly next to her, Red draped over his back, Lacey glanced over her shoulder at the black eyes of the house's windows, feeling more vulnerable than she had since she'd been reunited with the Boy Scout. The glass in them was perfectly black, as if they weren't windows at all but gaping chasms leading to a place where no light existed and everyone was blind and pale-skinned and cold. So very, very cold.

They stayed crouched and hidden, with Lacey throwing uneasy glances over her shoulder every few seconds, but the voices didn't get any louder, the muffled clomps of their shoes and the odd clink of gear and weapons fading as they moved off down the street one over from theirs.

The Boy Scout made them wait a further five minutes, their legs cramping from kneeling so long, silence all around, before allowing her to stand and move back on to the sidewalk. Lacey had to knead out her thighs before she could walk without hobbling, but she was relieved to get away from the black-windowed house with its gaping, blind eyes. From then on, he became extremely wary, walking ahead to each junction to check the way before coming back for her. It made their progress excruciatingly slow, and left Lacey torn, her impatience mixing with her gratefulness for the delay.

Soon, lavish three- and four-storey Victorian houses hemmed them in. The towering oaks eclipsed them in size, their thick, gnarled branches twisting every which way as if trying to claw upwards to the sky and, in failing that, simply clawing outwards at the obscuring structures built all around. The oaks were scary in their contorted majesty but staggeringly beautiful nevertheless. They made Lacey feel small and pathetic.

She halted at the steps leading up to her sister's house, dread opening up hands inside her that reached to grip her by the throat and heart and stomach. She was barely aware of the Boy Scout moving past. It was raining freely now, and she was already soaked through, but the evening was warm and the rain didn't chill her.

She gave the house a long look. The single gothic-style turret jutting skyward on the house's right flank made her think of locked-up princesses and evil stepmothers. The windows were all dark, and the rain made a comforting pattering sound on the roof's slate shingles, the rainwater trickling like mini-rivers along the guttering and spilling down pipes with soft gurgles. The house was alive with noises. She thought she saw a glimmer of light dance past the turret's top window, and the dread that gripped her reared up and became a fearful kind of excitement. But then the flickering light disappeared so quickly she couldn't be sure it hadn't been a reflection of some distant star, now lost behind the rainclouds.

Maybe it was Tinkerbell on her way up to visit Rapunzel.

Lacey wanted to *scream* at Voice, open her mouth and let out all the terror and frustration and blind hope in one breathless shriek.

He must have felt how close she was to breaking, because Voice backed off immediately. *I'm sorry. That was a bad time to crack a joke. Are you sure you're ready for this, Lacey? You might not find what you're looking for.*

'It'll be OK,' she whispered, more to herself than to Voice. 'It'll all be OK.'

PART FOUR

The Man Who Was Flooded

CHAPTER 1

Pilgrim waited for Lacey to try the door. It was unlocked, and it silently swung inwards on well-oiled hinges. He could have easily imagined a loud squawking issuing from the joints, but this wasn't a haunted house. At least, he hoped it wasn't.

He warned the girl to be careful, and she nodded while she fished out the flashlight and flicked it on. Only gloom greeted them from beyond the half-opened door. The flashlight's beam slashed through the darkness as Lacey cautiously stepped inside.

She softly called out to her sister. Her voice trembled as it echoed up the dark, wooden stairs.

The house felt like a shell. Vacant and dead.

A mausoleum, that small voice whispered.

The floorboards beneath Pilgrim's boots were shiny and worn, smoothed over by hundreds of passing soles.

Or souls.

He carefully stepped over to a padded, straight-backed chair set in the corner of the foyer and lowered the dead girl into it, his back muscles screaming as he bent at the waist, sitting the body so it wouldn't slide to the floor. When he straightened and looked at her, Red was slumped over to the left like a ragdoll, the arm of the chair holding her in place. Her scarf-covered face and the slight depressions of her chin and nose beneath the cotton gave her a macabre appearance, as if at any moment she might slowly rise from her seat and begin walking around these empty rooms. He placed the car battery on the floor beside her and briefly cupped his palm over his ribs, the warmth of his hand easing the soreness a little.

The creak of a floorboard had him glancing over. Lacey had advanced to the bottom of the stairs and was looking upwards, her flashlight dispelling enough of the gloom for Pilgrim to make out picture frames hanging staggered along the wall every few steps. Family portraits.

'David?' Lacey called. 'Addison?'

The names of her niece and presumably her sister's husband. No one answered.

Ghosts cannot talk.

'Can't they?' he whispered, as if he knew better.

Lacey looked over at him.

'Let's search the house,' he said. 'From the ground up. We'll find something.'

She nodded, a hint of relief in the movement, as if in action she could disperse her uneasiness. Pilgrim didn't feel a sense of unease; he felt only resignation.

They started in the sitting room. It was a big house, and old. It was all dark woods and fake lamp sconces and wainscoting. There were shelves upon shelves of leather-bound books, gilt lettering on their spines, and Pilgrim stood for a moment simply to appreciate the view. But the scene was tinged with sorrow; a purplish-black vein that had sewed itself through it.

The downstairs rooms were remarkably untouched, as if they had been preserved in some mysterious Victorian time loop. The house hadn't been ransacked, or vandalised, and although there were untidy piles of clothing and bedding and miscellaneous items sat in the corners or on side tables or draped over the backs of overstuffed chairs, it didn't detract from the mournful beauty of the place.

'Look at this!'

Lacey stood at the far end of the bookcases, where a neat little alcove housed a small writing desk. Papers were strewn haphazardly across the blotter. A cork noticeboard was pinned to the wall beside it, a multitude of letters and postcards tacked there, none of which Pilgrim could read. It was the sheet of paper sectioned off into blocks that Lacey was pointing at.

'They're alive! Look, they've been keeping track of the date!'

He squinted at the place her finger marked out. 'What's the last date say?'

There was a pause. 'August 8th, three years ago.'

Neither of them spoke. Pilgrim could hear Lacey breathing.

'Whose writing is it?' he asked.

'My sister's.'

'OK, that's good.' It was better than good. It was far more than he'd expected. 'Let's keep looking.'

As they moved from room to room, ghosts in their own right, rain lashed at the windows, showery, back-handed gusts that rattled the glass in its frames. Pilgrim shivered in his damp clothes, not chilled but in sympathy with the shivering of the house in the storm's onslaught.

On their way to the kitchen, he opened his mouth to suggest lighting a fire – they had already walked past two cast-iron fireplaces, one in the parlour and another in the attached dining area – when a cracking thud came from above their heads.

They both looked up at the ceiling. The brass light fixture rocked gently on its chain.

They waited for another thud, a scuff – *anything* – but nothing came. Eventually, they lowered their gazes and looked at each other.

Lacey moved off, her stride purposeful, but Pilgrim caught her by her arm.

'I'll go,' he said, his voice low. 'If there's anyone, I'll flush them out and down here to you.'

She pulled her arm from his grip. She did it easily, his hand too weak to hold on to her. 'No. I should go.'

'Chances are they'll hear me coming and run in the opposite direction. Your face should be the first one they see.'

She looked undecided. *Worried* and undecided. 'You won't shoot anyone, will you?'

He made a sound somewhere low in his throat. It was a non-committal kind of sound, one that could be easily dismissed if ever questioned. Lacey didn't question, and he left her with his Zippo while he took the flashlight and found his way back to the staircase in the foyer.

He made sure to examine the family portraits as he ascended – he wanted to be able to identify them in case he did come face to face with someone upstairs, didn't want to blow their head off before realising it was Lacey's long-lost sister. This scenario was unlikely; Lacey had already called her sister's name upon entering the house, and no answer had been forthcoming. The last sign of her existence was three years ago. More likely, he would find a stray animal, or an open window where a blast of wind had entered and blown a standing lamp or coat stand over.

He stuck to the left-hand side of the steps, a less travelled path compared to the more creak-heavy middle. He had to go about halfway up before he came across a good picture of all three family members. Karey, Lacey's sister, was bigger-boned than Lacey, broad across the shoulders, square-faced with widely spaced hazel eyes. Although her demeanour was sturdy and no-nonsense, the dimples on each of her cheeks softened her almost to the point of cuteness. David, her husband, had thinning, sandy-blond hair, so fine as to appear almost wispy as it brushed over the gold rims of his glasses. The man compensated for being folically challenged by having a studiously serious countenance and a full beard.

Cradled in her mother's arms and staring into the camera's lens, Lacey's niece had the best of both her parents. She was perhaps three months old in the photograph and had a head of dark wispy curls, and dimples to die for. There was no guile in the baby's eyes, just the innocence of the young – totally unaware that the world was getting ready to take a huge, painful bite from her.

Pilgrim reached the top of the stairs and turned left, making his way along the carpeted hallway to where the thump had come from. He gripped the shotgun in both hands, the flashlight held along the barrel and pointed at a partially closed door. He steadfastly ignored the muscle-deep trembling in his left arm. Beyond that door was a bedroom or, if not a bedroom, a study or playroom. Whatever the room's purpose, inside was where the noise had originated.

Be careful. We don't want to spook anyone.

Pilgrim kicked the door open and charged inside.

He had a moment to see the flash of an alarmed face, pale and dirt-streaked, on the other side of the king-size bed, and then it darted out of view, disappearing behind the wall.

Behind the wall? How . . .

As he leapt over the bed in pursuit, he spied a wooden panel retracted back from the wall to reveal a hidden space behind. And, from the scuffling sounds rapidly moving away and down from him, the hidden space went far deeper than appearances indicated.

Rats in the walls.

'*They're on the move!*' he bellowed.

The space was so narrow he had to turn sideways in order to fit. His flashlight revealed bare bricks and steeply ragged steps leading downwards.

A secret passage.

Christ.

'*There's a hidden stairwell. They're coming down!*'

Pilgrim took the steps as fast as he dared, which wasn't as fast as he'd have liked. He scraped his elbows and shoulders on the rough brickwork as he went down, the flashlight bumping along with him, throwing distorted shadows on to the walls. The fleeing figure couldn't be far ahead of him, but the enclosed stairwell amplified sounds and made him think there were only a few feet separating them, the twisting and claustrophobic nature of the steps keeping them out of sight and just beyond his reach. There was a low scraping – another panel sliding out of the way? – and Pilgrim increased his speed a little, meeting the last turn in a rush and running into the wall, rebounding off it with a grunt of pain and almost falling, catching himself with a hand on the wall and stumbling forward, wedging himself into the narrow gap and squeezing out.

A gunshot went off.

The bullet *thunked* into the panelling not far to his right, the distinctive sound of splitting wood making him flinch back.

'*Watch out!*' he shouted.

Lacey yelled at whoever it was to wait, to come back, don't run! and then a clatter of feet as she took off after them.

CHAPTER 2

Lacey cursed herself as she dashed out of the kitchen. What had she been *thinking*, firing her weapon like that?

Calm down. You weren't *thinking*, Voice said.

The sitting room was a dark landscape of lumpy furniture and shadowy hillocks – in her haste, she'd left the Zippo on the kitchen table. At the far end, backlit by the large picture window, a figure darted past an armchair and disappeared through the doorway.

'Wait!' Lacey called.

They didn't wait; a light patter of feet scurried across the hard-wood floor of the entrance hall. Lacey ran, grabbed the doorway and swung herself around, skidding to a stop in the middle of the foyer, listening hard and holding her breath.

She heard a creak through the archway to her right, which opened up into a large parlour fitted with more sofas, a dead entertainment system and two coffee tables. She rushed into the room, her footsteps falling silent as they hit the rug. There weren't many places to hide in here; behind the heavy drapes or the sofa, maybe. Possibly even inside one of the wall-length cabinets next to the TV system, where DVDs and Blu-rays and PlayStation games were undoubtedly stored.

The door, Voice pointed out.

A second door led out of the room. It was open a crack. That wasn't how she and the Boy Scout had left it. She hurried across the carpet, whacking her shin off the corner of one of the coffee tables, gasping as pain streaked up her leg. She hobbled the rest of the way and opened the door: the dining room, three doors leading off it, all of them shut. She stooped to look under the table. Only chair legs; no human ones. No more creaks or clattering footsteps clued Lacey in as to where to go next.

She went for the nearest door, footsteps thudding hollowly on the floorboards, and pulled it open.

Watch out!

She ducked and cried out, lifting a blocking hand as a cascade of chaotically piled boxes toppled down on top of her. The corner of one clipped her in the neck, eliciting another sharp gasp of pain.

When the last box fell, she stood silently in the wreckage of the storage cupboard, her shin throbbing, her neck stinging.

'*Shit,*' she whispered.

CHAPTER 3

Pilgrim squeezed out through the opening in the wall and spilled into the kitchen. He placed a hand on the table for support, inhaling a few deep breaths, wincing as his ribs creaked in complaint. Straightening up, he wound his way around the table and chairs and headed back down the hallway. He was halfway across the sitting room when Lacey cried out – a sound like a mini-avalanche crashing through the ground floor.

His heart clenched in his chest and he burst into a run, sprinting past the overstuffed armchairs and into the foyer, shouting her name.

She called back. Told him to wait where he was, that she was coming to him.

His heart thundered far too fast after such a short sprint. He'd halted next to the straight-backed chair and unconsciously backed up a step, putting some space between himself and the dead girl. Her mummy-like appearance seemed to fit in with the rest of the house, as if she'd been on display here the whole time and not on a cross-state journey in the back of a truck with a motorbike and a dead man for company.

'Look where you ended up, Ruby-Red,' he murmured.

Lacey appeared in the archway and Pilgrim couldn't pretend he didn't feel a flood of relief at seeing her whole and unharmed.

'Did she come back through here?' she asked, speaking again even as he shook his head. 'I almost shot her. *Shit*. I freaked out when you yelled, and then it was like the wall was caving in from the inside. She just popped right out of the wall in front of me. I panicked.' She paused to catch her breath, twisting to look behind her again, as if hoping the elusive stranger had waltzed back in to say hi. '*Shit*,' she said again, louder this time.

'I take it you know who it was,' he said.

'Yeah.' She inhaled deeply, the next words coming out on a long stream of expelled breath. 'I'm pretty sure it was my niece.'

It made sense to Pilgrim. The kid had slipped down those steps like an eel, easily keeping ahead of him – only a smaller, slighter person could have done that.

They called out for Addison, moved from floor to floor and room to room, but the girl was well and truly in hiding.

Lacey rubbed at her face, looking defeated. 'I scared her to death, firing a shot off like that. I'm such an *idiot*.'

'We're all a little jumpy.'

'We need to find her.'

He nodded, but he knew the girl wouldn't be found unless she wanted to be. Not this time. He had caught her off guard once. According to Lacey, the kid was seven, which made her old enough to be wily but young enough to hide in any tiny nook of the house. She could be anywhere. They went from room to room and, at least in the searching, Pilgrim satisfied himself that the rest of the house was unoccupied and there weren't any more surprises waiting for them.

There was a small wood-burning stove in the kitchen – probably more of a decorative piece, as there was an expensive-looking cooking range along the opposite wall – that would serve them nicely, and Pilgrim soon had it lit, the nostril-tickling scent of dust burning along with the wood and paper he had stuffed it with. If anything would bring the little mouse out in the open it would be the smell of cooking. Plus, Pilgrim was hungry. In less than five minutes he had both cans opened and emptied into saucepans, and they were bubbling nicely on the stove top.

Lacey sat at the table, arguing with herself and shaking her head, still upset. She periodically got up and went to the hidden staircase behind the kitchen wall and peered up it.

The third time she came back from doing this, she said, 'Karey never showed me that hidden staircase. You'd think she would've, it being such a neat little feature of her home and all.'

'Maybe she didn't know it was there.' He brought the hot saucepans over to the table. 'Chicken soup or alphabet—' he tried to say 'spaghetti' but the word stuttered at his lips and refused to come out.

'I always say "noodles" anyhow,' Lacey said. 'I'll have them, please.'

They sat and ate quietly, listening to the house creak and the rain lash. The soup burned a hot path down Pilgrim's oesophagus and pooled like lava in his gut. The only sounds in the kitchen, apart from the muted crackling of the stove's fire, were the occasional scrape and clang of their spoons as they dragged pasta and soup up from the saucepans and into their mouths. No more thumps came from upstairs.

Pilgrim watched the girl poke her spoon into the tomato sauce, push and nudge at the spaghetti shapes for half a minute before she showed him what she had done.

'Can you read what I put?'

He studied the pasta, even tilted the saucepan this way and that, but, although he knew that the spaghetti was letters, *knew* that each one she had lined up could be only one of twenty-six shapes, it was like trying to catch fish with his eyes, each letter squirming away from his comprehension.

He shook his head. 'Your name?' he guessed.

She drew the saucepan back to herself and dug her spoon in, scooping up the letters she had arranged and stuffing them in her mouth. 'No,' she said around the food. '*Eat me.*' She gave a weak smile as she chewed.

Without discussing it, they both left a little food in the bottoms of their saucepans and returned them to the stove, the aroma of hot broth still hanging thick in the air. The longer Pilgrim sat in the warm kitchen, his stomach as full as it had been in a while, the more his aches and pains leached out of him. It would be nice to settle down in front of the stove and not move. But he couldn't afford to relax – not yet – so instead he dried off and checked both guns, unloading each one, making sure the firing mechanisms, as well as the bolt action on the rifle and the pump action on the shotgun, all worked smoothly. Then he reloaded them.

The girl hadn't spoken for a while. He caught her a time or two looking up at the ceiling.

'She won't leave the house,' he told her. 'She's been here all her life. It's her home.'

Lacey nodded.

A minute's more silence went by.

He placed the rifle on the table in front of her. 'It's full dark outside. It'd be a good time to head out to the casino.'

He would have preferred to go by himself, but Lacey knew the area, at least more than he did. To a degree, he needed her, and he highly doubted the niece would make another appearance while they were here, at least not for a while.

'We'll come back,' he said. 'She'll have calmed down by then, and we'll try over.'

'I shouldn't leave. I only just found her. She's probably scared out of her brain.'

'I thought you wanted to help Alex.'

'I *do*.' The way she said it made Pilgrim think she'd either start yelling at him or burst out crying. He didn't want her to do either.

He reached over and briefly touched her hand. A few seconds' contact, a gesture of comfort that didn't come easily to him, but he recalled the weight of her hand on his foot, the hours she'd spent with it resting on his boot while he slept in front of the crackling fire, the barn doors closed to the night, his head throbbing with so much pain he thought there was a possibility he might not wake at all.

'Your niece doesn't want to be found right now,' he told her. 'She knows this place better than we do. We can search, but we'd be wasting our time. Alex we *can* help. Your niece will still be here when we get back.'

The girl didn't speak but gazed at him, searching his eyes. He could see the dejection in them, a dark shadow hiding at the back in a place she probably thought was hidden from him.

Finally, she nodded and pushed up from the table. 'I need to do something first.'

He wasn't sure what she meant, but he nodded in turn. 'I need to go hunt us out some wheels anyway. I'll be back in a short while.' He stood up, already lamenting the fact that he'd have to leave the cosy kitchen.

'It'd be worth checking next door. Karey was always complaining about Mr Thomas revving his new project at stupid hours in the morning. Might be something useful in his garage. They had a spare set of keys by the back door there. For when they went on vacation.' She nodded behind him to a key rack, half of its six hooks occupied.

She left the rifle on the table and crossed to the hallway. At the doorway, she paused, her head down. 'This isn't what I wanted.'

There was a world of meaning in those words, not least the fact that she had lost her niece almost as soon as she'd found her. Pilgrim understood that hopes often didn't align with reality. The easiest option would have been for her to keep her hopes modest, but she'd been unable, or even unwilling, to contemplate the reunion with her family as being anything but a happy one. Her high hopes had set her up for a long fall.

And it was never the fall that killed you in the end. It was hitting the bottom that did all the damage.

★

Lacey went upstairs, plodding her feet so that each shoe fell with a hollow *clomp*. She turned right on the landing.

Thump thump thump, she stomped.

Come out, come out, come out, she thought.

On their search, the Boy Scout had shut every door after checking each room, so now the hallway was a narrow, closed-off tunnel. She paused in the shadowy gap leading up to the tower. The dark was so dense she was sure she could reach out and touch it if she wanted.

This hadn't been her destination, but she sat down on the bottom step and looked up into the darkness. Addison might be up there, might even be sitting on the top step, gazing down at her, for all she knew.

'I'm sorry it's taken me this long to get here,' Lacey said, her voice hitting the darkness and disappearing, like musical notes in a soundproofed room. 'I wish I'd come three years ago, but it's been kind of hard, what with Grammy not being well. You'd have liked her, though, your great-grammy. She was tough. Like she was part of the rocks under the ground, something that could never, ever be uprooted. And you know, it's kind of funny because I guess she never was uprooted, not really. Everything that hurt her came from the inside. She didn't have any control over the things breaking down in her head, confusing her and changing who she was. None of us can control what goes on in our minds.' And wasn't that the truth, she thought.

She waited for a reply from Voice, maybe something sardonic or even defensive, but none came. He was giving her some space for now.

She scooped out the St Christopher from under her collar and stared at it. The design was lost in the darkness, but it didn't matter; she knew it by heart now. She brushed the coin against her mouth, feeling the embossed image warm itself on her lips. Look how far it's gotten me, Red. All the way to where I need to be.

She took a deep breath – held it in – then let it out in a rush. 'I'd love to meet you, Addison. Can we do that when I get back?' Not a whisper of sound reached her ears. 'I've never done this aunt thing before, but I know how to be a sister. I'd be good at that, at least.'

The dark remained silent, impassive. Lacey tucked the St Christopher safely away and stood up. 'I'll be back soon. You don't need to be afraid, OK? I'm going to take care of you. You're not alone any more.'

Lacey paused a second longer, but nothing stirred. She walked to the end of the hall, opening the last door on the right, and stepped into her sister's cold bedroom. The bed was made, the comforter neatly turned down at the top as if waiting for Karey to climb in with a hot cup of cocoa and a good book. Inside the wardrobe, Karey's clothes would be hanging. Inside each drawer, her jumpers and slacks and underwear would be neatly folded.

Lacey lay down on the bed and pressed her face into the pillow. Underneath the stale mustiness there was a faint, lingering aroma of perfume. Floral and sweet. Like stepping into the backyard at home in the summer.

Lacey allotted herself the same five minutes she'd spent at her grandmother's graveside before leaving home. For those three hundred seconds, the pillow's cushion caught her sobs and her grief twisted her grip on the comforter. Five minutes, and then she stood, her face damp, her breathing deep, letting the painful tightness rip through her chest, *wanting* it to hurt, needing her grief to be so powerful it urged her to turn away from it or else be consumed. She had no time to be consumed. Alex needed her. She neatened the pillow and smoothed out the bedcover. Then she left her sister's room, shutting the door behind her, and went back downstairs.

Thump thump thump, went her feet.

Alex, Addison, Alex, went her thoughts.

CHAPTER 4

The rain had slowed to a drizzle, a mist that settled in their hair like jewels and beaded on their jacket sleeves and shoulders. The sister's neighbour had a fine taste in projects; it was a shame the man wasn't still around – Pilgrim would have liked to shake his hand. The modified Triumph TR7 hadn't been too difficult to get up and running. It glided like a phantom, her parallel-twin-engine growl echoing off the buildings, burbling beautifully back at him as they passed through the darkened streets. He didn't worry about the noise or attracting attention any more; they would soon be leaving the city behind. He saw only two other vehicles, crawling along different streets as if in search of something, but neither car altered course when they sped by.

He didn't think he'd be on the back of a motorcycle again so soon, and not with Lacey huddled up against him. There had been a 1970 Dodge Charger in the garage, too, but he couldn't resist the pull of the motorcycle after spending so many hours confined inside the truck's cab. He had some difficulty squeezing the stiff clutch lever in with his weakened left hand so kept his gear-shifting to a minimum, and it was painful to have Lacey's arm curled around his middle, pressing over his ribs, but the ride would be short, and he was happy to contend with the discomforts for the pleasures he gained.

Too soon their four-lane-split highway passed into a factory district, businesses colonising the dry land up top with the distant gambling establishments lining up at the ends of gently sloping roads, each casino built on the banks of the Mississippi like kitschy children's playsets, the only things missing their flashing Mattel lights. He cut the engine and coasted the last half-mile silently, the night air warm and damp through the neckerchief he'd pulled up over his nose, the only sounds the motorcycle's spinning wheels and the rustling of the wind in his ears.

He remained unsure if the TR7 would fire up again without the car battery to jump-start it, but now wasn't the time to let such troubles concern him. He let the bike drift to a stop and planted both boots while Lacey climbed off. He left the motorcycle hidden behind what was once an old iron-working factory. Lacey unhooked the sling he'd made to strap the guns to her back, and he helped her untie them, retaining hold of the shotgun. She fiddled with the hand-held CB radio, two muted blips beeping when she turned it on. She held the speaker up to her ear.

'Anything?' he asked.

'Not yet.'

'Keep it on for now. But keep the volume low.'

She nodded and clipped the radio to her waist.

They carried onward on foot. Pilgrim heard Lacey sniff a time or two as she walked alongside him, her chin down and her hands stuffed up her sleeves. Under the cotton of his necker-chief, his warm breaths blew back at him in small, even puffs. It was a regular, countable thing. So were their footsteps, eating up the sidewalks, two of her smaller-spaced steps to one of his wider ones.

They jogged across yards and skirted empty parking lots, hopping over drunkenly tilted wooden fences and hugging the buildings' walls. Street by street, they moved steadily closer to the river. As they crouched down against one wall and caught their breath, Lacey leaned into Pilgrim's side and whispered in his ear. The casinos along here housed hundreds upon hundreds of visiting gamblers on their entertainment floors, she told him, and had almost as many guest rooms, as well as a variety of restaurants and gift shops. She also described the steamboat building she remembered visiting, but until he saw it he didn't quite believe the picture her words drew.

The Riverboat Casino sat on the river's swollen banks, its expansive parking lot flooded in places, the water dark and fathomless. The hotel-casino itself was designed after a multi-tiered steamboat. In its heyday, Pilgrim imagined it would have been lit up in strings of gaudy bulbs and neon lights, the paddle box and its wheel encrusted with illuminated balls, the two tall smokestacks painted red and blinking a welcome seen from miles upriver. It was an impressive sight even unlit and unloved, one towering mast listing dramatically off centre, windows smashed, paint flaking.

'You're sure this is the place?' he asked. There were no lights shining from any of the windows; nor were there signs of any visitors intent on gambling.

He got the sense she nodded. 'I loved this place as a kid. I didn't believe Karey when she told me about it – a building that was a boat, too. It sounded crazy. But she brought me here, and she—'

She stopped talking when a solitary figure emerged from the building adjacent to the hotel-casino, passing under the raised arm of a security barrier and ambling down the ramp. The guy wasn't in any hurry and didn't appear to be too concerned with checking his surroundings as he walked from what Pilgrim could only assume was a parking garage. An arm detached from the guy's side and rose to head height.

The radio at Lacey's hip crackled to life.

'*Vehicles all clear. Get those cards dealt out, Ove. Be back in two.*'

The figure disappeared from view behind the corner of the casino, heading back inside.

'*We're already two games in, buddy*' came the reply. '*Better get a shake on.*'

362

'This is it,' Pilgrim said.

He and Lacey were crouched behind a waist-high wall at the top of the road that led its snaking way down to the parking lot. Pilgrim had never understood this country's predilection for assuming that every single person drove everywhere, thus making the progression of the pedestrian difficult. The switch-backs in this winding road made the walk three times longer than necessary. It also meant they would be visible to anyone happening to glance out of a window for three times the duration.

If it is any consolation, said his new voice. *I'm sure the builders of this country now deeply regret their non-pedestrian-friendly road systems.*

It wasn't any consolation to him, and Pilgrim half crawled, half scurried further along the wall to the top of the road in search of another way down.

There wasn't one. Not unless they wanted to swim.

He sighed.

I'm at a loss as to how you get yourself into these situations. And that sounded far too much like something Voice would say for Pilgrim's liking.

He went back to Lacey and nodded to the road. 'This is the only way.'

'I figured it would be,' she said.

Pilgrim kept to cover as much as possible but there was nowhere left to hide by the time they reached the bottom of the winding road – the open expanse of the flooded parking lot was the only thing between them and the hotel-casino's entrance. Of the three hundred car-park spaces, only a handful was occupied, and Pilgrim didn't have to investigate the vehicles to know they had already been picked clean.

'What's the plan?' Lacey asked breathlessly, hunkered down next to him as they both surveyed the layout ahead.

There wasn't any plan. To plan something when you had no idea what waited for you was practically impossible. He was beginning to consider sending her back to wait by the bike but suspected she would start a heated debate with him right then and there, and that was the last thing he wanted.

'The plan is not to get caught,' he said.

He was hesitant to step out into the open. The night crouched alongside him, a dark presence at his back, lurking in his periphery. There was a heavy sense of waiting in the damp air, of cunning anticipation, as though something just out of sight were readying itself to pounce. He wasn't sure if the girl sensed it, too, but she had pressed herself up against his side, a warm, solid weight from his armpit to his hipbone. He could feel her breathing, her ribs expanding and falling with each heavy breath. For a moment he flashed back to how it felt to have her slotted on the back of the motorcycle with him. She had been the first living human he had willingly made physical contact with for 151 straight days, and Voice had warned him not to get used to her presence. Now he feared he was more than used to it: he found, increasingly, that he didn't want to be without it.

You're drowning.

Yes. And the feeling wasn't an entirely unpleasant one.

In the sudden deflation of her ribs, he felt as well as heard the girl huff her breath out at him. 'That's about as helpful as a concrete life-vest,' she said.

He smiled in the dark, although it couldn't be seen. 'We go in quiet. We stay quiet while we're inside – which means no shooting, no shouting and no knocking anything over. We look around. We find Alex. It's a big place, and you said there are about thirty of them? So there'll be plenty of places to hide if we need to.'

'And what if we *do* end up making noise?'

'You remember me telling you to keep your boots on when you sleep?'

'Yeah?'

364

'Remember why I said it?'

'Because most times it's better to run like hell than to fight?'

'Exactly. If they find us, we run.'

They agreed that, if they did have to run and were somehow split up, they would meet back at the metal-working factory where they had left the TR7. It was a simple plan overall, but it suited the situation.

Pilgrim did a strange thing, then, one he couldn't entirely explain to himself. He placed a hand on the girl's head, palm cupping over the fragile curve of her skull. Her hair tickled and the crown of her head pumped out heat like it was her very own wood-burning stove.

She must be burning a lot of logs.

That made him smile, but again the dark hid it from view.

He sensed her lips part, felt her lungs inhale in readiness to release words on her next breath, but he didn't give her chance to voice them. He whispered, 'Let's go,' and took his hand from her head and placed it back on the cold shotgun. He dashed out into the parking lot.

He first aimed for an old station wagon fifty yards away. It sat low on its belly, wheels gone, hood raised, doors and rear hatch open as if the car had sprouted wings in an attempt to fly. It wasn't going anywhere, however, and wouldn't be for a long time to come. He covered the distance quickly and ducked low at its rear fender, waiting for the girl to drop down beside him. He looked through the missing windows and searched the hotel-casino's front. No more sign of anybody. He found it peculiar they had no lookouts posted.

Scanning the parking lot, the moon slid from behind a soot-black cloud, streaks of light silvering over the top of the floodwater. A lot of the flooding blocked their way, making a stranded island out of the steamboat-shaped building.

It might sail away yet.

It would make a lot of noise to wade through all the pools, and it would slow them down considerably. Pilgrim spotted a single, narrow pathway through two bodies of black water, just wide enough for a person. It angled to their right, away from the main entrance. Pilgrim directed Lacey's attention to it. She nodded. As if on cue, the clouds scudded back over the moon, and Pilgrim slid around the back of the station wagon and broke cover, running in long, loping strides, his wincing eyes fastened to the building, stubbornly ignoring the lancing pain shooting through his ribs. He heard the girl behind him, her footsteps swift and rabbit-light.

They made it to the corner of the building, all puffing air and thrumming blood. Pilgrim hopped over a railing and waited while the girl ducked under it and moved to his side. As soon as he felt her arm brush his elbow, he took off again, jogging along the building's east flank, shotgun held ready, his one good eye scanning, scanning, scanning.

They entered a large covered portico that joined the main casino building to the neighbouring three-storey parking garage. Above them, the stern of the steamboat jutted out, joining the garage on their second levels.

A secondary entrance welcomed them, the ghostly spirits of valets and door greeters beckoning them in. The automatic doors had been wedged open with an upended garbage can. Pilgrim cautiously approached.

'Look,' the girl whispered, but he'd already seen.

On the glass of the automatic doors two large heads facing each other had been spray-painted. And inside each were black whorls, thick and heavy.

'They're tagging the places they've been,' the girl whispered.

Or they're warnings of what's coming, Pilgrim thought.

He lifted his leg high and stepped over the can. Inside, the silence crushed down on him, the wind and misting rain evaporating almost at once. He pulled his neckerchief away from his nose and mouth. The place smelled of cold water and rot.

The interior of the building didn't resemble a steamboat at all. The highly polished floors had barely lost their gleam, and the tall ceilings were decorated with lavish hanging strands of multicoloured glass: oranges and bronzes and ochres, and every colour in between.

Their footsteps echoed no matter how lightly they placed their feet, although their attempts at being silent appeared to be wasted. The place was a ghost ship, evidence of the man they had spotted nowhere in sight, as if theirs were the only two living souls aboard.

They passed an unmanned pretzel parlour, the warm, salty smell long since dissipated. Next came a gleaming stainless-steel cotton-candy stand. There, the sticky, sweet aroma of sugar lingered in the air, and Pilgrim knew that saliva flooded the girl's mouth as she went by; he heard her swallow. Doors to restrooms and janitor cupboards were the only others they passed.

Next to an oversized plant pot, big enough to house an oak tree, a detailed colour-coded map was framed on the wall. Although Pilgrim couldn't read the names of the different rooms and areas, he could plainly see where the escalators and elevators were located, as well as all the restrooms, ATMs and emergency stairways and exits.

At the end of the shining corridor, down a handful of steps, the area opened up into a cathedral-ceilinged atrium with two sets of frozen escalators leading up, and a ransacked gift shop directly opposite. A set of heavy-looking doors stood closed behind the escalators on the north wall. Moonlight spilled in from the main entrance, as the hotel-casino's frontage was made up almost entirely of glass panels, some broken, most still intact. The gleaming floor shimmered under knee-deep water. Leaves and dirt and other bits of collected waste, including discarded gifts from the shop, floated in the impromptu pond, some of it batting up against the escalators' bottom risers.

Man and girl sloshed their way slowly across like jungle explorers wading through a swamp. It was at the base of those metal-grilled stairs that they heard the first, distant signs of life.

Laughter. Followed by a crash as something heavy was overturned. More raucous laughter followed, but there was angry shouting, too, which fuelled a flurry of loud, mocking retorts. More crashes came.

Pilgrim and the girl exchanged looks.

Potjack, that new, separate part of him whispered.

They listened a while longer as the voices lost their volume and dispersed. Pilgrim knew it was a trick of the acoustics; the people were still up there, they were simply too far away to hear now that the storm of the argument had blown over.

He told the girl to keep close. He ascended the escalator, the hushed clang of their feet and the metallic drops of water pinging from their pant legs not loud enough to carry. Nearing the top, Pilgrim laid himself out along the cold, crooked steps, their serrated edges painfully digging into his sore ribs, and peered over the top riser. His eyes were jarred by an offensively patterned carpet. After a dozen yards of the concentric-hexagonal motif, the first line of slot machines stood in a dark row, each with its own stool perched in front. There were many machines, row after row, soon fading into darkness as the moonlight from the atrium failed to reach past the hulking gambling kiosks.

He watched for a long minute and then rose, motioning the girl to follow. He stepped on to the thick carpeting, his boots sinking into the plushness, and moved silently away from the wide centre aisle, weaving his way through the slot machines, using them as cover. His eyes quickly adjusted to the dark, although he could feel the heavy weight of the flashlight in his jacket pocket if he needed it. They met a wide intersecting aisle of carpet that led west to east, hundreds of gaming machines of all kinds standing mournfully tall like monoliths in a graveyard.

A bank of roulette tables spread out on their right, maybe twenty in total. One had been heaved on to its side, gaming chips scattered, the red, black, green and blue tokens camouflaged against the garish designs of the carpet. The surrounding stools had also been knocked over.

A hand tugged on the back of his jacket and he leaned down to the girl so her lips could reach his ear.

'Someone wasn't happy about losing,' she whispered.

Pilgrim wondered what these people could be worried about losing, other than a handful of plastic chips.

'See the door?' She pointed.

Sure enough, on the back wall behind the roulette tables, an 'Employee Only' door had been wedged partly open with a red fire extinguisher. He couldn't see it was red from this distance, it was too dark for that, but he knew what colour it was, what colour all fire extinguishers were. It worried him, that fire-engine red. It reminded him of the swinging service doors in the loading bay of the mall. Of how he'd seen a hole blown through them and phantom blood spurt out. His whole plan hinged on not being seen and yet, without walking deeper into the snake pit, where someone could be waiting around any corner, they would never locate the woman.

In careful advancements – keeping slot machines between them and it, and then dashing over the wide, carpeted aisle and staying low behind roulette tables – they headed for the back wall. They had almost reached it when voices came again, this time from somewhere behind the 'Employees Only' door, drawing closer.

Pilgrim dropped and crawled into the space beneath the nearest roulette table, reaching back to grip the girl's shirt at the shoulder. The door wheezed fully open on its hydraulic arm, and he dragged the girl under the table so she ended up mostly sprawled across him.

The voices spilled out, a pool of amber light coming with

them. Pilgrim froze. The girl stopped moving, too. Her bony elbow dug painfully into his gut. He could barely feel her breathing, although her jack-rabbit heart knocked clean through her body and into his.

A gravelly thirty-smokes-a-day voice said, 'But he's such a cock-sucker.'

A second, older: 'Don't matter what he is. You best do what he says or else he'll carve your nose clean off your face and say he was *told* to do it by that thing in his head.'

'He can damn well come and try it, the faggot.' The words were filled with false bravado. The man was obviously scared.

'Turn your face into scrimshaw.'

'*Scrimshaw,*' a third, younger voice hooted. 'Good one, Teller.'

'You don't even know what scrimshaw is, you damn fool.'

Pilgrim had recognised that third voice. Lacey stiffened against him, and he knew she'd recognised it, too. He still gripped her shirt in his fist, and he tightened his hold on her in silent warning.

The three men moved close enough to smell, walking down between the roulette tables, heading for the carpeted aisle, needing to pass by the table where they hid to reach it. The lantern light glided along with them. Pilgrim noticed Lacey's boot sticking out, clearly visible beyond the table.

'I know what scrimshaw means,' Posy said defiantly.

'Oh yeah? Then why don't you *enlighten* us.'

'Ah, leave him be,' said Teller. 'He don't know when to take a dump, never mind anything else.'

The two men laughed, very loud now, their voices practically on top of them, the pool of lamplight illuminating the floor, seeping in under the table where they lay hidden. Pilgrim loosened his hold on Lacey's shirt and reached down, snagging the denim of her jeans at her knee and carefully, *slowly*, pulling her leg under the table, sliding her foot into the shadows.

The three men trudged past, Posy complaining while the other two continued to heckle him. They reached the aisle and headed back the way Pilgrim and Lacey had come.

The radio on Lacey's belt bleeped twice to remind them of its dying battery. The girl flinched, and he felt a fissure of panic pin him in place.

One set of footsteps stopped walking. 'You hear that?' Teller said.

'Screw you, guys,' Posy whined. 'I don't gotta put up with this from you.'

The same set of footsteps that had halted now reversed course and came back towards their hiding place. Pilgrim watched a pair of boots appear and pause at the end of their table, where Lacey's boot had been seconds before. He could imagine the guy's head cocking, his ears straining, and Pilgrim had to fight his instinct to reach for the radio at Lacey's waist and click it off. All it would take was one more bleep . . .

'You're right, Pose, it's a free world,' the smoker said from over in the aisle. 'So why don't you express your right to freedom and fuck off someplace else?'

'Hey, you shouldn't talk to me like that—'

Lacey flinched again when the roulette wheel above them spun, the grinding of ball-bearings reverberating through the table as the wheel revolved over their heads.

'Only reason you got any leeway with us was because you was Red's lapdog,' Smokes said. 'Right, Teller?'

Teller, no more than a foot away, grunted in agreement. 'And she ain't here any more. You don't have any Get Out of Jail Free cards, boy, so you'd best watch your step from here on out.' The roulette wheel continued to spin, slower and slower, as Teller's boots turned and walked away. Pilgrim listened as the footsteps rejoined his companion's and the two sets continued on their way, the muted yellow light going with them. Posy stood somewhere off to the right and muttered to himself for a short while until another light bloomed, this one whiter and more intense. Posy left the aisle and traipsed back through the roulette tables, still bitching under his breath.

The sound of his name stopped his muttering.

Pilgrim gently called it again, and the man cautiously, with uncertain steps, came to stand beside their table.

Posy bent down and pointed his flashlight in at them.

Pilgrim pointed his shotgun right back and said, 'Unless you want another hole to breathe through, don't say a single word.'

CHAPTER 5

Lacey watched Posy's eyes go very wide, his mouth drop open.

'Close your mouth,' the Boy Scout said.

Posy closed it.

'Good boy. Now back up.'

The ginger-bearded man retreated a couple of steps, and the Boy Scout gave Lacey a nudge. Taking the hint, she wriggled down under his arm, being careful to not block the shotgun, and squirmed out from under the table. The first thing she did once she was clear was to turn the hand-held radio off. She wanted to throw the stupid thing across the room, smash it and then stomp on the bits for good measure – her heartbeat still hadn't recovered from the scare it had given her – but having a hissy fit over it would be a Bad idea with a capital B.

As the Boy Scout pushed his way out from under the roulette table, she noticed he was careful never to let the shotgun's muzzles waver from Posy's narrow chest.

'H–how'd you get here?'

It took her a second to figure out that Posy was talking to her. He was gaping, obviously shaken by the fact that she was standing alive and well in front of him.

Don't think his scarecrow legs will hold him up for much longer, Voice said.

She shrugged and offered a smile. 'Drove Lou's truck here.'

Posy slanted the Boy Scout a look, as if searching for confirmation that her claim was true, but before he could ask the question he blinked and his mouth fell open all over again.

'C–christ—' He trailed off and stared.

Perplexed, Lacey looked at the Boy Scout again, confused as to what Posy was gawping at. Then she got it. The last time these two were in each other's company, Posy had been trying to lift the Boy Scout's dead weight into the back of Jeb's jeep.

'Move over to the wall,' the Boy Scout ordered, gesturing with the shotgun to indicate a corner where they wouldn't be seen.

Posy didn't move. All his concentration seemed to be focused on gaining control of his flapping mouth. When he spoke it was as though he were talking to a priest after witnessing a miracle from God. 'You're *him*, ain't you?'

'No,' said the Boy Scout.

'Who?' asked Lacey at the same time.

'Y–you *are*. Jeb killed you. I saw it. You was dead.'

'I think you're mistaking me for some other person who got shot in the head.'

Lacey almost guffawed, but her amusement quickly died when the Boy Scout squared off, lifting the shotgun up to point it at Posy's face.

'I won't ask you to move again,' he said quietly.

'You better do as he says,' Lacey advised.

Whatever Posy saw in the Boy Scout's eyes did the trick; he wisely got moving, hurrying to the corner behind a rank of slot machines, away from the main aisle. He threw a pathetic *Please don't hurt me* glance over his shoulder, which only made Lacey pity him more.

The Boy Scout asked Lacey to pull out the Zippo, and she did, flicking it to life. Its weak flame was preferable to the harsh white beam of Posy's flashlight, and when he was ordered to switch it off, he shakily fumbled it until the bulb went dark. Lacey took it away from him.

'Sit,' the Boy Scout ordered.

Posy sat, sliding his back down the wall.

Lacey stayed standing while the Boy Scout hunkered opposite Posy, using his up-raised knee as a shelf for his elbow and, in turn, a brace for the gun. He pressed the barrels of the shotgun against the man's scrawny throat.

Posy squeezed his eyes shut, his face collapsing in a mess of pockmarks and patchy beard fuzz.

'P–p–*please*. I ain't *done* nothing!'

'*Hush*,' the Boy Scout snapped, his voice a harsh whisper.

Lacey rested a hand on the Boy Scout's shoulder, felt the slight tremble in it and glanced down at him in concern.

He's hurting.

She knew that. She crouched beside him so she was on the same level as them both, wanting to diffuse the tension. It wasn't good for either of them.

She spoke directly to Posy. 'Listen, Posy, we just want some answers, OK? We don't want to hurt you.'

Posy chanced opening an eye. 'Y–you swear?'

'We're reading buddies, right?' She made her voice as soft and persuasive as she could. 'I don't lie to my reading buddies.'

He opened both eyes and nervously shifted his attention from her to the man at her side and back again.

'All we want is to find our friend,' Lacey told him. 'That's it. Then we'll go.'

'You . . . you mean Alex?'

Hearing her name, Lacey felt a dizzying tilt, the floor suddenly becoming the heaving deck of a real ship, plummeting out from under her. If she had been standing, she would have staggered.

She could barely get enough air to speak. 'Yes. Alex.'

'Hmm, Dumont got her.'

'*Where?*'

'Upstairs.' He made that humming noise again. 'In the Lounge of Stars.'

After a little prompting – the majority of it done by the Boy Scout, if Lacey was honest – Posy also told them that the two men he had been with had gone to keep watch at the front of the casino and that most of the others were in the hotel part of the building in the west wing (raiding the guest rooms' minibars), in the buffet dining hall, which could be accessed by the staff corridors through the 'Employee Only' door, or out in search parties and not due back until morning. Dumont, however, was on the third level.

'Search parties for what?' the Boy Scout asked.

'People? Who can hear stuff? Boss wants 'em rounded up.'

'Why, Posy?'

'I don't know,' he whined. 'I don't get told nothin'.' Two fat tears welled, making the Zippo's light split into twin reflected flames, one in each of his eyes, dancing and flickering as his gaze shuffled between them. 'He'll . . . he'll hurt me if he knows I talked.'

They look like fire devils, she thought, the Zippo hot in her hand.

He's another empty soul, Voice said sadly.

The Boy Scout drew the shotgun away, no longer pressing it to Posy's throat. He kept it aimed at him, though.

'We won't tell him,' Lacey promised.

But the man wasn't looking at her any more, his attention fixed on the man knelt beside her.

'W–what happened to your eye?' Posy whispered. One tear spilled over and left a silvery track on his cheek, disappearing into his beard.

Lacey watched the Boy Scout cover his left eye, hiding it from view, and then drop his hand again to meet the man's gaze steadily. He said very quietly, 'When I was dead, I only dared open one eye. It saw Hell.'

Lacey nudged him in the side with her elbow, silently admonishing him for teasing the poor man. 'He's just kidding,' she told Posy.

'Am I?' the Boy Scout said, arching an eyebrow at her. The flicker of firelight added a wicked gleam to his eyes, especially the bloodied one.

She shook her head at him, giving in to a small smile, and got up.

Posy didn't speak much after that. When the Boy Scout pulled the man's laces free from his shoes and tied his hands behind his back, he began to weep, but his snuffles and drooling remained quiet, and Lacey was grateful for that: she didn't want the Boy Scout to scare him any more.

She attempted to reassure Posy that he wouldn't be hurt, but he didn't seem to hear her.

CHAPTER 6

They located a cleaner's closet and Pilgrim sliced a strip off Posy's shirt, stuffed his dirty sock in his mouth and tied him into silence. Only when the girl went to shut the door did Posy sit up and shake his head violently, so hard to the left and right that tears and snot flew from his face.

'What?'

A strangled whine came from his throat and his gaze dropped to the handle, where the girl's hand rested.

'Shut the door,' Pilgrim told her. 'We can't leave it open.'

Posy gave a pathetic, guttural mewl, his eyes big and wide and terrified.

'Is it the dark?' Lacey asked him. 'Are you afraid of the dark?'

Looking miserable, more tears sliding down his face, Posy nodded quickly.

The girl looked at Pilgrim, and Pilgrim could read her thoughts as plainly as if they had spilled from her lips.

'We need the flashlights,' he told her.

'We don't need two.'

They did. There were two of them. One for him and one for her. But he said nothing when she stepped into the small closet and flicked on the flashlight they had taken from Posy. As the beam flashed across him, his front awash in light, an arc of bright colour blotted out his features for a second, his face hidden behind an iridescent rainbow made up of blues and purples – the exact colours of a new bruise. Pilgrim blinked, momentarily taken aback, and then the colours were gone, the flashlight now standing upright between the man's legs so that it beamed a perfect white circle on the closet's ceiling.

'There,' the girl whispered. 'No need to be scared.'

They shut and secured the door by wedging a stool under the handle. They were gambling on it holding the man inside long enough for them to get upstairs. Pilgrim didn't like to gamble, but he had little choice under the circumstances. The man was too pathetic to kill but too dangerous to let go. Once Posy was out, he would go straight to one of his people and announce they had unwanted visitors.

They didn't have much time.

Pilgrim glanced at the red fire extinguisher as they hurried past and headed for the far end of the huge casino floor. It seemed its colour had indeed been a warning, for if they had decided to go through that door they would have undoubtedly come across a group of Dumont's people in the buffet hall.

They made quick progress, the plush carpeting muting their footfalls and allowing them to move at a jog, weaving in and out of the gaming machines, the beam from the flashlight he had taken out of his pocket picking out their lurid names, none of which Pilgrim could read, but their colours covered the spectrum from spectral red to violet.

Why the limp?

There was no pain or discomfort in his left leg, his thigh muscle felt only weakened somehow, shaky, like his arm did, and he found it put a weird hitch in his stride. He paid it no mind and paused just long enough at the threshold of the casino floor to gauge the way ahead as safe. The new lobby they entered was smaller than the entrance lobby downstairs. As the map on the wall had indicated, two more escalators slanted up to the next floor. A pair of elevators waited on the far side of the escalators, along with another group of restrooms. To the north, a main corridor branched off, leading to the buffet dining hall –

the more standard route for gamblers and visitors to take. (A faint murmur of voices came from that direction, proving that at least part of Posy's information was accurate and that some of Dumont's men were in there.) And to the east, a wide walkway opened on to another thoroughfare that travelled all the way back to join with the parking garage on its second floor.

Past the dual, motionless escalators to the south, the thick carpeting stopped and became the warm, honeyed wooden flooring of a saloon-type bar. Empty booths and a square central bar dominated the view, with numerous blank flat-screened TVs bracketed to the ceiling. There were no lights back there, so Pilgrim wasted no more time on it – he clicked his flashlight off and, keeping the wall to his left, crossed to a door marked with an unlit green sign with a man running towards a white doorway on it. He briefly pressed his ear to the cool door leading to the emergency stairs. Hearing nothing, he pulled it open and went through into the pitch-black stairwell.

When the door clicked shut behind them, all he could hear was the girl's panting. It made a ghostly wind-like whistling that echoed around his ears. His shirt under the arms was soaked with sweat, and more trickled down his ribs and along his spine. He waited, the girl beside him gradually catching her breath, and they listened for furtive, sneaking noises approaching.

After thirty seconds, Lacey nudged him and he clicked the flashlight back on. Together they stepped over to the railing and he shone the light up into the gloom above their heads. Pilgrim expected to see a line of white faces staring down at them with wide eyes and silent mouths, but none greeted them.

'Up we go,' he murmured.

His knee folded on the first step, and he grabbed for the railing, dropping the flashlight. The light rolled around in a disorientating circle, flashing white on the walls before Lacey bent and picked it up. It took a great effort to pull his weight on to his left leg.

'You OK?' the girl whispered, concerned.

'Fine. Just a slip.'

It's lies that slip so easily from your lips. Nothing more.

He let the girl hold on to the flashlight and kept his hand on the railing, gripping it hard as he took the steps quickly but jerkily. When he reached the door to the third floor, he had to wipe sweat from his eyes. More than his arm and leg were shaking now. His entire body trembled.

He felt the girl's eyes on him.

Again he pressed his ear to the door. He heard nothing, but there was *something* out there. A tension lined the door frame like an invisible barrier, unbroken but tightly stretched.

Something alive? he was asked.

Yes. Alive.

He motioned for the girl to turn off the light and, a second later, with a soft *click*, the world went dark.

Pilgrim didn't immediately move, not even when the girl pressed closer against him. He waited for a break in his trembling, although the sickly beat of his heart didn't calm, before slowly unlatching the door and easing it open.

A warm rush of air blew in his face and along with it came the brassy stench of blood. It entered his nostrils and fused inside his brain, lighting it up in a sharp, crackling snap, all colours leaching away except for *RED*. Even in the darkness, a wall of red dropped over his eyes, a pall of colour so rich and thick it was like he could reach out and touch it, inhale it, *taste* it. He saw the floors below them rapidly filling, silently churning with floodwater, except it wasn't the murky overspill from the river but the colour of burgundy wine, and it was hot and salty and as viscous as syrup. The blood gushed up the dead escalators leading to their floor, the serrated steps running red, the tide rising in a rush that exploded at the top in a cresting wave that burst into the air, splattering the gleaming floor in a messy, vibrant claret. The flood quickly pooled outwards, expanding in a growing lake, reaching out to him, reaching for the door he stood behind, blood seeping through the gap and touching his boot.

He stiffened and, when he stiffened, the girl did, too. She said his name in an unsteady whisper, a whisper that roared in his ears like a gale, and the red veil over his vision blinked out and all was dark again. Black, velvety darkness. The smell of blood receded quickly, still there but fainter, copper-tinged. The floods retreated from his mind.

He breathed in a trembling breath, and the girl whispered his name again.

Pilgrim.

Not Boy Scout.

He really needed to speak to her about that when they got out of here.

His instincts were to withdraw, to find another way around, that entering a place which smelled so much of fresh blood, that had triggered such a strong reaction in him, would be a dangerous mistake.

But he couldn't retreat. The woman waited for them. And the girl waited on him. Lacey had already lost her sister – he'd noticed the blurred redness of her eyes when she'd come back downstairs to him. He didn't want her to lose anyone else.

Maybe it's the woman's blood that has been spilled.

Possibly. Even likely. But they couldn't leave without finding out.

Pilgrim put his boot in the opening and let the door rest on it. He leaned the shotgun against his leg and turned to the girl, cupping her head in both his hands, tilting her ear up to him. Her face was very hot and sweaty between his palms. His words when he spoke them were a mere breath, barely a sound at all, and he breathed the instructions directly into her ear: to keep the flashlight off, to put it away, that they must proceed in darkness, mustn't be spotted, mustn't be heard. That if he tapped the top of her head it meant he wanted her to get down and to stay down until he came back for her (he felt her rebel at that, her body tensing, but he tightened his grip on her head and she was still). He told her to keep a grip on the back of his belt if she couldn't see well enough to follow him, and that if she understood everything he'd said she should nod.

A second later, she nodded.

He didn't immediately let her go but leaned his brow against the side of her head and closed his eyes. He was so tired. All he wanted was to go back to her sister's warm kitchen, lie down by the stove and fall into a deep, exhausted sleep.

The girl had already put the flashlight away, her hand empty when she laid it over the back of his. Her fingers curled around his hand and held fast. He lifted his head and looked down at her. They stood in pitch-blackness, but he knew she was looking him dead in the eyes, just like she had when she'd looked over her lemonade stand at him that first day. He had always liked her directness.

Keeping hold of her hand, he brought it down, turning himself and placing it under his jacket at the back of his belt. He felt her fingers curl around it, gripping on to him, effectively tethering them together. He picked up the shotgun and touched the edge of the door. He took a deep breath, deliberately drawing that heavy, wet stench of blood into his lungs, and silently pulled the door wider and stepped through.

With a gentle tug at his belt, he took the girl with him.

In his head was a clear diagram of the map he had seen on the first floor. He knew that if he were to keep left, the wall would lead him past an expansive room that housed something to do with high-stakes gambling (he had recognised a number of dollar signs on this part of the map). Next would be a corridor that led from this main part of the building to a series of smaller rooms – around ten – most likely guest suites. Then another set of restrooms (three in total, including one for the handicapped). On the east side of the escalators were the non-working elevators. There was no walkway leading out to the neighbouring parking garage, like on the floor below; they were now effectively on the large bridge level of the steamboat, where access was reserved for only the most affluent of guests.

Finally, in the north section, was the Lounge of Stars. Pilgrim knew this because there had been numerous stars imprinted all over that section of the map, the only ones in evidence on its entirety, at any level.

It wasn't completely dark when he stepped into the third-floor lobby, but it was a near thing. There was some natural light filtering in from somewhere because his night vision was able to pick out vaguely the black rubber escalator handrails that rose up from the floor below and the marginally darker recesses that marked doorways and the opening to the corridor. However, all the doors were closed, as far as he could tell, which prevented any ambient light from entering.

Pilgrim kept the wall at his left shoulder and started forward, his and the girl's shoes making faint squeaks on the floor. He held the shotgun down at his side and ran his left hand along the wall, pausing only for a moment when he reached the first set of double doors (to the unknown gambling room), and passed over it. The black maw of the branching corridor, leading off into the guests' suites, gaped a few feet ahead of him, and he had the awful feeling someone was standing in the dark opening, a handful of steps back, waiting for him and the girl to pass in front. Maybe the unknown assailant would reach out and drag them into the unyielding blackness with him. Or maybe he had an axe that was even now held high, ready to chop down into Pilgrim's skull as soon he stepped into view. He knew that, however indistinct, he and the girl would be faintly backlit to anyone looking out at them from the corridor. Two black, shifting shadows, detached from the surrounding darkness, visible by their movement.

The smell of blood grew stronger with every step. His fingers ran along smooth wall and stopped as they reached the corner that turned into the corridor. He crouched down against the wall, and his movement translated to the hand holding on to his belt and the girl crouched with him.

You're letting your fear control you.

It wasn't fear for himself. It would be foolhardy simply to walk into this without caution.

Holding the shotgun by its stock, he lifted it and held it out in front of him into the opening of the corridor. He expected something to grab it, or hit it, to try to knock it from his hand, and was tensing already, his muscles burning from holding on to the gun so tightly.

But nothing happened.

Pilgrim dared to lean his head around the corner. Let his eyes probe hard at the darkness, scrutinised it so intensely that flashes of colour danced in his vision. But no amount of staring made the darkness open up.

Only thing to do is chance it.

He remained mostly crouched as he went forward, keeping low, and stepped in front of that sucking blackness, in front of the dark unknown. His heart was a hammer-beat in his chest, and he was acutely aware of Lacey's hot hand clutching at the back of his belt as she followed.

They almost made it, too.

Pilgrim's left hand was stretched out, reaching, and it touched the far corner, his palm sliding thankfully back on to the cool surface of the wall, when a door burst open nearby, smacking into the wall with a flinchingly loud *CRACK.*

Behind him the girl gasped, but already he was turning and grabbing her off her feet and taking them both into the corridor that had only a second ago been a threat. He slid them into the darkness and flattened them against the wall, covering the girl's mouth with his palm as a storm of controlled rage crashed on to the third-floor landing. Energy crackled, but there was no sound other than the quick march of footsteps. A wash of light had spilled out from the newly opened doorway, a muted yellow that slunk outwards and crept into their corridor. It revealed they were alone, no axe-wielding maniac waiting to decapitate them. It also meant that, if anyone glanced over, they would immediately be seen.

The footsteps had originated from the Lounge of Stars and were now crossing the lobby, heading towards them.

Pilgrim turned his head. There was a door to a suite no more than ten feet away, a potential place to hide, but there was a black box stuck to the wall beside it. A card-activation slot. He couldn't trust the door would open if he went for it.

'My dear, why the dramatics? You know this is what I do.'

Two hot streams of breath blew hard on to the back of Pilgrim's hand. He didn't need the girl's reaction to know the man who had spoken was Dumont. The cultured New Orleans drawl was exactly how Lacey had described it.

The footsteps stopped, presumably so the person could turn and reply to Dumont, who had remained near the lounge. This voice when it came was clipped and coldly precise.

'It is not dramatics on my part, Charles. It is a little something called reprisal. You owe me more than this.'

All the warmth left Dumont's voice. 'And what exactly do I owe you, Joseph?'

Lacey had told him of another man. Pilgrim had watched her chew at four of her fingernails, one after the other, while she spoke about him. For reasons the girl couldn't articulate to Pilgrim, this bowler-hatted man had scared her more than his actions towards her had warranted.

'*Loyalty*.' The word resounded, echoing off the floor tiles and closed doors and empty spaces, and Lacey flinched under

Pilgrim's hand. He could feel her trembling. This man was Doc, all right. 'Red is not the only pet who deserves special care. You and I have been a team for years; not to consult me when decisions are to be made is disrespectful. The rules are changing. More than ever we need to be strong, or else there'll be no place left for us. Don't presume you can do this alone.'

The chill injected into the air by this man's speech made Pilgrim shiver, but now the low-burning anger in Dumont's reply added an undercurrent of heat.

'Choose your words carefully, Joseph. It is me these people look to for leadership. Not you.'

'The Flitting Man isn't the only one who has plans. We may be doing his work right now, but it won't be for ever.'

'You shouldn't be so openly seditious. He has ears everywhere.'

'Ears, voices, it's all the same. All the people we've gathered so far hear only weak, undeveloped whispers. I don't see the point. No one has a strong voice like ours.'

'Not any more, no. You made sure of that. You had no right to hurt her,' Dumont said, his words quiet and deadly. 'Or think that you could hide what you did.'

'I wasn't trying to hide it, Charles. I *wanted* you to know. Red was using you as much as the Flitting Man is using us. She fed you just enough information to fool you into thinking she was helping, but all the while she was playing mind games with you. You honestly believe she *chose* to stay? She stayed because you threatened to hunt down her family if she didn't. She hated you. She hated everything we're doing. She'd have released those people we've captured if she could have.' Joseph didn't wait for an answer, his footsteps starting up again, coming their way. 'You need to wise up, old friend. There's no room for sentimentality any more. This is a new world, pure and simple. And anyone who doesn't accept it will be left to rot alongside everyone else, including your precious Red.'

Pilgrim quickly released Lacey and tapped the top of her head. She dropped into a crouch, just as he'd instructed her to, and he lifted the shotgun, aiming it at the mouth of the corridor.

Another resounding *crack* sounded and the soft light vanished. The door to the lounge had shut. Dumont had retreated.

The coldly calculating man didn't light his own way but continued onwards in the dark.

A tattoo of panic beat in Pilgrim's temples and thudded to the back of his head, making the tender area behind his ear fizz with pain. He gently squeezed the trigger, felt it depress inwards by a fraction.

If he fired, the blast of the shotgun would bring them all running. Then it would be a crazy dash out of these dark hallways and into the rain, all their progress lost and the building put on alert. It would be impossible to re-enter and find Alex if they gave away their presence now.

The smell of blood was so thick it clogged the back of Pilgrim's throat, filled it up like a stopper. He was close to gagging but ruthlessly pushed down the reflux.

His finger twitched when a shadow passed across the mouth of the corridor, almost firing off a shot. He quickly released the pressure on the trigger, and stared hard at the dark shape. It was strangely bulky and heavy-footed, lumbering its way past them. Was Doc injured? Had his and Dumont's disagreement turned to violence? Although his tone of voice had conveyed no signs of pain, it would explain the strong stench of blood.

Pilgrim had two seconds to study the bulky shadow before it passed, the emergency-stair door opening with a vacuum-sealed *whoosh* – as if it had quarantined itself from the bloody atmosphere smogging the landing – and the man went through, the door *clunk*ing shut behind him.

The girl sucked in a long, ragged breath, as if she had been holding on to it the entire time. He had lost her hand but now reached for her again, finding her arm in the dark and sliding his hand down to grasp her cold one, tugging it back to his belt. He felt her fingers curl into his back as she gripped on.

Time was even shorter. He felt it. Very soon their opportunity would be gone and they would be hunted down like rats in a sewer. The time for hiding and sneaking was over.

He stood and pulled the girl after him, not sticking to the east wall any more but heading directly for the doors that had been open only a few short seconds ago. The doors leading into the Lounge of Stars.

The doors leading to Dumont.

The interchange between the two men had been intimate. Pilgrim believed that neither man would choose to talk so candidly in front of an audience. As such, he trusted his instincts and didn't pause when he reached the doors, pulling the right one open. Muted light from inside fell over him.

The man had his back to them and didn't turn when Pilgrim and the girl entered.

'I'm sorry, Joseph,' Dumont said, his head down and his wide shoulders slumped in apparent remorse. 'You know I value your friendship, your loyalty.'

While he spoke, Pilgrim surveyed the room. The Lounge of Stars was an impressively sumptuous bar. Expensive-looking leather armchairs and sofas, a dark mahogany bar lining the back wall, where a bow-tied barman had once respectfully mixed drinks while a straight-backed sommelier waited at the far end with a wine list. Pilgrim was surprised to see a number of intact optics attached to the wall above the bar, filled with a wonderful array of warm ambers and honeys, a veritable line-up of cognacs, bourbons and whiskeys.

'We must not argue between ourselves,' Dumont continued. 'Not if we want to survive.'

But most eye-catching of all was the ceiling, circular in design and segmented like a spider's web in a transparent mosaic of glass panels. It opened up the roof to the sky and allowed all inside to see the dark expanse of the night laid over them, adorned with its millions of flickering stars.

The Lounge of Stars had rightly earned its name.

The rainclouds had mostly cleared, and the scattering of cold, blinking stars was an apt backdrop to Dumont's speech of repentance.

When no response came, Dumont turned. The man's shirt-sleeves had been rolled up to reveal thickly muscled forearms. What caught Pilgrim's attention, though, were the sleeves of blood that streaked him from fingertip to elbow. In this luxurious room, amidst the sophistication of dark woods and leathers, lay the stink of pain and suffering.

It was hard to read Dumont's reaction. In fact, the man barely reacted at all, other than a slight narrowing of his eyes. Speckles of blood dotted his face on the left side like gory freckles.

His eyes widened to normal size when Lacey let go of Pilgrim's belt and stepped into sight. The tall man broke into a smile, seemingly genuinely delighted to see her.

'Lacey! You made it! What a surprise!'

Lacey didn't spend time on chit-chat. 'Where's Alex?'

Dumont's smile grew. 'I don't even get a hello? Well, that's not very friendly, is it?' He slid his wry smile over to Pilgrim, including him in his amusement.

'You're not my friend,' Lacey said. 'I don't even like you. I just want to know where she is.'

'I'll meet you question for question – how's that? Where's my Red?'

'We have her.' It was the first time Pilgrim spoke.

Dumont returned his attention to him, smile still in place, his stare sharpening. 'I don't think I've had the pleasure—'

'And you won't. We only want the woman. Let us have her, and we'll get the girl back to you.'

Dumont looked him over silently, smile fading. His eyes did

390

a thorough journey from the top of Pilgrim's head right down to his boots. Maybe he was considering the offer, but Pilgrim got the feeling the man was trying to unnerve him by not speaking. What he didn't realise was that silence was Pilgrim's friend and he would gladly allow it to stretch out for as long as Dumont wanted.

Lacey wasn't so immune. He heard her shift anxiously beside him.

Dumont finally broke the stand-off and moved to sit down, lowering his long body into an armchair. He winced and reached behind his back, plucking a handgun from under his belt. He left the gun resting flat on his thigh, pointed at them, and gestured to the other armchairs, indicating they should sit.

Pilgrim and the girl stayed where they were.

Dumont stroked his chin while he considered them, apparently unaware he was using bloodied fingers to do so.

'What happened to Louis and Rink?' he asked.

'Dead,' Pilgrim said.

Dumont regarded him a moment longer and then turned to the girl. 'That's four of my men you've been partially responsible for killing. That's four more than I've ever let anyone get away with.'

'I didn't kill them,' Lacey said, and Pilgrim could hear the defensiveness in her tone.

'She's right,' Pilgrim said. 'I killed them. Three intentionally, the fourth by accident.'

The bloodied fingers at his chin stopped their stroking. Pilgrim couldn't recall having seen the man blink since they had entered.

'You're the man who stabbed Jebediah?' Dumont asked.

Jeb. The dead man's name.

'Yes.'

'You're the one he shot? I was told you were dead.'

'You were misinformed.'

'I can see that. It's very perplexing.'

'Who's the Flitting Man?' Pilgrim asked.

Dumont smiled, unperturbed by the change in subject. 'You must have heard the tales by now. The boogeyman with a cloak made up of the night sky, who breathes fire over his enemies. Or maybe the version you heard was that he *was* the night, a man made of darkness and stars with black holes for eyes. He passes like a ghost into encampments and takes those he wants, and leaves to burn any he doesn't. He's quite something, if you believe all the stories.'

'I don't believe them.'

'Well, you should,' Dumont said, all traces of good humour gone. 'You should believe them. He's gathering his people.'

'People who hear voices.' Again Pilgrim felt Lacey shift beside him. 'Tell me why.'

'What purpose is any army for? To fight for something it wants. The Flitting Man has his own voice, and it's a voice unlike any I've come across before. It has grown in ways you cannot even imagine—' Dumont's gaze drifted, became unfocused, as if he were looking upon a world that was majestic and terrifying in equal measure. He came back to himself slowly. 'Like I said, he's quite something. Almost lives up to all the tales. He can't do all the work himself, of course, despite his abilities. That's where all the stories come unstuck: he's only one person, after all. He's had to enlist a little help.'

'From people like you?'

The man smiled again. 'Yes.'

'But why now?' Pilgrim demanded, uneasy to hear so much anger in his voice. 'It's been seven years.'

Dumont blinked for the first time, and a shrewd look came into his eyes. 'It's taken this long for him to be ready. You'll understand when you meet him, which I'm sure you will. Everyone will know his name soon enough. You'd best think about which side you're on and be sure you can live with it after all the dust has settled.'

The meanderings of a madman or the truth? Pilgrim didn't know. This could all as easily be the work of another manipulative voice, one that was as unhinged as its host, whispering away inside this man's head.

'I just want to know where Alex is,' Lacey said, a faint plea in her tone. 'Please.'

Dumont's attention shifted to her. He didn't speak.

'I'm sorry for interrupting,' she added.

The man's eyes crinkled. 'Manners. There's still a place for them.'

'Doc was just in here,' she said. 'I heard him.'

'Joseph? Indeed he was.'

'What did he mean by "reprisal"?'

'Ah, he's punishing me for having my fun.' Dumont lifted his hands to show the blood that had dried there. There was blood splashed in much larger spots on the carpet at their feet. 'He becomes quite annoyed when I don't include him in my decision-making. He was upset with me for letting you go, for example. Thought there were better uses for you. Do you know why?'

The girl had no answer for him, and even took a tiny step closer to Pilgrim, as if unconsciously seeking his protection.

'He sat for some time outside the freezer you were held in, Lacey. Seems you like talking to yourself. Joseph enjoys listening and watching. It's how we find the people we're hunting for, by looking for certain signs. It's how we learned of Red's gifts.'

'What gifts?' Lacey had found her voice again. 'What's so special about her? I don't get it.'

Pilgrim went back to studying the blood spatters on the carpet. They hadn't fully darkened yet, were still damp. He followed the stains, tracking them past his boot and back towards the main doors.

'She knows how to survive in this world,' Dumont said. 'Better than anyone else I've met. And that's all anyone wants, isn't it? To survive. She knew about the voices before anyone even suspected they were coming. She knew about the Flitting Man when the rumours were merely whispers on the wind. And she has lots more secrets locked up inside her, but it takes a certain finesse to get her to open up. Like playing chess: you lose as many pieces as you capture, but it's always a game worth playing. It's the *only* game worth playing. Joseph doesn't understand that. He lacks delicacy. Especially with what he calls my "pets".'

'He did that to Red's mouth,' Pilgrim said absently, thinking about the bulky shadow of the man walking past the corridor where they'd hidden. How heavy-footed his steps were, how cumbersome. Lacey had never mentioned Doc being fat or hunchbacked. Doc with his lack of finesse, with the coldness in his voice, the complete lack of emotion. 'Doc,' Pilgrim clarified. 'It was him who pulled out her teeth.'

'You saw Red's face?' Dumont sounded sad. 'He thinks disfiguring my pets will stop me looking at them. He wants me to see them as he does, as objects to be used and nothing more. I get so easily distracted, you see. He'll be as delighted as I am to hear you're back, Lacey. We're quite fascinated by you.'

Pilgrim didn't like the smile he gave Lacey when he said that. Didn't like it one bit.

Enough of this.

'Yes,' Pilgrim murmured. 'Enough.' To Dumont, he said, 'He took Alex from you. Just now. She was in here. Doc was carrying her.'

For the first time, Dumont regarded him not only with curiosity but with sharp appraisal. 'Yes. I let him take her. I'd had my fun, and he wanted to ask her some questions about our dear Lacey here. But he shouldn't have touched Red.' Dumont's face suffused with blood and his eyes narrowed into slits. 'The visit from our patron had spooked her enough. And it made Joseph question his place, too. The Flitting Man wanted her kept safe. He entrusted that to me. And Joseph hurt her. So she ran.'

'And that upset you.'

'Yes, it upset me! Don't you *see*? She is *like* him. She has a foothold in this world, just like the Flitting Man does. She *fits*. She doesn't have to grapple and claw to find her place, like you or I. It has already been carved out for her. And if I cannot have that, then she will give me the next best thing.' Pilgrim noticed the man's hand *squeeze* around the butt of the handgun. 'She warned me that a new chain of events would start if she left, and here we are. Here *you* are. Joseph understood what the Flitting Man would do to us if we didn't look after her. He *knew* how valuable she is. And now I want her back. And *you*' – he jabbed his finger at Pilgrim and the girl – 'are the only ones who know where she is. And you're going to give her back to me.' His flush had deepened to puce, and his eyes sparked with a dark, desperate need.

'If you've hurt Alex—' Lacey began.

'Of course I've hurt her!' Dumont snapped, mouth twisting. 'I've hurt her so badly she'll be wearing the scars I've inflicted the rest of her miserably short life! And Joseph will give her even *more*. She will be so grotesque even you'll want to scratch out your eyes rather than look at her!'

'Get behind me, Lacey,' Pilgrim ordered.

Dumont rose up from his seat, gun in hand, a vein throbbing in the centre of his forehead. 'She didn't even know what suffering *was* until she met me! I broke her down until she pissed in her pants and begged me to stop! And I will do the same to you, so help me God, *unless you give me back my Red*!'

'Lacey! Move!'

'TELL ME WHERE SHE IS!' Dumont roared, spit flying from his mouth.

Lacey leapt behind Pilgrim, brushing up against his back as Dumont's arm rose, handgun coming up. But so, too, was Pilgrim's. The bark of gunfire caused the crystal glasses and decanters to sing in reply, and the shotgun bucked in Pilgrim's hands. Dumont's fist exploded in a bloody splattering of meat and bone, his gun flying away to smack up against the bar.

Dumont howled, grasping at the pulpy remains of his wrist.

Pilgrim jacked another round in the chamber, but Dumont was already charging, his howl becoming a ferocious, wounded bellow. Pilgrim had a second to brace himself before Dumont crashed into him.

Pilgrim's muscles and joints locked together. He was knocked back three paces and probably would have fallen if Lacey hadn't shoved herself against him. The shotgun's barrels were pushed up, trapped between his and Dumont's chest, and Dumont wrenched at the gun, almost ripping it out of his grip; even with one hand shot to bits, Dumont's strength was astounding.

'Get out of the way!' Pilgrim shouted at Lacey. '*Now!*'

Her bracing support disappeared. He heard her scurry for cover.

For Pilgrim there was only heat and unyielding power and slippery blood. Dumont made a guttural growling deep in his throat, the steam of his breath basting Pilgrim's face, making him sweat.

He's too strong.

Pilgrim's left leg shook. His knee began to buckle. His fingers slipped along the blood-smeared gunstock.

'*WHERE IS SHE?!*' Dumont screamed.

Something struck the side of Pilgrim's head. Hot and wet. It hit him a second time and the world blurred as a shock of agony blew out the back of his skull. Dumont hammered his pulped hand into Pilgrim's face a third time, and Pilgrim did the only thing he could. He pulled the shotgun's trigger.

The thunderous blast sent white-hot needles lancing into his eardrums. Dumont's cry of pain joined his own.

Above them, the glass-vaulted ceiling exploded.

Pilgrim shoved the shotgun into Dumont's hands and had a split second to enjoy the man's shocked expression before he bolted away, a clinking sound of giant ice-cubes chasing after him. The first bits of glass hit Pilgrim's shoulders as he vaulted the nearest armchair and dropped behind it. Lacey crouched only a few feet away, eyes large, her rifle cradled in her arms. She was too near. Shards of deathly glass began to rain down around her, and Pilgrim scrambled from behind the armchair, larger pieces now smashing on to tabletops, shattering in glittery explosions, others smacking into leather with meaty slaps. Under the sound of mini glass-grenades detonating behind him, he heard a clunking, ratcheting sound and knew Dumont was pumping another cartridge into the shotgun.

Pilgrim threw himself at Lacey, knocking her flat, covering her with his body. She curled herself into him. Her breaths blew hot against his throat.

But no shotgun blast came; instead there was a heavy, solid thump, followed by a short, sharp crack like a small-calibre gun going off.

And then the world, which had sounded like it was coming down around their ears, very quickly grew quiet. Small smatterings of chinking glass, accompanied by the odd thump or crack, were all that was left.

Pilgrim raised his head. Glass sparkled everywhere: the stars that had glimmered above them in the dark skies had settled on every surface. Dumont lay stretched out on his front, a five-foot-wide sheet of glass laid over his head and upper body, split down the middle so it tented over him in two large sections. Through the transparent pane, Pilgrim saw the crushed side of Dumont's skull, grotesquely flattened under the heavy window, as if it were a specimen under a large slide waiting to be studied beneath a giant microscope. Pinkish-white meat oozed from the crushed skull, pushing up against the glass.

It's not meat. It's brains.

One bulging eye stared at Pilgrim.

It blinked.

Lacey's head twisted, turning to see, but he cupped his hand over her eyes and said, 'No.'

'But—'

'*No*,' he said more firmly.

The shotgun lay beyond Dumont's outstretched hand.

'Up,' Pilgrim ordered as he climbed off the girl. Glass tinkled as it fell from him.

'What happened?' Lacey asked breathlessly. As she rose to her feet she tried to look again, but he stepped in front of her to block her view. He wasn't protecting her from death; that was one aspect of her life now that she would have to get used to. But cracked skulls and exposed brains were a different kind of death altogether.

'What *happened*? Is he dead?'

'Yes. He's dead.' He gripped her shoulder and turned her to face the main doors. Boots crunching, he quickly retrieved the shotgun, hissing as all his pains flared when he bent to scoop it up, and then he hustled her ahead of him, not giving her a chance to ask more questions but firmly guiding her out of the lounge.

The darkness was a welcome shroud when the door shut at his back, but one that was no longer necessary, so he asked for the flashlight and the girl handed it to him, her movements jerky and robotic. He turned it on and directed the beam on the floor. Like he'd thought – like he'd *hoped* – droplets of blood dotted and streaked the gleaming tiles at their feet.

Alex's blood.

'I thought you said no noise. No shooting.' The girl's words were hushed, and even more breathless. Her eyes were still too big, her face pale in the white backwash from the flashlight.

'Plans change. Let's go.' If he kept her moving, kept her mind occupied with action, she wouldn't have time to think about what had happened in there.

How many is it now that you've killed in front of her?

Pilgrim didn't answer.

'But there's blood all over you.'

He glanced down at himself. His hands were covered in streaks of dark, wet blood. Attempting to wipe them clean would be futile: his shirt was a sopping, bloody mess, too.

'It's not mine.'

The girl reached for his shoulder, and he felt a quick, sharp sting. She held up a sliver of glass two inches long, pinched between her fingers. A ruby droplet hung from its point.

'Some of it is,' she whispered.

He met her eyes for a second. She dropped the glass and it clinked to the tiles, echoing prettily through the lobby. The drips of his own blood had joined Alex's on the floor, and he stepped around the girl, tracking them back past the escalators and to the emergency door Doc had gone through. He checked to see if the girl was following and found her still standing outside the Lounge of Stars. In a low voice, he called her name. Even from twenty yards away he saw her flinch and shake herself off. She hurried over to him.

With the girl at his heels, he pushed through into the stairwell and went down the steps, leaning heavily on the railing to prevent his leg giving out beneath him. His head continued to hurt from the blows he'd taken, and his left eye was practically useless now; not even a myopic blur muddied his vision, only a dark, dense fog, as if half of his body were readying itself for the grave.

Not yet.

'No, not yet,' he muttered.

The blood trailed from the bottom step and under the door, leading back into the second-floor lobby. The floor where the remainder of Dumont's people waited.

CHAPTER 7

As she stood outside the Lounge of Stars, Lacey's mind whirled. All the gunshots and crashing glass had made her ears ring, deadening all sound, as if she'd submerged her head in a tub of water. She'd jumped when the shotgun had gone off a second time, ducking instinctively as the ceiling above their heads exploded in a shattering crescendo. But before she could see what that falling storm of razor-like shards would do, the Boy Scout was pushing her to the floor and sheltering her with his body. He'd given her no time to ask questions or see the scene for herself but bullied her to her feet and manhandled her out of the room before her brain could scrabble to catch up.

She didn't know why he felt the need to protect her. She understood what had happened. In fact, she *wanted* to see.

Muffled ears didn't mute Voice – he came through loud and clear. *No you don't. You don't want to see that.*

But she did! Dumont was responsible for hurting her friend. For *torturing* her. She wanted to see his face frozen in open-mouthed agony, the blank death-stare, the broken bones, the bleeding wounds. She wanted to see him get everything he deserved.

No, Lacey. Someone deserving it and you seeing it are two different things. You learned that with Jeb. You don't need to see the cracked-open skull, or his dead, bulging eyes, or the obliterated bones of his hand sticking out like snapped twigs.

Lacey pressed a hand over her mouth, closing her eyes for an instant when Voice's description conjured a gruesome scene in her head. When she opened them, the Boy Scout was scanning the ground, the flashlight sweeping the floor at their feet.

She swallowed when she saw the dribbles of blood down there, some his, the rest not. Dabs and speckles and drizzles, as though someone had taken a treacle dipper, dunked it into a vat of gore and walked with it across the floor tiles. Something unlocked inside her at the sight – she almost heard an audible *snick* – and a flood of horror and dread surged out. So much blood. She'd seen pools of it in the last four days. A lake's worth. From the siblings at the motel, to the Boy Scout getting shot and Jeb bleeding to death, to Lou taking a bullet to the chest, and now more blood at their feet, as if, everywhere she went, the spilling of blood either preceded or followed her. She was leaving tracks of it in every place she visited.

Her hand had snuck to her St Christopher and she held on to the medallion tightly. 'I thought you said no noise,' she whispered, unable to take her eyes from a particularly heavy swirl of dark, viscous red. 'No shooting.'

'Plans change,' the Boy Scout replied. 'Let's go.'

She dumbly looked up at him. 'But there's blood all over you.'

He dispassionately studied the mess. 'It's not mine,' he said.

Something glinted at his shoulder and before she knew what she was doing, she had released the St Christopher and was pinching the cool glass between her thumb and forefinger and pulling it free. It slid out of his flesh easily, like pulling fork tines out of a slab of steak. Blood welled up through the material of his jacket and she felt a hot tingle rise up the back of her neck and into her scalp.

'Some of it is,' she whispered to him, the shard of glass slipping from her numb fingers. She barely heard it hit the tiles.

He dropped his eyes from hers, becoming alert again as he went back to investigating the floor. No more words passed between them. He headed off across the lobby, a hunter tracking his injured prey.

She was left facing the closed doors of the Lounge of Stars, the light from the flashlight fading quickly as the Boy Scout moved away from her. Soon those doors would be in complete darkness, and what they'd left behind them would be in darkness, too, all that blood and death hiding in there like some grisly banquet waiting to be fed on. Evil things glut themselves on such bloody feasts, don't they? If she listened hard enough, couldn't she hear the slick and meaty chewing of something feeding in there?

Let's go, Lacey, Voice said, breaking into her thoughts.

'Lacey!' the Boy Scout called out simultaneously.

She hurriedly turned away from the doors, fear quickening her pace as she ran to catch up. She followed the Boy Scout through the emergency door and into the stairwell. The atmosphere seemed to alter as the door *clunked* shut; it became cold, almost frigid, and the oppressive smell of spilled blood disappeared as if a mist had been lifted. Lacey breathed in deeply: once, twice, three times. The grey cement stairs led downward into darkness. Lacey could see the dribbles of blood swirling along the treads, black as oil. She shivered.

As they descended, their steps echoing eerily, Lacey couldn't help placing one hand lightly on top of the Boy Scout's uninjured shoulder. She told herself it was to help guide her, the bright shine of the flashlight not sufficient to show every step. But that wasn't the real reason. Not the real reason at all.

CHAPTER 8

After reloading the shotgun, Pilgrim held the door handle to the second-floor lobby for a beat of four seconds. He knew it was impossible to feel any transference of intent through an inanimate object, that there was no way he could interpret what was on the other side, yet he held the handle and *tried* to because what else could he do? Their time was up. Or, more accurately, *Alex's* time was up. Whatever questions Doc wanted to ask her, she wouldn't have the answers he sought.

Go.

He opened the door and swung the shotgun in a low sweep, the beam from the flashlight stabbing through the dark. The lobby and escalators were clear. He checked the floor, found the trail and, like a bloodhound, followed it to the right and into the corridor he knew led into the buffet dining hall.

You can't go in there. There are too many of them.

Even with Dumont dead, Posy locked up and the two men out on watch, potentially, over twenty men and women were left between them and Alex. Too many to take on.

'He locked me in the freezer,' Lacey whispered from behind him. 'Remember I told you?'

The service and employee areas of the hotel-casino hadn't been marked on the map, but he knew the kitchens must be vast in order to supply the large numbers of diners visiting the buffet hall. He only hoped they could access the kitchens without being spotted.

'Keep your ears and eyes open,' he told her.

Still following the blood, he slowed them down to a walk, now more cautious, his ears pricked up, straining to hear. As they turned the third corner, there was a low, indistinct drone that steadily clarified into a number of voices, all talking at once. Pilgrim knew that the kitchens and cafés would have been the first areas to be plundered, that stores of food were their number-one priority. And now that they had left the kitchens and stockrooms empty, they had moved elsewhere to stockpile their stolen caches and to indulge in their findings. Indeed, all the voices sounded boisterous and jovial, with bursts of laughter and shouting.

The gunshots from upstairs had gone undetected.

Pilgrim turned off the flashlight when a faint, sallow glow lightened the corridor in front of them, the source of illumination coming from somewhere around the next bend. The voices became louder still, and Pilgrim guessed there must be at least seven or eight people. He cautiously edged a look around the corner and immediately pulled back. The last part of the corridor opened up into a huge canteen-style hall. In the short glimpse he'd had, there had been seven people sitting around the tables nearest to the hall's entryway.

A gunshot rent the air and Pilgrim jerked, dropping into a crouch so fast his stomach gave a weak flip, but the bang was followed by a wild braying of laughter.

Fun and games.

'They're wasting their ammunition,' Pilgrim muttered.

It's one less bullet to shoot us with.

In his brief glimpse, Pilgrim knew there would be no way forward, not unless they wanted to walk in on the live-fire party going on in there. They needed to find another way.

'What about Posy?' Lacey said, her voice pitched low. The girl was strung tight with tension, obviously desperate to move, to get to Alex, her anxiousness notching up steadily the longer they stood doing nothing. For all they knew, the man known as Doc may have already started carving.

Straight away, Pilgrim knew what the girl was getting at, and he baulked at the idea. It was too brazen. They'd never get away with it.

There's a chance it could work.

'No,' he murmured. 'It's impossible.'

But the more he thought about it, the less crazy it seemed.

Why is it impossible? They've never seen you before.

'They've seen the girl,' Pilgrim pointed out. 'They'd recognise her.'

He'd been talking to himself, but the girl didn't comment. Instead, her expression closed down and turned mulish. He could see how much it killed her not to argue with his train of thought, but she simply stared at him. He wondered if Voice was advising her to hold her tongue and wait him out.

If he was, it worked.

'OK,' Pilgrim said. 'Let's try it.'

They backtracked swiftly, the speed of their retreat verging on reckless. The stool was still jammed under the door handle of the closet. When they pulled the door open, Posy drew his knees up instinctively and a low whine rattled from his throat, muffled behind his makeshift gag.

With the explicit understanding that Pilgrim would shoot Posy's spleen out of the side of his ribcage if he blew their cover, the two men walked side by side around the last bend of the corridor and casually strolled into the dining hall.

It was a disconcerting thing to approach a group of unpredictable strangers armed with knives, cleavers and a scattering of firearms. Not one of them looked like a rational, civilised human being, which wasn't a surprise, considering they didn't live in a civilised, rational world any more. The three people who sat facing the entryway – one older woman and two stocky, bearded men – were the first to look up, and when the four remaining people who had their backs to Pilgrim saw the shift in their companions' attention, they also turned around.

Another group was huddled around a set of tables against the western wall. Only two of them bothered looking up when they came in. Lacey had told him she'd seen four people tied before she left; now there were six. One man was slumped over the tabletop and didn't stir when the woman opposite him shoved at his shoulder. Her dark eyes met Pilgrim's. Distrust, anger, suppressed fear: it was all there. In the seat beside her an older captive in his fifties shook his head and murmured something. She dropped her eyes and stared angrily at her bound hands.

The male-to-female ratio in the armed group was 5:2. Women didn't last long in these types of set-ups, not unless they were as physically strong as the men or had something else to offer. The rest, if not abused and left bleeding in the dust, were kept alive for a protracted amount of time to be repeatedly used. You had to be a strong woman to survive. Or a strong enough woman to take yourself out of the situation altogether.

An older female, grey-haired and weathered, any beauty she'd had long since faded, watched Pilgrim with canny eyes. Sitting across from her, the second female was younger, with a mass of dark, tangled hair and a puckered scar that ran from her eyelid to the corner of her mouth. It made the eye droop and her lip quirk up unnaturally on one side.

Dumont's cast-off maybe, his small voice suggested, *and Doc's handiwork*.

A bundle in a tatty blanket lay swaddled against her breast. She had her shirt unbuttoned down to her navel, leaving the entire left side of her chest exposed. A tiny baby suckled on one dark nipple, a newborn, no more than a few weeks old. It made soft snuffling noises as it fed. The woman sat very close to the man beside her – a gruff-looking, wiry guy of indeterminate age. He had narrow features and cagey eyes, and he scrutinised Pilgrim closely as he and Posy approached. Pilgrim reasoned that the woman and baby belonged to him, and that he was extremely protective of his property.

The rest of the men were comparable. Beards, dirty, a coiled, wired energy barely restrained. The only one to stand apart was Buzzcut; he had a full, bushy beard as rough and coarse as the head of a broom and a closely shaven skull that revealed the silver nicks of many scars and a homemade tattoo behind his right ear: a black, spidery-thin spiral. He held a large hunting knife and was absent-mindedly sticking it into the table, levering it out, jabbing it in again. *Thunk-snick-Thunk*. He didn't look at the knife while he did this. Instead, he eyed Pilgrim.

'Hey, Pose. Who's the tall drink o' water?'

Posy didn't even look over at the old woman, which appeared suspicious as hell to Pilgrim, but no one else seemed to notice.

'Um, new guy,' Posy muttered to the floor. 'Yep. He's new. Boss just got done clearing him.'

'Oh yeah? What's your name, sweetcakes? Got yourself a woman?'

The narrow-faced, wiry guy spoke up. 'Chrissakes, Dolores, leave the fella alone. Why'd you always gotta be such a skank for?'

'Fuck you, Frank!' The old woman threw an open soda can at him and it *clonk*ed off his head, its fizzy contents erupting in his face. He shot up from his seat, his chair crashing to the floor, and yelled a long stream of abuse at her. For an old-timer (although Pilgrim suspected she wasn't as old as the wrinkles suggested), she had an impressively coarse vocabulary herself, which she hurled right back at him. The younger, wild-haired woman had risen with Frank, one arm cradling the baby while her hand tried to wipe the soda off his shirt. She was slapped for her trouble and quickly sat back down, her head bowed in contrition. A guy with a tidier, plaited beard laughed, picked up the fizzing soda can and lobbed it at the table of captives. It hit the wall with a thud and cola exploded, splashing the dark-eyed woman in the face. She twisted her head aside, squeezing her eyes shut, but gave no other reaction. The older man angrily swept the can off the table and glared over at them. It landed on the floor, dribbling the last of its contents on to the linoleum as the guy with the plaited beard continued to laugh.

The distraction was helpful, and Pilgrim and Posy made it past the occupied tables and were almost in the clear before another voice pulled them up.

'What's going on, Posy?'

Posy stopped walking, and Pilgrim clenched his jaw, forced to stop next to him. It was Buzzcut. He'd levered the knife out of the table and was holding it nonchalantly in one hand.

'Hmm. Showin' him the kitchen, Pike. Tha's all.'

'What for? There's nothing back there. We picked it clean already.'

Posy didn't reply. He obviously couldn't think fast enough to come up with an adequate lie.

'He wanted to show me the walk-in freezer,' Pilgrim answered. 'Said it'd be a good place to lock up fresh meat.' He made sure to say 'fresh meat' in a significant way and reached over to pat the seemingly unconscious girl slung over Posy's shoulder. Pilgrim hadn't been able to figure out a way he could bring Alex back through the dining hall to meet up with the girl without these people becoming suspicious, so Lacey got to come along after all.

Buzzcut smiled, an ugly curling of his lip to show he'd caught the inference. What few teeth he had left were brown and chipped. 'Fresh meat, eh? What kind we talking about here?'

'Young meat,' Pilgrim clarified. 'Very tender.' He knew Lacey was listening to every word, but she remained limp and motionless. He could barely register her back move with her breathing. 'She put up some fight.' He plucked at his bloodied shirt for emphasis.

'You sure we need to lock her up right this second?'

Pilgrim understood what the man was asking. Wasn't there time to take a look first? Maybe get a little feel?

'Your boss wanted her locked up, safe and sound. I'm just following orders.'

Buzzcut snickered. It was a dirty, depraved sound. 'I get your drift – Boss's laid his claim already, eh? No matter. There'll be plenty of time to get a sample later.' He jabbed the knife at them, waving them on. 'Go ahead and show him the freezer, Pose. Don't want him thinking we're not the accommodating sort.'

Posy nodded jerkily, turned and went to lead Pilgrim through the swinging kitchen door.

'Watch out for Doc in there,' Buzzcut called after them. 'He just took his own meat through. Didn't look half so fresh to me, though.'

The men around the tables laughed.

CHAPTER 9

As soon as they were in the kitchen, Posy bent and set the girl back on her feet. Pilgrim handed her the rifle, and they both turned on their flashlights. All this was done wordlessly. Pilgrim nudged Posy in front of him, prodding him to lead the way, and they walked in file – Posy, Pilgrim, Lacey – past stainless-steel counters and centre benches, pot racks and bains-marie, alongside an array of six-burner oven ranges, three pizza ovens and a line of commercially sized dishwashers along with three pot-wash sinks, to the two storage rooms at the back. One was used to hold dry goods, the other was a walk-in freezer. The four-inch-thick steel door to the freezer was open, and light came from inside, pooling out on to the floor.

A strange hissing noise, like a brief, sharp release of pressurised gas, slashed through the air, a harsh *ssshhhht* that ended as quickly as it had begun. Another one quickly followed. Then a third, and a fourth.

Posy faltered, and Pilgrim poked him with the barrels of the shotgun to encourage him forward. A low, metallic creaking came from inside the freezer, like the muted clanking of iron manacles. Posy halted in the door's opening. The man didn't make a sound, but Pilgrim saw him stiffen.

'Posy.' The voice was quiet, composed, as if he were in the middle of flower arranging or crocheting and not in the process of interrogation and torture.

'Doc,' Posy whispered.

'What do you want? I'm busy.'

'Th—there's a dead man here lookin' for you.'

Pilgrim shoved Posy into the room and out of his way. What he saw in that walk-in freezer made his mind reel unnervingly, his senses shrinking back as if they were shadows thrown into a blazingly bright room. He was snatched upwards, his perceptions ripped outside of himself, and they dived across that small space and slammed into the man in the bowler hat.

Through Doc's eyes, Pilgrim saw himself. He stood in the doorway, the shotgun in the other Pilgrim's hands pointed disconcertingly right back at him, and again his mind lurched drunkenly as he struggled to comprehend that he was seeing himself from someone else's eyes – and yet another, smaller part of him was back in his own body, watching Doc, understanding the fact he was inside the man, hitching a ride. His sanity unravelled a little, then, the duality of his consciousness fracturing him, sending him two ways at once. He see-sawed, the yawning space between the two polarities pulling him apart, and then it stopped and *locked* into place.

From inside Doc, he observed the blanched expression on his own face, the ugly shock in his eyes – even the bloodied left eye, where the haemorrhaging redness had crowded in on his iris.

I see you, Agur, an unknown presence whispered to him from a dark corner of his mind.

No, not *his* mind. *Doc's.*

Pilgrim felt like he'd been spotlit, caught where he shouldn't be, and there was a brief struggle as he tried to slither his way loose and go back to where he belonged, but claws held him fast, dug into him, wouldn't let go.

I see you, Agur, that unknown presence whispered again. *I. See. You. What are you doing here? How are you here?*

Giving an almighty psychic *heave*, Pilgrim wrenched free, the divided part of his mind shooting back across the small space, retreating fast. With a nauseating roll, he was thrust back inside his own body, his stomach muscles clenching as he reeled, his left knee almost buckling. He breathed heavily, inhaling that heavy smog of spilled blood, and stared back at the behatted man, but Doc appeared unaffected by what had just happened.

What *was* that? he thought shakily.

A voice, said his own, the one he was slowly growing accustomed to. *An Other. This man is just a puppet.*

Pilgrim was glad to hear this voice again, its presence strange yet familiar, a growing part of him, much like Voice had been. He never wanted to hear again the other awful sibilance of that unknown presence which had whispered to him from inside Doc's mind. His eyes slid to Lacey, fear gripping him. It had sensed Pilgrim immediately, a trespasser in its domain: could it as easily sense Voice and how he'd come to be in the girl?

I don't think so, his voice answered. *Not yet. She must be careful.*

The warning weighed gravely in his mind and sent another shiver of apprehension through him, but he ruthlessly reined in his spiralling thoughts. Everything was hanging by a thread, and some things hung by decidedly less.

In a lot of ways, the scene before him was reminiscent of how Pilgrim had first found Alex, hanging in the shower at the motel. Except that had been the handiwork of two amateurs, and this was the work of a professional. Alex was naked and strung up by her wrists, and it was a good thing she was, because the time-consuming act of fastening her hands together and lifting her on to the meat hook from the ceiling was probably the only reason she hadn't been carved down to the bone already. She was covered in darkly clotted blood, every inch of her, as if a barrel of the stuff had been dumped over her head. No clean patch of skin remained. New blood continued to dribble from the deep lacerations on the woman's breasts and sides and flanks.

She hung limp, all her weight dangling from her pulped

wrists. Not even Lacey's agonised cry could induce a reaction from the flayed woman.

You're too late. She's already dead.

But she wasn't dead. Pilgrim noted the shallow breaths that moved the woman's chest and the quick pulse of her heartbeat in the soft hollow below her sternum.

The man they called Doc stood behind Alex, holding a long strip of leather. Pilgrim didn't need to see the stripes of blood on his hand and arm and face to know he'd been using it to whip her. Other than the leather belt, the man was unarmed. Doc's clear green eyes cut right through Pilgrim like an ice adze through a frozen pond.

Pilgrim realised he was shaking, as if the freezer unit were turned on and pumping out chilly air. It wasn't. It was warm inside the room.

'Step away from her,' Pilgrim said quietly.

The man didn't respond. He simply wound the leather strip back in.

'I said, step away.'

The movement was shocking in its suddenness; Doc's arm whipped out, the leather strip whisking through the air and striking Alex's back. Blood misted. The light dimmed for an instant.

Lacey cried out as if the strike had landed on her. She brought her rifle up to bear on the bowler-hatted man.

'*Stop.*' Her voice broke.

Doc regarded the girl calmly and slowly wound the red, dripping strip back in. 'Hello, Lacey.'

'What's *wrong* with you?' she whispered.

'Wrong? Nothing's wrong. I'm glad you're here. We wanted to speak with you.'

'Please, just give me back my friend.'

Pilgrim heard the quaver in the girl's voice, and he understood why. There *was* something wrong with this man.

413

He was dangerous, even more so than Dumont had been.

'Don't you feel it?' the man said, lifting his hand to the air. 'The world is changed. They're here to stay now, and there's nothing anyone can do to stop them. They hide in us, like sleeping dogs.'

'No,' the girl whispered. 'No, you're wrong.'

The bowler-hatted man smiled. 'I'm not wrong. You hear. I know you do. And judging by how you conversed with it after our little visit with Jebediah, it's a well-developed one. That worries me. You're so young, much younger than Red – how are you so young with such a mature voice?'

Were these words coming from the man himself, or were they being fed to him by the *other* thing living inside? It didn't matter: Pilgrim was beginning to see everything clearly; he'd been trapped inside a rain-washed car, all the windows blurred opaque with sheets of misty water, but he'd found the windshield wipers and now they were feverishly working. This group was actively expanding its numbers, gathering in strength, and in other parts of the country similar groups were no doubt doing the same, each one encouraging (forcefully or otherwise) anyone who could hear a voice to join their ranks. All for one central purpose: they were readying themselves for a war. All people, everywhere, regardless of whether they heard a voice or not, would have to fight to keep their place in the world. The Flitting Man was tidying up the remainders, sifting out the voices, finding *his people* and leaving all others to perish. And it wouldn't be some faceless battle with unknown soldiers on each side, a battle Pilgrim could stay out of. No, everyone around him would be forced to join: young, old, men, women. Everyone. Including Lacey.

He'd known she was different from the start. She'd been an empty, defenceless vessel, waiting for Voice to jump into her. All the elements had aligned: the shot Pilgrim had taken to the head, her unique ability to house a voice, Voice's strength. It was a perfect storm. And if this man or, more accurately, the *voice* that lived inside this man, ever discovered such a thing were possible, this knowledge could potentially be disastrous, not least of all for Lacey. They'd turn her into a lab rat, poking and prodding until they had extracted every last scrap of understanding they could about her.

'We have lots to talk about,' Doc told her.

'She's not going to talk to you,' Pilgrim said. 'No one is.'

The man's head cocked, his green eyes sparking so that for just a moment they were flat and inhuman. 'You're not what you appear, either, are you? What an intriguing pair you make.'

Pilgrim knew this man wouldn't listen to reason. It wasn't in him to – the steadiness of his hands, his detached demeanour, the *otherness* in him, were all evidence of something lacking. His humanity, perhaps. Pilgrim wondered if a scuffle, probably a loud one, would bring the people in the next room rushing to investigate. (He couldn't chance firing his shotgun in such a confined space, not with Doc standing so close to Alex: the buckshot might hit her.) He wondered, too, which side Posy would fall on in the event of a fight. Posy could go either way, but Pilgrim suspected his long allegiance with these people would define the man's instinctive reaction, and it would favour neither Pilgrim nor the girl.

If you think you can end this quietly, you're deluding yourself.

He wasn't in the game of deluding himself.

And you're weakening. I feel it. You're not strong enough to fight anyone.

Flexing his hand, trying to still its fine-motor trembling, Pilgrim kept his good eye trained on the behatted man. Lacey, standing on his left, was lost in the dark graininess of his failing eyesight. He only knew she was there because of the harsh rasps of her breaths and the long, slim barrel of her rifle – up and pointed in Doc's direction – which had entered Pilgrim's narrow field of vision.

Pilgrim spoke into the silence. 'Dumont won't be talking to anyone, either.'

Doc stilled, the leather strip momentarily forgotten in his hand.

That hit something.

'In fact, he's done all the talking he'll ever do. Even to the voice in his own head.'

The only sounds were the *tink*ing drips of Alex's blood on the floor and the multiple strands of their breathing. Posy sat watching them from where he'd slid down against the wall. Pilgrim imagined he could feel Lacey's gaze, too; not on him, but boring down her rifle's sights like a laser, zeroed in on the man who was hurting her friend.

'He doesn't hear a voice,' Doc murmured. 'He never has.' For a split second something tightened across the man's features. 'What have you done to him?'

Pilgrim hadn't been wholly convinced this man was capable of feeling strong emotions, but now, with Doc's head slowly lowering and the brim of his hat casting a shadow over his piercing, emerald eyes, Pilgrim thought that maybe there was more to him than merely coldness and control.

There's always more. Dig for it.

'Oh, I didn't do anything,' Pilgrim told the man. 'But the large pane of glass that crushed his skull did plenty.'

With that, the dam quietly broke. The man didn't flinch or make a sound, but he slowly shook his head from side to side, an almost ponderous motion.

'I will not,' Doc muttered. He shook his head more forcefully. '*I will not.*'

'Brains everywhere,' Pilgrim added.

'*NO.*'

In the shadows beneath the brim of his hat, something slid out from behind Doc's eyes and a blind was dropped. What lived behind it was a terrifyingly visceral animal. It manifested itself not in a direct attack, which Pilgrim was anticipating, but in a tumult of unexpected violence directed at Alex.

Doc let out a throat-tearing howl that made Pilgrim's hackles rise and his jaw clench, and attacked Alex in a savage flurry of blows, the leather strip crackling with a manic energy as it hissed and cracked, flesh tearing from the woman's back on each lash. It was as though Doc understood *exactly* how best to hurt them, because, as the whip snapped and ripped and shredded – Alex flinching and shrieking awake, the whites of her eyes flashing wide open – Lacey screamed.

A gunshot went off, loud enough to vibrate the bones in Pilgrim's head painfully. He'd already lunged forward and was reaching for Doc's striking arm when the man staggered back, a hole appearing above his right eyebrow.

'Not the head!' Pilgrim shouted, but it was too late. Like a faucet turned to full spigot a stream of blood flowed out and sheeted the side of Doc's face. It filled his eye to overflowing. His bowler hat had been knocked askew and now it fell, tumbling to the floor, where it rolled away on its brim. Doc didn't seem to notice the loss of his hat, and he made no attempt to stop the blood decanting from his head – his hands shuddered at his sides, the belt falling from his grasp, its end coiling like a dead snake over his foot. And while Doc's right eye brimmed with blood, iris lost behind a sea of red, his other, cut-glass green eye gazed coldly past Pilgrim to the girl.

She stared back at Doc, a small curl of smoke rising from her rifle's muzzle as she silently watched the man bleed.

Her first blood spilled.

To Pilgrim, that sounded ominously like an omen of more to come.

Alex's pain-filled keening broke through the ringing in his ears. He became unstuck and dragged his eyes away from the smoking gun. He didn't bother watching the mortally wounded man slide to the floor but went to Posy, hauling him to his feet and grinding out orders in the man's terrified face. Next, Pilgrim went to the girl.

'Hey hey hey,' he whispered, putting the shotgun aside so he could cradle her face between his hands. 'Hey, it's OK. Look at me.' He said her name three times before her gaze moved away from the dying man and lifted to his.

He peered hard into her eyes, searching desperately for any difference. Would she even know if another voice had entered her? Voice would know, surely. Pilgrim had never heard of anyone housing more than one voice, but then he'd never heard of voices hopping from person to person, either.

There was nothing but dull shock in her eyes. He gently ran his thumbs across her hot forehead, a cleansing gesture, wishing he could erase everything the girl had just seen and done. He told her he needed her now more than ever, that he needed her to be strong, that he couldn't do this without her. She gave him a slow nod, her eyes shell-shocked but beginning to clear.

'Help Alex' were his final words, and he left her there and hoped to Christ she did what he'd asked.

At the far end of the kitchen Buzzcut was pushing through the swinging doors.

'What the fuck's going on?'

Pilgrim kept his voice conversational as he walked towards the man. 'Just a slight problem with the woman. It's been dealt with.'

Buzzcut looked past Pilgrim towards the freezer. 'Where's Doc?'

'Still in there. You should see what he did to her. Jesus, man!' Pilgrim laughed through the words as if impressed. 'That guy's really fucked up.'

Both men slowed down as they met each other in the middle of the kitchen, a tier of pot racks to one side and two pizza ovens on the other. Buzzcut held his knife down by his side in a hammer grip. From the next room, Pilgrim heard the baby crying and loud, heated voices.

The shaven-headed man nodded, the left side of his beard lifting in a half-smile. 'Yeah. He's one you don't wanna fuck with. He'll mess you up faster than a skinned cat in a—'

Pilgrim grabbed the side of Buzzcut's head and slammed it into one of the ovens. It connected with a deep, clanging *thuuunng!* and the man dropped to one knee. The knife clattered on the tiles. Gripping the man's head, Pilgrim yanked it down and brought his knee up in a hard, vicious snap, catching the man full in the face. Buzzcut crumpled to the floor.

Pilgrim cast a quick glance over his shoulder and caught sight of Posy coming out of the freezer, his movements furtive. The kid's stare was wide and terrified. He'd frozen comically in place when Pilgrim spotted him, his knees bent, arms stuck out like a tightrope walker's, but before Pilgrim could make a move towards him, Posy stiffened as if he'd been zapped with a cattle prod and fell into an awkward scampering run, hurrying past the sinks and racks of trays and disappearing behind a partitioned wall in the back corner of the kitchen.

Pilgrim let him go. The raised voices from the canteen were getting louder.

'Better get used to it, dog. Only place you're going is to boot camp with the rest of the freaks.'

The sharp bleat of a woman's cry signalled a new round of angry shouts, and something – a chair, the woman herself – was thrown to the floor with a skittering of flung furniture. The baby's cry built to a howling squall.

Pilgrim snatched up Buzzcut's dropped knife and ran back to the freezer.

Alex had been cut free. The girl knelt next to her. The woman was slumped on her knees, bowed over and rocking back and forth. Hisses whistled through her teeth as she tried to ride through the pain.

Looking down at her, Pilgrim doubted he would be able to carry her far: neither his dwindling reserves of energy nor his cracked ribs and weakened leg would hold up under the extra weight for long. He ripped off his jacket and threw it around her shoulders, covering her nakedness, knowing they would have to peel it away from her wounds later.

He crouched down in front of her and roughly gripped her chin, jerking her face up so he could look into her pain-racked eyes.

'*Pilgrim*,' Lacey hissed, stunned at his cruelty.

He paid her no mind and spoke to the woman. 'Can you understand what I'm saying?'

Her gaze was bleary.

He slapped her. Hard.

He gave Lacey a quelling look when she grabbed hold of his wrist. The girl scowled and released him grudgingly.

When he returned his attention to Alex, her eyes were latched on to his face.

'You're dead,' she whispered.

'So everyone keeps telling me.'

The woman's face screwed up tight and she moaned and tried to curl in on herself again, but Pilgrim held her face firmly and wouldn't let her.

Time time time, his voice reminded him.

'Did they break you, Alex? If they broke you, we might as well leave you here. Because you'll end up killing us. Killing Lacey.'

Alex opened her eyes again and, when she looked at him, behind the wall of agony twisting her features, there was a hard glint of something more. Something these people definitely hadn't broken.

Pilgrim nodded, gentling his hold on her. 'You need to get up. Right now. They're coming.'

He released her face and gripped her arm, his fingers sliding over her slippery, blood-covered skin. She whimpered and groaned and couldn't straighten fully, had to hunch over, but she was on her feet. Lacey helped her into Pilgrim's jacket, fastened it, and then slid herself underneath the woman's arm.

Pilgrim picked up the shotgun and went to the door. The kitchen was dark and silent. He waved the girls over to him and moved into the room, gun held ready. Posy must have known there was an alternative way out, and Pilgrim found it in the back corner, hiding behind a huge stack of dinner trays and an unused service elevator. He was holding the door open for Lacey and Alex when the doors at the far end of the kitchen swung inward and Frank came through.

They saw each other.

Frank's eyes shifted to Buzzcut, who lay unconscious on the floor. He looked back at Pilgrim, lifted his arm and fired. Pilgrim ducked, the bullet slamming into the wall near his head, the gunshot reverberating through the pots and pans and off stainless-steel surfaces, a high, melodic hum ringing through the kitchen.

Pilgrim didn't wait to see if Frank would fire more shots but dashed through the exit into a carpeted hallway, much wider than the others he had passed through. Girl and woman were shuffling their way to its far end, where it opened up into a vast, furnished lobby. There must be many windows up ahead because the area was aglow with moonlight, everything lit by a pale, ghostly luminance that bleached the carpets and walls of their gaudy colours.

Limping, Pilgrim ran after them, glancing back over his shoulder, waiting for the door to open and Frank to burst out, followed by the rest of the people from the dining hall. Lacey had stopped and was pushing open a second door, the clunking sound of its depress bar marking it as a fire exit. Pilgrim came up behind them and hustled them through, grabbing the door before it could bang shut and easing it closed.

He didn't let them catch their breath but took hold of Alex's free arm and steered them down the concrete stairs.

'What about those people?' Lacey gasped, stumbling along with him, Alex propped up between them. 'We can't just *leave* them.'

'We can barely save ourselves,' he muttered, leaning heavily on the handrail and concentrating on not losing his footing. 'Just keep going.'

He expected her to argue but, for once, she kept her thoughts to herself. The weight of the shotgun was pulling at his hand, and he wanted to drop it, to drop everything that was holding them back so they could run faster, slip like ghosts through the darkness and escape into the night, but Alex's pace was faltering – she gasped and flinched and almost fell a number of times as they descended the two short flights. Floodwater pooled in the bottom of the stairwell, and it snatched a gasp from the girls as their feet sank into chilly water up to mid-shin.

Pilgrim sloshed over to the door leading directly outside, but it was secured by chain and padlock. He cursed in frustration, and Lacey whispered for him to leave it, struggling instead to pull open the door opposite. He moved to help her, shunting the door open far enough for them to squeeze through, taking them back inside the hotel-casino.

The parking garage next door.

'Yes, the parking garage,' Pilgrim agreed. He knew they wouldn't be able to run very far or very quickly with the woman in her current state.

The girl looked at him a moment, uncomprehending, her gaze turned inward, listening. And then her expression cleared and she hissed, 'Of course! The *garage*.'

From within the stairwell, the emergency door on a level above them crashed open.

★

Pilgrim didn't recognise the area they had entered and relied on his inner compass to lead them south. They had come out in an unmarked service zone. The stale chemical smell hanging in the air most likely marked it as being part of the cleaning staff's storage areas. They hurried as fast as they could past an open door, the water kicking up around their legs, dragging their pace down to a crawl. Pilgrim glanced inside the room – some sort of staffroom with lockers, waterlogged seats, a kitchenette and nothing else. They kept going. At the end of the corridor was a heavy-duty set of double doors. Pilgrim waded on ahead, but they were locked and weren't budging. There was a card-access panel to the door's left but, without any electricity to power it, there was no way to force the doors open. He came back, panting heavily, the slog through the water exhausting him. Lacey was already shouldering a door open on her right.

She nodded to the unreadable sign pinned to the wall and gasped, 'Gift shop.'

There was a loud splash as Frank fell through the emergency exit into the corridor, landing on all fours, water bursting up and drenching him.

'*Go.*' Pilgrim pushed the girls through the doorway, Alex crying out at being shoved in her lacerated back, and went in after them, throwing his weight against the door to shut it. Frank called out and more splashes came from the corridor. More voices joined Frank's.

Lacey's flashlight picked out metal shelves filled with boxes of merchandise. Stock had spilled out, boxes had been ripped open and floated around their legs, their contents bobbing around: sodden towels with the hotel-casino's emblem stitched in the corners, loose playing cards, plastic poker chips, parts of a shaving kit, stuffed toys, fridge magnets, keyrings, pin badges.

'The other door. *Quickly.*' Pilgrim pointed and the two girls waded awkwardly across the stockroom, holding each other up. Pilgrim shoved his shotgun on to a shelf, grabbed the metal shelving unit nearest the door and yanked. It was heavy, but it moved. He strained and tugged harder, his side giving an excruciating pop, and he cried out as he pulled the shelving down, jumping out of the way as it fell with a tremendous crash, a wave of water sloshing up his thighs and knocking him back a step.

The door burst inward, shouts and pounding bodies ramming against the other side. It jammed to a stop when it met the fallen unit, opening to a gap of six inches.

Vicious curses were hurled in at him. Frank was there, trying to force his wiry frame through the small gap. Pilgrim reached for the shotgun he'd left on the shelf and had to stumble back when Frank pushed his arm into the room and unloaded his gun. Shots *zinged* off the metal shelving. Pilgrim felt a hot sting zip past his cheek. He abandoned the gun and dived for the floor, freezing water smacking him full in the face. He spluttered and scrambled blindly after the girls.

He heard his name shouted, high and scared, and headed towards it. Hands grabbed him, snatched up his shirt and dragged him out of the storeroom, bullets blatting into the walls and hissing through water. He was hauled up, and almost fell again, but Alex and Lacey steadied him.

'I lost the shotgun,' he gasped.

Lacey shook her head at him, her hair plastered to her head, eyes wild. 'Who gives a shit?'

They were behind the cashier's counter and had to waste precious seconds skirting around it. Pilgrim took hold of Alex, clamping his right arm around her waist and pulling her arm over his shoulder. Lacey waded on ahead, her rifle in both hands.

'Just l–l–leave m–me.' Alex's voice shook so much it was hard to make out her words. 'I'm s–s–slowing you d–down.'

'Hush,' Pilgrim said. He was practically dragging her along now, holding up most of her weight, her legs trailing through the water. The back of his head hurt like hellfire. Adrenalin pulsed through his body, his muscles twitching crazily.

More crashes and bangs came from the storeroom.

Twenty more seconds. Then they'll be through.

Ahead of them, Lacey splashed past an oval table filled with a ruined display of soggy books and went out through the gift shop's entrance. Pilgrim hauled Alex after her and once again found himself in the high-ceilinged atrium of the hotel-casino's main entryway.

Lacey looked back at him, her desperate indecision clear in her expression, and Pilgrim was tempted to tell her to go straight out the front so they could be free from this place and back under the night sky. But they would be completely in the open outside, with no place to hide and no cover. They would be picked off before they were halfway across the parking lot.

He nodded past the escalators. 'Keep going. Get to the garage.'

She nodded again and turned, leading them across the width of the atrium, the water frothing up around their knees, moon-light rippling in the waves, an undulating wake stretching behind them.

Pilgrim heaved Alex up the four steps and out of the water, his thigh muscles trembling. His sodden pants weighed down his legs; his boots were filled with lead. The gleaming corridor stretched out before them, the silent pretzel and cotton-candy stands beckoning. Their shoes squeaked as they hurried past the oversized plant pot. They could see the sliding-glass doors to the outside, the slashes of moonlight painting the tiled floor in white rectangles, and there, the overturned garbage can wedging the exit open.

Whoops and yells and a huge splashing crash came from the gift shop as something large and heavy collapsed.

'Lacey,' he gasped. 'The rifle. Give it to me.'

The girl was already ten feet ahead of them, but she spun

425

around and ran back, passing it over without question. He handed off the woman in exchange and Alex slumped into the girl's arms.

Holding on to her, Lacey whispered, 'Come on, Alex. We're almost there. Just a little further.'

The woman sobbed and somehow straightened, and the two shambled onward in painful, lurching steps.

Pilgrim watched them for a second and then hurried over to the cotton-candy stand. The hatch wasn't up, so he lifted it and went through. Sighting over the counter, he planted his elbow on the stainless-steel top and held the rifle steady, watching and waiting, listening to the girls stagger further away from him.

Their shambling stopped.

'*Pilgrim!*' the girl shouted.

'Keep going!' he called, not taking his eyes away from the four steps leading down into the flooded atrium.

'But—'

'Go, goddamnit! Do as I say!'

Their pursuers must have seen Lacey and Alex, because a cry went up and the first two people splashed through the last yards of water and leapt up the stairs. Men. Stocky. Moonlight flashed on the bladed weapons they carried.

Kill them.

His heart beat hard and fast in his chest, thudding like a bass drum, but Pilgrim released his breath on a long exhalation and squeezed the trigger. He slid the bolt back and chambered another cartridge even as the first man stumbled and went down. The second man, the one with the plaited beard, was still staring at his fallen comrade when he was slammed back a step, the bullet striking him in the chest. Pilgrim levered another round into the chamber, caught a dart of movement near to the escalator and, making sure not to aim for any headshots, fired a third time.

A yelp.

Shouts.

Splashing.

Then silence, apart from the lapping of disturbed water and a pained groan from one of the downed men.

You're not going to be able to hold this position for ever.

His legs shook. A droplet of water hung off the tip of his nose.

'Time to give it up, buddy!' Buzzcut called in a slurred voice, his words echoing off the tall ceilings and silent stalls. 'I have no clue who the fuck you are, but there's no way out for you!'

Pilgrim didn't bother pointing out that Lacey and Alex were already on their way out and there wasn't a damn thing Buzzcut could do about it.

Unless some of them went out the front entrance and were heading round to cut them off, his voice said.

Pilgrim crouched down in the scant cover offered by the counter's hatchway and glanced up the walkway. There was no sign of Lacey or Alex.

Buzzcut yelled, 'If you put your gun up and come on out, I'll kill you quick. How's that? A better option than me cutting every single fucking organ out of your body, eh?'

You've angered him.

Pilgrim was surprised the man was even awake. He'd slammed the guy's head pretty hard up against that oven.

Pilgrim guessed it was a fifty-yard dash to the sliding-glass doors. He'd taken out at least two men. Even now, one or more others could be moving to flank him, skirting the front of the building and coming around to the secondary entrance where the girls had exited.

Who's to say all the noise hasn't alerted those two men on lookout duty, too? And any number of others hanging around upstairs.

But all he kept thinking was: I left her unarmed. I took the rifle off her and now they have nothing to defend themselves with.

'Fuck,' he muttered. He raised his voice. 'Dumont and Doc are dead!' He let that news settle for a couple of seconds. 'Way I see it, there are two new job openings here, so maybe you should expend your energy on working out who's in charge now, instead of chasing down three strangers who mean nothing to you!'

He listened closely as the echoes of his voice faded and heard a low murmur start up as the remaining men began talking.

At first it had been difficult to pinpoint Buzzcut's location from the man's shouting, especially the way the acoustics of the place made it echo and bounce, but as he'd continued his taunts Pilgrim narrowed down the man's hiding place and now had a fairly good idea of where he'd taken cover.

They're as distracted as they're ever going to be.

Pilgrim stepped out from behind the counter and fired at the huge plant pot.

It shattered on impact.

Pilgrim ran.

He heard a cry of surprise but already he was ten yards up the walkway, his head tucked down, the rifle gripped mid-barrel so he could pump his arm good and fast.

More sounds erupted behind him. Shouts, sloshing water, heavy footfalls running in pursuit. He expected gunfire, but none came. Either they wanted him caught alive or they were conserving what ammunition they had left for when they could accurately take him down. They had already wasted a clip in the storeroom.

He didn't slow when he reached the sliding doors but vaulted over the garbage can holding them open, stumbling when his left leg touched down. He staggered like a drunk for a few yards, regained his balance and sprinted under the covered portico and up the ashphalt lane to the parking garage.

This was his last burst, he knew it. His lungs burned, his

breaths rasped like gravel through his throat, his legs were slender saplings, bending, trembling, near to snapping. He just needed to get into the garage; the ink-black maw of its 'Entry' gate whispered encouragingly: 'Just a little further and the darkness will swallow you up', it seemed to say. 'All these lovely shadows waiting to welcome you, friend, waiting to invite you inside. Just a little further now . . .'

But before he could reach the raised barrier a pair of dazzlingly white eyes found him, two harsh beams of light stabbing into his eyes. He squinted and turned his head aside. The scream of a lost behemoth tore the air and shook the ground beneath his feet, the newly awakened beast rising up from the garage's bowels and coming straight for him. With a shrilling squeal, the creature veered and shuddered and showed him its flank. It was off-white and rectangular, once shiny but now faded and grubby.

An RV. A Coachmen, maybe, or an Itasca.

Pilgrim had a brief, blinding moment to be astonished and wondered if he would ever get used to the girl's surprises.

There wasn't anything smaller?

The side door flapped open, rebounding off the RV's siding, the latch either broken or unable to catch.

The driver laid their hand down on the horn again and the off-white behemoth bellowed a breathless, birthing *HOOOOUUUUNNN!* What Pilgrim wanted was the opposite of birthing. He instinctively switched direction, darting to run alongside its flank, planning on climbing *inside* the belly of the beast and not on being expelled from it.

Shots rang out. Bullets *thunked* into the RV's siding, chasing Pilgrim to the swinging door, where he leapt, throwing the rifle inside, and gripped on to the frame with both hands, hanging there for a moment, the dark, pungent interior clinging on to him with fingers fastened to eyes and nose and throat. A rain of bullets hammered into the swinging door, shoving it into his shoulder, one bullet blowing out a slim Perspex panel, plastic shards cutting his face.

The same vertigo he had felt when the girl placed her hand along his cheek struck him once more, and he felt himself tipping backwards, his fingers fumbling their hold. He had a vision of falling and tumbling under the vehicle's wheels, the tyres trampling over him like a wild, stampeding elephant, leaving meaty smears of him on the asphalt. The RV turned sharply, whether by design or by accident it didn't matter, because he was thrown inside. He tripped over the ratty carpeting and crashed into the dining table, its edge delivering a cracking blow to his pelvis and hips. He hunched over it, collapsing, whining for breath.

'*Pilgrim!*'

It was the girl. She was half turned in her seat, scared eyes desperately searching for him in the darkness.

More bullets punched into the exterior panelling, some piercing the thin walls and smacking into the RV's sink and cupboards. More glass shattered.

Pilgrim managed to rip one word up and out of his ravaged lungs.

'DRIVE!'

The girl's driving skills were not great, but they were serviceable. By the time they had sluiced through the flooded parking lot and wound their way back up the driveway to the top of the ridge, Pilgrim had left his post at the rear of the vehicle – where he had been watching the scattered men and women run around like lost little ants before disappearing back into the hotel-casino – and swayed his way up to the driver's cabin.

Alex was sitting slumped in the passenger seat, flinching and stiffening each time Lacey took a corner, but she was awake and lucid. When she saw him she reached out a hand. For a moment he was unsure of what she wanted – he had nothing he could give her: no pain medication or clothing or water. But she interpreted his confusion and whispered that all she wanted was his hand.

He looked at her open palm, at the slim, elegant fingers, the same fingers Lacey had told him drew beautiful pencil sketches, and he suddenly yearned to see the shapes and sweeps and delicate grazes they could pull out of a pencil, to see the gliding strokes she committed to paper in intricate drawings that would hold his eyes captive for hours, a hundred hidden details lost inside the grey-leaded lines.

He placed his hand in hers and watched those slim fingers close over the back of his hand and hold on. Her grip was warm and surprisingly strong.

He met her eyes.

'Pilgrim?' she whispered. 'That's your name?'

He nodded.

'Pilgrim,' she repeated. 'Thank you.'

He nodded again, because he could find no words. When she turned away and went back to watching the road, she kept hold of his hand.

CHAPTER 10

They parked the RV two streets over inside a bricked-up backyard, hidden from view. They didn't leave the keys in the ignition like the previous owner had but took the keychain with them. Although no pursuers had chased after them on their drive back to Vicksburg (Pilgrim could only guess dissent had already set in after their leadership had been so thoroughly wiped out), he turned the hand-held radio on and, with the last of its battery, monitored the airwaves for activity. There was some – most of it incoherent and unhelpful – but nothing that caused him concern. Still, he would have chosen to leave the vehicle further away from the house, but the woman was unable to walk far; he and the girl had to hold her up between them. By the time they reached Lacey's sister's street, they had resorted to carrying her.

They took the stairs slowly. Pilgrim paused at the top to give the street a probing sweep. He would've liked to have spent longer at the task, but Lacey said his name in a low, fretful voice. There was still a possibility Dumont's people – or maybe *Buzzcut's* people now – would look for them, this Pilgrim knew, but they'd soon realise the task of finding three people in a city so large verged on the impossible and would quickly abandon the endeavour. That didn't mean there weren't others watching, though, the cunning-eyed man they had spotted earlier, for example, or another well-hidden onlooker who recognised an opportunity when he saw one. Pilgrim was still worrying about such threats from the shadows while Lacey awkwardly shuffled the last two steps across the stoop under Alex's weight. She said his name again.

Pilgrim went to the front door and turned the ornate brass handle, using his shoulder to push the heavy door open. He didn't see the small child sitting on the floor of the foyer – he was too busy glancing back over Alex's head, giving the street a final scan – didn't see the child, who had been sitting at the feet of the dead girl he had left in the straight-backed chair and staring up at Red's scarf-covered face, start in surprise and jump to her feet. He didn't see the unwieldly item the child had been clutching in her lap. All Pilgrim heard was Lacey call out the child's name –

Addison!

– and the sharp retort of igniting gunpowder. That's when he *did* glimpse the antique Civil War-era pistol that the child held out – probably in exactly the way her mommy had taught her to back when she was still around.

It was a relic of a pistol, which should have been consigned to a museum long ago rather than used for home defence. Pilgrim knew it must have taken the girl a while to draw back the hammer, the mechanism old and stiff with age, the gun cumbersome in her small hands. It was a miracle she was able to hold the pistol at all let alone hold it steady enough to fire. Indeed, the recoil from the shot made her stumble backwards, knocked the pistol up and out of her grip, although Pilgrim doubted she would've had time to recock the gun before Lacey rushed at her.

As it turned out, all it took was one shot. It hit Pilgrim high on the left side of his chest, knocking a hole clean through him. It rocked him back on his heels.

A sense of weightlessness came over him, as if gravity had reversed and was buoying him up instead of holding him down. His ears closed, stuffed with a beating silence that should have alarmed him but which he found lulling and peaceful. He watched Lacey run at the girl, except it was in slow motion, everything wound down in speed, and Pilgrim had all the time in the world to watch the child's pale, dirt-streaked face tighten in fear, watch her spin around and bolt out of the foyer, Lacey going after her, her foot connecting with the dropped pistol and sending it spinning away to smack up against the polished mahogany wainscoting. Then something made Lacey stop and turn, her eyes finding him, her face tightening with some emotion of her own – not quite fear but something close to it, something Pilgrim couldn't quite identify or put a name to. And then it floated up to him out of nowhere.

Devastation.

Speed was still slow, so slow it took a while for Lacey to reach him. Plenty of time for him to lean back against the wall and for Alex, who was still at his side, to try in vain to prevent him slumping down, down, all the way down to the floor.

He calmly watched the two faces in front of him, how intense their expressions were as they reached for him, lifted his shirt, pawed at his chest, their hands gleaming like the polished wainscoting, except their hands were red and wet and not like the dark mahogany wood at all. He couldn't help but think back to when Lacey had talked of living alone in that old house of her grandmother's, about how it was like existing outside of the world, being a drifting phantom whose actions and thoughts affected nothing and no one. How it was like being dead.

Sound fitfully filtered back in, and all he heard was someone saying the same words over and over again: 'It's OK, it's OK, it's OK,' and he realised it was him saying them, that he was trying to reassure, to comfort. But neither the girl nor the woman was listening. So he grabbed their hot, slippery hands, gripped on to them as tightly as he could, and said, 'Listen.' But they *still* didn't listen so he said it again, louder. '*Listen.*'

They stopped, frantic-eyed and breathless.

'It's OK,' he told them.

The girl started crying.

He held on to her hand. 'No. Don't. You have your family now. Alex, and Addison, and Voice.'

With her free hand, the girl wiped her tears away, a streak of his blood smearing across her cheek. '*What?*' she whispered.

'You called me Pilgrim. Only he knows that. You can hear him. I know.'

'How—'

He didn't let her finish. Already darkness waited for him each time he blinked; he had to snap his eyes open again because the dark called to him, wanted him to stay. 'You mustn't tell anyone . . . how you got him. Not *anyone*. Do you understand?' He must have squeezed her hand too tightly, because she winced. '*Promise me*,' he gasped.

She nodded. 'I promise. I won't tell.'

'Good . . . that's good.' He relaxed, his hold loosening. 'I had . . . a real name once.' The words were harder to get out now, coming in gasps between his struggles to draw in wet, broken breaths. 'And a sister. I told you . . . about her. I wanted to be a ghost, wanted to forget everything. But I can't forget the colours. Or maybe it's the colours . . . that won't forget me,' he mused, losing his train of thought. 'Violet,' he murmured. 'My sister. Her name was Violet. And there's Ruby-Red.' He fought to focus back on the girl. 'And *you*,' he whispered to her. 'You're a colour to me, too. So bright . . . you hurt my eyes.'

He let his eyes close, not because it hurt to look at her but because he could see her whether they were closed or not. She was *all* the colours. Rubies, reds, violets; every colourful spark flying away from her.

His chest was a sun going supernova. It burned from the inside. Even as the life poured out of the hole above his heart, he held on to that searing image of colours and the girl.

'Don't go,' the girl begged, and she was so close he could feel her words like gossamer on his face, like spun, rainbow-coloured webs, heavy and light at the same time. 'I don't want you to go. *Please* don't. You're my family now, too. Please don't leave me.'

He fought to speak. 'You shouldn't . . . be afraid.'

She sobbed his name. *Pilgrim*, not Boy Scout. He liked how the sound of it fit the shape of her mouth.

'You're not alone . . . any more—' He desperately wanted to speak her name, but time blew it away from him.

The voice whispered in his head: *Defend her.* And Pilgrim tried to speak these final words on his last, rattling breath, because they were important – he knew they were, the same way he knew the dirt would soon be parting to welcome him to sleep – but he wasn't sure if he'd said them loud enough to be heard. The girl and all her sparking colours drifted away from him, and in the dark, floating in nothingness, the voice spoke again. It wasn't his own voice any more, he wasn't sure if it ever had been, although it had matched the intonations of his speech very well. Now Pilgrim had distance he could hear the individuality, the separateness. It had its own identity.

After everything, it's a child who fells you.

Pilgrim wanted to shake his head, but there was nothing attached to his head. No neck, no shoulders, no nothing. Everything was slipping away, soon to be forgotten. And that was OK; he was good at forgetting.

A seven-*year-old*, the voice said.

Pilgrim disagreed, but his thoughts were like snowflakes, ungraspable and melting, and he couldn't form them into words, no matter how hard he tried. She wasn't just a child, he wanted to argue. She had Lacey's blood in her veins, and that made her special.

And for the first time, in all his experiences with the girl, he was unsurprised by how this was to end.

It made him smile, although no one would ever see it.

THE LAST PART
The Girl Who Was Pilgrim

CHAPTER 1

It's time, Voice said.

In the kitchen, Lacey stood at the back door, staring out over the porch and into her sister's backyard. She had spent a lot of time here during the past fourteen days. She had a good view of the rectangular patch of disturbed earth that marked the graves. It had been hard, digging into that slab of mud. It had taken her hours, despite the rain having softened the dirt, and she hadn't stopped until blisters formed on the bases of her fingers, and a seven-by-six-foot hole had opened up before her. She was getting depressingly good at grave-digging.

It's time, Voice said again.

'Maybe I'm not ready yet,' Lacey replied, staring out at the wooden cross. She had constructed it by lashing two broken chair legs together.

Maybe you'll never be ready, but we can't stay here for ever.

Two weeks ago, she had carried Red out to the grave she had prepared and placed her on the left, arranging her as best she could, which meant in the position the girl had stiffened into while she had been left sitting in the foyer chair. She lay gently curled on her side at the bottom of the shallow hole as if settling in for a long, peaceful nap. Her fingers were black, as though dipped in ink, and her skin was livid and marbled in green, but the smell of death and decomposition was strangely distant, detected at a low level but never overwhelming.

Next, Lacey had gone back to the foyer and looked down at the Boy Scout for a long while. He looked . . . content. That was an odd thing to say, she knew, but there was no other way to put it. He looked like he was sleeping. His face lay in unworried lines; the grimness that had often bracketed his mouth and narrowed his eyes was gone.

She had whispered his name. It still felt new to her.

He's not Pilgrim any more, Voice had said sadly. *He's reached the end of this journey.*

She'd tried lifting the Boy Scout up by the backs of his shoulders, hands jammed under his armpits, but he was too heavy. She had resorted to dragging him backwards by his booted feet across the polished wooden floor. His head had bumped down the steps when she pulled him off the back porch, and she'd winced at the *thunk*ing noise, offering a word of apology for the unintended mistreatment.

She had laid him to rest beside the girl. The red scarf she left draped over Red's face, but after a moment Lacey had leaned down and untied the Boy Scout's cotton bandana from around his neck and stuffed it into her pocket. In return she slipped the paperback copy of *Something Wicked This Way Comes* inside his shirt, next to his heart. She had first started reading it to Posy in the walk-in freezer and had finished it at Alex's bedside while the woman lay feverish and restless, Lacey's eyes constantly flicking over the top of the book until the woman grew quiet and settled back into sleep. Now, she gave the book back to him, because she wanted him to have something to read on his next journey, and something that would serve as a reminder of her.

She had touched the St Christopher through her shirt – something she found she was doing more often these days – and said her last goodbyes. Then she filled in the hole. And all the while she shovelled soil on to Pilgrim and Red, she was glad they wouldn't be alone down there, that they had each other; two travellers whose journeys, against all the odds, had converged.

With the chair-leg cross, she'd hesitated, not sure what to write. Neither Boy Scout nor Pilgrim was his real name. Finally, she had decided on a single word, one which she whittled in slow, careful lines.

DEFENDER.

It had been Red's dying message, a cryptic word that Lacey hadn't understood. At first, she had believed it to be a warning, to stay away from the truck bearing that same word, to steer clear of its occupants. In itself, the warning had been sound, and it was only later that Lacey had realised the full scope of its meaning. It was as clear to her now as the dawning sun indifferently shining over the graves: she, Alex and Pilgrim were the defenders. Defenders of each other. They may have started out as strangers, but together they were stronger than they could ever hope to be on their own. She was sure 'defender' was the right word to use on his grave. After all, he had been the strongest defender of them all.

Maybe that was what he'd been saying at the end, with his talk of defending her. He was bequeathing the role to her: her new responsibility was to defend her niece and Alex in his absence, to be the one now to keep them safe. She was ready for the task, and the fact that Pilgrim had trusted her enough to give it to her only strengthened her resolve. This may not be the family she had envisaged, but she loved it fiercely all the same.

Lacey?

Voice didn't have to say anything more. Lacey left her post at the back door and made her way upstairs. She found Alex and Addison in the master bedroom, Alex sitting cross-legged on top of the bed's comforter, Addison directly opposite, mimicking her pose. Although Lacey's niece didn't speak much – her vocabulary was mainly restricted to basic sentences and nouns, her favourites being about food, her teddy bear and all the places she could hide – she had quickly picked up their names and was adding words to her lexicon daily. She was a fast learner.

A few days after finishing the engraving on the cross, Lacey had been sitting on the backyard's porch steps, listening, as she did every day, for any vehicles or search parties roaming the streets around the house. It was getting cooler, the sun on its way to setting, and she'd been thinking about moving back indoors. She hadn't heard Addison approach until the girl sat down beside her. She had a keen way of sneaking up on you. Lacey figured it had been a survival skill quickly learned. The same as hiding. Addison was a whizz at that, too.

Lacey smiled gently at her. 'Hi.'

The girl didn't meet her eyes. She folded her arms tightly around herself and rocked a little in place, perched on the very edge of her step.

'Cold?' Lacey asked. She raised an arm so Addison could see her intentions and carefully slipped it around her niece's shoulders. The girl stiffened, but she didn't move away, so Lacey left it where it was.

They sat quietly like that for a time, watching the sun touch the last parts of the yard, gilding the grass in gold, and then Lacey began to talk. She spoke about how Karey had helped raise her, looked after and protected her, that Karey had loved Lacey almost as much as Lacey loved her back – because no one could love anyone as much as Lacey loved her big sister – the same way she was going to love Addison now. And maybe, one day, when Addison thought she was able, she could tell her what had happened here and where her mommy had gone. Tell Lacey *all* the things Karey had ever told her, because that way Addison would feel close to her mom again, and it would be as though Lacey had been here the whole time with her and Addison had never been alone.

Lacey was still in awe of her niece and, if she were totally honest with herself, a little wary. To survive alone in a city for so long, without any adults to care for her, was extraordinary. Lacey wasn't sure how she'd done it: she and Alex had spent many nights puzzling over it, but all they could agree on was that the girl must have barely left the house during the previous three years. Although Lacey also stuck to the argument that Addison came from brave, hardy stock, particularly on Lacey's side of the family, so, if anyone could do it, she could. Alex had smiled and conceded that it was certainly a valid point.

As they sat on the porch steps together, Lacey continued to talk to Addison, and with each star that twinkled into being the girl softened, imperceptibly leaning closer and closer until she was fully wedged against Lacey's side, tucked under her arm. Lacey talked until her throat was dry, and then talked some more, about Grammy, about her life at the farm with Karey when she was only Addison's age and finally, when the girl was completely slumped against her, Lacey began to hum. Her number-one favourite Beatles song of all time.

Addison smiled at her when Lacey entered the bedroom. Three rucksacks were leaning up against the wall under the window, packed and ready to go.

'Lecks and me playing pat-the-cake.' The girl held up her hands, palms open, showing them to her. Her nails were long, tapering almost to talons, but it had proven difficult to corner Addison long enough to trim them. Ever since Lacey had been forced to crop the kid's hair short after being unable to untangle her mass of matted curls, Addison ran and hid at the sight of scissors.

'Pat-*a*-cake,' Alex corrected from her place opposite Addison.

Lacey nodded, but didn't speak. Her niece hadn't shown any reaction to having shot and killed a man. Possibly, she didn't understand what she had done, or maybe she wasn't a stranger to such things. Lacey had lived out in the middle of nowhere, with a grandmother who'd done everything in her power to shelter her from the outside world and the horrible things happening in it. Who knew what Addison had seen in her seven short years, as much as Lacey was sure Karey would have tried to protect her. Age meant nothing any more. You lived and survived by doing what needed to be done, and a survivor could be a seven-year-old girl left to fend for herself in a hostile world or a sixteen-year-old who'd been in it for less than twenty days.

It could simply be that Addison felt no guilt. This tall stranger had invaded her home, her safe place, and she had defended herself. Who was Lacey to judge her for that? Hadn't she herself taken the life of a man who was sadistic and merciless and was mutilating her friend? She didn't feel remorse for that, either. Or, at least, that was what she told herself in the bright light of day; her sleep brought nightmares that argued otherwise.

On the bed, Alex had lowered her hands and was regarding Lacey quietly. 'Everything ready?' she asked.

Lacey nodded again, moving nearer so she could run a gentle hand down the back of Addison's closely shorn head. It was soft and warm and a bit bristly. 'We're all set. How's your back?'

'It's better. Just a little stiff. If I keep my movements slow, I'll be fine.'

'Good. We should go. We can't stay here for ever.'

'Did the voice say that?' Alex asked, frowning.

Lacey nodded a third time. Alex hadn't asked for details about Voice, and Lacey hadn't provided any. It was obvious Alex was uncomfortable with the subject; she'd never hidden her mistrust of the voices, and Lacey didn't want their friendship to be damaged by the secret she had promised to keep. So the matter remained unspoken. It pained her to hold back such a big part of herself. More than anything, she wanted to talk to Alex, be honest, explain everything that had happened and have her understand and accept that Voice wasn't bad, that he *could* be trusted (it was Voice who had advised her on how to care for Alex's wounds, after all; without that, Lacey wasn't sure Alex would have improved as quickly as she had), but she didn't think her friend would take kindly to knowing he had directly helped in looking after her.

So Lacey ignored the occasional guarded look Alex sent her way when she thought she wasn't looking. Maybe she thought Lacey was crazy, and you can't argue with crazy (although she never belittled or outright refuted any of Lacey's claims whenever Voice was brought up). Lacey found she didn't mind being thought of as nuts, if that's the way it had to be. There were worse things in the world. Besides, she was kind of getting used to having Voice around.

As far as Alex's memories went, she remembered only snatches of what had happened to her inside the freezer. She did, however, recall some of the questions Doc had asked.

'He wanted to know where you were from,' Alex told her. They were lying face to face in Karey's bed, close enough so Lacey could feel Alex's warm breath on her cold nose. Addison was asleep nearby, curled up in a duvet on the floor. Lacey and Alex whispered to each other in the dark, lying on their sides with hands cupped beneath their cheeks for warmth, eyes shining with flecks of moonlight from the curtainless window. 'He wanted to know where we'd met, where we were going. And, God help me, I think I told him. I told him everything.'

Not wanting to disturb Addison, they kept their voices so low Lacey had to watch the movement of Alex's lips as she spoke.

'I overheard talk of this Flitting Man while I was there,' Alex murmured, 'but I didn't know who it was. Didn't realise it was the same nameless man from all those stories my sister and I heard. That he was real.'

The mysterious man from Alex's campfire story had a name, and they had come within spitting distance of him. Some nights, Lacey felt like she'd stepped outside of the safe if lonely existence at her grammy's farmhouse and into a nightmare world inhabited by monsters and murderous henchmen where there were no safe places left to hide.

'They talked about him in whispers, Lacey.' Alex's voice had dropped to the merest breath of sound. 'There was fear, but there was respect, too. And that's what feels so dangerous about all this. They're not doing what they're doing because it's a job to them, they're doing it because they believe in it.'

She let Lacey digest what she'd told her, and then said, 'They loaded a truck just before we got to Vicksburg. Sent it off with maybe twelve people, including three they'd kept tied the whole time. I heard it was going to a place up north. Some camp. No one argued about going. They just climbed aboard and left. Everyone toed the line.'

Everyone except Doc, apparently. He hadn't seemed to like or trust the Flitting Man much, Alex told her. But then Lacey didn't think Doc liked anyone much, other than Dumont.

'He didn't want to hand all their power over.' They'd pulled their covers up higher, almost to their ears. Their muffled whispers and murmurs breathed heat into the material at their mouths, but no matter how much Lacey snuggled closer to Alex, she couldn't banish the chill from her bones. 'He resented Dumont for that, I think,' Alex said. 'But all Dumont wanted was to be on the winning side. His motivation was survival. He must've believed that his best chance of that was to throw his lot in with this . . . this *Flitting Man*.'

Dumont may have been cruel and self-serving, but he wasn't a fool.

Hearing all this had only deepened Lacey's fear. In her nightmarish version of the world, the Flitting Man had become a winged creature with the black eyes of an insect, and he flew the skies, hunting the Earth for her.

Posy had told her that Red had been scared of the Flitting Man, too. He wanted people with voices, like Lacey, and had little need for anyone else. There wasn't only herself to worry about any more, she had Addison and Alex to look after. Her family. She had plenty of reasons to be afraid. And, from what Dumont had said, it wasn't only Lacey who should be.

Everyone should be afraid of what was coming.

CHAPTER 2

Posy scratched at the sore lump in his armpit, his dirty fingernails picking at the coarse hair stuck to the weeping boil. As he fingered his pit, his eyes followed the rabbit sniffing around the run. He knew the scruffling of his scratches were well hidden by the leaves of the bush he was squatting behind. He was downwind of the animal, too, his bodily stench fetid and rank, a mix of unwashed body, piss, shit and wildness.

He didn't understand what downwind was, or know how to make a rabbit snare, but it had all been explained to him and one thing he did understand was how to follow orders.

As he watched the rabbit hop a step closer to his trap he had to cram his dirty hand against his mouth to smother his giggles. The animal froze, its head coming up, glass-button eyes watching, *searching*, little twitching nose smelling the wind.

Posy did his own freezing, his shoulders hunching up around his ears when he was admonished sharply to be quiet, to stay still. He bit at his fingers so hard they turned white in his mouth.

The rabbit darted away so fast Posy's eyes were a second delayed in going after it. As if snatched by an invisible hand, the animal was yanked to a stop, its legs flinging past its pinned head and shoulders. The rabbit flipped on to its feet and shook its head back and forth, fighting the invisible hold, but the more it pulled, the tighter the noose cinched around its neck.

Posy giggled and stood, his feet shuffling excitedly in place as he watched, gnawing on his hand, saliva sliding down his wrist. Hungry moans whined out of his throat. When he was told to, he hurried forward and knelt next to the struggling rabbit. And again when he was told to, he deftly avoided the rabbit's sharp teeth and snatched hold of its head, wrenching it in a vicious twist, the snap of its spine sending a tingle of pleasure down to his groin.

He extricated the rabbit's body from the trap and set it aside, even though he was desperate to rip into the still-warm body and start feeding on its steaming insides. With shaking hands he reset the snare, patting down the ground around it. He was getting good at setting traps. He had a good teacher. But they had bigger traps to set, yes sir, and larger prey to catch, and a *much* wider field to cover. They had a lot of work to do.

Posy shook his head and smacked his palm off his temple. 'Yes, *yes*,' he muttered, 'I'll cook it prop'ly this time. I *know*.' Tears welled in his eyes. 'I was hungry. Not stupid, not worthless. Jus' hungry. No, don't *say* that. *Don't say that*.' He clutched two fistfuls of his hair and yanked savagely. He hit his temple again, harder than before.

Sometimes, when the *other* was being especially mean and asking him to do things he didn't want to do, Posy wished the man with death in his eyes had done away with him, too.

CHAPTER 3

Lacey had spent most of the previous two nights carting their supplies two streets over to where they'd parked the RV. Her sister – who had been married to a retail manager at the local Walmart – had stockpiled an impressive inventory of foodstuffs and provisions in the pantry, but Addison had exhausted a lot of it during the past three years and it was now down to the last shelf of powdered goods and two cardboard boxes filled with four dozen cans.

At the time, Lacey had been unhappy that the only vehicle she could steal from the parking garage had been the unwieldy RV. It was hard to drive, slow-moving and difficult to hide. But now, with all their supplies loaded into it and it effectively being a home on wheels, her attitude had changed. It stank, the carpeting and cushions were all stained, but she had swapped the bedsheets with clean ones from her sister's closet and flipped the mattress and cushions where she could, and it wasn't so bad any more.

Carrying the last few things in packs on their backs, the three of them trudged downstairs. Lacey asked the other two to wait and went to the sitting room alone. She approached the wall-lined bookcases and walked along them, running her fingers over the leather-bound spines, pulling the odd one out and hefting it in her hand, trying to *feel* if it were the right one.

'Which one do you think he'd like?' she asked Voice, sliding a copy of *Moby-Dick* back into place.

All of them.

She rolled her eyes. 'I can't carry *all* of them. Help me out a little here.'

She had pulled out another slim hardback novel and was in the process of sliding it back when Voice said, *That one. He'd like that one.*

She pulled it back out and read the gold lettering embossed on the brown leather spine. *The Lord of the Flies* by William Golding.

'It's good?' she asked, as she fanned through the pages.

No clue. I haven't read it.

'Then how—'

I just do. Take it.

She did, and was about to turn away from the shelves when Voice spoke again.

Take that one, too. Same shelf, on the right.

She reached forward.

Your other right.

Her fingers drifted back to the decorative silver scrollwork on a pitch-black woven spine. She traced the delicate filigree design with a fingertip.

Yes. That one.

Her eyes travelled over the title. *The Princess Bride.*

He's read that one before. You'll like it. So will Addison.

She slid the book out of its place and packed the two hardbacks into her pack.

She passed back through the house to the kitchen, where Alex and Addison were waiting for her, and told them she was ready to leave. They all filed out of the back door, locking the house up tight behind them. Crossing the backyard, feet whispering through the overgrown grass, their steps faltered and slowed as they passed by the graves, but they didn't stop. They went through the gate into an alleyway and walked its length until they came out the other end. There, facing the deserted street, they stood side by side.

Addison's hand sought hers – it was small, a thin membrane of skin covering all the slight bones beneath – and Lacey gripped it gently. Addison reached for Alex on her other side and took hold of her hand, too.

Alex looked over the girl's head and met Lacey's eyes. 'You ready for this?' she asked.

'Not really,' Lacey admitted.

The girl beside her, whose head barely reached her shoulder, gave her hand a squeeze. 'Time to go,' she murmured.

Alex smiled. 'Addison is ready.'

'Well, I guess if *Addison* is ready—'

Alex laughed quietly and stepped off the kerb, the ancient pistol held ready at her side. Her arm stretched back, hand linked to Addison's, and pulled her along after her. In turn, Addison – the middle link in their concatenated line – tugged at Lacey's hand to follow. But Lacey didn't move, and the line came to a standstill.

Lacey avoided Alex's eyes when the woman glanced over her shoulder. Instead, she dug her chin down into the Boy Scout's bandana that was tied around her neck and hunched up her shoulders, an irresistible urge to look back bearing down on her, simply to turn around and go back to the house where she'd buried her friend.

Voice stopped her. *You leave pieces of yourself everywhere you go. Looking back doesn't return them to you. Best thing to do is place one foot in front of the other and keep moving forward.*

It sounded like something the Boy Scout would say, and she liked that.

She breathed through the warm cotton over her mouth, counting her breaths. When she hit ten, she lifted her head and straightened her shoulders and, fingers firmly gripping her niece's hand, moved up level with Alex so that they bracketed the girl between them.

DEFEND HER.

The words seemed to echo in her head, unspoken yet clear.

The three of them started forward again, hand in hand.

Lacey didn't look back.

A Note

The theory behind the bicameral mind argues that there was not such a thing as an internal mindscape, that we didn't learn to internalise our thoughts until well after the Bible was written (sources such as Homer's *Iliad* bear no evidence of 'self-conscious introspection'). Only an external dialogue existed between people.

Bicameral man heard auditory hallucinations. He believed them to be gods.

Remnants of the bicameral mind remain. As much as 10 per cent of the population hear voices and as many as 35 per cent report sensing a loved one's presence after their passing. Other examples include the Third Man Factor (a guiding presence detected by mountaineers in extreme conditions) and the muses of artists who visit in the dead of night to bestow inspiration. And let's not forget that around 65 per cent of children admit to having imaginary friends or anthropomorphic toys that protect them. For some, imaginary friends continue to appear well after adolescence.

On the cusp of sleep, have we not all heard a voice call out our name?

ACKNOWLEDGEMENTS

This part of the book is where I get to express my gratitude to everyone who has helped me along the way, so batten down the hatches – I'm going in.

Much love to my mom for generally being the most supportive mom ever. Thanks, too, to my wonderful dad, who always told me to do something with my life that would make me happy, irrespective of money or prestige. I never expected writing to bring me either of those things, but it's always made me happy. I wish you were here to see this, Pops.

Also, thank you to the rest of my family and friends for their patience; I know I spend a lot of time in front of a screen, which may be brilliant for an introverted day-dreamer like myself, but not so great for when I should be socialising and generally being part of the 'outside world' (which I still think is largely over-rated). I know my nieces will be excited to see their names here, so bundles of love to Isabelle and Scarlett for being my two favourite people in the whole wide world.

An especially big thank you goes out to my beta readers, Tom Bissell and Cath Hancox, who've kept me on the straight and narrow, writing-wise, and still do.

Huge admiration and authorly love go to my agent, Camilla Wray, and everyone at Darley Anderson for their constant enthusiasm and hard work. CW, you're truly the Elton John of the literary agent world!

And last, but certainly not least, my thanks go to my editor

Mari Evans (a Wonder Woman in her own right) and the talented folk at Headline – especially *Team Defender* – for taking a massive gamble on an unknown element. They have been passionate advocates for Pilgrim and Lacey from the start, and for this I am eternally grateful.

RESOURCES

This book is a work of fiction, but suicidal thoughts and auditory hallucinations are very, very real. I spent a lot of time researching and reading within these areas, so if you'd like more information, or need help and support for yourself or a loved one, please take a look at the following websites.

Mentalhealth.org.uk
Papyrus.org.uk
Rethink.org
Mind.org.uk
Hearing-voices.org
Samaritans.org (their helpline is free and available 24/7 on 116 123)

EXTRA MATERIAL

#HearTheVoices

LACEY'S LEMONADE

*'When life gives you lemons, squirt lemon juice
in the booger's eye' – Grammy*

Ingredients:

1 cup of sugar (or whatever you have left – old fluffy boiled sweets will do, tree sap, out-of-date tinned fruit syrup also doesn't kill)

1 cup water (rainwater collected in buckets: boiled, fine. Well water if you're lucky enough to have it)

1 cup lemon juice (squeezed from the lemons on Grammy's lemon plants)

More water to dilute (rainwater fine again – preferably cold – bury underground for 1 week+ or immerse in lake or water well)

Method:

1. Squeeze lemons. Use whatever you've got – a bucket, rocks, furniture, your shoes (jumping helps)

2. Add in the sugar (tree sap, boiled sweets, or old syrup) and stir with your pocket knife

3. Add cold water

4. Shake or stir

5. No ice. There's no ice anywhere

6. Blend to taste

7. Serve as follows:

    a. Set up stall: siding from a crate – paint sign – attract your customers somehow. Grab your old fold-up table, find a chair – you'll be waiting a while. Don't forget your sunscreen!
    b. Pour into a can or flask (whatever receptacle you have left) – or straight into mouth if customer wants
    c. Serve with a rifle

Tip: If a customer drinks, they owe you. Never take 'no' for an answer.

Tip: You have that rifle. Use it if you have to.

Author

Title **Pilgrim**

Due Date	Borrower's Name
Vehicle of choice:	Motorbike/legs and feet (boots compulsory)
Shelter of choice:	Motel (without sadistic siblings)
Favourite book:	*Lord of the Flies* by William Golding
Favourite things:	Books, time alone
Darkest fear:	Remembering the past
Most craved refreshment:	Beer or strawberry milkshake
Words to live by:	Worry about the future later
Most important things left:	Not much: lemonade, Lacey, cigarettes

Author

Title
Lacey

Due Date	Borrower's Name
Vehicle of choice:	RV
Shelter of choice:	Sister's house in Vicksburg
Favourite movie:	Frozen
Favourite things:	Family, her grammy, The Beatles
Darkest fear:	Never finding her family
Words to live by:	'Best thing to do is place one foot in front of the other and keep moving forward' – Voice
Most important things left:	Food, fresh water, health, family

Author	

Title **Voice**	

Due Date	Borrower's Name
Age:	Been around for a while
Vehicle of choice:	Pilgrim, Lacey
Favourite movie:	Harvey with Jimmy Stewart
Least favourite kind of holiday:	A post-apocalyptic road trip
Darkest fear:	Being viewed as a parasite not a friend
Most craved refreshment:	N/A
Most important things left:	The people he likes

Author

Title **Alex**

Due Date	Borrower's Name
Favourite book:	The Very Hungry Caterpillar
Favourite movie:	Thelma and Louise
Favourite thing:	Drawing/sketching (portraits mostly)
Darkest fear:	Hearing a voice
Words to live by:	Don't trust a voice, especially if it's in your head
Most important things left:	Lacey, Addison, Pilgrim, fresh supply of pencils

Turn the page for a glimpse of the next instalment
in the *Voices* series

HUNTED

G X TODD

HEADLINE

LETTER #271
January 12th, Thursday

Dear Stranger,

Do I even call you that now? Stranger? We've come too far for that, I think. We know each other, a little bit, if only because we share the same world. We survive it by hiding — from ourselves, from each other, but I must tell you there is coming a time when hiding will no longer work. We have been dragged down into the mud, we have crawled through its muck until we are unrecognisable, and now there is nothing left to do but climb free and wash ourselves clean.

You're wondering if I hear one, aren't you? I do. My voice's name is Jonah, and he wishes we could all just get along. It makes me laugh, the way he says it, as if 'getting along' is as easy as inviting someone over for milk and cookies. But there are people out there who want us gone — want me and people like me gone. They want you to believe that voices are bad and that those who hear them cannot be trusted. I'm here to tell you that it's not so simple. But then nothing ever really is.

Have you heard the stories yet? Of a man who knows all our hiding places? He comes in the night, if you believe the tales. He finds you in your sleep and, with a whisper, steals you away. He is a ghoul and a ghost and he's called the Flitting Man by some. He's the fear that rides these lands. He is the voice that non-voice hearers believe will wipe them from the earth. I think the Flitting Man is all of us, hiding in our little holes, alone and too scared to come out.

Some of us have already begun to climb clear of the mud. A teenaged girl whose name I don't know but who I see with lemons in her hands and a rifle over her shoulder. A man of lost wisdom, a pilgrim who carries us all on his back yet is too fearful to ask where he must head. And my brother — oh, Al, I miss your face. I miss singing to you and seeing your eyes light up as they lift to see the colour spill from my lips.

No, I will call you 'stranger' no more, dear reader. I will call you 'friend', whether you hear a voice or not. Because you can never have too many friends in a world where strangers are so plentiful.

Always yours,
Ruby

HUNTED

GX TODD

The birds are flying. The birds are flocking.
The birds know where to find her.

One man is driven by a Voice that isn't his. It's killing his sanity
and wrestling with it over and over like a jackal
with a bone. He has one goal.

To find the girl with a Voice like his own. She has no one
to defend her now. The hunt is on.

But in an inn by the sea, a boy with no tongue and no Voice
gathers his warriors. Albus must find Lacey . . . before the Other
does. And finish the work his sister Ruby began.

Coming 2018
Pre-order now

#HearTheVoices

HEADLINE

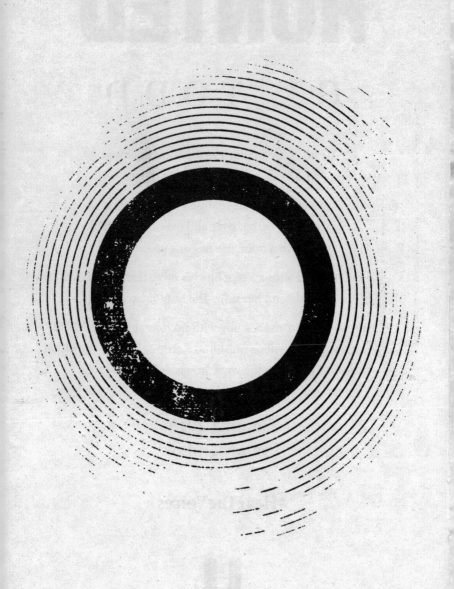

'A delightfully dark dystopian journey with compelling characters and a provocative plot. Highly recommended' *sfbook.com*

'A chilling vision of a world gone feral, yet strangely triumphant. You can taste the dust and blood and sweat; the fear on every page. Readers should approach with caution, those voices will burrow into your head and heart' Karen Maitland

'Yes it's dark, violent and bloody. Yes there's gore, guns and grief. But there's also friendship, loyalty, fantastic characters and writing that will keep you hooked from the outset . . . This is a series to be really excited about' *strupag.com*

'*Defender* is lifted way above the other novels in the over-subscribed post-apocalyptic subgenre by Todd's sympathetic characterisation, and superb pacing' *Guardian*

'G X Todd is not just going to be "The Next Big Thing", she's going to be the benchmark for other "Next Big Things"' *ebookwyrm.blogspot.co.uk*

'Promises to be the start of a wonderful series. A superb debut novel' *bluebookballoon.blogspot.co.uk*

'Wow . . . A brilliant debut novel . . . I can't wait for the next book in the series' *jacob-reviews-books.blogspot.co.uk*

'Quite simply an unputdownable page-turner. Seek it out!' *booksmonthly.co.uk*

'The best dystopian novel I have read for a long time . . . Impossible to put down' *bookerworm.com*

'*Defender* is one of those absolute rarities – a book by a debut author that is genuinely mind-blowing' Mike Craven

'One of the best debuts for 2017' *fantasy-smorgasbord.blogspot.co.uk*

'It'll grab you by the hand and take you on a dust-soaked ride across the wilderness . . . A stunning debut' *espressococo.com*

G X TO͏... Midlands. Since complet͏... iversity, she has work͏... de and currently holds ... .cenc... ...oot-long library van around the borough. *Defender* is her first novel and the first in the four-part *Voices* series featuring Pilgrim and Lacey.

Follow G X Todd on Twitter @GemTodd, on Facebook at Facebook.com/GXTodd or visit her website www.gxtodd.com to find out more.

#HearTheVoices

'It's not often you read a debut this assured, this confident. *Defender* is simply majestic' Adam Christopher

'A rich blend of horror and heart . . . sharp, gruelling and gripping, and we can't wait to explore this harsh world further and see what Todd has to offer us in part two' *SciFiNow* magazine

'An incredibly accomplished and impressive debut. The novel is of a piece with Stephen King's *The Stand* . . . *Defender* stands head and shoulders above most recent post-apocalyptic offerings' *Independent*

'Extremely refreshing . . . a brilliant thriller' *Starburst* magazine

'*Defender* is insane, intelligent, beautifully plotted, intensely absorbing' *lizlovesbooks.com*

'Compelling, suspenseful, and altogether extraordinary . . . You won't forget this one in a hurry' Lee Child

'So accomplished that it's difficult to believe it's a first novel, *Defender* is already worthy to take its place alongside *The Stand* in the canon. An absolute gem of a book' John Connolly

'Highly entertaining . . . *Defender* portrays a vivid picture of the cruelty of humanity and highlights the destructive power of the mind' *thebookbag.co.uk*